F KL 09/26/2017
Coonts

MW01420093

WITHDRAWN

DEEP WATER

A NOVEL BY

DEBORAH COONTS

Copyright © 2016 by Deborah Coonts

All rights reserved. No part of this book shall be reproduced, stored in a retrieval system, or transmitted by any means, electronic, mechanical, photocopying, recording, or otherwise, without written permission from the publisher.

This is a work of fiction. All incidents and dialogue, and all characters with the exception of some well-known historical and public figures, are products of the author's imagination and are not to be construed as real.

Book published by Deborah Coonts

Book Formatting by Austin Brown, CheapEbookFormatting.com

Cover Design by Andy Brown, ClickTwiceDesign.com

Paperback ISBN-13: 9781944831974

Hardcover ISBN-13: 9781944831721

V032617

Also by Deborah Coonts

The Lucky Series

"Evanovich....with a dose of CSI"
—*Publisher's Weekly* on *Wanna Get Lucky?* A Double RITA(tm) finalist and NYT Notable crime Novel

WANNA GET LUCKY?
(Book 1)

LUCKY STIFF
(Book 2)

SO DAMN LUCKY
(Book 3)

LUCKY BASTARD
(Book 4)

LUCKY CATCH
(Book 5)

LUCKY BREAK
(Book 6)

LUCKY THE HARD WAY
(Book 7)

Lucky Novellas

LUCKY IN LOVE

LUCKY BANG

LUCKY NOW AND THEN
(PARTS 1 AND 2)

LUCKY FLASH

OTHER BOOKS BY DEBORAH

AFTER ME

DEEP WATER

CRUSHED

CHAPTER ONE

I'm a killer. The thought tortured Jake Walker. Matt was dead. Jake's fault. At least that's how he saw it.

Bile rose in his throat at the image of his boss thrown back in his chair, one neat hole in the center of his forehead, a once brilliant mind reduced to splattered bits of gore. Jake's hands shook as he closed his laptop and gathered his things.

They had asked him to let the bad guys into the software, to allow them to wander and hide in the millions of lines of code. A huge gamble. He'd tried to warn them. Yes, he'd told them he knew where to look, how to follow, but still...the stakes were so high they were out of sight.

They told him to keep his head down and report what he saw. He'd done that. The game had been fun...until an innocent man paid with his life. Jake knew he'd been the target. Or maybe Matt had been a warning.

Either way, Jake had blood on his hands.

They hadn't told him the cat-and-mouse game could be deadly. They promised they had his back. They were supposed to be the good guys.

They had dangled the carrot. This was Jake's chance to be somebody, they'd said. Jake was the only one with the skills, knowledge, and access. Ego and idealism—and he'd fallen for it.

Had his back. Fuck that.

He'd called the number. They'd said sit tight; they'd get back to him.

Right.

Jake Walker might be a fool, but he drew the line at being a martyr.

The bad guys killed with precision and then vanished as if they'd never been. A shiver of fear knifed through him. What chance did one pansy-ass software geek have?

Matt was dead.

Forced into action, Jake didn't really hold out much hope, but he clung to the flotsam of desperation with the strength of a drowning man. Jake willed himself to slow, to act casual, as if nothing was wrong. He had to get out of here, to run, to find help.

He squeezed his eyes tight against the image of Matt branded on his brain with the singe of horror and guilt.

Right now he felt spotlighted, the lights of his office holding back the darkness of the night outside his window. Through the interior glass walls, he scanned the sea of cubicles. An ominous quiet lurked in the shadows. In the half-light, Jake felt exposed and at a disadvantage. If someone wanted to hide, the geometric patches of darkness cast by the security lights would shelter them—the overheads had been doused when the last of his staff had left hours ago.

A noise startled him. Jake froze. He held his breath and waited.

The sound didn't repeat.

Perhaps it was the air conditioning kicking on. The noises of the empty building sounded strange, creaking, groaning as if collapsing without the human energy to keep it inflated. Or perhaps it was his imagination. But he hadn't imagined Matt, dead, half his brain splattered on the bookcase, the window, the photos of his wife and kids.

Jake pulled in a deep breath, squeezing his eyes shut,

then let the air out with measured precision, willing his nerves to calm. When he opened his eyes, the world had steadied a bit.

He could do this.

As he stuffed the papers into his briefcase, his hand brushed against cold metal. A gun—a Glock 19, so new there was no shine on the metal and no sign of burn on the muzzle. Jake had never owned a gun before. And he'd never broken the law—not intentionally anyway. He'd felt like a felon scoring the piece off the kid in Hell's Kitchen.

How the hell had he gotten into this?

Jake didn't even know who the killers were. But he'd chased them through the code, and he knew where they were and what they were trying to do. He had to stop them, but he needed help.

And he needed to get as far away from here as he could.

He knew they were there, watching, waiting. So clever how they by-passed the trading programs with all the tight checks and rechecks and security redundancies. And so easy, too. Had he not been looking, watching, no one would've known the bad guys tampered with the inventory numbers, or made phantom trades to manipulate the price of oil. His trip to Oklahoma had confirmed the inventory anomalies—the only time he'd gone off the reservation. Well, that and the phone call to his IT contact in Conroe. But those were it. After that, nothing had felt the same.

He tried not to look out the window, to squint into the night, scanning for those who wanted to know how much he knew, who he told. He didn't know all of it, but he knew enough to be afraid. Big players: Drayton Lewis the tech magnate, Senator Herrera from Texas with a lifetime of political IOUs, and others—he could sense them, but he hadn't turned over their particular rock yet.

Hurry, Jake. Hurry.

Jake booted up his desktop, his foot bouncing a staccato rhythm. They were clever, all right, clever to the point of arrogance. And that's how he'd found them.

With a few quick keystrokes he started the scrubbing

program on his hard drive and the backup that would overwrite both drives. Then he stuffed the new laptop into his shoulder bag, killed the lights, and headed out the door.

With no one at work to help, Jake knew he had to get word to someone. Without a whole lot of luck, and some serious help, he was a dead man. Shelby would know what to do.

But the information could get her killed.

He'd thought long and hard about how to show her where to look. He'd been careful, but had he been careful enough?

At this point, out of time and using up luck by the second, he had no choice.

They had to be stopped, and, of everyone he knew, Shelby was the only one who could handle the heat and crack the code. Together they could outmaneuver these guys. His sister had more lives than a cat and a bite more vicious than a pissed-off Doberman. And she could dig—if anyone could take what he'd found and put names to it, she could.

The elevator dinged its arrival, tripping his heart, which already pounded. As the doors opened, he paused. Looking back, he took a quick look around; he couldn't help himself. He'd liked it here—writing the security for the trading programs, being a cog in the wheel of global trade. With a sigh, he flicked off the lights and stepped into the elevator.

The clock was ticking.

After the doors closed and he was alone with his thoughts, Jake punched the button for the fifth floor. The guard wouldn't be at the monitors—he still had a lot of real estate to check—nonetheless, Jake would have to be quick.

They watched.

The elevator slowed to a stop. Fifth floor. As the doors eased open Jake fought the instinct to cringe, to hide—he half believed they'd crawled inside his head and knew what he was doing. They'd been in every other crevice. He ran a hand through his hair. *Calm down. If they knew... Stop! Think!*

After punching the hold button to keep the car there, he ran for the mailroom. The pre-addressed FedEx box waited where he'd hidden it. Each floor had a mailroom. He'd chosen this one at random, but primarily because he had no connection with anyone or any department that had offices there. After wrapping the laptop quickly in two layers of bubble wrap, he shoved it in the box, sealed it, and then put it in the early pickup box. It'd be on its way before the workday got fully underway. Filling his shoulder bag with a thinner box so it looked as it had when he'd left his office, he took a deep breath and bolted for the waiting elevator. Less than thirty seconds and he was back riding down to the lobby.

Jake had calmed himself by the time the doors opened, disgorging him into the large marble and glass atrium that never warmed, not even in the heat of the New York summers. The perfect heart for a corporate collective where "survival of the fittest" and "he who dies with the most toys wins" were rules branded on men's souls.

His footfalls echoed as he strode across the lobby, working hard to act as if today was the same as any other. But it wasn't. After today, there would be no going back. And Jake was fine with that. If not exposed, the secrets would eat at him until there was nothing left. So, either way, he was doomed.

Sorry to draw you into this, Shelby.

A year apart, he and his sister had been close once, until Shelby had taken up the sword against big business and Jake had sold himself to her devil. As much as he hated to admit it, his sister had been right. She was making a career exposing those whose greed ruined it for everybody.

The security guard met him at the door with a smile, pushing it open. "All work and no play, Mr. Walker."

Jake gripped the man's shoulder—a quick connection that felt final. "Some days are like that, Ethan."

The man nodded as if he had a clue. For a moment Jake was envious of the guard. *Four advanced degrees and I'm jealous of the night watchman.* Jake chided himself, but he recognized his emotion—the last dying gasp of idealism. But somehow having taken a stand, having put in motion things that would stop them, Jake felt better. A surging sense of relief rushed through him—he would do that, he was that kind of guy, even when his life was on the line.

Jake stepped through the door, then stopped once outside the penumbra of light cast through the glass. The night air, muggy and dense, smothered him like a plastic sheet. Sweat popped, beading on his skin still cool from the air-conditioned office. The discomfort proved he was still alive, which, all things considered, was a good thing and by no means assured—although his prospects were looking up.

He'd done it. He'd really done it. The vise around his chest loosened, and he took a deep breath, letting it out slowly.

Night had scoured the streets of people. A random can, skittered by a silent breeze, made him jump. Jake crossed the strap of his shoulder bag across his chest. The doorways stood empty, the storefronts shuttered, One World Trade Center a beacon of light standing high above.

New York's fabled financial district—the beating heart of capitalism. Now a sleeping lion, it would awake to consume its fill again tomorrow.

A frisson of fear shivered through him, making the hair on the back of his neck rise.

So close. He'd made it this far. All he had to do was get to the airport—a ticket to Houston in his breast pocket. He'd paid cash, but computers remembered, and there was always a trail if someone knew where to look and how to follow it. He ought to know—he was a master at that game.

Head facing forward, eyes scanning as he maintained an outwardly casual interest in his surroundings, he turned and strode toward the Ritz. It wasn't far. He could catch a cab there.

He whirled at a noise behind him. Pausing, his heart accelerating, he stared into the darkness.

CHAPTER TWO

Sam Donovan was in her usual position—flat on her back.

Even though she'd pulled the small plane into her hangar that hunkered between the larger Coast Guard Air Station Houston Hangar and the even larger NASA one, the heat from the floor burned through her thin shirt—a vestige of the sun on its path, the light angling in through the open hangar door. Her east-facing hangar took the worst of the morning sun.

Only June and already the temperature and humidity in this reclaimed swamp south of Houston were off the charts. Cicadas sang from hiding places among the leaves on the few trees stubborn enough to live despite little water and intense reflected heat. A lone seagull called. Moisture beaded on the relative cool of the hangar floor. Sam had no doubt that if she tossed some water on the tarmac, she'd hear it sizzle and pop in the summer skillet.

Seattle would be misty and cool....

How had her father convinced her to give up the bushplane charter company and move to this hellhole? Sam shook her head in disgust. Her mother had come, too. They'd done it for family, even though theirs was as fractured as any, and more than most here in the sanctimonious South, which itched like a hair shirt.

Clearly, some boundaries needed to be drawn, but,

when it came to her father, Sam wasn't good at drawing a line in the sand. Patrick Donovan was known for crossing most lines anyway. All other areas of her life were ordered, precise—each tool in its spot, each plane centered on the markings on the hangar floor. Yet, her father defied all efforts at pigeonholing. Something Sam found irritating and oddly admirable. Perhaps she wanted the father he couldn't be.

But, thankfully, right now she wasn't searching for the glue for a fractured family. Her current problem was something she could actually solve. The spring assembly on the tailwheel of her 1946 J-3 Cub had popped on landing this morning. Thank God she'd been making the landing and not her student. The memory of the plane's immediate turn when she set the tail down on rollout shivered through her. Experience and quick reflexes kept them from leaving the runway, ground looping, or worse.

Then she would have had to fix more than a spring.

"Wrench." Sam stuck out her hand.

Nothing.

"Geraldo! Dammit." The heat had eroded her good humor. She blinked at the sting of sweat that trickled into her eye. Wedged under the tail, she couldn't reach to wipe it away. She shook her open palm. "Geraldo. Wrench, please." Where was the boy?

"What manner of wrench would ya' be needin'?"

Sam froze, the voice a taper lighting her already short fuse. Her father.

She wriggled from under the plane's elevator, which sat low to the ground, and gazed at the man looming over her. Full head of white hair, ruddy complexion, a bit of a paunch, his chin held a bit too high, as if willing someone to take the first punch—Patrick Donovan in the flesh. Today the scar across his chin—an old oilfield battle wound inflicted when the pressure got too high on a well and it blew the valve, launching a spear of metal three-hundred yards—was etched in bright red. He'd been lucky. His partner, not as much—the metal shot through both his knees. But that scar on her father's chin had served as a bellwether of his mood for as long as Sam was wise enough to take heed. Red was not a good sign—something had amped him up and raised his blood pressure, although she couldn't see any other outward sign. In fact, if she didn't know better, he looked snake-bit, although he was working to cover it up with a grin that barely lifted his lips into an anemic curve. His eyes, bright green and normally dancing with a joke, looked flat and dark.

Lately, he'd kept his distance, ever since their last row, but that one was on him. By Sam's way of thinking, stealing someone's plane, even if you brought it back, was just plain bad form.

"Paddy. Been awhile." *Think of the Devil.* Sam shook her head and stifled the urge to cross herself. Like the Devil, Patrick Donovan often rode in on a random thought. She had only herself to blame.

"Aye." A frown darkened his face briefly like a cloud passing across the sun.

"Whatever you're selling, I'm not buying." Sam leaned over to root through the toolbox at her father's feet. After finding the wrench she was looking for, she glanced around the hangar, scanning for Geraldo. The King Air, an older model twin turboprop that was her workhorse, still nestled tail-in in the far back corner. Her Jet Ranger, one of the older models but still an amazing machine, took up the center of the hangar, its rotors aligned along its body. The J-3 she was working on, a post–World War II tube and fabric trainer, she'd pulled just inside the doorway. The floor with its new coat of Epoxy gleamed like china ready for the plating of a holiday meal. A small office, with a subsistence-level apartment above, jutted from the north side of the hangar.

Her helper had vanished.

Wrench in hand, Sam dove back under the plane. "What did you do with Geraldo?"

"The kid launched out of here looking for all the world like he'd been shot from a cannon."

The wrench fit over the bolt but slipped when she put her elbow to it. "Goddamn it!"

"Mary Catherine!" Paddy actually sounded a bit shocked, which irritated the hell out of her.

"Now I know you didn't come here to make nice," Sam growled from under the plane. She hated her name. Hated to be spoken to like a child. And was on the verge of hating her father for it, which didn't sit well with her at all. Sam counted to ten and then decided she needed another trip through—ten wasn't enough. This time she held each digit in her brain until thoughts of patricide passed.

"You'll need to remember that one when you confess to Father Flanagan," Paddy continued, unaware of how close he was to dying. "He's been asking after you."

"Been working overtime on your soul, I'm sure. But tell him not to worry on my account. I gave up hypocrisy for Lent. So Geraldo jackrabbited. Thank you for that. But, really, it's little wonder considering the last time you were here." Sam knew there wasn't much good that could come from worrying that knot, but she couldn't resist.

"Aye. You were a bit cheesed."

"More than a bit. You stole my plane."

Patrick Donovan, Paddy to his friends, pressed a hand to his chest in mock indignation. "Stole! I was just borrowin' it a wee bit. I returned it."

Sam needed a different wrench. After rolling out from under the stabilator, she returned the wrench to its slot in the toolbox. With a clean mechanic's rag, she worked at the oil staining her hands to little effect, then pressed herself to her feet. "With bullet holes in the stabilator, no explanation, and the DEA hot on your heels. Took me a month to get my plane out of impound."

Paddy spread his arms wide. "See there, nothing lost."

"Except for the legal fees and the revenue I would've earned had I had the plane in service, not to mention parts and labor." He started to argue, but Sam waved his words away. "I'm taking it you are not here to apologize."

"Ah, you be thankin' your mother for that tongue."

"Don't you be speakin' of Ma. She's a saint." Sam clamped her lips closed—words, once spoken, couldn't be unheard. Those said in anger often provoked regret.

His cheeks flushed, his eyes all misty, her father stared at her, seeming at a loss for words, and then he said, "I *am* sorry. Sometimes life..." He sighed and then started over. "Sometimes I miscalculate."

Despite being hardwired to the self-preservation mode, Sam lowered her shield a hint. She'd never seen him without a ready gambit. "Is that what you call it?" She softened her tone. Asking someone to be what they weren't never worked out well, not that she'd forgiven him for stealing the plane. She knew he hadn't planned it; it had just happened. But, despite the almost near perfect futility, she had a mind to try to teach him a lesson. Things had to change—*he* had to change—for all of them. He needed a good scare, but, if her father was afraid of anything, Sam had yet to see it.

Jamming his hands in his pockets, Paddy turned to look through the hangar door into the heat of the day. It shimmered off the tarmac in waves, distorting the world like a funhouse mirror. "I've made mistakes—left the wrong woman, trusted the wrong people, tiptoed on the wrong side of the line more than once. When I make my way to the Pearly Gates, I'm sure Saint Peter will have a one-way ticket to Purgatory for me." He angled a glance at his daughter. "I'm not saying I won't deserve it. But I will say, when I made my choices, I thought they were the right ones. Perhaps I didn't think it through."

Sam snorted. She'd heard it all before. "Thinkin'—not your strong suit." She clamped her lips together. He was doing it again, sucking her in, poking at the beehive of worry that she might have far more Patrick Donovan blood coursing through her veins than made her comfortable.

"You've made yourself a nice place here." Paddy clasped his hands behind his back as he let his gaze wander.

"Paddy, I'm working fourteen hours a day, barely

keeping the lights on and the lender off my ass, and the Coast Guard wants to get rid of me." As the only civilian operation in the secure area of Ellington Field just south of Houston, she'd become a thorn in the side of the Homeland Security folks, a tempest stirred up by her neighbor, the Coast Guard's Air Station Houston.

"Your father's daughter." Paddy sounded proud, but not happy. "You'll figure it out—you always do. And the Coast Guard won't evict you. Commander Wilder won't let them." Backlit by the sunlight behind him, his expression was unreadable.

"Wilder! He's leading the charge."

"Don't be too sure."

Sam hated it when her father used that superior tone. "Is that why you came here? To fill my head with ideas that Commander Wilder is going to be my Galahad? You're wasting your time. Men! They always have an angle. You taught me that."

Her father deflated, a balloon pierced by the sharp point of her cynicism. "Aye. Leavin' your Ma and you—that'll be a sin I carry on my soul. I might not be able to make it up to the Almighty, but I aim to try to fix what's between the three of us."

"I saw what your leaving did to Ma. I'll not be forgivin' you."

"Then that'll be a burden you carry. But don't let my haymes ruin your happiness." Paddy turned and grabbed her hands in his, surprising Sam before she could retreat. "I'll say it again: I *am* sorry. I was a fool. Lessons often come too late, but now perhaps it was for the best."

"How can breaking a woman's heart be for the best?" Sam vibrated with anger—this was not the discussion for today, maybe not for any day. She'd shut him out; it was the only way she knew to protect herself. And she'd rather die than see him hurt her mother again.

"Break her heart. Maybe a small price to pay to save her life," Paddy murmured, looking pained.

"What?" Sam wrenched her hands from his then pushed

at a lock of curly red hair, tucking it back under her ball cap as she flipped the brim around to the back.

Paddy's expression opened, as if he wanted to explain, reaching for the words before he gave his head a quick shake. "You've got your mother's eyes. So green—a piece of the Emerald Isle."

They were his eyes, not her mother's. Sam had always chaffed under the comparison, but he knew that. She narrowed her eyes as if focus would give her a clue as to the game he was playing. It didn't. It never did.

He dug into his front pocket and pulled out something silver that reflected the light. "Here. Take this." He pressed the object into Sam's hand.

A key.

Small and light—a key to a padlock maybe? "What's this to?"

"The answers, if you ever find yourself lookin' for some." He tried for a smile and then leaned into her. "If something happens, if I don't come back, look where you would expect to find something I hold dear."

A niggle of worry chased a chill down Sam's spine. "Never come back? What are you talking about?"

Patrick drew back, running a hand through his hair, standing it on end. "Phillip has a story. I'm tellin' ya', lass, it's a wild one. Didn't believe him at first. But, they got him spooked for sure."

"Uncle Phil? Spooked?" Sam couldn't imagine what it would take to scare the senior senator from Texas. Worried now, she couldn't keep the sharpness out of her voice. "About what?"

"I can't be tellin' you." His voice shook.

Sam could tell he was afraid. She grabbed his shoulders. "Da? Does this have something to do with your new well? The one you've leveraged your soul to drill?"

"You may be right there, lass."

"You need to tell me."

He shook his head. "Promise me you won't go looking

unless I'm not there to give you the answers."

"No."

"Promise. It's bad business." He gave her a slight smile. "Please?"

Her father never asked nicely. "Okay."

"Say it."

"I promise."

"There." He seemed satisfied.

Whirling at the sound of running footsteps echoing off the tarmac, Paddy stiffened. Fear sliced across his face as he pulled away and then stepped back. He relaxed as two figures, one tall and broad, one small and slight, pounded around the corner and through the door.

"Over here." Geraldo motioned. A lean and lanky refugee with shaggy black hair, skin the color of pecan shells, a tentative smile, and a love for anything that flew, the kid had showed up out of the blue one day and stayed, despite Sam's best efforts to run him off.

Commander Wilder, the taller, broader of the two, followed on the boy's heels. Both of them skidded to a stop in front of Sam and Paddy. The boy's eyes, dark with worry, darted between Sam and her father. A look of bemused consternation softened the angled planes of the commander's face. A flush of embarrassment rose. The boy had oversold the danger. The commander should know Sam and her father lived life at the top of their lungs, and, while death might be threatened, they hadn't yet started shooting at each other.

Sam stashed the key in a pocket then crossed her arms and stepped back. Just like Wilder to dash into her hangar, loaded for bear like...Galahad. She snuck a look at her father. He knew what she was thinking, and he raised an eyebrow to tell her so, which made her smile.

Family.

Suddenly a bit self-conscious, Sam tugged at the damp white tank top that clung to her skin. Not a good choice in hindsight, but it was the coolest thing she had that was clean. Under the intensity of the commander's gaze, she tried not to squirm.

Commander Kellen Wilder. Just his voice warmed her to the core and sent her thoughts tumbling in a direction she didn't want them to go. She'd been fantasizing about him since she'd met him. Tall, broad, and tapered, with blue eyes and dark, almost black hair which he wore a trifle too long to suit his higher-ups, Commander Wilder was a perfect poster boy for the Coast Guard. Whether he intended it or not, his mere presence demanded attention.

Yep, he'd been the stuff of dreams...right up until the Coast Guard focused on getting her operation kicked off the airport. "Can I help you?" Sam kept a mildly interested expression on her face as she met him eye-to-eye. When his gaze shifted over her shoulder to the plane she'd been working on, she allowed herself a moment to appreciate all of Kellen Wilder. She didn't feel bad about that—he invited the attention in the almost-too-tight flight suit, which he wore well, damn him.

The commander looked a bit curious as he glanced between Sam and her father. "The boy here told me I needed to hurry. Apparently he was worried about a future homicide."

"Homicide?" Sam said as if the idea appealed to her. "None imminent, but my finger is still on the trigger."

Donovan shifted, but he let her do the talking, which put her guard up.

Wilder extended a hand as he clasped the older man's shoulder with the other. "Paddy."

There was warmness between them, and affection—a respect of sorts. "Wilder." The older man gave the commander's hand a solid shake, then stepped back.

To Sam, the fact that her father liked Kellen Wilder was a huge red flag.

Paddy cleared his throat. "I've got to go, Mary—"

Sam silenced him with a shake of her head. Despite the hundreds of times she'd lectured him on the difficulty of being taken seriously as a woman in the man's world of aviation, he refused to understand her adoption of a more gender-neutral moniker.

"Sam," her father quickly corrected. When he said her name, it had a note of finality to it.

She felt a frisson of panic, a need to keep him there, to keep him safe from himself and whomever he was running from this time. "Da?"

"You'll know." He gave her a wink.

With that, he turned and was gone.

Sam stared after him, working to breathe, as if he'd taken all of the air with him.

CHAPTER THREE

Shelby Walker stopped in the middle of Fifty-Seventh Street to glare at her phone as the constant Manhattan traffic snaked around her, most drivers honking and gesturing their displeasure. Jake's text message had been succinct—that, of course, was after she'd spent an hour trying to crack his code. In riddles and a rudimentary childhood cipher they'd spent one summer developing to keep secrets safe from their parents, the thing resembled hieroglyphics. The message had come in last night after she'd turned off her phone. This morning, late for work, but not so late she couldn't stop for a coffee and an egg on a roll, she'd picked up the message and then spent far too long deciphering the damn thing. Jake was lucky she even recognized the code game they'd played, much less remembered how it all went.

She read the message one more time—probably the hundredth since she'd broken the code.

Houston. Be careful. Senator Herrera. Drayton Lewis. Push but be careful. More. The normal place. ASAP. Locked and loaded. Leave now!

Her brother always was a bit dramatic, which made her smile. And he knew she was headed to Houston for the big interview in a couple of days—Drayton Lewis! As she'd researched for the interview, Shelby had found Jake and his computer skills invaluable. They both were on the same page regarding Herrera and Lewis, but locked and loaded? *Right, Jakey.* The guys were scumbags, but that was as far as the trail Jake had found led.

Unless...

That thought wiped her smile. Jake was a stickler for detail. Give him a task and he'd stick to it like a tick on a dog. Shelby clung to the bottom rung of the corporate ladder at *Straight Talk,* a national prime-time news show. A year into the gig, she'd done her time and Drayton Lewis was a huge stepping-stone on the way to being Diane Sawyer. Huge!

Not today, Jake. Not now.

Horns sounded and a car whipped by her, almost brushing her thigh. Message delivered: the light had changed.

Shelby shot the vanishing car the finger and took her time getting to the other side of the street—five-inch heels on New York streets littered with potholes and flaking asphalt were killer. Tugging down her short skirt, she stopped in the doorway to a pizza place. Ignoring the enticing smells and the irritating looks of the counter help, she thumbed open the screen on her phone and hit a familiar speed dial number.

Shelby was about to hang up when Tracy picked up. "Hey, I need a favor," Shelby launched in without pleasantries.

Tracy's bored Jersey-Shore voice came back. "No, girl, you need to get your ass to Houston ASAP."

"Have you been talking to my brother?"

"What? Jake? Honey, I wish. That boy is *fine.*" Tracy, like every one of Shelby's friends, married or single, old enough to know better, or young enough not to care, lusted after Jake Walker. They had good taste if they wanted a kindhearted geek who communicated in code. "What does he have to do with you going to Houston?"

"I'm not sure." Jake's warning raised every hackle she had. Drayton Lewis. Locked and loaded. What did that mean?

"Honey, I'm confused. Let's start over. You need to get to Houston ASAP. The C-level suits have their panties in a wad."

The visual made Shelby smile. "What now?"

"Lewis upped the time frame for the interview."

Shelby's adrenaline, already redlining after Jake's missive, didn't even spike. Max overload, that's what it was. "When?"

"Tonight."

"They want me to interview Lewis tonight?" Her brain clicked into overdrive as she ran through her preparation.

"His office. A local crew has been arranged. They'll be there to set up around eight."

"Damn." Shelby focused on breathing. She could do this. She knew she was ready. "Okay, I got this. But after the interview, I really need a couple of days of PTO."

"PTO? Are you shitting me? Girl, you pull a Houdini, and the Assholes are gonna shit. They jumped through their asses to get this interview. No way are they going to let you go gallivanting with the interview to edit."

"Don't you think I know that? I've been talking to his people for weeks now. I'm ready, but see if you can work it so I can edit from Houston. I can tie-in from my laptop. Tell them I'll hang around in case Lewis wants to clarify anything." That sounded weak, Shelby knew, but it was all she had at the moment. Jake's note had derailed logic and started a sinking hurt in the bottom of her belly.

Tracy's voice dropped to a stage whisper. "It's your big break, girl. You fuck it up, you're toast."

Shelby could picture Tracy leaning back in her chair, examining her too-long, bright pink acrylic nails as disbelief dripped off of her. "I'll head to the airport now. Anything you want from Texas?"

"Texas! That backwater? Maybe a rich cowboy with a butt 501s were made for."

"Rich cowboy—an oxymoron if there ever was one."

"Not if your ranch is sittin' on a boatload of oil."

"Oil. There is that." Shelby disconnected and stuffed her phone in her purse. "Jake," she said under her breath. "What the hell do you know about Drayton Lewis? And why couldn't you just tell me?" She tried calling him…again. Voicemail, like all the other calls she'd put in to him this morning. *Come on, Jake. Where are you? You can't leave me dangling like this.*

Stepping to the curb, she put two fingers between her lips and blew—a shrill whistle that turned every head in the block. Three cabs careened across traffic. She winced as one clipped the bumper of the car it cut off.

As the cabbie and the driver got into it, Shelby opened the door of the first unscathed cab and slipped into the back seat. She thought about going by the apartment. Jake's note stopped her. She could buy what she needed when she got there. "They have shopping malls in Houston, right?"

The cabbie shrugged. "I'm from the Bronx. How would I know?"

"LaGuardia."

"You got a bag or something?"

Shelby gave him a slant-eyed look in the rearview mirror. "Do you see a bag?"

He shrugged, then threw the car into gear and slammed back into traffic. The only way to drive in New York, take a position and expect everyone to get out of your way. Worked most of the time.

"An extra twenty bucks if you hurry." Shelby leaned back. With a little bit of luck, she could make Southwest's 5:00 nonstop to Houston Hobby.

She dialed Jake one more time.

Still no answer.

CHAPTER FOUR

"I'm sorry," Commander Wilder said to Sam as he shot a disgruntled look at Geraldo, who stood mute at his side. "We've intruded."

"Not at all." Sam tore her gaze from the doorway that had swallowed her father. Rearranging the worry from her face, she reached over, giving the boy's arm a squeeze. "My father and I tend to bring out the worst in each other these days." It hadn't always been that way, and the thought didn't make her proud.

Geraldo's rigid posture relaxed, and once again Sam saw the boy who spent every moment he could at the airfield, peppering her with questions until she'd relented and taught him what he wanted to know. Although she never was certain how much got through his rapidly improving English and her halting Spanish.

All arms, legs, brown skin, a wicked smile, Geraldo couldn't hide his excitement behind his longish black hair that swept across his forehead and brushed his eyes. The two of them shared the same love of aviation—a love gifted to her by her father. A pang hit her heart.

Da.

Today had done little to dissipate the meanness between them. Words needed saying. Damn him for running off again, leaving her with nothing but questions, worry, and an unfulfilled need to set things right.

The commander nudged the boy. "Won't your mother be worrying about you? Aren't you supposed to be in school or something?"

The boy looked with old eyes between the two adults, and Sam swore he knew. She counted out some bills from the wad in her pocket and handed them to him. "Here. You're worth every penny."

Geraldo smiled as he stuffed the bills in his pocket, not bothering to count them. "That's okay, Miss Sam. I need to go home. My mother..." He glanced at the commander with a knowing look. "She will be worried." The boy waved and trotted off toward the north side of the field.

"That kid's a friggin' Houdini." Wilder stepped closer, turning so his face wasn't shadowed anymore. "No matter what we do, he still gets in here. I'd love to know how he does it."

"Growing up on the streets in El Salvador, he probably has all kinds of skills that would shock the hell out of you and me."

"How'd he find you?"

So, the Coastie wants to chat. Secretly more than okay with that, Sam lowered herself back to the ground. "Just showed up one day. I've got to get this spring assembly back on."

"Understood. Let me help?" He actually waited for an answer.

Sam curled her arms around her knees, pulling them to her chest as she looked up at him. "I'm not going to get a bill for using government resources, am I?" She almost rolled her eyes at herself, but she found her thoughts captured by some interesting visuals in the game of what-if.

"This one's on me." The commander kept his face impassive, but Sam heard the husky warmth in his voice.

The guy probably has a medal for flirting above and beyond the call of duty.

He squatted next to her as she shimmied her head and

shoulders under the elevator. "You and your dad okay?"

She could feel the warmth of him next to her. Why did being so close, so very close and not touching fire all her nerves? There was something so...electric about it. A charge building before the lightning arced. "Working our way back." She stuck her hand out, hoping it didn't shake. "Wrench."

After glancing at the bolt, then touching each of the wrenches as he worked through them in the toolbox, Kellen chose one and handed it to her. "When are you going to let me take you out to dinner?"

Sam fit the wrench over the bolt and put some muscle into it. This one worked like a charm. Of course it did. She smiled to herself. *Dinner. If only...* "Do you really think that's a good idea? Our jobs put us on opposite sides of the equation. Nothing but trouble can come from that."

"I don't have anything to do with the decision whether to renew your lease or not. Way above my pay grade. But, to the extent I have any sway, I'll work on keeping you around. I like having you near."

The way he said it, she knew it was true. Of course, that didn't mean she wouldn't use it as a weapon when she felt vulnerable, which was pretty much always when around him. Not inferior...vulnerable. Like break-my-heart vulnerable. Old fears and hurts taunted her. Wilder wasn't her first rotorhead, or her first Coastie for that matter. When it came to flyboys, past experience had built a wall around her heart. "Where would you take me?" Sam asked, surprising herself. Yes, the commander had knocked a few bricks out of her wall, and that made her nervous.

"You strike me as a Thai kind of gal. Foreign Correspondents is supposed to be off the charts."

Sam tested the spring and the guide wires on the tailwheel, then worked her way from under the plane.

The commander didn't move, so when she rolled onto an elbow, he was right there smiling down at her. "Did I guess right?"

Thai was her favorite by far, and Foreign

Correspondents had been at the top of her list since she first read about its opening. Pricey and popular, it would take more than the few meager bucks she'd managed to save. "Yep, you guessed right. A bit too easily for my comfort level. I'm going to have to be a bit more wary."

"Wary? You're as skittish as a white-tail buck on opening day." He stood, then gave her a hand and pulled her to her feet.

"That's an interesting analogy." Sam worked at a casual attitude. Heat and electricity shot through her when he'd grabbed her hand, as if his touch completed a circuit.

"Not one of my best." He gave her a grin that probably was one of his best. Then the grin faded. "I pay attention, Sam Donovan." He sounded like he meant it.

For a moment Sam thought he'd move in. Her breath caught. She didn't move.

His eyes turned dark and serious. He leaned closer.

Sam froze.

The commander took a deep breath, then stepped back. "Thai it is. When?"

The spell was broken. Sam snagged the rag from her back pocket and busied herself wiping at the grease on her hands. "Shift change this week on the rigs. I've got a full flying schedule."

"And we're watching the hurricane trying to form south of Cuba. It's throwing off bands of storms but looks like it could be one hell of a ballbuster later in the week."

Sam knew what that meant—thirty thousand folks on the rigs in harm's way and three Coast Guard choppers to pluck the stupid ones to safety.

"But we'll make it happen."

Between their jobs, the storm, and the looming turf battle at the airport, Sam didn't see how. Probably best that way, but it was nice to dream.

CHAPTER FIVE

Night was Drayton Lewis's favorite time of day.

Lewis mopped his brow; klieg lights amped up the temperature in his office by double digits. He checked his appearance in the camera monitor. Tall, thin, not yet fifty, with dark black hair and piercing blue eyes above an aquiline nose, thin mouth, and strong jaw, he had an aura of power and the look of a merciless despot. He liked what he saw.

Tonight he wanted to be at his best. *Straight Talk,* the most influential prime-time news show, was setting up to interview him at the end of his business day regarding his recent investment in alternative energy, a staggering sum by anyone's standards, so it garnered a lot of media attention, as was Drayton's design. Success accrued to those who stacked the deck in their favor.

Lewis was a man who took chances, bet on the dark horse, and won. He'd made a fortune betting against the collective wisdom. First in technology, now in energy. He'd funded a huge solar farm in Nevada, several wind farms across the west, and battery technology to move the world electrically. Contrary to popular wisdom, he had leveraged his net worth and put it all on the dark horse sector in the race. Of course, he hadn't left it entirely up to chance, along the way buying a few congressmen and senators influential enough provide a hedge for his bet, although that was far from a sure thing. As Warren Buffet was the Oracle of Omaha to his generation, Drayton Lewis intended to be the Emperor of New Energy, and right from Houston, the beating heart of the oil business. Hit 'em where they lived, someone had told him once. Lewis liked the sound of that. But the current price of oil, now at a several-decade low, put a crimp in his plans. When oil was cheap, no one really cared about alternative energy. Time to change their minds. He had a fortune riding on it.

A young assistant, cute and bubbly in painted-on jeans and a tight tee, with a face curiously unadorned with pancake makeup so popular in Texas, approached him, a mic held reverently in one hand as if it were a snake, or the man in front of her was. "I need to wire you, Mr. Lewis, and then check the levels for sound."

Lewis opened his arms wide and shot her a grin of equal proportion. "Honey, you can do anything you'd like to me. Sky's the limit."

Without a smile, or any reaction at all that Lewis could see, the assistant mic'd him up, weaving the wire under his shirt. Drayton thought about copping a feel. The Texas women were used to it, but the New York thing made him wary. The local girls were taught to take what they were given. He'd heard it wasn't the same up north. Although pushing the limits a bit *was* fun. Always interesting to see what you got. "You want a job, a good job?"

The girl didn't even bother meeting his gaze. "I have one, thanks."

He shrugged. "Your loss."

Done with her job, the girl stepped back. This time she looked him square in the eye, her gaze never wavering. "No...sir."

"Touchy," Drayton muttered as he settled himself in the limelight and watched her ass as she moved away. Nice ass; too bad. Shifting in his chair, he figured the angled shots and then worked out how to play them.

Shelby Walker took the chair opposite him, smoothing

her skirt and tugging her suit jacket into place. An up-and-comer, they'd assured him—but she wasn't their top dog, which miffed Drayton, but he didn't let it show. He felt relaxed, in control. He'd approved the questions in advance and had been assured they would be soft-served. A pro-alternative-energy piece, he'd been told.

"Are you comfortable, Mr. Lewis?" Shelby Walker asked, all sweetness and light, her youth on beautiful display. "You ready?"

A cakewalk, he thought as he nodded, then unbuttoned his coat button, letting his jacket fall in an easy, casual style. Open, like he had nothing to hide. "This isn't my first rodeo."

"Okay." Shelby took a last flip through her notes. "I'll do a quick lead-in—it's not like I have to introduce you to the world—then we'll dive in. Sound good?"

She was cute, Drayton thought, with her take-me-seriously attitude. Her light brown hair in a short bob, her eyes dark and intense, her makeup overdone for the cameras but right for Texas, yes, she was cute. Probably a bit on the young side for him—he liked women who were a bit more...seasoned. Trim and buttoned-up in her East Coast clothes—those would have to go. He idly wondered what she would be like in bed. "When will this segment run again?"

"Next show. Thursday."

Three days. Enough time. He adopted an air of calm control through the intro and then readied himself for the first question. He'd pretend to be surprised, disarmingly unguarded.

"Thank you for being here, Mr. Lewis. You are quite a legend, an iconoclast." Shelby smiled an easy, deferential smile.

"You follow the pack, you're just another lemming, you know?" He raised an eyebrow as if he expected her to not know.

"Right off the cliff." Shelby's eyes challenged him.

Drayton settled back. Maybe he imagined the challenge.

She'd been spoon-fed the questions, and he'd been assured she'd follow the script. "Our reliance on fossil fuels is growing, our supply dwindling. We're leveraging our country's future, getting in deeper and deeper to foreign suppliers. What's going to happen when they cut us off?" He asked the question, knowing the answer.

"Why would they?" Shelby wasn't buying it.

Not the answer he'd been told to expect. "Mutually assured destruction." Drayton laughed, giving the impression he thought she was naïve, bordering on stupid, then shot her a warning glance. Shelby Walker had veered off the script.

"More mutually assured survival."

So she wanted to sail into rough seas. Lewis smiled, an easy affable smile. He ate reporters much more seasoned than Shelby Walker as appetizers. "But at what cost, really? Global warming. The ozone hole."

"Any correlation remains speculative. What is known is the temperature of Earth has fluctuated through millennia as evidenced by the various ice ages. And no one can say that there never has been a hole in the ozone layer at each pole. For all we know, they are natural phenomena."

Drayton narrowed his eyes. The sheen of sweat, curiously cold, oiled his forehead. The girl had a plan; he could see it in the flat cold of her eyes. "That's your interpretation." He gave her a relaxed smile. Just a kid, an upstart, hoping to make her mark besting him. Drayton would've laughed if the film hadn't been rolling. She didn't have any idea who she was taking on. Hell, he'd been playing the game longer than she'd been alive. For some reason, that realization wasn't as comforting as he thought it would be.

Shelby let her victory hang there for a moment. "First the tech world, now Big Oil. Hoping to wean us off our addiction to fossil fuels?"

Drayton settled in. Now they were on track. "It'd be better for the planet, better for all of us. And, given enough time, we're going to outrun our supply, and then where will we be?"

"And your solution, one that you've risked your net worth on, includes solar, wind, and electric?"

Drayton gave a confident smile. "It's not a risk, really. Solar makes sense—we have an enormous supply of sunlight in certain parts of the world. Wind as well. And electric, the battery technology is developing so fast that the excitement is palpable."

"Perhaps there's a place for each of them, but at what cost?"

Drayton shifted, sitting upright. "Excuse me?"

A hint of a benign smile lifted the corners of her mouth. "Let's take wind. The turbines are unsightly, most folks hate them, and they are killing raptors by the thousands. The technology wouldn't be profitable without serious federal tax incentives, rammed through by two senators and three congressmen, all of whom have received seven-digit contributions from you or your affiliated companies."

Drayton's anger spiked. The little twit, trying to make her name by tearing him down to size. "What are you implying?" He tried to keep his voice light, conversational, but even he heard the edge in it.

"I'm not implying anything, just stating the facts." She started laying out papers on the coffee table in front of him. "Here are the 990 disclosures. The contributions are a matter of record." She leveled a stare. "You connect the dots."

"I contribute to a number of politicians. I have a multitude of companies. I can't keep track of everything they do." He could tell the statement came out sounding like a lie, which infuriated Drayton further. He felt his face flush with anger. Not good.

She let silence stretch for a beat or two in manifestation of her disbelief. "The Man With a Finger on the Pulse of Every Employee, as *Newsweek* called you? I find that hard to believe. But, okay, I think I can connect the dots." She leaned forward, extending a piece of paper to him.

He knew not taking it would make him look worse, so

he snatched it from her hand. He didn't glance at it.

"That outlines the flow of money, timing of phone calls from your private line to a certain senator in a western state. Curiously, right after all that, he changed his vote on a bill providing federal funding to a huge wind farm in the northern part of his state, ensuring you millions."

Drayton leveled his gaze and lowered his voice. "You'd better be careful. Slander is a serious charge."

"And truth is a complete defense," Shelby said with the confidence bred by her two bar association memberships. She thrust a second sheet of paper toward Lewis.

This one he ignored, his hands folded neatly in his lap as his mind whirled. *Where had she gotten that information? A mole, it had to be. But who?*

Shelby retracted the paper, returning it to the small pile in her lap. "This one implicates Senator Herrera, the poster-boy for scum-free politicians. He took a chunk of change which you deposited in a dummy account in Guatemala, for which it seems he was pulling some strings to get some oil leases in the Gulf nationalized. National security, it says."

God, she knew stuff only a few people knew. Drayton felt a trickle of sweat run down his side. He resisted wiping his forehead. "That's crazy. I have no interest in that."

"Yes, but your friends in Washington would have their hand on the oil spigot, wouldn't they? They'd control some of the largest finds to date, the bulk of this country's major production. Especially since the environmentalists, who you also fund heavily, have effectively eliminated drilling off the coast of California and in Alaska, not to mention South Dakota."

"A clever little theory, but you have to prove it."

"I just did."

She was a born interviewer, Drayton grudgingly admitted to himself. He had underestimated her—something he wouldn't do again. Getting cocky, he'd let his defenses down. A guy like him had a target on his back, especially for gung-ho reporters gunning to make their mark. Granted, she'd made it to network news, something he should've been more appreciative of. Too bad she'd never get the chance to see how far she could go. He'd bury her as a stand-in weather girl on the early morning news in an obscure market somewhere nobody gave a rat's ass about. "Clearly, you don't want to talk about the energy issues facing the nation. This interview is over."

Shelby nodded at the producer.

Lewis waited until the red light on the cameras all blinked out. "This was nothing more than a witch hunt. Tell your bosses no more interviews. Ever!" Drayton ripped the mike from his shirt, pulling the wire like he was ripping stitches from a wound. He hurled the device at the assistant who had materialized at his elbow. He pointed a menacing finger at Shelby. "I'll have your ass."

"You wish." Shelby breathed under her breath, making the assistant who hovered at her elbow smile.

Lewis turned and stalked off as he shouted, "Who the hell is in charge? I want that woman's head on a spike."

Shelby and her assistant both watched as Lewis stormed out of his office. "What you just did, Shel, was either brilliant or stupid beyond measure."

CHAPTER SIX

Shelby Walker's career was over. Drayton Lewis slammed through the doors into his private apartment. As he expected, his personal assistant, Becca Molinari, waited at her desk. She jumped when the door hit the stops and bounced back.

"What the hell bit of bullshit did you feed the newshounds?"

Her smile fled at his bark. She fisted her hands in her lap where he couldn't see her knuckles turning white. "The regular press packet. Why?" She kept her voice even.

Lewis narrowed his eyes, looking for a twitch, a hint. Vibrating with anger, he kicked her chair around and then placed a hand on each arm, jailing her in the full force of his wrath.

Her unblinking gaze held his.

Moments ticked by.

Then he relaxed, the tension leaving his face. Plucking a few strands of her blonde hair he coiled them around a finger.

She met his eyes with a steady gaze. "What happened?"

With the flick of his wrist, he jerked her hair, wrapping it around his fist, and pulled tight.

A quick flinch and a slight uptick of one corner of her

mouth was Becca's only response. "You are in a state." Her eyes shone.

Lewis pulled tighter.

Slowly, she licked her lips.

Oh, he liked this woman; he liked her a lot. He uncoiled his hand from her hair and then backhanded her across the cheek.

A red welt bloomed where his ring met bone. Grabbing her around the neck, he squeezed. Hard. Still, she smiled. Harder. The grin faded; her eyes turned dark. Harder. One hand twitched in her lap. His turn to smile. He knew what she wanted—to reach up, to fight, to pry his fingers away. Her blood tripped faster under his fingers.

"Drayton, you're hurting me," she gasped, her breath all but gone.

"Isn't that the point?" He kept the pressure on, enjoying the dullness that crept into her eyes. "You haven't hurt me, have you, Becca? You didn't tell Shelby Walker any of our secrets now, did you?"

With her last bit of air, Becca Molinari laughed.

And Drayton Lewis had his answer. He released her. "I didn't think so." He grabbed her hand, jerking her out of the chair. "You know what I need."

CHAPTER SEVEN

Presley Davis, senior agent with the Cyber Division of the Federal Bureau of Investigation, mopped his brow with a folded and creased square of pristine white cloth. As he stared at the body, he rearranged the cloth, point up, in the breast pocket of his jacket. New York in the summer—the bowels of Hell as far as he was concerned. Today did nothing to change his mind, the heat rose in undulating waves off the concrete, moldering the garbage in the dumpsters lining the alleyway. This was one of the hard ones—this one was one of theirs. Worse, if he was who the Medico-Legal Investigator from the Office of the Chief Medical Examiner standing to his side said he was, he'd been Davis's responsibility. "You sure his name is Jake Walker?"

The MLI, a young blonde woman in her early thirties—Davis couldn't remember her name; they all looked the same—shrugged under the weight of the chip on her shoulder and read from her notes. "Jacob Charles Walker. Age thirty-one. Several advanced degrees from MIT. Senior software engineer at the NYMEX. Worked late last night, according to the security guy. Left around eleven."

Shit. Their inside guy.

Davis hadn't met Walker. Jeffers, his head geek, recruited him and was running him. But, as the agent in charge, Davis felt responsible...hell, he *was* responsible. Squinting behind his shades, he looked up and down the rabbit warren of narrow concrete canyons. "Walker live in the Battery?"

The MLI consulted her notes again. "No. Upper West Side." She tilted her head as she stared at Jake's body. "Looks like a professional hit."

The woman had a flair for the obvious. One shot to the head, point-blank range. But the killer had worked him over before delivering the bullet. So much so, Walker had probably welcomed it.

Davis flinched as he recorded each wound on the battered and broken body, imagining the pain, the torture. "One sick son-of-a-bitch did this."

"Should I put that in my report?" The MLI asked.

Davis didn't smile, even though he understood her need for humor in a situation like this—it helped with the fear. "So what was Walker doing over here? If he left from work, he'd try the One World station, I'm sure. Looks like he was going in the opposite direction."

"I'd say, and I'm not the expert so this is just an educated opinion, but it looks like he probably was snatched at some point, taken somewhere and," she motioned to his body, but didn't look at it, "all of that was done to him. Then they dropped him back here to be found."

Davis had come to the same conclusion, although he'd need confirmation from the Medical Examiner. "Any more ideas?"

"You'll have to talk with Detective Martinez." The MLI lifted her chin in the direction of a heavyset man standing at the entrance to the alley. "He's the detective in charge."

A young NYPD officer cleared his throat and angled into the light. "Excuse me, sir." He nodded to Davis. "Ma'am, we found this in the dumpster two blocks over." He held out a computer bag, distressed leather.

"Walker's?" Davis asked.

The officer shot a look at the MLI, who gave him an

almost imperceptible nod. "Yes, sir. A couple of business cards, but nothing else."

"What else did you find in the dumpster?"

"Trash had been picked up yesterday by the looks of it, so there wasn't much in there."

"What else?"

"Fast-food bags, some old clothing, a FedEx box."

"Address?"

"None. It hadn't been used."

Davis filed that away. "Laptop?"

"No, sir."

"Bag it and label it," the MLI ordered. The officer nodded once and then eased back into the darkness.

"I'm assuming the cause of death will be the bullet to the back of the head?" Davis asked the MLI when they were once again alone.

"That'd be a good bet, but we won't know for sure until the autopsy and the tox screen." She let her eyes linger on Jake Walker's body. "But the bullet could have been delivered post-mortem."

"A message." Davis nodded.

"Or a reprieve."

That one he took personally. His people, his family. He'd lost some before, not many, but each one carved off a piece of his soul until he had little left.

A hit on a software engineer at one of the most important exchanges in the world. One who his staff had recruited and who had looked to him for protection. Agent Davis contemplated all that could mean, none of it good.

While figuring out who thought it was a good idea to take this kid out would be interesting, Agent Davis really wanted to know why. Whose toes had Jake Walker stepped on? Knowing that would bring him one step closer to the endgame. Lately, his higher-ups had been climbing up his ass to get some answers, which raised his antennae a bit. Squatting down next to the body, he rested his forearms across his knees. "What game were you playing, Jake

Walker? Where did you step outside the lines?" *And why the hell didn't you wait like we told you to do?*

This wasn't the first hit Davis was chasing on this particular trail. And he'd heard there was another one waiting for him at the NYMEX—Jake's boss.

He hoped to God that was the last target, but somehow he knew it wouldn't be. These guys, whoever they were, were cloaked in a darkness he'd never encountered. The stakes were high. His higher-ups were taking orders from somewhere even higher. The entirety of Davis's mission was above his pay grade, but he felt the ripples, could feel the tug of the riptide.

"The bullet will be a 9 mm, a tight twist, but an identifying gouge down the middle." He'd seen the guy's work before.

The MLI snapped to attention, her eyes locked on his. "You holding out on me, Davis?"

He blew out a breath, keeping his anger, his frustration, on simmer. "I've been chasing this guy across three continents. I've seen his handiwork."

"So, who is he?"

"Haven't a clue." Davis felt his anger start to boil.

"What does he want?"

"What his boss wants."

"Who's his boss?"

"Now there is the question."

That got a raised eyebrow and a disbelieving look.

Not getting any answers from the dead man and with distrust emanating in waves off MLI What's-Her-Name, Agent Davis pushed himself back to his feet, grimacing as his knees protested. One bad knee normally would've taken him out of the field—two would give him a gold watch. He'd take it…once he got the bead on this guy and those who hired him. His mission was clear. Identify then step out of the way. He flipped open the phone and dialed a familiar number.

Andy Jeffers, Davis's team leader and in-house head

hacker, answered before the first ring. "Don't ask." At first word of Jake Walker's murder, Davis had tasked Andy and his team of barely respectable geniuses with sifting through files and computers at the NYMEX, remotely, of course.

"Got anything?"

"I told you not to ask." Andy was all of maybe twenty and had come up the hard way, learning his skills in the Stygian world of the Dark net. When one of his hacks got busted, jail or the FBI had been his two options—it had taken several countries working together over a year to bring him down. Davis could picture the kid with full sleeves of tats running up both arms, an angular face roofed by thick, short, cropped jet-black hair, and skin so pasty anyone who looked twice—and most did—would know the only light he saw was fluorescent. And he could hear him chomping on his ever-present wad of bubble gum, occasionally blowing a bubble, then popping it with a loud smack. Irritating, but Davis didn't have to work in the same room with him.

Andy lowered his voice. "He was one of mine. It's my fault."

"Don't go there. Walker left when we told him to stay." Davis remembered his first loss. Jeffers would remember Jake Walker, too. Perhaps that was a good thing. Somebody would remember why he died.

"Hell, there was a killer in the building. I wouldn't have stayed either."

The truth of that statement hit Davis pretty hard. "Okay. But that was my call. So if anybody is at fault, it would be me. If you do your job, Walker won't have died for nothing. So do your job."

Jeffers audibly worked the gum. "Davis, sometimes you're an asshole."

"Only sometimes? I must be slipping. Tell me what you got."

"A maze even a rat couldn't get out of. Whoever's doing this, they got skills."

"Andy, stop sounding so impressed."

"The guy's good; that's all I'm saying."

"So the answer to my question, then, would be nothing?"

"Well, not definitively. This dead dude, he was working a pretty elaborate trading scheme."

"*He* was working it?"

"His credentials. If not him, then somebody was in the system pretending to be him."

"It wasn't him." Jake had opened the door on his suggestion, and Davis felt while the burden of his own guilt was bad enough, carrying the condemnation of his team would be staggering. "The trading scheme? Is it active?"

"Yeah. Oil futures."

"Oil? Usually, this sort of thing happened in the precious metals market. What's the game?"

"Not sure exactly, yet. Trades that bypass the security and reporting constraints. Most of them forward-dated."

"Like a trigger—all going to hit at once. How much?"

"Enough to move the market."

"Can you trace the money?"

"Working on that. I got a theory, but chasing it will take time."

"I'm listening."

"Remember Hammertoss?"

"Sure. A bunch of Russians hiding code in plain sight—in the pixels of a seemingly innocuous GIF or JPEG."

"Right, folks were downloading normal stuff, e-cards, photos of crap for sale on various sites, music, never knowing there was a coded time bomb riding into their machines piggybacked on the innocuous stuff."

"And, at a certain time, the bomb explodes and the code gathers itself and performs its designed function."

"I think the same thing is at play here."

Davis whistled. Once they found the code, reading it would be easy. But finding it? "Get all our resources on it. We have to find it and shut it down before it takes the market, and the world, for a ride. You got it?"

"Sure."

Davis ignored the undertone of sarcasm. "I want names. Amounts. Locations. I want these guys. I want them bad. Do what you have to do to get me a lead."

"Okay," Jeffers's voice sobered.

"I got your back."

"Sure, boss. One more thing."

"Yeah?"

"This has a different feel to it."

"How so?"

"It's like part of the hack is super sophisticated—the whole steganography angle we just talked about. And then they'll leave a crumb anybody could find."

"Like a trail?"

"Or a clever misdirection. I'm sure it'll take me down a few blind alleys before I see the light."

"Let me know when you do."

Snapping on a set of plastic gloves, Agent Davis stepped over the body, straddling it as he worked through Jake Walker's pockets. He found the kid's cell in his inside breast pocket. It had a broken screen but still lit when Davis punched it on. A long list of contacts, a few favorites—pretty normal for a single guy. The recent calls proved more enlightening. One with a Houston area code—made yesterday afternoon. He pressed the number, calling it back. An answering service picked up, "Senator Phillip Herrera's office." Davis hit the *end* button. "Shit!" The killer had the jump on him. What else was fucking new? He handed Jake's phone to the MLI and then turned his back, moving a distance away.

Using his own phone this time. Davis typed in another number. He waited while it went through the clicks and pings of encryption.

"Yeah?" The voice was hard, flat, the voice of a killer.

"You got eyes on the senator?"

"Roger."

"Don't lose him." Davis stuffed the phone in his pocket as he turned back to the MLI, who was ordering the forensics team to secure and transport the body back to the office for an autopsy. "You got a rundown on this guy's family?"

"Don't want to talk to the local cops, huh?"

"They always want to tell me they have their own cybercrime specialists. What they fail to appreciate is our reach is a bit wider than theirs." Truth of it was he hated dealing with folks who hated the Feds just because, and Detective Martinez had that look about him.

"At the risk of being annihilated by jurisdictional crossfire, here's what we've got." She read from her notepad. "Parents in New York. One sister. Shelby. Also New York-based. Works for that news show, *Straight Talk*. Trying to locate her now." She jotted a note, then ripped out the page. "Here's her address and phone."

"Family been notified?"

"Looks like you drew the short straw, Agent Davis."

"Everybody hates the Feds."

She didn't argue. Davis looked at his phone, the list of missed calls. Jake Walker's number was the last. Davis had seen the call. He hadn't taken it. Figured the kid was getting spooked. He'd planned to get Andy to settle him down.

Too late for that.

No wonder everyone hated the Feds.

CHAPTER EIGHT

The boat rocked as Senator Phillip Herrera stepped aboard. With dual outboard engines, a flybridge, and a lower cabin filled with extra fuel, the boat was the Senator's escape—from life...and from death.

He'd known this day would come.

You lie with snakes... He shook his head at his mother's admonition. Dead all these years, the woman could still reach him from the grave. *Sometimes, Mama, you have to lie with the snakes to learn how to kill them.*

And with this particular snake, cutting off the head wouldn't solve the problem.

Although he felt eyes on him, he tried to be casual as he paused in the rear of the boat to attach the fuel line. He then gave the bladder a couple of squeezes, moving fuel into the engine. The cool fingers of fear brushed the back of his neck like a scorned lover as he scanned the small estuary as if eyeing the eddies, the calm, cool waters where fish would gather. He had to make them believe, those who watched, that this was like any other fishing escape—he was known for running away from the office occasionally.

But this wasn't any other day. Far from it.

The sun still climbed toward its apex; yet, heat and humidity already gelled the air, making it hard to breathe. Without thinking, the senator slapped at the prick of a mosquito on his forearm. The Texas Gulf Coast in the summertime was as inhospitable a place as any on Earth.

Nothing moved. The water slick, unruffled, the light yellow-green sheen of undisturbed algae covered the areas closest to shore. A blue heron, imperial in its fragile beauty, blinked at him from its perch among the grasses and reeds fortifying the shoreline. A lone seagull hidden in the early morning haze called, a plaintive cry, common and disturbing.

He'd known for some time someone had been watching, like a predator slithering through the grass, hidden yet raising the hackles on the back of his neck. Recently they'd been bolder, careless in their arrogance, and he'd known time was short. After taking a lead role in the oversight hearing that led to the breakup of the Mineral Management Service, the senator had met his share of snakes. But these guys, they were the proverbial wolves in sheep's clothing—and nobody was seeing it. But they would. He'd expose them...if he stayed alive.

That's why he'd taken the risk, shown his hand. He needed Donovan's help, but the stubborn Irishman needed proof. Fairly reasonable, since the senator was asking the oilman to risk his life. At first Donovan hadn't believed him, forcing the senator to give him more than he dared.

And they watched. They listened. And they killed. He had the photos, the documentation. No going back now.

The senator pushed the boat away from the ramp with a quick shove of his foot, letting it drift into slightly deeper water. The prod of panic strong, he fought the urge to hurry. To anyone watching, this would appear to be one of his normal days of fishing.

Donovan's rig perched at the edge of the continental shelf—a long trip in a small fishing boat meant to dart in and out of the bayous, keeping close to shore. The senator had been secreting fuel in extra tanks in the cabin below for over a week.

The swells were growing—pushed by a storm gathering strength in the Caribbean. But, if the weather held, he'd make it. If not, he'd be a headline.

And God help all those left behind.

At the helm, he turned the rotating switch to the "rear battery" indicator, giving the engine and the instruments power. With one hand, he cracked the throttle. A turn of the key and the engine roared to life—a thrumming growl that vibrated through his chest. After a couple of grunts and puffs of exhaust, the outboard settled into a steady rhythm. Pushing off from the pilings, pointing the bow to the bayou, the senator opened the throttle. The boat sprang forward with an adrenaline-inducing jump. As the water flew under the hull, the wind ripped at his shirt. For the first time in weeks, the senator felt in control, a sense of personal power he could use to wrest back his self-respect.

Slowing as he approached the flats, the senator killed the engine, then pulled the prop out of the water. The air barely stirred under the growing heat of the day, the brackish water lending a musty odor. A dead fish or two added a disconcerting pungency. The scent of death, the smell of the salt flats. Combined with the hint of sulfur carried on the scant breeze from the refineries in Texas City just to the north, it was the scent of his hardscrabble youth.

The senator breathed deep. Stepping to the bow, he dropped the small trolling motor down. After turning the battery power switch to "Battery 2," he stepped on the seat and then climbed on the console. He reached back for his rod, setting it in one of the tube holders attached to the side of the console—he'd baited it last night. Propping his knees against the windscreen, he held on to the high bar, controlling the trolling speed with the small throttle attached near his thumb. From this vantage point, he could see down into the water. Scanning the bottom drifting by underneath, he looked for dark shapes moving against the sandy bottom—a habit. Then he eyed the sky, the clouds gathering. He'd give it a few minutes before drifting into open water and heading south.

CHAPTER NINE

Patrick Donovan's mind raced as he climbed aboard his helicopter perched on the helipad of the San Rafael Oil Company Building in the heart of downtown Houston. Senator Herrera's warning had him on edge, looking over his shoulder for phantom ghosts. He glanced at his watch and cursed. The day had gotten away from him.

His meeting had taken longer than he'd thought it would. Farrell Bishop, CEO of San Rafael Oil, had turned up the heat. If his staffer hadn't pulled them apart, there was a good chance he would've choked the life out of the S.O.B. He'd been a fool to take San Rafael on as a limited partner.

Donovan normally loved playing the game of Big Oil and Big Money. But this time, the stakes were higher than ever, the rules shifting like sand under his feet. Hell, he wasn't even sure he knew who all the players were. When he'd asked the senator, he'd acted like someone had a gun jammed in his back. Not like him. Not like him at all.

But the senator was on his way to meet him—a hell of a jaunt in that bucket of bolts he had, but there'd been no talking him out of it. And he'd promised he'd come clean. If things went as planned, Phillip ought to be at the rig by now, and for a moment Patrick wondered what he was getting himself into. But Phillip was an old friend—chosen family. Besides, no use worrying—he'd know soon enough.

Donovan's mind switched gears, whirling with worries about keeping the bankers off his back, his limited partners out of his office, and the environmentalists out of his hair. On top of that juggling act, he had an upcoming safety inspection, fifty employees he had to figure out how to pay, and a secret so big it threatened to blow the lid off.

And the sharks were circling, using their clout to try to pull his lease out from under him. *Safety concerns, my ass.* For the first time in a very long time—since his first partner had stolen their first big find right out from under him—Patrick Donovan found himself contemplating homicide. Most folks weren't worth the killing, but Ferrell Bishop was proving to be the exception.

Donovan hoped like hell the senator could keep the slime ball under control. Phillip had always managed to keep the playing field, if not level, then at least open to the little guys like Donovan, but lately Patrick had felt the senator's control slipping. He wondered what Bishop had on the Senator. Whatever it was, it must be good. Was Bishop involved in whatever it was Phillip had uncovered? He'd know soon enough...if Phillip made it.

As Donovan started the engine, he waved the pilot around to the left seat. No way was he letting the kid fly tonight. When Donovan took the controls, life settled into some semblance of order. Whether it was the act of flying itself that centered him or the fact that, while flying, he couldn't think about anything else that brought life into focus, he didn't know and he didn't care. After securing the door and then himself in the co-pilot seat, the kid donned his headset and gave a nod in answer to Donovan's thumbs-up.

With the RPMs up, engine temps in the green, and the blades beating a fast rhythm, Donovan pulled up on the collective. The helicopter shuddered, struggling against the ropes of gravity. It rose, slowly at first, then soaring, a leaf riding the wind.

He kicked the rudder, pointed the machine southeast toward the ship channel, then dipped the nose to pick up speed. Once over the channel, he would follow it to the Gulf, then let the GPS guide him to the production vessel. His petroleum engineer and drilling supervisor, Benji Easton, was waiting.

Donovan tried to loosen his tie, but the thing refused to budge. After a brief battle, he surrendered. He'd never learned the proper technique needed to tie a necktie. Well, actually he could tie the thing, but once he did, he was as hung up as if someone had put a noose around his neck and a bag over his head. Today more than ever. Every time he met with his investors he felt like Bishop had his hand on the lever, waiting to drop the floor out from under him.

Oil was big money business, dirty, cutthroat, and, occasionally, downright dangerous. Donovan Exploration was a small-time player—always one step away from being squashed like a snake on the Interstate. Nerves chewed at him a bit, an unusual unease. Benji had been guarded and edgy over the phone, not like his normal pragmatic self. And he hadn't wanted to talk about it. Better in person, he'd said. There seemed to be an epidemic of that going around, and Donovan didn't like it.

The stakes were really high on this well—deep water, lots of money...too much interest. Donovan feared he may have mortgaged his life to the wrong folks. The senator had heightened his fear. In all likelihood, depending on what Benji and Phillip each had to say, he'd be rich or he'd be dead. He'd as much as told Sam that when he gave her the key, but he wasn't sure she believed him, not that he blamed her. Sam was a cookie-cutter image of himself except for the obvious. If the roles had been reversed, he wouldn't have believed her either. Not something that made him proud. Family shouldn't be that way, but he'd earned the distrust, and he and his girl butted heads more than they should. His fault. Somehow he'd try to bridge the current chasm between them. He couldn't even remember what had set them at each other's throats, and the realization shamed him. Some things were more important than winning...even to an Irishman.

He hadn't been the father she deserved. The Almighty

ought to give parents a do-over, especially when it came to their first-born. But God apparently didn't see fit, and Patrick didn't think Sam would be that magnanimous.

To Donovan, the flight seemed to pass quickly as the helicopter skimmed across the swells at fifty feet; enough of a margin above the swells in the gathering darkness but low enough to keep it interesting. Worry nipped at him—the swells were higher than normal, much higher. That tropical depression forming to the south in the Caribbean was having an effect, tendrils of storms spiraling from the massive low-pressure center. The weather guys were touting it as the storm of the decade. A bit premature in Donovan's opinion—the storm was still a long way off. Pretty soon it would have a name, if it didn't already—something Donovan found silly.

Phillip's boat wasn't meant for the swells, not swells like these.

The ceiling came down, and the fog thickened the further south they went. In the dwindling light, Donovan found himself relying on the GPS to find his target—a tiny speck in a vast expanse of nothing. Every day, pilots put their lives in the hands of technology they barely understood—took a certain kind of person, Donovan thought, wondering why that occurred to him now, after all these years. The reflections of an old man with more behind him than in front. Not the most comforting thought.

But tomorrow was never promised.

Soon he could just make out the odd Erector-Set outline of his drilling rig positioned where the gentle slope of the continental shelf dropped off a cliff, turning the muddy water of the shallows a deep blue. As if drilling for oil on dry land wasn't hard enough, Donovan and his crew had to go through seven thousand feet of sea water before they even started drilling—an extraordinarily costly proposition and dangerous as hell.

Normally the helipad was empty, but today Donovan had to hover while members of his crew boarded another helicopter resting on the pad. Today was shift-change day and apparently something had thrown their schedule off—the chopper should've been long gone. Guys still milled on the level below, so the chopper spooling up wasn't even the last one. Generally, crews worked three weeks on, then three weeks off. Today the weary were going home to families, and the fresh were back, hopefully ready for the grind of a twenty-four-hour-a-day, seven-days-a-week drilling operation. The chaos on the vessel was certainly more than normal, thought Donovan, as he hovered the helicopter, his fingers only lightly touching the stick. So many bodies moving, people coming and going...

Soon it was his turn, and he settled the machine precisely, taking a brief bit of joy in his still-sharp skills. Flying—easy to learn, but hell to keep sharp.

He didn't shut it down, idling the engine—they couldn't take up the helipad, the helicopters working the shift circled to the west, hanging in the sky like a fireflies on a summer night. His co-pilot took over. As Donovan slid from the helicopter, he motioned to the kid to gather a few folks waiting for a ride to the mainland, then spool it up and head back to shore as they'd planned. Benji had promised he'd find Donovan a bunk, if he could sleep after they'd talked. Donovan hadn't liked the sound of either.

Ducking at the waist, Donovan moved to safety, then watched the kid lift off and head for home. An ominous feeling settled over him as he watched the night sky swallow the delicate machine—his link to the safety of land. The wind had freshened—it licked at his face like a lion contemplating dinner. Lightning strobed in the distance, briefly illuminating the towering clouds advancing on them. Perhaps that's what made him nervous—a tiny platform in the middle of an angry ocean reinforced the truth that man was but a small, powerless animal at the whims of forces far greater than himself.

Donovan didn't like the ocean. He didn't like storms. He didn't like feeling powerless. And he didn't like secrets, something he'd reminded Phillip of but to no avail. As twitchy as a dog on summer concrete, he tried to shrug off the uneasy feeling, but it wouldn't let him be. Taking extra care with the ladder—the trip down those few treacherous rungs was far more dangerous than the flight out—Donovan arrived unscathed in front of his engineer.

"Sorry you had to wait, Paddy." Benji pounded Donovan on the back, shouting to be heard above the rotor beating the wind.

Thankfully, he had braced himself for the blow. A bear of a man, Benji stood a half-inch over six and a half feet tall—he always said the half-inch made all the difference. With his shock of unruly brown hair, his broad shoulders and hands as big as a grizzly's paws, he had the look of someone who should be heading into the forest with an ax in his hand.

"Jesus, Benji, easy on the old man." Donovan scanned his friend's face for a hint. Nothing. "We got a storm coming."

"Been watching the radar. Coming up from the south. Just a tropical depression right now, but they're watching it. Saying it might be a bad one, but too early to tell." Benji's eyes, flat and dark, held Donovan's for a moment. "Not going to be good."

"And the dynamic positioning system? Will it be able to hold our position?"

"We're anchored pretty good. The system can help keep the load off the ropes, but if the storm builds like they're saying and it heads our way, we'll have to button up the well and boogie."

"Not unless we have to." They were at drill depth and had just completed logging the well. The data so far was crazy.

"You putting pipe back into the hole?"

"Yep, it'll take a while. Then we'll circulate the mud to test the hole. Then drop the last string of production casing."

"Will you make it before the storm?"

"*If* it sticks to the track and timetable they're calculating right now." Paddy started to smile. Benji held up his hand.

"And *if* nothing goes wrong. Those are huge ifs, Paddy."

"We'll just assume life is going to work out, and it will." Paddy didn't believe that any more than his production engineer, but it sounded good—and it couldn't hurt to throw it out to the Universe. Maybe, just this once, the Fates would listen and smile kindly on him. "Any sign of a fishing boat docking below?"

Benji cocked an eyebrow. "No. Are we expecting someone?"

"Yes." Donovan waved away the question he saw lurking in the big man's expression. "Let me know if a boat comes close, okay?" Phillip should have been here by now.

"Sure." Benji turned and scanned the agitated waters, patches visible in the lights directed downward from the platform. "Whoever we're expecting, he'd better hurry. Seas are coming up."

Donovan didn't look; he didn't need to. That worry had been chewing on him all the way from Houston. A lot of fishing boats had been out in the Gulf as he passed overhead, but most of them were scurrying back toward land. If the senator was out there, Donovan hadn't seen him.

Benji gave the storm a last once-over, then motioned Donovan in front of him. "This is just the first wave. The really big one is still forming south of Cuba. Pressures are lower than anything we've seen in a while." He gave a shrug that didn't dislodge his worried expression. "We've weathered worse."

Donovan didn't know whether they were still talking about the weather. "What's this about? Smoke and mirrors is so unlike you."

Benji gave a quick shake of his head as his eyes darted side-to-side. "Not here." Before Donovan could object or take the lead, Benji grabbed his boss's briefcase, then turned and disappeared down the ladder.

Donovan followed, but turned at the sound of engines spooling up. Another helicopter, the only way off this tiny bit of human audacity other than the pods below, which weren't a viable option for him—his claustrophobia would kill him before he crawled into one of those—lifted into the darkening sky. The dark smudge of clouds on the horizon loomed closer, riding in on a freshening breeze with the hint of ozone. Tonight's storm would hit before his pilot could return. Donovan couldn't shake the feeling that he shouldn't have let the chopper go.

He ducked as the first few drops pelted him and ran for the control room. As he shook off the droplets, he faced the worried frown of his chief engineer. "I keep the logs in there, locked up tight, like you said." Benji pointed at the filing drawers, narrow and shallow, bolted to the far wall of the operations control center one floor above the main deck. A gray metal table bolted to the deck and the two chairs tucked under it were the only pieces of furniture in the room besides two stools in front of the control panel. With the two men packed in as well, there was hardly enough room left for them to breathe.

As he worked the lock, Benji's eyes were wide as saucers, black with a dose of serious. "We got a problem." He had to shout to be heard over the thunder of the big diesels, which pulsed through every surface of the metal vessel like a heartbeat. "I told you not to take those people's money. Bad partners."

"This is about our *partners*?"

"In a roundabout sort of way." Benji looked at the logs like they were his last dose of poison.

"Jesus, Benji. You're spooking the hell out of me." Donovan crossed himself, a reflexive move—Irish superstition etched into his soul.

"A bunch of other stuff came for you on the first chopper this morning, including a letter from the bankers. Price of oil has them twitchy. You want it?" Benji pulled at the papers in the drawer.

"It'll wait—I can do a lot, but changing the price of oil isn't one of them."

"Don't be too sure."

Donovan started to laugh, but Benji's serious expression

as he handed over the logs shut him down. "It's all there. You won't believe it at first. Then, you'll be over the moon..."

"And then?"

"You'll be scared as shit. That old adage, too much of a good thing?" He raised an eyebrow at Paddy. "More than a drop of truth in there."

Benji hooked a thumb over his shoulder. "We're losing mud into the reservoir faster than I've ever seen. We're going to have to be careful with this one, Paddy, real careful. I know these wells, can read them almost as well as I can read my wife, and this one is in a mood. She wants to get away from us."

"Mud in the reservoir could mean a big strike." Paddy felt his spirits rise.

"And a big problem casing the thing. The pressures are really high. Been pumping mud like crazy. The mud man has really amped up the heaviness."

"Who knows about this?"

"Just the mud logger." Benji thought about the copies of the logs he'd sold, as a wave of fear and self-loathing shuddered through him. "And you and me. But you're the petroleum geologist. You know better than anyone what they mean."

Paddy looked like he wanted to say something, but didn't.

"While you're letting it all sink in, I'll go get us some supper. Kitchen won't close, but the best stuff will be gone soon." He paused before he stepped out of the room. "Here." He pulled a handgun from under his shirt at the small of his back. "I won't be long. Watch your back."

"A gun?" A shot of cold adrenaline hit Donovan's heart as his hand closed over the steel warmed by contact with Benji's skin. "Watch my back?"

"We just pay these guys; we don't own them. And I've been seeing a bunch of new faces lately, more so than normal. There's something going down. Don't know what, but I don't like it."

CHAPTER TEN

Juan Garza scanned the horizon through his night-vision binoculars. The storm licking at him from the west kicked up spray off of each swell, clouding the lenses. He'd been using his shirttail to mop up the water, but now that too was a wet mess. The shivers chasing through him had more to do with the wind that cut like a knife than the fear of being on a small vessel this far from shore riding waves that grew as the storm pushed them, or at least he liked to think so. The salt water wasn't doing the Glock tucked in its holster under his arm any good—not that that was supposed to matter to a Glock—but the TOPS knife strapped to his calf would be fine, wet or not. One couldn't be too careful out here, a small speck in the vast Gulf. One of the last, vast frontiers where the law was far away and the lawless plentiful, well-funded, and creative. Hell, just last week he'd lost two of the guys—one took a knife in the back; the other one they just found pieces of. Could've been a shark...or not.

Squinting into the night that was quickly turning inky black as the clouds behind him erased the dying daylight, he caught a rare flicker of lightning as it painted the waves a translucent blue. The lights from the Donovan Oil rig glittered in the distance. El Jefe had assured him he'd take care of the problem. His instructions to Juan, which had come through the man he answered to—there were many layers between Juan and El Jefe—were to bring one of the

Waverunners and to sit out here and wait.

Juan watched the choppers come and go—he could sense an urgency in front of the storm. Once the activity on the platform died down, he was told there would be a signal—a light from the lower platform, the one at water level. Then he was to go in and grab the guy and take him to the old abandoned platform, he knew which one, where a boat would be waiting for them both.

The growing swells sheltered him. Timing each crest, he'd take a quick look, then ride the swell down, staying hidden. The storm complicated matters. One good thing: the Coast Guard wouldn't be out patrolling, working their routes. That was the *only* good thing. The storm was gathering strength, breathing down his neck. Cool fingers of sinking air off the thunderheads cut through his already soaked clothes. Being out here when the storm hit would be sure suicide.

The guy had better hurry.

CHAPTER ELEVEN

Drayton Lewis hadn't been raised to be an eco-terrorist, but the lifestyle fit him. His father had had dreams of Drayton joining his Wall Street firm—that was before the old man had blown his brains into the next county—but Drayton had had other ideas. In his more reflective moments, he fancied himself a modern-day pirate of sorts—robbing from the rich and keeping the spoils for himself. By his father's measuring stick, Drayton had achieved all the old man had hoped for and more. Both ruthless, financial barbarians, Drayton pillaged a slightly different segment of the economy than his father and in a less overt way.

Most saw Drayton Lewis as the savior of the environment—something he didn't care about but it was an image he'd cultivated with great care. All of this made him a darling of the celebrity crowd. With all of the A-listers on speed dial, Drayton worked them like a pimp worked his whores. Dim-witted do-gooders, so easy to manipulate. Sheep, one and all. And having the national stage was worth a small fortune, maybe even a large one.

Short, with a physique an Italian designer would salivate over, Lewis wore the wolf's clothing well. Jet-black hair he had cut every other week. High cheekbones and a strong jaw formed the framework of his face, but Nature hadn't taken advantage, clustering an angry, mean mouth and small feral eyes too close together. But Lewis had money and that was the only thing that mattered. Not a day went by that he wasn't amazed at how quickly the world attached credibility to anyone with enough money to throw a lavish party and land in *People Magazine*.

Tonight, artifice and pretense of gentility sliced away, he looked like what he was—his lips curled in a sneer, his eyes cold, flat. Dressed in faded blue jeans, a torn sweatshirt from the Texas A&M School of Engineering—not that he had ever graced those hallowed halls—deck shoes, and smoking a Cuban cigar, he paused to peer through the telescope mounted in the bridge of his ship *Vengeance*. The ship bucked beneath him, a hint of ozone mixing with the salt spray.

Lewis loved the ocean—so many places to hide.

He'd left Becca sleeping. Things had gotten rough. They both liked it that way.

"That the target?" He directed the question to his captain, a former South African drug-runner working for the cartels. The man knew these waters better than Drayton knew his own reflection.

"Yes." A handsome man, tall and blond, and dreams of avarice far beyond sensible, the captain would nail the Messiah to the cross himself if the money was right. "We've been watching. Our men aboard are ready. You make the call."

"You're sure the pressure is high?"

"It'll be worse than the Deepwater Horizon blowout."

Lewis smiled. Deepwater Horizon. BP had really fucked that up—a string of mistakes that ensured the disaster. Arrogance coupled with greed—often an incendiary mix, especially when drilling in the depths they did and as Donovan was doing now. The pressures, hell, the sheer physics of the thing was incomprehensible. One mistake. Too little cement. Too much mud lost to the reservoir. The pressure would build and nature would take its course. An inferno reducing every man-made scrap in its path to ash and twisted metal, spilling millions of barrels of crude into the delicate ocean ecosystem. Drayton bared his teeth, a predator's smile.

His guys had been there, too, on the BP rig. And their tip-off had come in barely ahead of the news, but he'd jumped into the market and made a mint shorting BP stock. But that one had been years ago, and his financial bloodlust gnawed at him, a beast desperate to be fed. Lewis needed another big score, and he was tired of waiting for corporate greed to override good sense. He had to make something happen, and Patrick Donovan was playing right into his hands. And the anti-corporate-fat-cat sentiment on Wall Street gave him the perfect opportunity to ride into battle waving the sword for Mother Earth.

"Our guys are in place?"

"Just waiting for the word. Shift just changed so we have a three-week window."

"They're using the mud?"

"Yep, it came through our guy. Delivered it myself. Don't worry, Mr. Lewis, we got it covered."

Lewis angled a hard look at his captain. "No," he said, menace curling around the single word. "*I* have it covered. And it's my job to worry."

"Yes, sir." The captain's eyes snapped to the view out the window. "That's Donovan's rig, sir."

"And the final ingredient?"

"On board. Our guys are waiting to add it. Once they do, forty-five minutes."

Drayton loved plans like this—once set in motion, even God himself couldn't stop it. "Any idea as to best timing?"

"Still looking for the right moment, when they're most vulnerable. The guys are skittish—something's got them spooked. Everybody's looking over their shoulders. The foremen are on top of everybody. Whatever's got them on the alert, it needs to die down a bit. But, even if it doesn't, there's a storm brewing south of Cuba. Looks like it's going to be a monster. We could use that to our advantage."

Lewis thought for a moment. A huge oil spill in the

midst of an angry hurricane, the damage to marine life, delicate coral beds, and coastal economies would be astronomical. Heads would roll—and Big Oil would once again be vilified. "Deep-water drilling, it's so dangerous. Anything can happen."

He scanned the water between his boat and the rig—the seas were building. On his second pass, at the apex of a wave, he thought he caught something. A reflection? A small light? Keeping the binoculars pressed to his face, he pointed. "Did you see that?"

The captain swiveled, raising his glasses to join his boss in the search. Both men waited, timing the swells.

The tiny light blinked. "There," Lewis said, his voice growing hard. "Did you see it?"

"Yes. Someone is watching." Anticipating his boss, the captain eased the throttle forward and brought the ship slightly to starboard. "I think we should find out who."

Drayton Lewis kept his eyes trained on the dark and angry seas, watching the light. "I think why will prove more interesting."

CHAPTER TWELVE

The storm broke as Donovan checked and double-checked each report. Captured by the data, by the reality, no, by the dream, he was only slightly aware of the rain pelting the window, the swells lashing the sides of the drilling platform, the lightning. And this one was only the harbinger of what was yet to come. But he wasn't worried about storms or hurricanes or fucking tsunamis right now.

He ran a trembling hand through his thick mane of hair, now white with the passing years. He slammed his hand down on the table, the echo reverberating in the small room, then dissipating, as if dampened by the unrelenting pulsing of the engines.

After all these years...

Donovan leaned back in his chair and allowed himself a sigh of satisfaction. All those years scrounging for money like a cur dog scratching for a meal. A dreamer, they'd said. Well, he'd dreamed all right, but never this big. A grin sliced his face. The payoff was going be huge, beyond all dreams of avarice. He could set Sam up, buy her that Sikorsky or whatever she wanted. Of course, she wouldn't want that, but he'd wear her down and she'd come around. And Brid, his sainted first wife, only wife by his way of thinking. He found her the fucking pot of gold at the end of the rainbow. The other wives? Momentary lapses in judgment when Brid had thrown him out and wouldn't take him back. She'd understand—he thought perhaps she already did and she was making him suffer for a bit...a long bit. But she, too, would come around, and they could be a family again. He'd bet it all on one throw of the dice if he could win that.

The dream enveloped him and he basked for a moment, letting the what-ifs carry him along. Then in a moment of shattering clarity, Donovan realized why Benji had mentioned their partners. A discovery of world-rattling magnitude, this was the sort of thing one had to keep to himself. For all of them. If anyone found out about his find, the barrel price would drop like a stone. Then where would they all be? Funny, he'd spent his life working for that big score. He'd never considered that a score could be too big and topple the whole house of cards. Supply and demand, immutable laws of value.

But how the hell was he going to keep something this big, this world-changing, a secret?

A trickle of sweat rolled down the bridge of his nose and Donovan blew it away. His shirt, soaked with sweat, stuck to him as if it had been applied to his skin with glue. God, it was hot. Even without the sun beating down, heating the air to flash-fry levels. The air was so thick it seemed to take twice the energy just to suck it into his lungs. *Almost like trying to breathe Jell-O.*

He tugged at his tie, still knotted around his neck. Wrestling with the thing, he finally got it loosened; then he shimmied it over his head and tossed it on a chair. He leaned forward and shrugged out of his suit jacket, which soon followed the tie. Suits and ties, his Houston Big Oil uniform, he hated the things.

Damned sissy clothes.

Give him a well-worn pair of Levi's and his old ostrich-skin Noconas and he was happy as a pig in slop. He watched as both the tie and the suit jacket slithered out of the chair and landed in a heap on the metal floor of the rig, which was dotted with beads of perspiration as if the metal itself was sweating. *South Texas in the summer—Hell couldn't be any worse.*

Donovan rose and stretched. He could really use a cold beer, but since alcohol was forbidden on the rig where reflexes and good judgment were the difference between doing your job and losing a body part, an ice-cold diet soda would have to do.

Where was Phillip?

Donovan turned at the sound of approaching steps. "'Bout time you got here. The seas, your boat, you scared the hell out of me." His smile froze at the sight of the man in front of him. He was pointing a pistol at Donovan's chest. "What the hell?" Pain exploded. Donovan's world went black.

CHAPTER THIRTEEN

Arms crossed, Sam leaned against the side of the open hangar doorway and stared out at the rain, a pelting curtain of gray that washed the color out of everything. The storms had been coming in bands thrown off by the tropical storm in the Caribbean. It now had a name, Abigail—the first storm of the season, and, if the weather folks were right, it'd be one to remember. The track would take it over Cuba, which hopefully would keep it from intensifying. But, once back over the warm waters of the Gulf, all bets were off—it could turn into a beast.

As to the track from Cuba, the models differed, but most showed a generally northerly path. Either way, Mother Nature was cooking up a bad problem for her father.

Grounded by the weather, she'd fixed every gripe on every plane and now found herself with the curiosity of free time, something she had no idea what to do with or how to fill.

Commander Wilder ducked around the corner and stepped into the hangar on the far side, peeling back his hood, then shaking the water off. He held up a bag. "I brought food, and, since my flying is done and I doubt you will be getting out in this stuff in the next twelve hours or so, I also brought a nice Napa Valley Sangiovese. It should pair well with Thai."

"Thai? I believe you promised me Foreign Correspondents."

"And so I did." He shrugged out of his Coast Guard slicker and hung it to drip off the end of the prop on the Cub. He ran a hand through his hair—the rain and humidity had made it curl a bit.

Sam wondered what it would be like to run her fingers through it, then shut that thought down. A nice little fantasy with a broken heart at the end. Flyboys were short-term fun, and she was a long-term kind of gal. She pushed off the wall and met him halfway. "God, that smells delicious. Where'd you score those kinds of smells in this neighborhood?"

"Bates, my JG, was heading down from the city for his shift." Kellen set the bag on the floor. Extracting a towel in swirls of neon, he shook it, snapped it open, then settled it between them. "Have a seat. I didn't have a blanket that didn't smell like a bunch of cadets trying to catch some midshift zzzs. This was the next best thing."

"Works perfectly." Sam reached to pull open the bag so she could see inside.

Kneeling across from her, Kellen lightly slapped her hand away. "All in good time."

"Seriously, where'd you get this?"

He pulled out a bottle of wine. "Del Dotto. This is their Sangiovese. Light yet really flavorful—it should pair well with the heat of the food."

Sam cocked one eyebrow at him. "So sophisticated, you are," she teased.

"How am I supposed to dazzle you if you have that kind of attitude?"

Sam leaned back, capturing her knees in an embrace. "Dazzle away."

"That's better." He gave her a long look.

Sam felt the heat of it. Just before she embarrassed herself, he broke away, reaching into the bag and pulling out cartons. "Like I said, Bates was heading down, so I asked him to swing by our place, Foreign Correspondent. I wasn't sure exactly what kind of Thai dishes you liked, so I got a sampling of a bunch of them. The food is supposed to be amazing—farm-to-table Northern Thai, if that means anything to you."

"I'm afraid I'm not that nuanced." Sam felt like a kid at Christmas—so many little boxes to open. "I can't believe you got takeaway from *the* most popular place in town. This is really so great. Thank you."

"I hope you like spice."

"Please! Thai without heat is like sex without..." She choked on the words.

"Go on." Kellen raised an eyebrow in bemusement.

"Never mind. Suffice it to say, I'm a spicy kind of gal."

"Interesting." He eyed her for a bit longer than suited her comfort level.

Sam felt the heat rise in her cheeks.

"Had you pegged as such," he said with a hint of self-satisfaction. A constellation of little cartons between them, Kellen went to work on the cork and then poured each of them a healthy dose of wine into plastic glasses with the Coast Guard logo on the side. "You hear anything from your father?" He slipped that question in as he took a sip of the wine, his eyes flicking to hers.

Sam went to work on the cartons. "My father? Not since he was here a couple of days ago. I've called him, several times, but I keep getting voicemail. He hasn't called back, but that's not unusual when he's out on the rig." Her hands stilled as she speared him with a look—he'd been out over the Gulf. "Why?"

"No reason. It was pretty crazy out there. You'd think people would be smarter." The shadow of a memory passed across his face, and from the looks of it, Sam didn't think it was a pleasant one. "We got them all, though, so that's a good thing."

"You look beat. Maybe some of this divine-smelling food will bring you back." Sam snagged a bite of chicken in red curry sauce with a pair of chopsticks, then groaned in delight.

"Lives up to the reputation?" Kellen asked.

Sam plucked another bite and fed it to him.

His eyes widened. When he'd savored it, he washed it down with a sip of wine. "Manna from Heaven."

"Well, divine, perhaps. But manna? May be overstating." Not that she didn't agree. And she wasn't above giving credit, but she intended to make Wilder work for—whatever *it* was he seemed to be angling for.

"Some of the rigs are evacuating," Wilder said through a mouthful. "The hurricane spotters flew through the forming eye this morning. Some of the lowest pressure on record." He turned serious. "I know your father."

Sam thought on that a minute. If Paddy was sitting on an ocean of oil, what would he do?

Wilder reached across and touched her hand, then squeezed it when he got her attention. "I know what he means to you, and I know how damned hardheaded he can be. This one's going to be bad."

The Coastie's concern softened her up a bit, just enough so worry could leak in. "I'm not a hundred percent sure where he is in the drilling process. Based on a couple of days ago, I'd say he's laying the last bit of pipe, then will cement the casing. It's a delicate time."

"How so?"

"The pressures are tricky. At the depth he's drilling, if he's hit good, the pressure will be very high. So, he has to counteract that, or..."

"Or what?" Kellen had paused, a bite pinched in his chopsticks halfway to his mouth.

"High pressure will rush to low pressure."

"A blowout." Kellen voiced the words Sam had been afraid to utter.

"Let's hope not."

"What about the blowout preventer, or whatever it's called—the thing that failed in the Horizon mess?"

"At the depths they're drilling now, they do the best they can, but this is sort of uncharted territory. It sounds irresponsible, but that's how life goes—you give it your best guess, then learn as you go."

Kellen popped the bite in his mouth and chewed, his brows pinched in thought.

Sam knew what he was thinking—he was weighing the logistics and the resources should a major blowout occur in front of a major hurricane. "Kellen, it's a possibility. The nature of the game. If it'll make you feel better, I'll find my father and do my best to make sure he doesn't contribute to a natural disaster."

"That would help. One less worry. You do know about the storm that's coming?"

Sam nodded.

"I expect evacuation of the Gulf to be ordered in the next week. A hell of a thing." Kellen's smile was weak. "But worrying won't solve the problem. However, it will rob us of the joy in this moment. Too high a price to pay." He reached for another carton.

Sam, beating him to it, shot him a grin as she dug in. But she offered him the first bite, feeding it to him slowly.

"God, that is good."

Sam sampled it herself and agreed. "You are so easy."

"I'm a man."

"Nothing easy about that. Simple, maybe, but not easy." Sam fed him another bite, relaxing into the ease between them. She shook her head, which Kellen didn't see since he had his eyes shut. There wasn't any upside with the commander. He'd move on like they all did. But maybe, just maybe, he'd make the short-term a bit more fun...if she could keep hold of her heart. She looked up and caught him watching her.

"Whatever you're thinking, you're wrong."

She sat up straighter. "How do you know what I'm thinking?"

"I don't, not exactly. But I do know you are looking for

all the reasons why I'm not right for you. Give it up. We're perfect for each other."

"Really? How do you know?"

He reached across, once again grabbing her hand. "Feel that?"

A bolt of electricity jolted through her, but she didn't acknowledge it.

Kellen's eyes darkened. "I feel it, too. Let me in. Give me a chance."

The heat, the connection—there was something different about this one. Sam didn't want it, didn't want the vulnerability followed by the sure hurt. But maybe he was different. Maybe they would be different. Sam started to agree, to let him in.

Before a word escaped, a voice called from the doorway breaking the spell.

"Anybody home?" The voice was raspy as if roughened by a cold.

"I'm not going away, Sam," Kellen whispered.

A man stepped into the hangar, his umbrella held in front of him. He popped it a bit to shake off the rain, then left it upended in the corner. "This weather is something." Whippet thin, hair short, posture military, the guy had Fed written all over him.

Sam pushed herself to her feet. After wiping her hands on her jeans, she extended one. "Sam Donovan. Can I help you?"

The man didn't take her hand. "Have a cold, sorry." He flapped open a wallet. His shield said FBI. "Agent Presley Davis."

Sam tucked her hands in her pockets and tried to fight the unfounded yet instinctive guilt that flooded through her at the subtle show of federal force. The guy could make her life hell if he wanted, and he didn't need a reason. "Agent Davis, what can we do for you?"

The agent, whose piercing eyes looked right through Sam as if recording every important detail, didn't try to hide behind a façade of nice.

"I'm looking for your father, Patrick Donovan."

"What would the FBI be wanting with my father?"

"That would be between me and him."

"I see. Well, you won't find him here." Behind her, Sam was aware that Kellen had stilled.

The agent nodded at Kellen. "Commander." The tone in his voice had chilled.

"You two know each other?" Sam asked, not really surprised. The miles of unguarded Texas coast and the vast expanse of the Gulf were a morass of competing jurisdictions and all kinds of lawlessness.

"Our paths have crossed." Kellen's voice was measured as he stood, brushing some crumbs from his flight suit. "You're looking in the wrong place on this one, Davis."

Ignoring the commander, Agent Davis kept his eyes on Sam as he wandered over to the nearest plane, the J-3. "Learned to fly in one of these. My father taught me. Turned me loose in it when I was 14. We lived out toward Big Bend, far from everywhere. Everybody had a truck and a plane in the garage. Used to take a plane just like this into town to get groceries for my mother."

Sam eyed the agent and the commander—like animals in the jungle they circled each other, keeping a wary eye. "Why are you looking for my father?"

"I told you, that's between the two of us. Just have some questions for him, that's all."

"Is he suspected of wrongdoing?" Sam cringed. She sounded like one of those officious twits on a TV cop show—the ones who always ended up dead.

"No, I'm just looking for answers."

"To?"

The agent gave her a tight grin, but clammed up.

"The FBI does the asking, never the answering." Kellen moved to stand next to Sam, shoulder to shoulder. "Isn't that right, Davis?"

"Kellen, really." Sam had no intention of getting caught

in the middle of this pissing match. "My father should be out on his drilling platform. I'm sure the FBI can figure out where exactly that is."

"Was out there yesterday. No sign of him." The agent's eyes captured hers. "Odd, don't you think? He went out there, sent his pilot back, and hasn't been seen or heard from since."

"What?" A shot of cold adrenaline bolted through her, chased by the heat of worry. "He should be there."

The agent shrugged. As Kellen said, the Fed had come here looking for information, not to give her any.

Sam wrestled her composure back into order. "My father is unpredictable. Was his crew able to help you?"

The agent gave her a flat look.

Sam bit down on a smile. *That would be no.*

"Do you have any clue as to where your father could be? He's not in any of the usual places."

"Given that it's my father we're talking about, the usual places are not the ones you should be checking out."

"You don't seem too broken up about any of this."

"Should I be?"

"Well, if my father had gone missing..."

"Agent Davis, first, there is no evidence my father has, as you put it, gone missing. You simply can't find him. And, second, you are not Patrick Donovan's child. He has a habit of going off, then popping up when you least expect it." Sam worked to keep her voice steady. What she said was true, as far as it went. But, with her father's veiled warnings and now this, even a daughter with a jaundiced attitude would be worried.

"Right. You let me know if you hear from him." The agent peeled a card from a rubber band-bound stack he extracted from the side pocket in his rain slicker and handed it to her. Then he grabbed his umbrella and nodded. "Miss Donovan. Commander." He glanced at the wide-open hangar bay door—Sam prided herself on the fact that a King Air fit through it easily. "I can let myself out." He paused in the doorway. "Miss Donovan? Be careful who you invite in. Ask the commander there about the one that got away."

Sam and Kellen stood there until they heard a car engine fire up and saw lights arcing through the rain.

"That was fun," Kellen said with a growl as he lowered himself back to the floor. He stabbed at the contents of various cartons with his chopsticks. "Now our food is cold."

"It's okay." Sam joined him, capturing his hand. "We can nuke it."

The agent's visit had wiped away Kellen's smile. His skin was warm, almost hot to the touch. Anger burned under the surface pulling his lips into a tight line.

"Want to tell me what that last little snipe was about?"

"No." A muscle worked in his jaw as he clenched his teeth. "Excuse me a minute. I'll be right back."

The commander caught Davis, his car idling as he looked at his phone. With a knuckle, he tapped on the window.

Davis jumped, then scowled as he rolled down the window.

Kellen, ignoring the rain that streamed down his face, put both hands on the window ledge and leaned down. "I don't know what game you're playing, but you need to back off."

Davis gave him a smile. "The folks I take orders from are a bit higher on the food chain than you, Commander."

A bit of contempt crept into the last word, firing Kellen up even more. "Last time you came sniffing around I lost a bird and my best crew." The loss of his men still hung heavy in his chest. Youngsters, kids really, four of them. Davis had caused it, but the commander held himself responsible. They were his men. And he'd let them down. First and last time he'd take the Fed at his word.

"Yes, that couldn't be helped."

"Nice to know you're taking it so well." Commander Wilder leaned down until he was face to face with Davis. "Don't try pulling rank on me again. It won't happen. And stay away from Sam Donovan. She doesn't need your kind of trouble."

"She's already in the thick of it." Davis shifted the car into gear. "Watch your back, Wilder. And hers."

Raking his hair out of his eyes and shaking the water off like a dog, Kellen settled himself back on the towel across from Sam.

"You going to tell me what that was about?" Sam pretended to be focused on making a selection from the cartons between them. "Better eat up, it's getting cold."

Finally, he relaxed a bit, although tension still pulled his shoulders up toward his ears. "A couple of FBI agents got their asses in a crack. They were out on an abandoned rig about ten miles out. Hell of a night. A storm not unlike the one they're predicting to hit in a couple of days." His voice cracked.

"What were they doing on an abandoned rig?"

Kellen shook off the anger that darkened his eyes and stretched his lips into a thin line. "With the Feds you only get half the story, and even then, you don't know which half—the true half or the one they spin to keep themselves looking good. Davis was running the operation."

"What happened?"

"I was flying. I lost one of his agents. Got the other one...barely. Lost my swimmer in the process. And a whole other crew went down trying to pull those suckers out." He ran a hand over his eyes. "I relive that night over and over."

"Any conclusions?"

When he looked at her, his eyes were clearer. "I wouldn't do anything differently. It was what it was. A real bad night."

"Then you've got to make peace with it."

"I have, to the extent you can ever resolve yourself to a situation where you have to make a decision knowing lives will be lost no matter what you do." He lifted his chin toward the door of the hangar that had swallowed Agent Davis. "But Davis, he held me accountable."

Sam reached over and squeezed his arm. "I'm sorry."

"A couple of agents drowned. Hell of a night and nothing I could do. One chopper. One swimmer. Three crew. But he blamed it on me—tried to get me court-martialed. Said I made us both look bad."

"But wasn't he responsible for his agents being out there in a storm?"

"He seems to have overlooked that."

Sam shrugged. "His problem."

Sam sensed a bit more to the story, but she could tell this was all of it she'd get out of the commander. "What he says is only his interpretation of how things went down." Obviously, the guy hadn't been right or Kellen Wilder could've kissed his career goodbye, but there was something else there—she'd felt it from both of them.

"Davis is a loose cannon. During the court-martial, I tried to find out more about him. Got stonewalled at every turn. I couldn't determine who held his leash, what his mission was; hell, no one would even tell me what his team does. That's need-to-know, I was told. But there's something fishy about him. I know it in my gut; I just can't prove it."

"Any idea why he would be interested in my father?"

"With Davis, who knows? But having him sniff around does make me even more concerned than I was before."

"So I should be worried?"

Kellen squeezed her hand, then smiled as he looked at their entwined fingers. Sam felt the connection, too.

Damn.

"Hell of a storm is brewing and, as the agent said, he went out to the rig but there's no record of him coming back. You can't reach him. But you know your father. What do you think?"

"I'm thinking this has a Patrick Donovan stench about it. He's got himself in a mess. I'd be willing to bet all I've got on that."

Kellen looked around the hangar at Sam's collection: a Bell Jet Ranger 206L, the King Air, an early model but spotless, the J-3. "I'll take that bet."

Sam waved her arm at the planes. "I don't own those—the bank does. All I have free-and-clear are the clothes on my back, a few tools, and my BMW F 800GS."

"Good enough. I need a new bike."

"You're a foolish man if you bet against this Donovan."

"Indeed. I retract my offer." His chopsticks poised, he eyed his next target. "You think he's in trouble"

"Don't know." Sam searched the cartons until she found the red curry with the avocado. That one she claimed as her own. "But I do know we'd better find him before the Feds do."

CHAPTER FOURTEEN

"This is better than sex!" Sam Donovan shouted into the mike arcing from her headset. A case of serious lust thrummed through her. The stick jutting up between her legs, the twin jet engines mounted above her vibrating a sensual, seductive pulse, the rotors beating the air holding the machine aloft. At one hundred feet, Sam had the helicopter's nose down, screaming south toward Galveston Bay. After the storm yesterday, today had dawned bright, the blue sky teasing and tempting Sam. Dark clouds scuffed up the horizon, but for the moment the sky was calm, the sun hot. The tropical storm had indeed stalled over Cuba for the moment. And, for the moment, it had been downgraded.

When the Sikorsky salesman had wandered in, she had jumped at his offer of a test ride. Her father was still radio silent, which didn't sit well. Benji and a few others on the rig hadn't been any help. In fact, they'd left Sam with the distinct impression they were stonewalling her.

Kellen had said they should look for her father, so that's what she'd do...look for him. If she got to fly a sweet machine she could only dream of having while she was doing the looking, well, so much the better.

"I get that a lot." The salesman sitting next to her didn't seem the least bit surprised. He patted the top of the instrument stack. "You'd be the first in Texas to own one of these babies."

Sam would give her right nut, if she had one, to own a Sikorsky S-76D. The latest and greatest, it was one awesome machine and could handle her work in the Gulf with ease. There was only one minor problem—actually there were eleven million problems. When the salesman had come calling, she had failed to mention that, had she sold everything she owned, she probably couldn't buy a one-hour ride in the thing, much less park one of her own in the hangar. But that could change. If she could close the deal with Farrell Bishop and San Rafael Oil, that would alter her bargaining position dramatically.

"My father would love this thing," she said before thinking.

I might even tell him about it, if I could find him. The thought hit her heart.

The salesman pulled a pad and pen from his shirt pocket. "Give me his name, I'll hook him up."

"Naw, this would only get him into trouble." Not that Patrick Donovan needed anything to get him into trouble. Buying a sweet machine like the Sikorsky was a long-term commitment, not one of her father's strong suits.

After a moment the salesman tucked his pad away. "Why don't you head down the channel a bit, get it over the water. You'll see how the instruments are readable even in the glare. Did you notice some of our new design features? The extra-large windows and doors are of particular interest with your offshore work. They are much easier to pop out in case of an auto-gyration into the water. Remember that bird that went down some time ago? The impact bent the skids up and they blocked the doors and windows? The folks inside were lucky to get out."

She'd flown a bird like that. She knew.

Sam mentally muted the guy—she probably knew more about the helicopter than he did. Instead, she focused on the physical act of flying, the feel of the machine. There were pilots, and then there were people who flew. Sam considered herself a pilot, one with the machine and all of that. Flying machines talked if one knew how to listen. This one had a rotor that was slightly out of balance. Even though infinitesimal, the vibration was there. She felt it through her two fingers on the stick, through her butt in the seat. And the machine didn't fly completely straight—someone had landed a bit too hard and tweaked the frame most likely. Pretty typical for a demo aircraft.

The salesman droned on, reciting his pitch as if by rote as Sam played, putting the machine through its paces. Just over the water of Galveston Bay, she pulled it to a stop, hovering, delighting in the shocked reactions of the pelicans as they lumbered aloft, struggling to get out of her way. Twenty feet under the copter, the sunlight dappled the water, the rotor wash scuffing it to a light chop. The smell of the sea rose up to tempt her. To Sam life was best lived within throwing distance of an ocean. In her low hover she moved the machine forward, then backward, then to the left and right, and finally rotating it in a slow circle, keeping the same spot underneath her. Landing on a rig with a heavy load in bad weather was a game of inches.

"This puppy will lift anything you can cram inside or strap onto it." The salesman wrapped up his pitch with a bit of hyperbole, which Sam found patronizing. "So what do you think? Want one of these horses in your stable?"

"Running any specials?" She shot a sideways glance at him. "Like maybe an eighty-percent discount?"

The salesman laughed like she was joking.

Sam decided to string him along. She'd probably not get another chance to enjoy this kind of aircraft, loaded with all the latest whistles and bells, *and* on somebody else's dime—Nirvana to a pilot on a tight budget. "What kind of service can you offer?"

He launched into an explanation of the various mechanical support packages as Sam kept her eyes scanning not only the sky around them, but also the water below. Situational awareness: an autonomic piloting skill. And, to be honest, although she didn't expect to find him here, she looked for her father amid the reeds and grasses lining the inlets.

The ass end of a boat caught her eye. *Texas 47* stenciled in red on the stern, with *Galveston* in smaller black letters underneath indicating its homeport. Her heart tripped—she knew that boat. Well, that was an understatement. She'd memorized every rivet, every turnbuckle, each bit of wood that needed sanding and shellacking.

Uncle Phil's boat.

Sam had spent many summer mornings baiting hooks and trolling for redfish from that boat with the man she knew as Uncle Phil, the man everyone else knew as Senator Phillip Herrera, senior senator from Texas. She'd never tired of hearing Uncle Phil and her father gas about "the good old days."

Her father. Uncle Phil.

Paddy's veiled warning chimed loudly now. *Damn.*

There was no good reason Uncle Phil's boat would be out here with no Uncle Phil. Sam tried to stay positive, to do what she knew needed to be done, but something unraveled inside, like a thread pulled, the fabric of her life coming apart one row at a time.

Barely visible, the boat had nosed into the grasses. Tucked in tight, either someone dumped it there on purpose or someone had fallen overboard and the engine drove the boat in. This part of the bay was so shallow that if someone had gone over, they could walk in, which, to Sam's way of thinking, eliminated the last possibility. If Uncle Phil had gone over, he could've gotten to the boat.

"Did you see anything floating in the bay as we maneuvered?" she asked the salesman who sat mute and apparently unaware beside her.

"Like what?"

"A body."

"What?" His voice quavered, ending on a high note.

"I'll take that as a no."

He leaned in close to her angling a look out her window. "What do you see?"

"A bay boat." This wasn't the place she expected to find Uncle Phil's boat. His was a flat-bottomed bay boat for skimming through shallow bayous, not cutting through the swells of the open ocean. Sam pushed her rising panic down as she tried to think. If anyone was aboard, the noise of the helicopter's twin jet engines should've attracted their attention, but no one moved. Focusing on her surroundings, she looked for anything unusual, anything out of place. Vultures circled on thermals above. They could be searching for dead fish left when the tide moved out. Sam hoped that was the case as she eased the collective up. A bit of altitude would give her a better vantage point to see inside the boat since she didn't want to hover over the grass—she had no intention of scaring up a bird or something and pulling it into the engines.

"What are you doing?" The salesman had stopped talking and was now casting a worried glance at her.

Sam ignored him as she inched the helicopter closer, then spun it around so the skiff was on her side. Yep, Uncle Phil's boat. A low-sided rig, twenty feet, with a center console, a high rail on top, and rigged-up rod still in the side holder. Shards remained where the windscreen had been. The Yamaha outboard, a saltwater 250, raised her eyebrows. He'd replaced the old Merc 125, and recently by the looks of it. Wherever Uncle Phil was planning to go, he apparently needed some horsepower. The high fishing seat in the stern blocked some of her view. She needed a better angle. "Take the stick." She waited for the waggle confirming the salesman accepted the flying responsibilities, then opened the door. Leaning out into the rotor wash, she held tight to her glasses with one hand and tight to the airframe with the other. The harness straps held her as she peered over the gunwale into the bottom of the boat. In addition to the high seat, the two low rear seats partially blocked her sight. She could make out two feet in topsiders, lily-white legs, a triangle of madras—the end of one leg of a pair of shorts. "Move it forward a few feet."

A body lay sprawled on its side, one arm bent unnaturally to the back. Blood pooled beneath it, a dark, thick pool that no longer spread with the rocking of the boat. From her vantage point it looked like part of the back of his head was gone, but the shadows from the chairs made it hard to tell. Curiously, his visor remained in place, tucked low over his eyes.

Oh, God. No! She fought the bile rising in her throat. *Uncle Phil! No!*

She couldn't make out the guy's face. The birds had been at him a bit, which unnerved her. A shudder of revulsion racked through her, but she pushed it aside. Although she couldn't be certain, on some visceral level, she knew it wasn't her uncle.

"See anything?" The helicopter dipped toward her side as the salesman tried to look.

"Straighten it up. The guy down there doesn't need our help."

That turned the salesman's interest into horror.

"Yeah." Sam pulled herself back inside and latched the door. Channel 16 was the Emergency channel in the Gulf. Her hands shook as she keyed the mike and called the Coast Guard. She gave them the details as succinctly as possible then finished with, "We'll stay on site until you guys arrive. Make a small sweep, see if we see anything." She was hoping Commander Wilder would be at the helm when a chopper arrived, but she wasn't about to ask.

"Please confirm the boat is the *Texas 47*." The Coastie sounded young.

"Roger that." She resisted telling him that she knew whose boat it was.

"Please stay on site until company arrives. Repeat, stay on site."

Sam glanced at the fuel gauge, then ran a quick and dirty fuel burn for the half-hour or so it would take the Coast Guard to scramble their equipment out here, then the burn back to Ellington with the mandated reserve. "Wilco. One Bravo Charlie can stay for forty-five minutes, until fourteen-thirty zulu, then we gotta boogie."

The salesman looked a bit pale. "You're sure the man is dead?"

Sam backed the helicopter away, letting it drift, her eyes scanning the area. "Yes."

"Poor guy."

"Yeah." *Where is Uncle Phil?*

And where is my father? Hadn't Paddy said something about Phil having a story, something he didn't believe at first? Sam thought back. Yes, Phil had a story, and her father was scared. Those two were up to their eyeballs in a very deadly game, by the looks of it.

Keeping the chopper steady with one hand, she pulled her cell out of her pocket and patched it into the sound system.

Kellen Wilder answered on the first ring.

Benji Easton cornered Wes Craven in the head. Wes was the lead mud man—not the technical term but that's what he was in charge of, drilling mud, the fluid that, at this point in the process, kept the well pressures under control. Every time Benji was around the guy he came within a nanosecond of firing his ass, but he didn't have a good enough reason...not yet anyway. Firing somebody because you had a bad feeling about them would have the HR folks climbing up his ass. He had a bad feeling about them, too.

Benji made sure he and Wes would be alone—the head was the only place to talk and not be overheard. The guy was just getting the last shake out when Benji grabbed him from behind, pinning him against the wall. "What the hell does your boss think he's doing?"

The man calmly zipped himself, then, with a mitt almost the size of Benji's, he peeled Benji's hand from his shirt. Stepping around the engineer, he straightened his clothing. "*My* boss? You're my boss."

"Don't bullshit a bullshitter, asshole."

"You came to us, remember?"

Benji vibrated with anger. "I sold you some information. Your employer is a limited partner. Hell, one of his subsidiaries owns this damned drillship. I didn't see the big deal. Gave you a jump on the rest of the world—insider-like."

"That's illegal," the man sneered.

"Not if you *are* an insider. You didn't say anything about..." Benji lowered his voice and looked around, even though he knew they were alone. "You didn't say anything about killing Donovan."

"Collateral damage." The man brushed by Benji. At the door, he turned. "You'd be wise to take that as a warning."

CHAPTER FIFTEEN

Thirty miles offshore, due south of Galveston, Texas, the Gulf of Mexico was a deep sapphire blue. Dewayne Niland popped the top of an ice-cold Bud and took a healthy swig as the boat rolled in the swells. Today he'd targeted the abandoned rig just west of some new deep water drilling stuff going in, but he wouldn't get in too tight. Last time he'd been shot at. Weird stuff happened out here far from shore. The less he knew about most of it, the better.

He leaned back in his captain's chair on the flybridge, pushed his ball cap ringed with sweat back on his head, and belched. The sun had been up about two hours, he guessed; yet, even this early in the morning, he had to squint as the rippling water fractured the sunlight into countless bits of sparkle. The cumulus clouds stacked on the unbroken horizon encircled him like Indians around a lone stagecoach—the remnants of the storm that had kept him in port the last couple of days. Dewayne was as alone as any man could be, and he liked it that way. His wife, Doreen, liked to say that Dewayne hunted two things: sharks and solitude. Doreen had a knack for reading him that bordered on scary.

With the big toe of his left foot, Dewayne lifted the cover on his cooler. One short of a six-pack. He'd started out with three. That'd be about right: a six-pack usually lasted six miles or so. Dewayne belched again and scratched his stomach where it bulged bare beneath his T-shirt. The engine pulsed its steady rhythm. The heat lay thick and heavy on the water like a gauze curtain until gray water melded into misty sky.

Usually he hunted sharks at night. He loved to troll the beaches after dark, hook him a big hammerhead or something, then hang it up for all the tourists to see what had been swimming where they'd been dipping their dainty little toes. However, last night Doreen and a couple of her friends had gone to a bachelorette party at a male strip club in Houston. Dewayne had no idea they had a club like that—near-naked men dancing for money...from women.

They'd had a fight about her going. Doreen had won.

He was pretty sore about it too until right before he was set to go after the sharks. Doreen had come home so horny she couldn't get his clothes off him fast enough. She'd worked him out like he was the only bronc at a cheap rodeo, then left him for dead when she went to work the graveyard shift at the hospital. The woman would be the death of him yet. At least he'd die with a smile. But she sure put a crimp in his shark hunting.

During the daylight, the sharks generally moved offshore away from the noise of the beaches. So he was heading out to the rigs. Fish came to feed on the trash and crap the guys threw over the side. The sharks came to feed on the fish.

Dewayne idled down. He retrieved his Smith and Wesson 4506 from its watertight compartment and tucked it into the band of his jeans up against the small of his back. A four-step ladder separated the flybridge from the cockpit. He eased down the stairs, then moved to the extra set of controls at the stern of the boat by the fighting chair. From here he could set his flat lines, or outriggers if he chose to use them, and still control his speed and direction. Even when he was strapped into the chair to fight a fish, his controls would be close at hand.

Sharks were different, and hunting them required

special equipment. The single barbed hooks, wide as a man's hand, were made of steel. Some guys used steel wire for the leaders; Dewayne found it simpler to use linked chain. He'd never met a fish that could bite through that, not that he would want to. Hooking a chunk off a tuna he'd caught the night before for bait, he tossed the whole thing over the side and watched as it trailed behind the boat, pulling the line out with it. The trick was keeping his speed right so the bait would trail at the depth the sharks usually traveled. When he got closer to the rig, he'd set his line and chum the water. For now, he'd just troll on in and see if he could hook something interesting.

Halfway through his beer, the first strike caught Dewayne off guard. The line whined, speeding off the reel. Unwilling to waste an ounce of Bud, he drained the can, crushed it in one hand, then tossed it on the floor of the boat. After strapping himself into the chair and making sure his belt was low and tight, he grabbed the rod out of the holder. He waited a few seconds, then thumbed down the drag and gave a big jerk to set the hook. The fish didn't sound. As he reeled in the line, it didn't put up much of a fight either. He'd had fish play coy with him before, so he braced his feet and tightened his grip. The fish would surely turn soon.

But the fish didn't turn. And Dewayne kept reeling, now sure that he'd hooked some flotsam even though it was unusual for anything other than a fish to be riding at that depth. As the line came in, Dewayne saw a dark object ascending toward him. He unstrapped from the chair and bent over the side of the boat. Grabbing the chain leader, he pulled the object closer. Cloth-covered, bloated, pasty white, loose skin, a shock of white hair drifted in the swells. He reached down and turned it over.

One look and he vomited over the side of the boat.

CHAPTER SIXTEEN

"Goddamn it!" Shelby Walker threw her shoe across the room. The six-inch heel survived but left a dent. She found that satisfying, so she threw the other one. This one bounced off the wall, no dent. She buried her face in her hands, but she was all out of tears.

The bastards had killed Jake.

The cop, a Federal Cyber Crimes guy, had been as nice as he could have been, given the nature of the call. Shot. Point-blank range. No witnesses. No suspects.

She'd been surprised when her brother hadn't beaten her to Houston. The St. Regis, there was only one. That was their usual place whenever and wherever they traveled. He'd left her a cryptic note at the front desk about being there soon with a story to tell. And he'd had a shotgun delivered to her room. She shook her head.

A friggin' shotgun! What, Jake? Can you just call room service and have it delivered? Houston was in Texas, after all. The case made it a little less obvious when she toted the thing out to the car—Jake had arranged for that, too, leaving the keys with the valet.

And not just any car. No, he left her a truck. His way of poking fun at her and her big-city sensibilities. They'd had that talk a thousand times. Jake never could understand the concept, much less the reality, of a two-thousand-dollar handbag or a pair of fifteen-hundred-dollar heels. Vuitton and Louboutin meant nothing to him. A sacrilege as far as Shelby was concerned, but today, Jake got the last laugh.

Oh, Jake.

Shelby swallowed hard. Any minute she expected her brother to stroll through the door, gloating that he had won. But he didn't. And he still didn't answer his phone. Shelby couldn't stop calling it.

He couldn't be dead. He just couldn't. The FBI guy had to be wrong.

The asshat Fed had intimated that there was some talk of Jake having played fast and loose with his software and allowing back doors and other holes in the security—hints that Shelby didn't really understand. However, the gist was perfectly clear—they thought Jake had been scamming the system and had crossed the wrong guys. And he was heading to Texas when they'd caught up with him...whoever *they* were.

Texas. *Why Texas, Jake?* Senator Herrera, he'd said. Turns out she'd been too late to catch him before he disappeared. So she was chasing ghosts and vanishing senators.

Damn it, Jake.

What information she had left to go on had come from the Fed, who had said more than he should. And he'd want Jake's laptop. She thought about telling him he was going down the wrong rabbit hole thinking Jake was the bad guy here, but they wouldn't believe her—the cops never did. And she sure as hell didn't have his laptop.

Manipulating the markets? For money? Please. That was so far beyond the capability of Saint Jake that it was laughable. If someone hadn't killed him.

And she'd spent the better part of the last forty-eight hours looking for a needle in a haystack of over four million people. This godforsaken hellhole was as far away from Midtown as it was possible to get and still speak the same language, sort of. If anybody said, "Howdy, Hon," to her one more time, she'd shoot them. But right now it was safer than New York. Drayton Lewis had made good on his promise...or at least he'd tried to. But her bosses had loved the interview, loved the controversy. The soft-spined idiots in the legal department had sung a different tune. So, the C-levels told her to lay low in Houston until legal signed off. Lewis wouldn't look for her in his own backyard. Funny how that had played into her hands, although she didn't really think it was funny at all. Jake's death sucked all the high out of her win, all the joy out of her juice, leaving a red-hot wad of revenge in the pit of her stomach.

With a nose for a good story, Shelby knew she was sitting on a powder keg and her brother had put her there, with the help of Becca Molinari. He hadn't told her Becca was his source, but she had been easy to sniff out. The two of them had been almost inseparable at school.

And now Jake was dead. Jake, who never hurt anything or anyone.

She'd find out who did this, who killed Jake, and she'd put the guy's picture on every news channel, in every social media feed, blasting it across the universe.

And then she'd kill him.

Her phone jangled and she nearly jumped out of her skin. Today she'd picked the siren ringtone. Seemed appropriate, but perhaps not the best choice. After swiping her finger across the face—it took two tries—she pressed the phone to her ear. "Shelby Walker."

"We need to talk," a whispered voice.

Shelby thought she recognized it. "Miss Mol—"

"Don't. Not over the phone. Pick me up. The corner of Kirby and Westheimer. Thirty minutes."

The line went quiet. She was gone.

Shelby leaned forward, her elbows on her knees, her phone dangling as she thought through the possibilities. It could be a setup, of course. What if Drayton Lewis tied the three of them together—Shelby, Becca, and Jake? Of course, Shelby had no proof that Drayton had done anything other than a few underhanded business plays, but still.... And Becca had given both her and Jake the scent that put them on the trail.

Clearly, the bad guys had figured it out. Jake was dead. Becca was afraid. And Shelby was pissed. She reached for the shotgun and wondered if she could point it at a human and pull the trigger. One never knew until put in that position.

Jake was gone. The reality would recede as if it never happened, then boomerang back, nailing her when she let her guard down. She better keep it up, stay on the defensive, if not for her own sake, then for her parents'.

If whoever killed him didn't get what they wanted out of Jake, they'd probably figure he might have shared with his sister. They'd be looking for her...whoever the hell *they* were. A faceless killer Shelby aimed to expose. But she had to stay alive to do it.

Her parents were in New York, wondering why she wasn't and how they could move forward without their son. Shelby felt a pang of guilt and overwhelming need. She needed her parents. She needed Jake. And if she couldn't have Jake, she could sure as hell have the person who killed him. And she'd delight while watching that person roast on a slow spit over the mouth of Hell.

The siren call of the phone dangling between her knees made her jump. "Shelby Walker," she said, on autopilot, feeling nothing other than the need for justice.

"Shel. Shit!" Ashley, one of her four roommates—a financial necessity in Manhattan—sounded relieved. She was the one who had flunked out of BU because of a guy. And *that* had worked out so well. He'd drained her bank account and left her with a pesky rash. Her fault, but still...

Ashley's voice pulled Shelby back to the present, the grim reality. "Hey, Ash. What's up?"

"The FedEx guy has been driving me nuts." She sounded out of breath, but then again, she always sounded that way.

If any guy liked that act, he wouldn't be anybody with a shred of dignity. Then again, guys and dignity? Sort of an oxymoron where women were concerned and sex was a possibility. "The cute one with the tight ass and the bedroom eyes?"

"Yeah," she sounded disheartened. "He actually had a package...for you. Someone sent it overnight. The guy tried to deliver it a ton of times; there were like a *million* of those notices on the door. But, God love him, he kept trying. I think he's got a thing for you. He finally caught me today."

The cub reporter and the FedEx guy. Shelby shook her head. "Okay." She thought through who might want to get something to her so bad they paid enough for three drinks at the Waldorf to get it to her that fast, but drew a blank. "I can get it when I get home."

"I thought so too," Ashley's voice dropped to a conspiratorial, sad, sympathetic tone, "until I saw who it was from."

Shelby sat up, wiping her eyes—they were dry, but they hurt from tears long spent. "Who?"

"Jake."

She sucked in a sharp breath. "What did you do with the package? You have it, right?"

"No, I thought it might be important, so I forwarded it on to your hotel."

Dear God in Heaven, the woman did have a brain. "It'll be here tomorrow?"

"No, I didn't have the money for anything other than three-day."

Shelby started to rip her a new one, explaining she would've paid her back, her brother was dead, her mother was in New York trying to plan a funeral for her only son and calling her only daughter every hour on the hour...but she didn't bother. It would all be wasted on Ashley. "Thanks. Tell me what I owe you."

"You can pay me back when you get home."

"I can put it right in your bank account. Remember that app we use for apartment expenses?"

"Oh."

Good as a "no."

"Shel, you doing okay?"

Ashley needed a yes, so Shelby gave her one.

"What the fuck?" Ashley sounded startled.

"What?" Shelby's pulse lurched.

"Who the hell are you? Get out of here." Ashley's voice rose on a wave of panic.

"Ashley, what's going on?" Shelby shouted into the phone as she bolted to her feet. "Ashley?" She heard crashing sounds, things breaking. Ashley dropped the phone.

Heavy footfalls. A man's voice. "Where is it?"

"What?" Ashley's voice shrill and tight.

"The package. Where is it?"

"I don't know. I...I...just noticed the sticky notes. Shelby Walker doesn't live here anymore. I assume the driver took the package and sent it back to whoever sent it."

"Don't lie to me."

Something broke, glass maybe.

"No! Go away. I swear I don't have what you're looking for," Ashley shouted. "What are you doing? Oh, God, no!"

A muffled sound. Something hit the floor with a thud. A door closed.

Silence.

"Ashley?" Shelby shouted. "Ashley!"

CHAPTER SEVENTEEN

When the shit storm broke, Commander Kellen Wilder was sitting at his desk staring at a pile of reports he'd already read twice. His flying time had been limited—the younger guys needed some practice—and he was getting a bit short-tempered. He chewed on a forkful of cold eggs he'd bought hours ago when he'd still thought breaking for breakfast had been a possibility, then pushed the plate away. Although his stomach churned, he wasn't hungry.

A dead guy on a senator's boat was bad enough. Now the FBI was nipping at his heels—the senator in question had disappeared. And not just any senator, the senior senator from Texas, Phillip Herrera. Thank God Sam had given him a heads-up.

Apparently the guy had a habit of disappearing for a few days, so his people hadn't reported it. When he'd spoken with the senator's Chief of Staff, Grady O'Dell, he'd sounded genuine in his shock, but distant, as if shifting into spin-mode. Politics. Not a trustworthy one in the bunch.

Almost as bad, the media vultures were already circling. He'd rolled the calls to the Public Affairs Officer, who was instructed to give them the standard, "No comment, this is an on-going investigation," which would hold them for a bit, but not for long.

The guy on the boat was missing the back half of his

head, according to the Medical Examiner, who'd given the commander a quick and dirty analysis over the phone as he transported the body back to his offices. A gunshot, but no gun found at the scene, the caliber of the gun still in question. No slug at the scene and the ME was too smart to try to guess at it like on those idiot CSI shows. The time of death he'd guessed to have been mid to late morning—a lifetime ago when searching for a missing senator.

And the senator was missing. The ME had run the dead guy's prints and had gotten a hit. Kellen blew by the irony—a hit indeed. The guy was some international assassin, suspected, of course—they hadn't proven anything. But, apparently, the Feds had enough to go on to put him on a most-wanted list.

What was some gun-for-hire doing after a senator from Texas? That was the question, wasn't it?

Currently in the midst a full-blown autopsy, the ME would know more soon. For now, Commander Wilder had to content himself with getting his mind around what they already knew. He needed a sounding board.

"Bates, get in here, would you?" The commander heard a chair scrape back, a muttered curse, then Lieutenant Junior-Grade Jeter Bates, all five-feet-ten inches and one hundred and fifty pounds of him, skidded into his office.

"Sir." Bates, with his ruddy cheeks, wispy blond hair, round face, and innocent eyes made the commander feel old. He'd probably lived and loved, saved many and lost a few before Bates had been even a twinkle in his mother's eye.

Commander Wilder swallowed hard at the memory of one particular night, a crew lost. *Goddamn Davis.* Sweat popped on his brow, his heart hammered, but his expression remained calm as he worked to stuff the memory back into the deepest, darkest hole he could find in his psyche. He'd lived that day a thousand times, and nothing ever changed. And now, with a missing senator, the FBI was going to be crawling all over his ass and everyone else's.

"You were first on the scene this morning." A statement, not a question. "I've got your reports here, but I want you to walk me through it, as you saw it."

Bates clasped his hands behind him and spread his feet as if he was adopting parade rest. Wilder motioned toward a chair. "Take a load off, kid. It's been a long day already, and things are just getting wound up." Incoming calls lit up every line on the phone in front of him.

The kid sagged into the chair, thrusting his legs out in front of him as he leaned back. With one hand, he doffed his ball cap, then wiped his eyes with his forearm before settling his cap back low over his eyes. His arms rested on the armrests, his hands dangling. "The call came in at 9:37 a.m. to Sector over channel 16. Sector about went ape-shit over the name of the boat. They deployed a bunch of assets—us and a small boat crew from Galveston. They actually got there a few minutes before we arrived."

Any news outlet monitoring the frequency could've picked up the call. That explained how they knew the senator could've been involved. "Ms. Donovan called it in?"

Bates looked at him with a bemused expression. "Yes, sir."

"Did she say what was she doing in Galveston Bay?" Sam hadn't mentioned it and he hadn't thought to ask, not with...everything.

Just the mention of Sam Donovan had Kellen's mind wandering where he didn't need it to go. That woman had gotten under his skin all right...like a sand flea, burrowing in beyond his reach and driving him nuts. An itch he longed to scratch but couldn't. Negotiating the real estate between them was like traversing a minefield. But he had to find a way. He'd never felt at peace like he did when he was with her.

"She wasn't *in* the bay; she was *over* it. Pretty sweet machine, too. One of the new Sikorskys. She stayed on scene until we got there. I dropped Mason in. The boat crew rerouted channel traffic and kept folks away. The guy was dead when we got there. Half his head—"

The commander held up his hand. "Got it."

Bates blinked rapidly as he clamped his lips together. "There was so much...and his brains...the color wasn't what I thought."

The commander swallowed hard and tried not to picture the scene.

The kid looked a little green. "It gets easier, doesn't it, sir? To handle, I mean?"

"God, I hope not."

For a moment, Bates looked confused.

"Even if the guy deserved it, murder is a pretty harsh punishment." Kellen strove for a casual tone. "Anyone talk to Ms. Donovan?"

"We gave her info to the State Police. It's their investigation, right?"

"Yep. It's theirs until the FBI gets ahold of them, if they haven't already—missing senators get the Feds all twitchy. Should be quite a battle, but thankfully this time it ain't my circus." He wondered who would be charged with handling Agent Davis. Wilder didn't envy the guy.

"And ain't our flying monkeys," Bates added without thinking. When his eyes caught his commander's, his face reddened. "Sorry, sir."

Kellen smiled a tired smile. "Have that on good authority, do you?" Truth of it was, he didn't mind the kid repeating one of his own tired phrases.

"Yes, sir."

"Describe the scene as you remember it, without the gore."

"Boat was nosed in to the grass on the northwest shore over by Annahuac."

The commander closed his eyes, letting the kid's words paint a picture for him. "Pretty remote."

"Yes, sir. Not sure where he put in, but if he put in on the Texas City side, with the heading that boat took, normally it would've headed out into the Gulf. Might've taken a long while to find. But the winds are a bit more southerly coming up and over the top of that tropical storm in the Caribbean."

"Perhaps a lucky break for us, if the storm doesn't intensify. Then all bets are off." The commander had worked Katrina, flying until he couldn't fly anymore. So many people to save, but only so much time, limited resources. He didn't need to see another storm like that one; nobody did. "Grass behind the boat...torn up, bottom muddied?"

"No, sir. Engine was shut down."

"Out of fuel?"

"No." The boy shifted in his seat. "Odd thing, the boat had extra tanks stashed below, all of them filled to the brim."

Wilder flipped back to the first page of the report. "But the boat was a small fishing boat. Not really seaworthy for the open ocean."

"Yes, sir."

"No sign of the senator?" Wilder asked, knowing his luck wasn't that good.

Bates shook his head.

Commander Wilder opened his eyes and stared at the ceiling, picturing the bay, the island, the boat. "I wonder where the boat was headed. Was the senator on board? How'd an assassin end up with half his head blown off?"

"All good questions, sir."

Wilder lifted an eyebrow at him. "Thank you, Lieutenant. Is there anything you do know that might be helpful?"

"Well, I checked the firearms registry to see if the senator had a gun. He does...did...does. A SIG-Sauer P227 stainless."

"Serious stopping power." Wilder thought you could tell a lot about a man by the gun he carried. And the senator's choice told him the guy was expecting a fight.

"Sir?" a worried tone crept into the kid's voice.

"Nothing." Wilder waved that train of thought to the side. "What else did you see? Were there any maps on board that might indicate where the boat was headed with all that fuel?"

"No."

Wilder pulled his phone from his pocket and opened the map feature then set the phone down in front of him of the desk. "With GPS technology, he could use his phone if he wanted to."

Bates moved forward for a look. "Until he got far enough out and the signal degraded."

"Wouldn't happen. Enough of the rigs have towers and repeaters to cover the Gulf. Lots of lonely men out there, Lieutenant. Cell is the cheapest way for them to call home."

Commander Wilder grabbed a pencil from his desk and flicked it toward the ceiling while he thought. He'd not stuck one in the acoustic tiles yet, so he wasn't in danger of damaging government property...not that he cared. "What else did you notice?" He caught the pencil on the bounce back.

"Boat was rigged for fishing. One line was still out."

"Was there anybody else fishing? Any witnesses? Someone who might've seen something?"

"Not that we saw. It's pretty remote, and a weekday."

Wilder punched up another app on his phone—a current chart of the drilling operations in the Gulf. "With the fuel the boat had onboard, how far, assuming high seas, do you think it could've gotten?"

Bates rolled his eyes as he did a bit of mental math. "There's so much we don't know: time, tide—"

"I know." Wilder put his finger on a spot on the screen, then tilted his head, trying to read the distance. "Let me put it this way. Could he have made it, say, seventy miles?"

Bates thought for a moment. "Yeah."

"Thanks, kid." The commander flicked the pencil skyward one more time. This time it went in pointed end first and stuck. "Well, I'll be damned." He left it there as he levered himself from his chair...a clue to the kid the interview was over.

"I think I'll wander next door and have a chat with Ms. Donovan myself."

"We've got training in half an hour, sir."

"I haven't forgotten."

CHAPTER EIGHTEEN

Shelby fought the afternoon traffic through Houston. Westheimer, one of the main east/west roads through the Galleria area, was slammed in both directions, even heading toward town. Pressing on the horn only got her the finger. So she waited, her hand draped over the top of the steering wheel; her fingers drumming was the only outward sign of her impatience as they all inched forward. A guy in a black Dodge rode her ass, which pissed her off even more. She motioned him to go around, but he stuck behind her. Squinting in the rearview, she tried to see his face, but he wore a set of dark glasses, and the side windows had been tinted black as night so they let in little light. In New York, it was illegal to tint windows that dark—now she understood why.

Finally, the Kirby intersection came into view. The shotgun Jake had left her sat across her lap—not exactly the kind of weapon for tight spaces. But she guessed it was better than nothing. Three lights later, she was at the head of the line waiting to cross, scanning the corners for Becca Molinari. Shelby knew what she looked like. As the personal assistant to Drayton Lewis, Ms. Molinari wasn't exactly low profile. Tall and blonde, she would stand out on any corner, even in Texas.

As it was, Becca spotted Shelby first. The passenger

door opened, and Becca slid inside on a rush of heavy, humid air, surprising Shelby, leaving her little time to react. But her instincts were good, her reflexes better. Gripping the shotgun, she raised it slightly. The traffic, still moving at a glacial pace, didn't require much attention, so she focused on Becca Molinari, who seemed amused by the gun rather than alarmed.

"You know how to use that?"

"Point and pull the trigger. What else do I need to know?"

The guy in the black Dodge honked. Becca swiveled to take a look. Her eyes narrowed. "How long has that guy been back there?"

"I'm not exactly sure, but I think he picked me up just outside my hotel."

Becca glanced down at Shelby's gun. "I'm glad you have that."

"Why?" Shelby flicked a glance at Becca. Her movements seemed jerky, nervous. Huge dark glasses hid half her face. A bruise bloomed around her throat.

"What happened to you? It looks like someone tried to strangle you." Shelby's insides turned to ice.

"What the hell did you do to Mr. Lewis?" Becca asked, her voice tight with anger.

"Me? What did *I* do? Seriously? You know perfectly well what *we* did."

That seemed to sober Becca a bit. "We weren't going to beat him over the head with it. What a stupid, self-aggrandizing thing to do. He was pissed."

"I did my job; that's what I did. The guy's a cockroach. We needed to bring him into the light." The haze of anger cleared. "Why?" The light dawned. "Did he do that to you?"

Becca looked out the side window.

Shelby saw the glint of a tear as it inched below her sunglasses. She reached over and squeezed Becca's arm. "Oh, honey, I'm so sorry. I had no idea."

Becca waved away Shelby's concern. "My fault, really. I

can take care of myself." Her tone left little doubt that she thought she could make good on that.

Shelby thought, from the looks of her, perhaps she was a bit overconfident.

"I heard about Jake. I'm really sorry."

"Yeah. It doesn't seem real." Becca had been a good friend of Jake's at MIT. Of course, that had been a few years ago, but Shelby had played that card with her brother when she had been assigned the research on Drayton Lewis. He'd made the introduction, and Becca had been the mother lode of information. Shelby couldn't have dug up the juicy bits without Jake and Becca. And then something changed. Becca and Jake had a side bet, something they were doing on their own. When Shelby had asked him about it, Jake had gone all weird, making her promise on her life not to go down that path, not to look any further.

"Do you know anything about what happened to Jake?" Becca asked.

"Only the what and the how, not the why." Shelby tried to concentrate on the traffic. The guy in the black Dodge still dogged her tail, which sent a bolt of adrenaline to jumpstart her heart. She willed herself to calm. *Stupid. Just relax. Nobody's going to come after you here—not with everyone around.* Easy to think; hard to believe. "So, if you'd wanted to extend your condolences, I assume we could've had a nice phone call. What's all this about? We didn't cross any lines as far as I can tell. If I know something worth killing for, then I'd sure like to know what it is. And I know you said you can take care of yourself, but you look like you're scared of your own shadow."

"I am." Becca rooted in her handbag. Shelby tightened her grip on the gun. Becca pulled out a well-used tissue and dabbed at her eyes. "You know I've worked for Mr. Lewis for a while now. At first, I was just one of the staff, but lately he's letting me into more and more of the sensitive side of his business dealings."

Shelby focused on the traffic and tried to keep her mouth shut. The best asset a reporter could have was the ability to shut up and listen—she was still working on the shutting up part. The guy in the Dodge was making her nervous, and when she was nervous, she tended to rattle on. So, she focused on keeping quiet and not running into the car in front of hers as the traffic stopped and started through town.

"Did Jake tell you about working with me?"

"No. I knew something was going on, but he wouldn't tell me."

Becca nodded. "I didn't think so. Anyway, not too long ago I was looking through my c-drive when I came across a series of emails. At first they didn't make sense, and then I realized they were orders."

"What kind of orders?"

"Puts and calls on the oil futures markets."

"Nothing illegal about that." Shelby felt a hollowness in her stomach. With Jake working his way to the top of the security section at the NYMEX, she knew where this was going.

"Well..." Becca glanced out the passenger window. "That's where Jake came in."

"I hate it when I'm right," Shelby muttered.

"What?"

"Nothing." Shelby focused on following the car in front. She had no destination in mind and all day to get there. "You told Jake about the trades?"

"I asked him to check them out."

"Why?"

"The email seemed off. I did a little searching of my own, but..."

"You needed an inside guy."

"Jake was intrigued. He said he'd help."

Of course he did. Shelby bet there weren't many men who could say no to a stunner like Becca Molinari. "What did he find?"

"Two interesting things. First, the trades were executed but never reported. And the source of the money was buried in a hidden trail that bounced from server to server around the world."

"So the identities of the parties making the trades couldn't be identified."

"Jake said he'd follow the trail. Next thing I hear is he's dead." Becca nodded as she blew her nose. Then she reached across and squeezed Shelby's hand tight. "Shelby, I think I may have gotten Jake killed."

Shelby took that blow, pausing to let it reverberate through her. "You couldn't have known."

"No. I mean, you always wonder what people are willing to do to hide their secrets and keep them hidden, but you never think of it happening in your world, to someone close to you. And that you may have unwittingly put them in danger in the first place."

"I understand. You can't blame yourself. Jake was a big boy. His job was ferreting out the guys who broke the rules. It could have been any one of those folks who killed him."

"You think?" Some of the tension tightening her voice eased.

"We just need to figure out all the different miscreants he was chasing." *Hell of a job, Jakey.* Then it dawned on her; his job hadn't been too different from her own—chasing the sociopaths who insist everyone was to be used for their own gain. Evil made good headlines. Shelby's thoughts whirled. At Becca's shout, she stomped on the brakes, missing the car in front of them by inches. Both hands white-knuckled around the steering wheel, Shelby took a moment, waiting for the sharp flush of adrenaline to subside. Prodded by the horns sounding behind her, she let the car idle forward as she worked to keep her voice under control. When she glanced in the rearview, the guy in the Dodge shot her the finger. Okay, clearly not following them—just an asshole. "Here," Becca said as she retrieved the shotgun that had fallen to the floor. Let's put this away before someone gets hurt." She turned and hung it on the rack in the back window.

"Is that legal, to hang a gun there like a threat?"

Becca shot her an incredulous look. "It's Texas. If you don't have a gun hanging in the window, they think you're gay. Not that that really applies to us."

"Did you talk to Jake at all about what he may have found?"

"Yes, he was narrowing it down." Becca worried at a tear in a beautifully manicured nail. Finally, she tore it off. "I sure wish I had his laptop." She pointed at the next street. "Take a right here."

Shelby turned, picking the center lane, since she had no idea where she was or where she was going. "Jake wouldn't be stupid enough to put what he found on a laptop."

"He said he was being careful; the computer wasn't connected." Becca sucked on the thin line of blood where her nail had ripped. "Do the cops have it?"

"Not that I've been told." Shelby felt Becca looking at her. They passed under a freeway. She made note of it: Highway 59.

"You have it."

"What? The laptop?"

"Yeah."

Shelby kept her eyes on the road. "I don't have it." Glancing behind, she saw the Dodge two cars back.

"He sent it to you." Becca sounded sure. "You were the only one he trusted. It has to come to you. You'll tell me if you get it, right?"

"Sure. The guy in the black Dodge is still back there, not that he could get very far in this traffic."

Becca reached up and angled the rearview so she could see behind. "Where?"

"Two cars back."

"How long?"

"Like I said, not sure, but I think he picked me up outside the St. Regis."

Becca relaxed a little bit. "It won't be one of Lewis's men, then. Anyone following you that we should be worried about?"

"I can't imagine who."

Becca re-angled the mirror. "Here, fix it so you can see. And keep an eye on him. If he makes a move, tell me."

"And what will you do?"

Becca gave her a tight grin. "I don't have a clue, but it sounds good."

Shelby glanced in the rearview at the shotgun hanging in the window. Not that she could hit anything with it, but at least the guy behind her knew she had it. Everything was coming at her so fast, she found herself struggling to keep up. Jake had been playing a dangerous game. Why hadn't he told her? "What else did Jake tell you?"

"The money came from some interesting places. Riyadh, The Hague, London, Houston, Hong Kong."

"And the pooled money was used to make the trades?"

"Yes."

"What ties those cities together? Any ideas?" Shelby had made a huge circle and was once again approaching Kirby, this time from the east and much further south, in the West University District.

"Pull in over there." Becca motioned to a shopping center on their right. "I know a great little Italian place. I could use a drink."

"I second that." Shelby piloted the car to an open parking space then killed the engine. The Dodge went on. Shelby was about to breathe a sigh of relief, when she saw him turn into the same parking lot at the next turn-in. She watched as he went around the far side of the building. Swiveling to look at Becca head-on, she asked again, "What do those cities have in common?"

"Each is the headquarters for one of the major oil companies in the world."

Shelby chewed on that for a moment. "Okay, let's play this out. If the major oil companies are in cahoots, manipulating the markets, or trying to, why would Drayton Lewis be interested?"

"Apparently, you haven't picked up on just exactly what

kind of wolf Drayton Lewis is. He's a master at using information to gain leverage. If the oil guys are running a game, you can bet Lewis wants in."

"Is he blackmailing them?" Shelby wasn't surprised. The news business had ripped off her blinders years ago. Corporate America had a stench about it, and, living in New York, it was hard to ignore it.

"Could be." Becca's face drained of color. "But I'll tell you this, there isn't anything Drayton Lewis wouldn't do to get ahead. Even murder."

CHAPTER NINETEEN

The man roped to the chair didn't move...he didn't dare. Rope stretched his arms around the back, lashed his feet, then looped around his neck. Any movement, any struggle to release the pain, would tighten the rope, choking him a bit at a time. His head hanging forward, dark hair matted with the salt from the ocean spray and slick with blood that dripped onto the floor, the man shivered, but he didn't make a sound.

"Again." Lewis's voice held a hint of curiosity, nothing more. The guy was a goddamn Timex. Frankly, he was amazed he'd lasted as long as he had. All night. As the morning bloomed into the full light of day, Lewis grew tired of the game.

With balled fist, the member of Lewis's crew sent the roped man's head snapping to the side. Blood arced, leaving a dotted streak along the gray metal wall, joining the dark brown of others. The man grunted, flinching against the hit. He tensed, then worked to draw a constricted breath.

"Who were you waiting for?"

"I told you." The choked reply. "A man."

"Who?" The single word, hard-edged, sliced like a blade.

"I." Gasp. "Don't." Another tortured breath. "Know."

"Who sent you?"

"*El Jefe.*" A wheeze and then a grunt when the crewmember hit him again.

Lewis grabbed the man's hair lifting his head. "Who the fuck is *El Jefe?*"

"He is a ghost." The man's eyes wandered, rolling back before focusing again. "*Mi hija.*" He spit blood, which splattered on the decking, barely missing Lewis's shoe.

"Your daughter?"

"*Si.*"

Lewis stared through the porthole at the gray skies, the gray water. "*El Jefe es un coyote?*"

The man said nothing.

Drayton released the man's head, which lolled forward. With a lift of his chin to his crewmember, Drayton stepped back. He plucked a white linen handkerchief out of his back pocket and dabbed at the blood on his hands.

A raised fist crashed down in a meaty thunk. A new arc of blood to join the others that dripped down the wall.

"*La luz,*" the man muttered as his shoulders sagged against the rope that bound his arms. Struggling for breath—ragged wheezes as he sucked in air, fighting the constriction.

"What about the light?" Drayton pressed.

"Boss, I'm thinking we got all he knows." The crewmember's voice was a low, menacing rumble.

Drayton arrowed a look at him.

The guy didn't look like he was getting queasy—he merely looked bored.

They both watched the bound man. Each breath shallower, the time between longer, until they stopped.

"Is he dead?" Lewis asked, not caring one way or the other. He would have liked a few more answers. The one he got was useless to him. So the man died for his daughter. But what was a *coyote* doing interested in Donovan's drilling platform? *Coyotes* smuggled people.

Lewis didn't buy it.

The rest of the blood had dried on Lewis's hands. He

dropped the handkerchief, leaving his man to clean up the mess...all of it. "Throw him overboard," he said as he stepped through the doorway. He didn't look back.

Lewis returned topside, working his way to his cabin in the stern of the ship above the engine room. The killing he could stomach, but he didn't really enjoy the disposal. Something about a body when the life had left disturbed him. Maybe it was from finding his father, his brains blown out by his own hand. Regardless, death didn't bother him, but what remained did.

After securing the door with two latches and a lock, Lewis poured himself three fingers of bourbon into a cut-crystal tumbler, then turned to stare out at the angry seas. Braced on wide legs, his knees slightly bent, he absorbed the movement as his ship rode the swells. The seas had built over the last hours. Someone else knew about Donovan. He didn't know that, but he had to assume it was true. Why else would they be watching, waiting, on a fucking Waverunner no less? In seas building in front of a hurricane. This was much more important than smuggling a bunch of wetbacks into Texas. Word would get out. And when it did, his gambit would be screwed.

Lewis took a mouthful of bourbon, holding it there, relishing the sting on sensitive skin before swallowing, and enjoying the fiery path it traced to his stomach. Pain, so elemental, yet so transitory. Pleasure equally so.

Both leaving you wanting for more.

CHAPTER TWENTY

Despite an early morning run to St. Charles in the King Air, and Geraldo dogging her every step when she got back, Sam Donovan couldn't shake the memory of the guy on the boat with his brains blown all over. She was pretty sure it wasn't Phil Herrera, but she'd like to know for sure—no, she needed to know. The hair color hadn't been quite right, nor the physique—but she'd only gotten a quick look. More definitive, Uncle Phil wouldn't have been caught dead in a pair of Madras shorts—one of those back-east styles that Texans scoffed at unless you hung out with the toffee-noses at River Oaks. Hardly something to hang her hope on, but that was the best she had.

"Miss Sam?"

Geraldo's voice brought her back—he'd caught her with both hands on the right strut of the J-3. The boy manned the left. They were poised to push it back, tail into the corner, when Sam's mind had wandered into dark places. "Sorry. You ready?"

They both pushed and moved the light aircraft easily, Sam pushing and pulling as needed to guide the tail to the proper spot. Geraldo was quick with the chocks, a set bracketing each of the wheels on the main gear. They met at the nose of the airplane.

The boy was like a sponge, absorbing everything he saw,

his English far outpacing the improvement in her Spanish. He made her feel old. Hell, at thirty-eight she guessed she wasn't exactly young, but she didn't feel old either. "If you get me that permission from your mother, we can take this old bucket into the air."

The boy pulled a folded paper from his pocket and extended it to her. "I got it." His eyes danced. "I...she made me write a paper for school on the safety of flight. And I think I did a year's worth of chores."

His eyes held hers, then darted away. She glimpsed excitement there, and a little bit of fear. Sam smiled inwardly. Fear was a good thing—it kept you from doing the stuff that could kill you.

Commander Wilder ducked in out of the heat. "A man's gotta do what a man's gotta do."

Sam had no idea how long he'd been standing there. Her heart did one of those funny little bounces that pissed her off. She felt her face flush, which pissed her off even more. With the greasy rag in her hand, Sam wiped at a trail of sweat trickling down the side of her face. "Twice in less than twenty-four hours, Commander. To what do I owe the pleasure?"

"Working on bad-penny status." He turned to the boy. "I need to talk to Miss Sam for a minute, alone."

"Yes, sir." Geraldo jammed his hands in his pockets. "I'm going to get a soda next door."

"Tell them it's on me," Wilder said.

"I always do." The boy easily darted out of the commander's reach as he made a playful lunge at him, then jogged into the sunlight and disappeared around the corner.

"If I didn't know better, I'd say that little shyster is your watchdog," Wilder said, his voice lacking any hint of a bite.

"He's a good kid. Just had some bad breaks." That sounded a bit more defensive than Sam intended.

"Agreed. I didn't intend to insult him, merely to express appreciation for his skills." Kellen stepped closer, stopping only when the look on her face told him he was close enough.

"Sorry. I'm a bit touchy. My father..."

"Can break open the scab and expose the raw."

Sam wanted to like the commander, to trust him. He said the right things, seemed to get her on a level no one ever had. Right now, he looked like he was caught in one of those awkward self-debates—should he hug me, should he not? With a bit of surprise, Sam realized she'd take the hug.

Instinctively, she stepped back, letting him off the hook and retreating to safety. The last thing she needed was to get hung up on some here-today-gone-tomorrow flyboy.

"I really had a nice time last night," Kellen said. "It rescued a deadly day."

"Me, too." It had been the perfect evening, until Agent Davis had crashed the party. And his parting shot did little to shore up Sam's rickety confidence in the commander. What really had happened out there that night? What had the commander done? "Do you have any information about my father or the senator?"

He raked his hand through his hair. "I've got patrols out, but nothing so far. That storm south of here is making a mess. Just this morning we plucked a group of refugees from a sinking bathtub...literally. Lost a few in high seas."

"I'm sorry." Sam couldn't imagine a job where death lurked in the shadows every moment. Of course, flying itself was an on-the-edge game.

"That's part of the allure, isn't it?" he said as if he could read her mind.

She gave him an eyebrow raised in disbelief. She hadn't pegged the flyboy as particularly intuitive.

"Right. Let me explain. No, there is too much; let me sum up."

"One might think you're trying to soften me up, quoting my favorite movie."

"*Princess Bride*. I've done my research. A man's gotta do..."

"What a man's gotta do."

That comment fueled both horror and delight, making Sam feel as if she was standing at the pivot point on an emotional teeter-totter. "Look, about last night." She couldn't look him in the eye. "That was really nice of you. I appreciate it. And I hope you're not trying to soften me up to take the sting out of your bosses wanting to kick me off the field."

"They kicked you off?" Kellen sounded surprised and more than a little bit angry.

"No. Not yet. No need to go to general quarters." Sam hadn't expected indignation from the commander. Maybe, just maybe, her father had been right.

Ah, Da, where have you got to?

"Don't scare me like that," Kellen sounded sincere.

"You don't look like the scaring kind."

A cloud passed across his face and his voice had a hollow ring. "You have no idea."

The silence turned awkward—unspoken questions hanging between them. So many things she wanted to ask him. "You want to help me with the King Air? If you entertain me while I work, I might buy you a beer."

"Deal." Kellen followed her into the relative cool comfort of the deeper shadows at the back of the hangar, looking relieved at having something to do. The Model B-200 was old, yet shone with love, care, and a new paint job. "What's wrong with her?" He ran his fingers along the leading edge of the wing as he followed Sam around to the door—she'd lowered the stairs to allow access.

"Not much. Just need to tighten up a few of the latches. Got a slight pressure leak on the run this morning; couldn't figure out from where. Turns out the door seal was going bad in a couple of spots. I replaced it, but now need to make sure the door seats right and the latches are tight."

"You lose a door in flight, you'll be calling the Coast Guard."

Sam turned and gave him a hooded look. "You'd come running?"

Kellen cleared his throat as pink flushed his cheeks, showing Sam's words had hit close to the mark. "Speaking of calling the Coast Guard..."

"Subtle, Commander. Like a sledgehammer." Sam laughed as she held out her hand. "Screwdriver." Someday maybe he'd come around without an agenda or an excuse. But he didn't strike her as the committing kind. Although she put up a good front, Sam wanted someone solid, someone to ride out the rough patches with. God knew she'd seen enough of the other from her father.

"Thought I might weasel some info out of you." Kellen watched her work.

Sam bit her lips as she angled to gain some leverage—one of the fittings was giving her trouble. Strong and lean, yet with curves that embarrassed her sometimes, Sam radiated cool efficiency. But the red hair and the way her green eyes narrowed and her face pinched when she was angry hinted at the fire underneath the calm exterior.

"Allow me?" Kellen didn't wait for permission. He eased the screwdriver from her hand. As he leaned in, she didn't move away. She smelled of jet fuel, hard work, and something sweet. Distracted by the nearness of her, he lost focus once and his hand slipped.

Sam didn't say anything. Instead, she brushed back the curls from her forehead as she watched him. He tried not to stare. She took the screwdriver when he'd backed the screw out a bit. "Thanks. Who was that guy in the boat?"

Kellen leaned back; his eyes widened. "You don't know? I thought the State Police would've been by to question you."

"They were here, but you know how that goes: they ask all the questions; I give all the answers. I told them what I saw, what I knew. They told me nothing."

"I'm surprised you didn't at least catch it on the news. What rock have you been living under?"

She looked around, her eyes taking in the aircraft filling the hangar. "You're looking at them. I'm a one-man show—fix it, fly it, fuel it, I'm it. I've been sleeping upstairs." She nodded toward a small landing above them where she had a bunk, a shower, and a hotplate. "Catching sleep when I could. I haven't been home in three days. First, it was rig shift change, so I was flying. Then with the weather, I took the time to do some maintenance and a few inspections. And you know how that goes; it's like decorating. Buy something new, and everything else looks shabby. I think I've touched every plane in this hangar fixing something." She worked as she talked, her face pinched in concentration. "You going to tell me or just keep rubbing my nose in the life I don't have?"

"ME ran the prints. Got a hit from Interpol."

"Interpol?" Sam said, as if speaking about another planet, another life, which she was, in a way. "How'd *that* end up on the news?"

"I don't know. These media-types, they can follow a trail better than a pig on a truffle hunt."

"Why do I get the idea you know more than you're telling me?" Sam put a hand on a hip as she eyed him.

"I'm not your father, Sam."

Sam flinched. "You're a man."

Kellen let that one go—Sam's skin was paper-thin when it came to her father. "The guy's fingerprints were in their database along with a couple of photos they suspect are of our guy. The ME is sending some DNA. We'll see if it matches some they collected from various crime scenes."

Sam looked at him like he was reciting the plot of a Ludlum movie. "Interpol? Various crime scenes? So, who was he?"

"Some gun for hire." Kellen watched for a reaction, trying to gauge what Sam knew.

"Seriously?" Sam seemed just as confused as he was. "What would international criminals want with Uncle Phil?"

"Not sure. Not even sure the guys who hired the gun were international. The shooter traveled worldwide, but that doesn't mean he wasn't working for homegrown assholes."

"Fuck." Tears welled. Sam swiped at the tears.

"I think your Uncle Phil, assuming he was on the boat, came out on the right end of that bit of bad business."

Sam used the oily rag to wipe her eyes, leaving a black smudge under one of them. "Okay." She nodded several times, as if trying to convince herself that a whole list of imagined horribles couldn't possibly be true. "I like that. But then, if he was there, and he blew the guy away, where is he?"

"I wish I knew. He's simply vanished." Kellen hesitated. He could point out the vastness of the Gulf and how the fish and crabs and birds could make short work of a body tossed out there. That kind of stuff was common knowledge. He searched for something comforting to say that didn't sound like a thin platitude but came up empty-handed. Of course, he was unsure as to how much comforting Sam wanted or needed. With her the two were never synonymous—a fact that kept him feeling like a boy at his first dance.

Sam remained rooted to the spot. Her hand shook as she brushed back a strand of hair that refused to be corralled. "When I got close, I could see the guy in the boat, but not his face. Something about him struck me as familiar, but I couldn't place him."

"Really? How would your path cross with a known assassin's?" Kellen didn't like the sound of that.

"I've been trying to remember where I might have seen him, but not being able to put his face together..." Sam grimaced and ground to a halt.

Kellen put the screwdriver back in the toolbox at her feet. The spring assembly she'd taken off the J-3 caught his attention. Needing something to keep his hands busy and offload some nervous energy, he grabbed it, running it through one hand like a set of worry beads. With the other he gently reached for her hand, needing to offer comfort and get some, too.

Her skin felt warm, soft—a connection sizzled through him. If she felt it too, he couldn't tell. "Come on. Let's go sit a bit." He led her to the bench outside off to the side of the hangar door—not much shade to shelter them from the heat of the day, but at least it was a place to sit. "I'll find us a couple of sodas. I've got training in a few."

"Diet for me," she said to his back.

He dropped the spring assembly in a pile of parts near the door. "That stuff can kill you."

"Not any faster than the sugar hit. The latest studies link sugar to all kinds of health disasters."

"Justifying."

"True."

When he returned, he found her standing where he had left her, staring across the field, a lost look on her face. He handed the soda to her, then parked a butt cheek on the rounded top of a concrete pillar protecting the door, letting it take a bit of his weight. "Why is it I always seem to be the bearer of bad news? I wish I had some good news for once."

She popped the top and drank deeply. Then she backhanded a tear that had the audacity to escape and run down her cheek. "All things considered, it wasn't the worst news you could've brought. My dad gave Uncle Phil his first job. The story of that job interview is a killer. Working for my dad is probably what propelled Phil into a legal career." Sam sank down on the lower step. Easing over, she patted the space beside her, inviting Kellen to join her. "I've known him my whole life really. Certainly saw him more when Dad was around. So not much for the last few months." Not that she saw her father all that much either, not that she was proud of that. As usual, she was as much at fault as he.

"Anybody want to kill the senator?"

"Well, he made some enemies in the Mineral Management Service dust-up a couple of years back."

Kellen nodded. "I remember. The guys in the Interior Department in charge of all the oil leases, including those in the Gulf."

"Those...men...were accepting drugs, sex, all kinds of things in exchange for favorable leases."

"And Senator Herrera led the witch hunt, didn't he?"

Her chest sorta puffed out "Yeah, he did. You think that could have something to do with his disappearance?"

"One of the questions. Still no answers."

"Somebody better start finding some." Sam bit off the words, her anger leaking through as she worked for control. Uncle Phil missing, presumed dead, and everyone was looking for her father. "I don't like it."

"Sure would like to talk to your father."

"You and me both." Sam looked like she was weighing what to say next, chewing on some words.

"What?"

"You know when you barged in on my father and me a couple of days ago? He was running scared. Although he tried to hide it, I could tell he was worried. I've never seen him quite like that."

"About what?"

"He didn't say. Not exactly. But it had to do with Uncle Phil. Paddy said Phil came to him with some story, but he only gave him enough to scare him and convince him it was true."

"Have you had any luck getting a bead on your father?"

"The guys on the rig weren't any help. I spoke with his production manager myself."

"No help?"

Sam drained the last of the Diet Coke, crunched the can, and then launched it in a perfect arc into the trash can bungeed to the hangar. "I know this is going to sound weird, but he left me with the impression he was stonewalling me."

"About what?"

"When I asked him if he knew where my father was, he didn't answer...not directly anyway." Sam squinted one eye at the commander. "He said he hadn't seen him in a couple of days."

"But he didn't say he didn't know where he was."

"And the production manager is an engineer. If he's about anything, it's the details." Sam shrugged. "Maybe I'm reading too much into our conversation, but he's always been square with me before."

"Maybe you can try again?"

"All I know is that, knowing my father, if he doesn't want to be found, he won't be. Something has forced him underground. I can feel it. I just wish I knew what."

Kellen unfolded himself from the bench, drained the last of his Coke, and then launched his can toward the trash. He missed. "I've got training in a few minutes. I'll try to stop at your father's operation while I'm out putting the new guy through his paces today. Do you think Senator Herrera could've been headed out that way when he got...intercepted?"

"In that boat? Suicide. Especially with the storm around Cuba—it's making a mess of things, but I don't have to tell you that. And it's only getting worse. The storm is deepening." Sam squinted against the sun. Bright in a bluebird sky, the day made it hard to believe a huge storm was gathering strength to the south and would unleash its fury by the week's end. "You asked that question for a reason. You think Uncle Phil was trying to meet up with my father?"

"The senator had been squirreling away fuel below deck. Enough to make a run as far as your father's rig, perhaps farther depending on the wind and seas."

Sam chewed on that a moment. "You don't get to be a Senior Senator from Texas and chairman of the Natural Resources Committee without making enemies." Sam felt the warmth where her shoulder touched the commander's. It heightened the cold she felt inside, but she found the connection comforting and unsettling in a way, as if she stood on shifting sand.

"Anything you shared with the State Police that you'd like to share with me?" Kellen asked.

Sam leaned back and stared straight ahead, casting an occasional quick sideways glance at the commander. The Coast Guard would have jurisdiction. Closing her eyes, she let her thoughts drift back. "I was out playing around. Talked some salesman into letting me fly his demo S76-D for an hour."

Kellen gave a low whistle. "It's a sweet ride, but a bit heavy for some of the platforms I've contracted with. Their pads are certified up to ten thousand pounds. The 76-D grosses out at over eleven thousand." She took a deep breath and ran her fingers through her hair. "Caught a glimpse of the boat, nosed in. A fishing boat rigged out, it didn't look right stuck in there the way it was. Thought maybe someone was in trouble. I was right, but too late. The rest you probably know from your man, Mr. Jeter. Great kid. He a good stick?"

"A natural, but he doesn't know it. Still trying to push the helicopter around rather than encouraging it to go where he wants."

"So a typical male flier." Sam nodded, then smiled at a thought she didn't share.

"Perhaps someday we can discuss the various inherent aptitudes of each gender over another, more traditional dinner sometime?" Kellen cringed. "Not real smooth, sorry. Bad time, I know."

"I liked your non-traditional approach." Sam let her eyes rest on him for a moment longer than necessary. "So dress-up and white tablecloths?"

"I have a special woman to impress." He made a move to go, stepping in closer to her. "I've got to get Bates to lighten his grip when he flies."

She shot him a look. "Men, always wanting to manhandle things."

He couldn't read her. Sometimes it seemed like she gave him a green light, only to switch it to red when he moved closer. "Anything else?" he asked.

"You mean about my theory of why women make better rotor wing pilots than men?"

"No. Not that I disagree. About the scene. Did you scout the area?"

He knew full well she'd been told to stay on scene, but

he also knew her pretty darn well...maybe too well. "I drifted around a bit. The only thing I saw that looked odd was a new set of tracks, not too far from the boat launch. They looked new, deep—a pickup maybe, pulling a trailer. To me, it looked like somebody launched a boat from there."

"Through the mud? They had a perfectly good ramp not far."

"I hope the forensics techs got a cast of the tracks."

CHAPTER TWENTY-ONE

Flying a helicopter was the nearest thing to being trapped alive in the bowels of a beast, thought Commander Wilder as he piloted the Dauphine H-65 low over the azure blue waters of the Gulf of Mexico. Clouds scudded, gray and dark, pregnant with water. The ceiling hung just above a thousand feet. That tropical storm, now expected to re-form north of Cuba, teased them, taunting them with the ferocity to come. A few days away, but it was shaping up to be one hell of a ride—if the weathermen could be believed. The NOAA had sent one of the hurricane hunters to check it out. The reports ought to be coming in soon.

Refusing to be desk-bound any longer, he'd penciled himself into the flight schedule, as much for the health of his junior officers as his own. The machine vibrated with life. Engines roared; the whap of the blades pulsed like a heartbeat through the stick, resonating in his very core until his heart seemed to pick up the same rhythm. His mother had told him he'd be lucky if he found a passion in life, and he'd be damned lucky if he could find someone willing to pay him to do it.

Kellen Wilder had been damned lucky.

And Sam shared his passion. Damn. A tough nut to crack, that woman. With his training schedule tight, he'd left her. He hadn't wanted to. She seemed okay, but she hid herself behind a thick wall.

With a practiced eye, he watched the needles on his HSI slowly center up. He pressed the mic close to his lips, "Okay, here we go. Last one, then we stop for fuel." Tipping his head toward Lieutenant Jeter Bates, his pilot-in-training in the right seat, he continued. "She's all yours, Mr. Bates. If you do it right the first time, we just might be in time for a late breakfast."

For the last hour and a half, Wilder and his crew had been on a training flight just west of the Mammoth Four drilling rig thirty miles out from Galveston. This last part of the flight included shooting instrument approaches, much as they would have to do in bad weather. Using the onboard computer, Wilder had designed an approach to a thousand yards off the west side of the rig. He had flown the first approach himself, then he had let the kid do it with the help of the computer coupled to the autopilot. This time he wanted the kid to hand-fly the approach. Autopilots had a nasty habit of crapping out when you needed them most, so a pilot had better learn how to rely on skill alone.

Jeter Bates wiped his palms on the legs of his flight suit and then took the stick with his right hand, the collective with his left. When Wilder checked off the autopilot, the helicopter bucked and rolled. Inexperienced pilots always over-controlled.

"Easy, son. Don't fight it," Wilder said. "Flying a helicopter is like making love to a woman—each move needs to be slow, gentle, and done with finesse."

Color rose in the kid's cheeks, but the helicopter settled down.

Sneaking a look at the kid out of the corner of his eye, Wilder wondered if the kid had ever made love to a woman. Despite his twenty-two years, he didn't look much over twelve.

As of last Wednesday, Wilder had given almost as many years as Bates had been alive to the U.S. Coast Guard. At the same point in their careers, many of his friends retired with their pensions and took up golf, but Wilder couldn't imagine doing anything other than what he was doing right now. But he was nearing the end of the flying, that he knew. As Commanding Officer of U.S. Coast Guard Air Station Houston, Wilder was on the top rung of the pilot's ladder. The billets above his did not include flying. Should he become a paper pusher or get out? And do what? As he watched the kid fly the approach, Wilder mentally cataloged that question for another day. This was too pretty a day to ruin, despite a missing senator and a guarded woman he couldn't resist.

"Keep it steady, kid. You're a bit high but otherwise right on." Wilder dialed in the radio frequency used by the rig and keyed his mic. "Mammoth Four, Rescue One inbound. ETA..." Wilder glanced at his watch, then at the computer screen. "Ten minutes. Is the pad clear?"

"Roger, Rescue One, come on in."

"We could take a load of fuel, and the guys are hungry." In addition to Bates, a swimmer sat quietly in the back in case he was needed.

"No prob. Bickerstaff has a heck of a spread laid out."

Wilder keyed his mic twice in response. On any given day as many as thirty thousand people lived in the Gulf of Mexico on the hundreds of working rigs. Three weeks on the rig, then three weeks at home—it wasn't a job Wilder would want, but he was glad they were there. Most drilling and production companies allowed the Coast Guard to use their rigs as fuel and rest stops. This provided safe landing areas in the event of an emergency and greatly increased the range the Guard could search.

"That's right, kid. You got it now." The kid was good, but Wilder wasn't going to let him know that just yet. A good pilot needed confidence, but cockiness could get you killed—you and your crew along with you. Confidence came from doing. Cockiness came from praise too easily earned. Wilder had learned that lesson the hard way.

"Easy. Watch the wind. It's pushing you to the right. See?" Wilder pointed to the barely discernible deflection of the needles on the HSI. "Watch the swells. They'll give you clues about the direction of the wind."

"It's hardly pushing at all, sir. I'm only a few feet off center," Bates replied, his face scrunched in concentration, his gaze not leaving the instruments.

"Kid, think of a black night, in the middle of a storm, and it's your job to pluck a family off the heaving deck of their sailboat. The mast swings with the pitching of the boat. The rigging is broken, flying in the wind. And you gotta drop a bucket on the deck—and bring it back aboard. A few feet can be the difference between a successful mission and something you'll spend the rest of your life seeing when you close your eyes. Trust me, kid, you don't want to go there."

Bates didn't say anything else.

The look on his face told Wilder he'd heard the rumors. No doubt some of them were true. The commander didn't know and didn't care.

"There you go, kid. Not bad for the first go. A bit of advice, stop trying to squeeze the juice out of the stick. You'll find she's easier to handle with a light touch." Wilder grabbed the stick and gently shook it. "She's mine now."

Bates relinquished the controls with a sigh of relief that made Wilder smile. The kid was green now, but with a few months under his belt, his nerves would be tempered hard as steel, his instincts and skill finely honed. He'd be a pilot his crew could count on. Wilder could spot the good ones right off. Bates was a good one.

Wilder banked the chopper over, righted it, maneuvered smartly into the wind, eased over the edge of the helipad, and set down with barely a discernible bump.

Several men waited, three or four more than usual.

"Looks like we have a welcoming committee," Wilder remarked almost to himself as he shut down and then removed his helmet. He turned to his crew. "Why don't you fellas tidy up? I'll go see what the ruckus is about." Then he levered himself out of his seat and dropped to the deck, staying bent at the waist until out from under the slowing rotor.

Homer Houston, Manager of Operations of the Mammoth Four production rig, waited at the head of the stairs.

"Hey, Homer." Wilder slapped his friend on the back as he eyed him. If he didn't know better, he'd say Homer was a bit spooked. A grizzled veteran, Homer had been on the rigs for thirty years. His small, wiry body carried the signs of his battles—two lost fingers and a puckered scar on the right side of his face from a big fire a few years back.

As twitchy as a kid trying to walk across the sand on an August afternoon, Homer shifted from one foot to the other. "Sorta fortuitous you boys showed up."

The men waiting on the lower rungs behind Homer stared at Wilder with flat faces and wide eyes. "What's happened?"

"Come with me." Homer turned and squeezed by the big men below him.

Wilder turned to follow, but not before he motioned to his crew to bring the medical kit. Homer Houston had taken off like a scalded cat, and Wilder had a hard time keeping up with him. "Hold on, Homer."

The rig reminded him of the imagining of a three-year-old with a giant Erector Set—built on a large square platform resting on four legs with ballast tanks below the surface and a Christmas tree of the rig sprouting amidships. The main structure of the vessel, comprised of several decks, housed everything from the laundry and sleeping quarters to the galley and ward room and the operations center. The helipad, one small platform jutting off the side of the top deck and braced against the lower deck, looked like it would bend from its load, but it never did.

The main level seemed a jumble of beams and pipe and unrecognizable machinery whining at a mind-numbing decibel level. Hoses snaked across the platform, ready to trip and grab the unwary. Huge diesel engines spit grease and belched exhaust. A tower in the middle contained the lifting mechanisms to hoist sections of pipe, which were then positioned over the hole and fed down into it. And all of it was coated in a layer of mud and oil that was as slippery as grease on a pig at the State Fair.

"Jesus," muttered Kellen as he found a third shin-knocker with his left leg, adding a bruise on top of a bruise. After working his way down two levels, he managed to straddle the ladder he'd seen Homer use. Sliding, he landed on the lowest level, the one just above the water line. Walking through the open hatch onto a platform he came face-to-face with Dewayne Niland.

"Dewayne. Hell, I shoulda known."

Dewayne held his ball cap in both hands in front of him, wringing it like a dishtowel. He didn't look happy. The odor of stale beer seeped through his pores like last night's garlic-laden dinner. "Hey, Admiral."

Dewayne always called him Admiral. Kellen didn't know whether he was sucking up or sticking it to him. He suspected a bit of both.

"You know this man, Commander?" Homer asked, his surprise evident.

"Sure. Dewayne makes it his mission in life to make sure the Coast Guard never stands down. When we don't have any other crisis to deal with, we can count on one from him. He tends to head to open waters in the middle of the night, with nothing but Budweiser to guide his way. You're late today, Dewayne. Tell me you didn't run into this big rig in broad daylight."

"No, Admiral, I swear. I was trolling for sharks a few miles east of here. Hooked something I think you need to take a look at."

Kellen eyed the shark fisher. Fat, sunburned, clearly nervous with probably two six-packs too many sloshing around in that big gut. But there was something else...a man who trolled for sharks by himself at night didn't scare easily, but the guy looked like he'd seen a ghost. He scanned the faces of the men surrounding him. Hell, they *all* looked spooked as hell.

"Okay, I'll bite. Show me what's got you all as twitchy as calves at branding time."

Dewayne pointed, but remained firmly rooted to his spot. "Over there. Tied it up-side my boat."

Following Dewayne's finger, the Commander could just make out something bobbing in the swells. It looked like a body—a very dead body—facedown. Kneeling on the edge of the platform, he reached down. Grabbing a handful of cloth, he turned the body over, then immediately recoiled as a startled crab skittered away and disappeared into the blue water with an almost inaudible plop. "Shit," he muttered under his breath, then sucked in some air, fighting the urge to vomit.

The crab or a gull or maybe even small fish had been eating on the one remaining eyeball. Apparently, they had been at work for a while. Most of the soft tissue of the face and neck had been eaten away. Only strings and bits of flesh remained. Fighting an urge to recoil, Kellen picked up an arm. As he suspected, the hands were eaten down to bone and sinew as well.

"Dang." Jeter Bates, the first of the crew to arrive on the lower platform, turned green and puked over the side, narrowly missing the commander. He stood, wiping his mouth on the sleeve of his shirt. "What the hell is that?"

"Better question. Who is that?" Kellen responded as he carefully snaked a hand into the man's coat pocket, mindful the crab might have a few friends he was sharing the feast with. Nothing in the first one nor in the second. Trying not to look at what remained of the man's face—the half-eaten eyeball bobbing in the gentle swells attached only by a thread of nerve tissue—Kellen pulled the man's jacket open. Paydirt—the man's wallet was in the inside pocket. And, better yet, a Texas driver's license.

Dewitt Patrick Donovan.

Kellen stared at the picture.

Those green eyes.

Sam had her father's green eyes. Eyes that challenged, that danced when she smiled. Eyes that, like the lady they belonged to, remained wary, aloof, unattainable—just out of reach.

And now he had to tell Sam her father was dead.

CHAPTER TWENTY-TWO

Ferrell Bishop, the CEO of San Rafael Oil, the largest privately owned producer in the Western Hemisphere, glanced at his watch, a Vacheron Constantin Tour de L'ille. With two faces and costing more than his first divorce—hell, more than the first two—it kept brilliant time, which was the problem.

Ferrell Bishop wasn't used to waiting, for anyone. Only partially interested, he watched the muted talking heads on the newsfeed showing on the television in front of him. The captions were enough to get the drift.

Senator Phillip Herrera was missing, presumed dead.

The thought didn't sit well. Herrera had been *his* man. And without the senator, Bishop's leverage just expired.

Of course, the senator wasn't technically dead, just missing. But Bishop was smart enough to read between the lines.

And someone had taken him out before Bishop had gotten what he wanted from Herrera. Pretty much the way his luck had been running lately. But he aimed to reverse that trend.

He settled back and tried to enjoy a world without that pompous, holier-than-thou prick.

The thought appealed to him, despite the heightened scrutiny a dead senator would bring. If there was anybody besides one or two of his blood-sucking ex-wives who deserved to be taken out, it was Senator Herrera. All of them seemed unduly interested in altering his cash flow—the senator most of all. But he wouldn't be a problem anymore. Bishop knew who had pulled the trigger—well, he knew the master and he knew the dogs, but he didn't know the guy's name. A bead of sweat trickled down his side. He'd have to move fast...before they sent one of their dogs after him.

In La Porte, an industrial town fronting the Houston Ship Channel on the outskirts of Houston, the limo stood out like a Vegas call girl at the Houston Oil Club. Two days ago, his man had set up this meeting. He'd wanted to keep it on the sly. The two of them had been great partners through the years, always under the radar, especially since their first deal involved stealing a great strike from Donovan Oil. Well, if he remembered correctly, it had been Donovan and Halloran Oil, but Bishop was an opportunist and Halloran hadn't been above selling his soul to the Devil himself if he could make a tidy profit. Bishop had used that first deal to leverage himself up the food chain. And now he and Donovan had come full circle.

Scuttlebutt had it that the Irishman had actually found the mother lode this time. Bishop didn't understand why the guy kept searching for the stuff when stealing it took out the risk and was a lot easier. Of course, Bishop hid his participation in these unsavory deals, burying the info in layers of corporations and offshore partnerships. Always easier to lead a lamb to slaughter if he didn't know you were the wolf.

Bishop had the television on mute—the CNN talking heads never had much of any substance to say. He glanced at the spot price of crude ticking across the bottom of the screen in real time.

Falling like a stone.

This spring had been a perfect storm—too many new rigs coming on line, the shale play adding to the overstocking of oil up in Oklahoma where they'd never seen the reserves this high. OPEC refused to turn off the spigot; Iran was about to be ushered back into the world community along with their crude production. For the first time in history, investors realized that the world had more than enough oil...and the price was tanking.

And now there was just a whisper through those closest to him that Donovan had a strike so large, so revolutionary, it was practically limitless. Word of that hitting the streets would be another knife straight to the heart of the oil business. It could ruin all of them. Armed with the proof his man on Donovan's rig had procured, Bishop had sent it on to his man in London. He'd convened a special meeting in Geneva. Rumor had it the meeting hadn't gone well. Apparently, the blame had been placed on his shoulders for his inability to shut Donovan down. They didn't understand that buying a senator or two wasn't that easy.

They also didn't understand killing a senator brought all kinds of bad, or maybe they didn't care—an even more troubling thought. The FBI interceded in every suspicious death of a civil servant. Bishop figured disappearing and leaving a guy on every international wanted list with the back of his head blown out qualified as suspicious.

And now, if he couldn't figure out what the senator had really been up to, Bishop figured he'd lost his usefulness as well. And he had no doubt that they would have a bullet with his name on it.

He could run, of course. And he had almost enough money squirreled away to buy a nice retirement in some place like Uruguay and to pay off the locals to keep him safe.

Almost.

One more score. And he had a plan already in motion to turn the tables on the big boys. Power bred arrogance, and he aimed to capitalize on that. Then *they'd* have to do the sucking up. He just had to stay alive long enough for the plan to work.

The thought had him reaching for a drink.

With a knuckle, he rapped on the glass dividing panel to

get his driver's attention. Leaning forward, he didn't wait for it to fully descend. "I thought I told you to keep Lone Star Rye stocked at all times."

"Yes, sir." His driver, Jorge, eased from behind the wheel and came around back. Without even looking, he reached across his boss and pulled out a bottle. "Right here, sir."

Bishop leaned back. "Two cubes. Make it a double."

Jorge handed him the glass and retreated to the driver's seat.

"Has he called?" Bishop never used his name.

"No, sir."

Bishop took a pull on his drink, relishing the fire that chased down his throat and knowing a bit of calm would follow...if he drank enough. Texas whiskey. Put hair on your chest. Lately, it was taking more and more to soothe his frayed edges. Another glance at his watch. Thirty minutes now. "We'll give him another five minutes, then head back to town. We don't want to be late for services."

Bishop threw back the rest of his drink in fury—he hated being stood up. As he reached for the intercom button, the door opened and his man eased inside, taking the rear-facing seat opposite Bishop.

"What took you so long?" Bishop eyed the young man, Grady O'Dell, chief of staff for Senator Phillip Herrera.

A short man, O'Dell was half Bishop's age, with thick legs, broad shoulders, a barrel chest, a ready smile curving below a crooked nose and intelligent eyes. He pointed at Bishop's drink. "Make me one of those. You think with all the publicity around the senator's disappearance it's easy for me to get away? I had to circle back a bit to make sure I wasn't followed. Those newshounds are damn good—better than you think."

Even though the kid's attitude pissed him off, Bishop figured he could be nice until the kid had served his purpose, so he poured him two fingers over a single ice cube. He wouldn't be staying long.

Bishop envied the kid his shock of reddish brown hair, green eyes he was sure the women would swoon over, and his knack for getting out of trouble, but he paid him to get information, good information. "Sorry about your boss."

"Save it for someone who cares. But seriously," Grady paused, keeping his voice low as he glanced around. The driver had his hat pulled down low over his eyes and didn't seem to be paying any attention. "Are you fucking nuts? This could ruin everything."

"They didn't kill him, just made him disappear," Bishop hedged.

Grady sipped his drink. "Same thing."

Bishop gave him a hint of a knowing smile. "Wasn't my call."

"Whose?"

"You don't want to know. Trust me."

"Yeah, I do. If I don't know them, how can I stay out of their way?"

"You'd never see them coming."

Grady chewed on that for a moment, then seemed to accept it. "I'm risking a lot just being here. The office is going nuts. The media is in a feeding frenzy."

"I appreciate that."

Grady leaned close, his elbows on his thighs, his glass dangling between his knees. "I don't think you do. We have a lot at stake here."

Bishop ignored the "we;" the kid hadn't a clue. "What do you have for me?"

A tic worked in the young man's cheek. "He was cutting and running. Had stored enough fuel in his bay boat to make it out to Donovan's platform."

"You're sure that's where he was going?" Bishop poured himself another drink. This time his hands shook as he settled back and raised the glass to his lips.

"No. But it makes sense. They had a meeting the day before."

"Why go out there? What was he after?"

"Proof."

"Proof of what? His well?" Bishop already sat on that information. He never took a large position in a well without having men on the inside who could give him a heads-up when things were going south, or, in this case, going far too well. Information was power. And to control a well that size would be the closest thing to being God—open the spigot and bury the little guys; close the spigot and bring large economies to heel.

"I doubt Patrick Donovan would share any information, if he even has any to share. We have a partnership meeting next week—the bankers are breathing down his neck." Bishop lingered over the thought, relishing the plan that was working. With the price of oil dropping, Donovan's find was diminishing in value, putting pressure on the collateralization of the operating loan. If the bank bailed, then Bishop and the other limited partners could force Donovan out and take over the project, and he'd be first in line. Then, if the oilmen working the trades could do what they said they could do, fortunes would be made. But, as the controlling partner of Donovan Oil—assuming he could get Donovan out—they'd need his cooperation.

Grady took a mouthful of whiskey, savored it, and then swallowed as he leveled a gaze at Bishop. "The senator wasn't looking to get info; he was giving it."

That wiped the grin off Bishop's face. "What?" Herrera changing teams in the middle of the game? Bishop hadn't seen that coming. They had enough to hang the senator by his balls in the rotunda of the state capitol. A life, a legacy, a family's reputation in ruins. "He'd never risk it," Bishop said with more confidence than he felt. He'd seen it before—some low-life finding Jesus.

"How much did he know?" Grady asked. The kid didn't seem to understand the gravity of his little bombshell, or, if he did, he felt unthreatened by it.

Bishop ran his index finger around the inside of his collar, tugging at it. This could change everything. Frantically he thought back...what *did* the senator know?

"You're asking me?" Bishop's voice rose. "Isn't that what I pay you for? To be my eyes and ears on the senator and make sure he colors inside the lines?"

"You mean colors inside *your* lines."

Bishop gave him a look of distaste mingled with disgust he normally reserved for the bums on the downtown street corners. "So what information was he in such a hurry to share with Patrick Donovan?"

O'Dell threw back the rest of his drink and shook his head. "I don't know. If the senator had what you apparently think he had, he's hidden it well."

"Fuck!" Bishop hurled his empty glass, which caromed off the partition.

Grady didn't flinch. "What is it he has on you?"

"It's not me you should be worried about."

He didn't seem overly concerned. "I'm not scared of any of you."

That pissed Bishop off even more. He preyed on a man's fear. But a man without fear was not only crazy, he was unassailable. "Are you sure? You've looked everywhere? You couldn't find anything, any information?"

"Look, I'm his chief of staff, and that gives me a certain level of access, but I can't just go picking locks on his files, at least not right now, not with all the added scrutiny *your* people have brought."

Bishop reached across and grabbed the kid's tie, pulling his face close. "Clearly, you have lost an appreciation for your position here. You've got a great reputation on the line here, a cushy job in politics, which I'm sure you can leverage into an even cushier one. But what do you think would happen if it got out that you took bribes to spy on your boss?"

"It won't."

"Really, how can you be so sure?"

"If that takes me down, it takes you down, too. Mutually assured destruction, and you're not willing to go there."

Bishop let the kid have that little victory. "Okay, a good

card to play. But what about that pesky little bit of jail time, your stint as a cracksman? Another name, another place, the same you?" Bishop had dug and dug until he'd found that bone.

Grady put his glass down, then dabbed at his mouth with a napkin. "I'm doing all I can. Your threats don't change anything."

With a slight push, Bishop let him go. He turned to look out the window while he thought. If this wasn't the ugliest corner of Texas, it had to be in the top three. Flat, dismal, not even a slight elevation change to make it interesting, a perfect breeding ground for mosquitos and rats.

But, in the spring and fall, the northwest sky would grow dark, as thick, menacing lines of storms would descend on the city. Bishop loved to watch that, waiting for the violence Mother Nature unleashed at the boundary between the stifling humidity from the Gulf, heat from the sun, and cool air rushing from the north. Built in the middle of a swamp with mosquitoes as big as cockroaches and as prevalent as dots of light in the Milky Way, Houston was the most miserable place on the planet, except for the oil, except for the money. When he'd worked through all solutions, he leaned into Grady, grabbing him by his jacket lapel. "Find your boss. Fix the problem."

"And Donovan?"

"Do you know what they met about, Herrera and Donovan?"

"No, the senator clammed up when I asked."

Bishop felt the trickle of a cold sweat. If Herrera had told Donovan ... "If he gets in the way, take care of him, too." With that, he made the sign of the cross. He toggled the intercom switch. "Time to go."

The man started the engine. O'Dell took the cue and let himself out the side door.

Grady watched the big car swirl dust as the driver gunned it for the blacktop. Bishop hadn't said how to handle the problem but the implication was clear. He hoped that was enough, but somehow he knew it wasn't...not quite...but it was a start.

Of course, this left O'Dell to improvise. Totally his kind of gig.

Once the car was out of sight and he was alone, Grady stepped into the shadows and out of sight of any security cameras. Pulling a wire from his shirt, he ripped loose the mic taped to his chest. Holding it to his lips, he lowered his voice. "You got that?"

Shelby Walker left her finger on the button as the camera took rapid-fire frames. Good thing she swung by the senator's offices after she'd dropped off Becca. Senator Herrera had disappeared, so she decided to follow the next best thing, his chief of staff. And Grady O'Dell was proving to be *very* interesting. He was up to something; she just had no clue as to what.

She couldn't see who was in the limo, but she bet whoever it was, he was in this thing up to his ten-gallon hat. The license number on the limo ought to tell her who the high roller was.

She had some good shots of O'Dell, who'd ducked into the shadows.

Jake had died, and somehow these men were involved.

Jake.

He'd put her onto Herrera. She just wished he'd told her why, and what to look for.

Senator Herrera.

How many more? And for what?

Grady O'Dell hung back in the shadows. Shelby stayed, waiting to see who or what he was waiting for. It didn't take long. A black Dodge with near-blackout windows eased around the corner, its tires crunching on the broken-shell road.

A black Dodge.

Like the one that had kept close to her when she'd picked up Becca.

She raised her camera and clicked away, zooming in on the license plates. The best shot was her last, as the car paused to retrieve O'Dell, then circled and headed back out to the main road. Once she was sure they were out of sight, she walked down to look for good tire tracks. She wanted the Dodge. Unsure of the quality and the light, she snapped a bunch of shots.

She scrolled through her contacts, then hit Ashley's number. She needed to call her anyway.

"Hey, Shel." Today she sounded stronger when she answered.

"How's the head?" Someone had broken into the apartment—of course, Ashley couldn't remember if she had locked the door or not. Shelby had heard it all. She thought they'd killed her, what with Jake and all. Immediately, Shelby had scrambled the police. Thank God the NYPD wasn't like these Texas outfits she heard the locals complain about, that showed when they felt like it.

"Better. I go in for a recheck tomorrow. Maybe then they'll let me actually *move*."

"They're trying to keep any brain injury to a minimum." Personally, Shelby thought Ashley's brain was about the size of a tangerine and rattled around in her head without help, but apparently the doctors weren't of the same opinion.

"I know. How's everything in Texas?"

"Going slow. But would you happen to be interested in a little project to alleviate the boredom?" Ashley might not be the brightest bulb, but she wasn't above a little bit of stretching legal boundaries.

"Oh man, that would be awesome." Ashley's enthusiasm vibrated through the connection.

Shelby glanced at the license plate she'd perfectly framed in the last shot. "I've got a little job for you."

CHAPTER TWENTY-THREE

Sam checked and rechecked the plane as she waited for her first paying client of the day. The sky called to her. Action would be a welcome reprieve from all the thinking. Although several hours had passed since the commander left for his training mission, the hint of him lingered in her thoughts—a weakness that irritated her.

The senator going AWOL and her father's silence coupled with his not-so-thinly-veiled warnings had her pacing, twitchy like a man awaiting the executioner as midnight approached. She'd seen the body, the blood.

An assassin.

The smart money would say Uncle Phil was dead already. The thought churned her stomach, balling it into a knot. She'd known the man and cherished the memories. A dispassionate distance no longer possible, a shudder of horror ripped through her. Then thoughts of justice...of revenge. Phil Herrera had been one of the good guys—he hadn't deserved to be hunted down by a killer.

And she couldn't shake the nagging feeling she'd seen the killer before. But where?

Her father would have some answers.

Sam pulled up DUATS on her iPad and checked the current weather and the forecast. Not many windows of decent weather in the near term—this might be the last if the hurricane forecast could be believed. Then she checked her schedule and shook her head. Enough business booked to make what she needed for the month. She'd booked herself solid to make up for the revenue lost to the storms. She glanced at her watch. In fact, she'd better check the fuel and do one more walk-around of the King Air. Her next hop, this one to Brownsville, would be here in thirty.

Her father wouldn't be going far—the State Police or whoever investigated a missing senator and a dead hitman would make certain of that. Equally certain was the fact he wouldn't tell them all he knew or suspected. Again, Sam fingered the key in her pocket. Why hadn't she told Kellen about it? Not that it mattered. What did matter was finding her father. He'd disappeared before—often, in fact. So she wasn't all that concerned. Hiding when things got a little hot had been one of his best tricks. She wouldn't put it past him to be holed up with Uncle Phil somewhere, probably on the rig, waiting for the cavalry to arrive.

But worry was starting to creep in.

This time her father was pushing the limits.

The day was quickly slipping toward dusk when Sam pushed the King Air into the hangar with the four-wheeler outfitted for the purpose, her paying rides for the day now complete. Of course, she still hadn't taken the J-3 for a checkout after replacing the tailwheel assembly. That needed to be done before her student showed up for his lesson at first light. She threw down her rag in irritation—getting out to the rig today wasn't going to happen. Maybe the weather and her schedule could align so she could pay her father's rig a visit tomorrow. Yeah, and maybe pigs will fly and hell will freeze over. But one could hope.

Sam eyed the sky. Maybe she could knock out the J-3 shakedown. A few hours of daylight remained. Nothing like a low-and-slow flight to soothe the soul—nothing strenuous, just a short flight around the area.

As if he knew what she was planning, Geraldo appeared in front of her, shifting from one foot to the other.

Sam flinched in surprise—she hadn't heard him walk in. But, then again, a lot of things had been flying right by her recently. "Where'd you come from?"

"School, then my mother made me do chores before I could come. Do you have anything I can help with?" He glanced around the hangar, looking a bit crestfallen when his gaze landed on the toolbox, buttoned up, each tool put away in its place.

"Well," Sam glanced out the hangar door, milking it and trying not to smile. "I have to take the J-3 for a check ride."

Large doe eyes widened, and with hope oozing out of every pore, Geraldo stilled.

Sam found his enthusiasm irresistible. "You think you're up for it?"

The boy lit up like a Roman candle on the Fourth of July. "You mean it?" At her nod, the boy let out a whoop and fist-pumped the air.

His joy muted some of her worry and frustration. The senator's disappearance—at least they weren't trying to put a gloss on it—had been the lead on every channel this afternoon. After the commander had left, she'd flipped the channels, catching the gist, then switched off the TV. News—what a joke. They'd attributed his disappearance to everyone from a drug dealer to the idiot ragheads trying to terrorize the world in small doses, never realizing there was nothing more uniting than shared anger at a common enemy.

Uncle Phil would've hated being used as a talking point for terror. Somehow, they left out the assassin with half a head.

Curious. What game were they playing? Sam shook her head and focused on the boy in front of her practically vibrating with excitement. "Let me make a call, then we'll preflight, okay?" she said to Geraldo. "Why don't you check the fuel?" She watched him trot away, a colt dancing in the sun.

With two fingers, she pried her phone out of her back pocket. Taking a deep and not-so-steadying breath, she thought for a moment and then hit her father's speed-dial button. After five rings, the call rolled to voicemail. Her eyes watered when the familiar Irish brogue started in, "Ye rang me, so ye don't need me a tellin' ye me name. Leave a message and I might be callin' ye back." Even a recorded message could make Sam mad and sad at the same time. At the sound of the tone, she hesitated, then killed the call and tucked her phone away. She'd reached out; the next move was his. He knew the play; hell, he'd taught her the game and donated the hardheaded gene to her DNA. But by Sam's way of thinking, kin shouldn't be played. And one should be willing to go the distance when necessary. Paddy Donovan had fallen more than a wee bit short...but he had given her flying. A salve for the soul that soothed the burn of many transgressions.

And he'd given her a key.

Sam made sure the key was secured at the lowest point in her pocket. Standing in the hangar door opening, she narrowed her eyes at the sky, gauging the air.

"We've got full fuel." Geraldo stepped back in front of her, a soldier reporting for duty with a catbird smile and serious eyes.

"How much is that?" Sam asked, always the instructor.

"Twelve gallons, two hours, maybe a little less with a reserve." The boy was a sponge.

"Hour and a half. That should do it."

The J-3 was a sprightly little tube-and-fabric plane put into production before the Second World War. Sam thought it the perfect plane. It cruised at about eighty miles an hour with the ninety-five-horsepower engine she'd installed and the door open. With tandem seating and dual controls, it could carry the pilot and a passenger.

"This first time, I'll sit in the back. You can sit up front where you can see better." She waited until she was sure she had the boy's attention. "Put your butt here on the side panel, grab the window strut there." Sam pointed inside the plane. "Now swing your feet inside and scooch your butt into the seat."

With agility Sam could only vaguely remember having, the boy quickly complied. Sam put the headphones over his ears and tightened the five-point harness around his slight frame, then settled herself in the rear seat, snaking her feet into the narrow space on either side of Geraldo's seat to reach the rudder pedals. The stick jutted up between her thighs. It was a tight fit, one of the charms of the little plane. You didn't so much fly the thing as wear it.

"I'll take her off," Sam said when she had settled in, their headsets firmly in place, and the radio and com on. "Keep your hands lightly on the stick, your feet touching your set of rudder pedals so you can feel what I'm doing."

The boy in front of her, the nod of his head, and suddenly Sam was transported back in time. Her father taught her to fly the very same airplane when she'd been just shy of her twelfth birthday. And she'd nodded her head then at her father's instructions just as the boy did at hers, too excited to speak.

The engine kicked over easily—she'd installed a starter when she'd started using it to teach primary students. Propping the plane herself was too dangerous with only a student at the controls. After getting clearance from the ground controller, Sam taxied the little plane to the runway.

"Ellington Tower, Cub 70906 ready to go on one-five. Request right turn to the south."

"70906 cleared for takeoff, right turn approved." *Cleared for takeoff, the three best words in the English language.* Sam positioned the little plane on the numbers.

"Ready?" Again, the boy nodded.

Slowly, Sam fed in throttle and the plane started to roll, watching out the corners of her eyes to gauge the distance between the plane and the edge of the runway. The plane sat with its nose in the air, obscuring the pilot's view out the front windscreen. Glancing side to side was the only way to judge whether you were going straight down the runway or not. As their speed picked up, she pushed the stick forward just a tiny bit, lifting the tail so the plane was riding on the two wheels of the main gear; and the runway, no longer obscured by the nose of the airplane, appeared in the windscreen. With each move, Sam explained to Geraldo what she was doing, how she was doing it, and why—a flight instructor's running commentary. But they weren't her words; they were her father's. She could hear his voice as she parroted his words, hear his joy to be flying with his only child. He had been her world. And, at this moment she knew exactly how he had felt.

She hadn't flown with her father in a long time. Time and harsh words had opened a chasm between them that neither had crossed.

She missed him.

Sam knew the J-3 better than any plane. She didn't need to watch the airspeed indicator to know exactly the right moment to let the plane lift into the sky—the plane told her, through the lightness as the wings took more of the load, through the pressures on the stick as the control surfaces bit into the airflow. Flying a plane like this was more about being still, staying out of the way, and letting the machine do what it loved to do. The boy in front of her had been gripping the sides of the plane. As the wings took the load and the tiny machine took flight, riding the wind like a leaf flowing on an unseen current, he loosened his grip. There was something magical about flight. Sam felt it every time. She could see Geraldo did, too.

The shift in the engine tone was the first sign of trouble. A slight deepening, laboring. Sam picked up on it instantly, bending to see around the boy in front to see the gauges. The oil temp was rising fast, the pressure falling. She'd just changed the oil a few days ago, when she repaired the wheel spring assembly and had triple-checked her handiwork before reinstalling the cowling, but the instruments didn't lie. A quick glance at the altimeter and airspeed—low and slow, not a good time to have an emergency. Still on climb-out, she pressed the button on the top of the stick and radioed the tower. "Ellington Tower, Piper 70906, heading one-three-zero, six-hundred feet, we appear to have an oil problem."

"Roger, 70906. Are you going to return to the field?"

"Negative. Hanging above a stall as it is." Sam lowered the nose so she could see in front of her and so she could keep the airspeed above that stall. Reaching around Geraldo, she closed the throttle. A few coughs and the engine fell silent, the prop windmilling as the air pushed through it. Any hotter and the engine would seize anyway—this way maybe she could save it. "We've just turned into a glider. I'm trying for the levee. If I overshoot, we'll be in Mud Lake. Have somebody come get us, would you?"

Geraldo's hands once again gripped the side of the airplane.

"You okay?" Sam asked him after releasing the radio button.

"Yes, ma'am." His voice was strong, determined.

"Good. Tighten your seatbelt." Curiously, her heart beat a steady rhythm; her focus tightened.

Sam scanned in front as the plane drifted down. The levee. Right in front of her—she could make it easy. But, man, it'd be tight. If she miscalculated, she could always pop it over the water. But that presented a whole other set of issues in the form of a dense copse of sturdy pines. The levee was their best bet.

The silence taunted her—the whisper of the wind flowing past only a breath, not even a sound, really more of an awareness. The wind would save them. She grabbed an old life vest she'd tucked behind the back seat. Pushing it over Geraldo's shoulder, she said, "Put this between you and the instrument panel. Make sure all your straps are so tight you can barely breathe. Got it?"

"Got it," came the reply, again without a waver.

Time slowed, her vision clear and crisp, her instincts sharp. Where her body met the plane, she could hear its voice in the vibrations, sense its comfort in the pressures on the stick and rudders. Flying easy.

Slipping, she dropped altitude and a touch of airspeed, but not much. Lowering, she kept the wheels just above the treetops, flirting with the highest branches. The levee was short and narrow. This would have to be perfect. There'd be no second chance.

Her heart rate slowed. The sweat on her palm as she gripped the stick was the only sign of nerves. With the other hand, she swiped the hair that tickled her forehead—her eyes never leaving her landing spot. She could do this; she knew she could. And she tried not to think about the boy in the front seat, his life in her hands.

At the edge, where the trees ended just off the end of the levee, she stomped on the rudder, bringing the nose around to align with the levee, and eased the stick back in a continuous pressure as she pulled the nose up, dropping the airspeed as the plane settled toward Earth. Fighting a slight crosswind, she also had to keep a little right aileron in, which necessitated opposite rudder. A tailwheel airplane separated the men from the boys. *You don't really learn to fly until you have to learn to handle a taildragger—a skittish beast if there ever was one.* Her father's voice echoed in her memory. Time to find out if he was right.

Sam worked the controls, changing the attitude of the airplane as needed to arrive at the landing spot with as little airspeed as possible. *Kill that momentum, lass. You want the plane nice and docile when the wheels kiss the Earth.* I know, Da. I know.

The trees at the far end of the levee rushed toward them, growing like giants.

It'd be close. Real close.

CHAPTER TWENTY-FOUR

After a stop in Texas City at the hospital to offload Patrick Donovan's body and hand it over to the Medical Examiner, Kellen Wilder and his crew were heading back to Ellington. They were monitoring the tower frequency, when Sam's transmission went out.

"Shit." Wilder's thoughts had been tied up with Patrick Donovan and the grim task of telling his daughter. But Sam's emergency derailed that pity party.

Jeter Bates shot him a sideways glance. Everyone knew about the commander and Sam, and what they didn't know for sure, they suspected.

Wilder grabbed the stick and shook it. "My bird."

"Yes, sir, your bird."

Wilder lowered the nose and cranked on all the power the machine could give him. "Let's see how fast this bucket of bolts can go without popping rivets." He didn't smile when he said it.

Bates gave him a wide-eyed look, which he ignored. "Watch the temp, Bates."

Sweat popped on Wilder's brow as he imagined where Sam was trying to put down that plane. No margin for error. None at all.

Bates radioed Ellington tower, identifying themselves,

then said, "We're *en route* to the J-3."

"Roger that. We'll scramble emergency."

There was nothing left to do other than sit tight.

"Let her be safe." Wilder hurled the words like an invective, cursing the Fates that hadn't seen fit to protect her. And, stuck where he was, he couldn't do a damn thing about it.

The first brush of the wheels on dirt had Sam pressing with everything she had on the heel brakes, which were iffy at best in a J-3. She pulled the stick back, eased it back really—they were too close to flying speed and she didn't need the plane to become airborne again.

Too fast! The plane juked and bounced over ruts and rocks. "Help me on the heel brakes," she said, her voice steady. "They're the—"

"I know." The boy added his strength to hers, which helped.

When she was sure the wings wouldn't fly anymore, she held the stick back tight to her stomach, trying to keep the nose of the plane from pitching forward at the rapid deceleration. As the plane slowed, the airflow over the elevator would be reduced and she'd have less ability to keep the nose up.

It had to be enough.

The little plane bounced and bucked, keeping Sam dancing on the rudders to keep a wheel from catching the edge and pulling the plane over the side. The levee wasn't much more than a few feet wider than the main gear. A few inches either way and they'd be hurtling over the edge into the water, which, at landing speed, would have the surface tension of concrete. She sensed the edges rather than saw them.

One wheel caught slightly, jerking them to the right, but

Sam slammed in the left rudder, then quickly the right. Just enough to correct then straighten.

Funny how she could hear the wind now. And the pounding of the bungees absorbing the rough surface. Keeping her head down, she avoided looking at the trees. She and the boy were at the mercy of physics at this point, and she didn't believe God would listen.

He never had.

"Do you guys see anything?" Wilder asked his crew.

Still four miles out from the levee, they both scanned into the haze that had thickened in the soft light of dusk. The swimmer in the back added his eyes through the side door, which he'd slid open.

"Negative."

Wilder's heart pounded, but he kept his touch light on the stick, the machine an extension of himself that reacted as if to a thought rather than a touch. The trees flashed by below in a river of green as he kept the speed up. He didn't want to try to raise Sam on the radio—she had her hands full. But he wished like hell the woman would get on the horn and let somebody know what had happened, if she was okay.

She had to be okay.

"Brace yourself!" Sam shouted as the trees filled the windscreen. Finding an extra bit of purchase on the tiny metal flanges that passed as brake pedals, she pushed with everything she had left and held her breath.

She resisted the urge to brace for the impact. If she was

going to meet her Maker, then she'd do it eyes wide open, head held high.

One big bounce and the wheels hit a hole...and stuck. The nose started to go over as the tail lifted. Sam threw herself backward as much as she could. They hung balanced on the main gear for a moment, as if the scales of Justice were deciding their fate. Then the tail settled and the small plane shuddered to a stop.

High and dry...and safe. With no more than four feet to spare.

For a moment, Sam sat there just breathing. Sweat had soaked her shirt, and a slight breeze now gave her a cool shiver. Or maybe it was the brush of death against the back of her neck. And she remembered telling her father that nothing bad would ever happen to her in the J-3. He'd laughed and then sobered. "Don't be fooled, child. That plane can kill you just like the others; it just takes you to the crash site more slowly." An old saw in the pilot world, but she'd remembered it.

Today had proven them both right.

"You okay?" She patted the boy's shoulder as she killed the electrical and pulled off her headset, then lifted his off from behind.

When he turned, his eyes shone, but not with fear. "You teach me to fly like that?"

Looking at his face, Sam saw her younger self. "You bet."

Maybe God had listened after all.

"There!" Bates shouted, pointing off the nose to the right. "Two o'clock."

Wilder squinted as he pulled back the speed and lowered the collective as he banked to the right. The tail of the J-3 was all that was visible from under the overhang of the tall pines guarding the end of the levee. He whipped the helicopter around so he could see out his side window. The plane was intact.

She'd done it.

"Holy Damn," Bates said. "That is some piece of flying."

Wilder felt pride, and he didn't know why. Okay, he knew why; he just wasn't ready to acknowledge it—of course, he couldn't really claim Sam as his own, much as he'd like to.

He backed the chopper away a bit and then landed across the levee—plenty of room for a helicopter, but damn tight, even for a J-3. As the engine spooled down and he and Bates hopped out, he could hear the sirens in the distance. "Better call off the cavalry," he called over his shoulder as he hurried toward the Cub.

Someone stepped around the front of the J-3 and waved at him. Geraldo. *Holy crap, she did that with the kid up front.*

"Hey, kid. You okay?" At the kid's grin, he relaxed and almost tripped over a pair of lower legs jutting out from under the J-3. Kneeling, Sam had the lower cowling off. Oil painted the underside of the plane, covering its signature bright yellow paint in a thick layer of brown. Kellen squatted next to Sam. "Find anything?"

"You going stay like that, pretty boy, or are you going to get down and dirty and see what I've got to show you?" Sam growled.

Kellen couldn't read everything in her tone, but he got anger, disbelief, and something else. He joined her under the plane.

Her eyes, hard and angry, met his for a moment, then he followed them as they lighted on something else. The screw-on oil filter was hanging by a thread.

"Not like you to make that kind of mistake." Before the words had landed, he regretted them, afraid he'd lit a fire.

"I didn't." She fingered the end of the safety wire that was required so that just this thing wouldn't happen.

The wire was still twisted and tagged, but the loop that held the oil filter was in two pieces. Both ends pinched, with a bit of bright shiny metal showing at the break. Sam had wiped them clean of oil.

Wilder's gaze found Sam's. "Someone cut this."

She nodded.

As the realization hit him, they both wormed out from under the plane. Wilder stood, then offered a hand to Sam.

She accepted it, letting him pull her to her feet. Brushing herself off, she braced her hands on her legs just over the knees for a moment. Then she stood, her lips pressed into a thin line, her eyes slits. "Why would anyone try to sabotage my plane?" Geraldo pressed next to her and she looped an arm around his shoulder, glad for the support.

As Bates joined them, the reality hit the commander. He knew. Well, not exactly, but he could for sure steer her in the right direction.

Someone had killed her father.

And now they were after Sam.

CHAPTER TWENTY-FIVE

Sam sat on the edge, peering through the open hatch, her legs hanging in the breeze, her hand woven through the netting the only thing tethering her to the helicopter. Illegal as hell, but Kellen hadn't said a word. Maybe he knew that without feeling the wind, without staring into a fall that would kill her, without a little fear to dissipate the adrenaline still surging through her system, her heart might explode—or at least it felt like it.

The ride back to Ellington had been quiet with Bates at the controls and Kellen beside him, a grimace on his face like he was trying not to scratch an itch. The lights were on, the rabbits strobing, darkness almost full but for a brush of purple on the western horizon. The wind had died as if the world held its breath.

She had strapped Geraldo in. He'd answered her unspoken question with a smile. Each of them kept their own counsel as the commander handled the tower. The ride had been short—too short. Sam had yet to even process what had happened—and deal with the list of horribles that hadn't. Once safe, she knew they would come—the punishment of fear unrealized. Fear was a funny thing—in the thick of the crisis, Sam was cool, her thoughts clear and precise. But, after the danger had passed and everyone was okay and all body parts and plane parts accounted for, then it usually hit her, the what-ifs cutting her legs out from under her.

Once settled, Kellen hopped down, motioning for Geraldo to do the same.

"Should I tell my mother?" Geraldo asked before jumping out of the helicopter as the blades spooled down.

She could see the boy's lie in his eyes, ready to spring to life. "Of course you tell her. All of it. That's only fair." Sam gave him a steadying hand, which he didn't need but used anyway. "Keep your head down." A reflexive warning.

"But what if ..."

"Don't worry about the what-ifs. Just deal with what's in front of you."

Geraldo didn't argue. "Are you worried about leaving your plane out there?"

Sam dropped to her feet, then ducked under the rotors that slowed with each pass as she followed the boy. "I don't think anyone will go looking for a plane on the levee." The idea sounded funny, but neither of them laughed. They'd come close. That was flying, though. Cheating Death. Moments of sublime peace punctuated by unadulterated fear, but hopefully not too often.

"Or be able to get it out of there if they do find it," Kellen said as he joined them.

"I'll have to take the wings off and truck it out. If someone else is that prepared and that skilled, they can have it."

"You don't mean that." He still had that irritated look on his face.

An uneasiness settled in Sam's stomach. Something was wrong. She couldn't place it, but she knew it. "What is it?"

The commander brushed off her question as he grabbed the boy's shoulder. "Your mother is probably good and worried. It's best you head home so she can count fingers and toes."

"How would she know?" Geraldo asked.

"Mothers just know, okay." His brush-off was

noticeable, even to the kid.

Geraldo's grin fled. "Yes, sir."

Sam gave the boy a squeeze. "You were very brave today. And calm. You're going to be a great pilot."

That perked up the youngster. Shoulder to shoulder, Kellen and Sam watched the boy's easy lope until the darkness swallowed him.

Sam crossed her arms and stared out into the darkness long after she could even sense movement, much less track the boy's progress. "You going to tell me what's got you all lathered up?"

"Let me walk you home while I find the words."

His hand brushed the small of her back, but he didn't push. Sam let him encourage her back toward her hangar. Home would feel good. *Cheated death one more time today, Da.* And she wondered if he would be as lucky. Death was close this night, lingering in the quiet where her fear resided.

Whenever she felt particularly adrift, Sam took solace in an imaginary conversation with her father. Of course, she could talk back, which was rarely the case in the real world.

She tried not to imagine whatever it was the commander wrestled with. *Don't worry about the what-ifs.* Sam needed to take her own advice, but it was damn hard. Funny how children's problems seemed so small when looked at from the adult perspective, but Sam remembered them feeling as large as the life-knots she wrestled with now. Maybe the Coast Guard and all the other government types had decided to finally kick her off the field—or at least out of their enclosed end of it. They had the right. Didn't mean she had to like it.

"First your father and now you," Kellen said. His voice, disembodied in the darkness, had a ring of anger to it.

Through his hand that lightly touched her back, she could feel his tension. "What about my father? What do you know that you're not telling me?"

"I'm not concerned about him right now." He tugged

her to a stop. "Damn it, Sam, somebody's after you."

"Somebody's after something, that's for sure. But aren't you overreacting a bit? I mean, really, what would anybody want with me?"

"You're overlooking the fact that someone made sure you weren't going to get far in that J-3—a sure emergency, usually fatal in a little popper like that."

Fear scratched at her bravado—the shield of adrenaline worn thin. "Okay." Suddenly cold, she rubbed her arms. "But who? Why?"

"I don't know. I was hoping you might have a clue." The commander again eased her toward the hangar.

"Kellen, I've got nothing."

Her hangar was open when they arrived, its doorway like the entrance to a cave. Sam always thought the hangar looked like an empty sound stage—well, empty but for a few props to be moved in and out as needed. That sense of adventure, of great stories to be lived, reeked from the rafters and hid in every corner. A magical place. Sam had never felt spooked here before. The fact that she felt a twinge of nervousness now pissed her off.

Home. She'd really miss it if she had to go. She'd fight for it before she left. And she'd kill the person messing with it.

"Stay here." With a hand on her arm, Kellen stopped her. "Let me check it out first. You stand out here in the light where the tower can see you."

She started to argue.

"Please." He gave a sign to the controller in the tower.

With a quick nod, she acquiesced, too tired to argue, too scared to walk into the dark—but she'd never admit that, not to the commander, anyway. Someone had been in there. Someone had sabotaged her plane. Now she'd have to go over all of them before she committed lift again. That thought alone pissed her off and threw fuel on her fear.

Someone wants me dead. The thought boggled her mind.

Kellen left her hanging under the halogen light on a pole to the left of the door as he disappeared into the dark maw of the hangar.

Night, an unwanted suitor, pressed up against Sam and breathed down her neck. She shivered away but couldn't escape. Kellen's steps echoed as he circled the interior of the building. Then she heard him rooting around in the dark. "If you tell me what you're looking for, maybe I can help you."

"That tailwheel assembly you were working on yesterday." His voice echoed like he was talking into a kettledrum. "I thought you dropped it into that box of parts."

"You dropped it. Remember?"

"That's right. Here it is."

A few scuffling steps and he materialized in front of her. Angling it to catch the light, he stared at the broken ends of the spring. When he looked up, worry creased his forehead and clouded his eyes.

"What?"

He handed the assembly to her. "Take a look."

Sam didn't need to; the look on his face told her all she needed to know. "Cut, too?"

He scowled as he looked over her shoulder.

"There's more, isn't there?" Sam put a hand on his arm to bring his attention back. "I don't have a pot to piss in. I'm not a threat to anyone. But you know something. You're an open book, Commander Wilder."

"Why is it my job is always on a collision course with my life?" His tone held a hard edge, harder than he intended.

"Just lucky, I guess." Sam didn't move—frozen by the knowledge she was about to learn something she didn't want to know, something that would change life, or her spot in it, forever. "Tell me. Your boss jerk my lease?"

"What?" At the look on Sam's face, he pulled in a deep breath. "Even if they did, no one would try to kill you over it. We're in the rescue business, remember?"

Sam couldn't read his tone and his circuitous route to the point punctured a hole in the threadbare fabric of her patience. "What is it then? Something new on Uncle Phil?" She tried not to grab him and shake the truth out of him.

"Would you just stop?" He visibly worked to control his emotions. He sighed. This time when he spoke, he had taken the hard out. "No."

Sam gave him a long look. Tired lurked under his tan; his eyes were bloodshot. Days spent squinting over the Gulf could do that.

The commander pulled a square of cloth from some pocket in his flight suit. Lifting his ball cap, he wiped his forehead, then reset the cap low over his eyes. "Could it get any hotter?"

"You've been here longer than me. You should know. And you're stalling." Antsy, feeling the need to do something, anything that might restore the balance in her world, Sam looked at all the planes. "Every one of these will need a going-over, but where do you start to look for sabotage?"

Kellen wiped his brow again. "It's been a hell of a day." He peered over her shoulder. "With the J-3 it was quick and dirty. It almost seems like they meant to scare you rather than kill you."

"Are you trying to make me feel better?"

"Well, it would make *me* feel a darn sight better—scared is transitory. Dead is pretty final." He winced, then shook his head. "Damn."

Sam pointed to the helicopter. "I'll start with that. Gotta check everything." The items she'd addressed earlier today, she crossed off her mental to-do list. Nobody had been in her hangar while she'd been gone; the security patrol had been keeping a close eye thanks to Kellen.

Kellen leaned over Sam's shoulder when she crouched down to check the gear.

"Don't do that." Sam wiggled and tugged at the various arms and screws, testing for loosening. "It bugs me. I feel like you're breathing down my neck. If you're not an A and

P and rotor rated, I'm not sure how much help you can be." She didn't add that he was distracting and tripping over him only made it worse.

"Not part of my duty list." Kellen stood fast, making no move to take her hint and leave.

Satisfied, she stood to move around to the nose gear. "You look pretty beat up, flyboy. You gotta tell me what you're wrestling with. It can't be that bad." Sam stretched her back. Two long days hunched over, buried in the bowels of some plane, were making her feel twice her age. Weariness tugged at her concentration—tonight was not the night to do this, no matter how much she wanted to. And the commander standing there looking like someone had killed his dog didn't help. She placed the screwdriver back in its slot in the box. "Whatever it is you've come to tell me, it'll go down better with a beer. Shiner Ruby Red, right?"

Kellen nodded. "Impressive. With a memory like that, you could keep me coming around."

Sam ignored him.

"Get one for yourself, too, and then let's go sit on the bench outside. It's suffocating in here."

Sam bit down on a retort; now was not the time. He looked one step from dead. "I'll grab one and meet you outside."

"Make it two?" Night brought little relief from the heat. Kellen squashed a mosquito that had dared to puncture his forearm. "Anyone who wondered whether life was nothing more than a test had only to move to Texas in the summer to find the answer," he muttered. "Hell of a place."

"What?" Sam appeared in front of him, the two bottles in her hand already beaded with condensation.

"Texas in the summer."

"Miserable." She handed him a beer. "Here. You look too pensive for a flyboy. What's eating you?"

"You're not joining me?"

"Like I said, I got to at least get one of these buckets of bolts ready to fly my schedule tomorrow. And sleep would be a good thing, too. So, could you make it quick? I'm trying to be kind to a man in uniform."

"You really need to hire some help."

"Since I'm just swimming in green?" Sam shot him a look. He was well aware of her financial situation. If she could get her father to come around to help like he used to, that would make a world of difference.

The commander tipped a bottle at her. "Normally, I don't drink alone, but today I'm not suffering from such acute sensibilities." He drained half of it, then set the other on the armrest of the bench. "It's been one hell of a day."

"You said that." Sam sat next to him, her elbow on her knees. "You okay?"

Elbows on his knees, his beer dangling from both hands, Kellen stared out at the airfield. Night added to the magic. Runway and taxiway lights patterned the darkness. The rabbit lights sequenced at the far end of the runway guiding planes in. Stars twinkled high above. Salt tinged the air. Night had silenced the birds as they roosted until morning light. Traffic from I-45 rumbled low and muted in the distance. A normal day. Life...and death.

"It's about your father." He felt Sam stiffen beside him. He rushed into the abyss, words tumbling. "I was training the new guy out over the Gulf. We stopped at Mammoth Four. Needed a break and some fuel. Turns out the choice was fortuitous. While trolling, a shark hunter had hooked a body." Kellen turned to Sam, trying to catch her eye, but she remained stoic, staring straight ahead. He touched her shoulder, but she didn't turn. He wanted to hold her, but was afraid of her reaction. "I found your father's wallet on the guy. I'm sorry."

Sam flinched. First Uncle Phil, now her father. "You're sure it was my father? You know him. You'd recognize him, right?"

"I don't know, not really. It looked like him, well, what was left of the body. The sea and the sea creatures... The body was..." He trailed off as if words had fled. "Look, a body in the water for a few days, it can get pretty messed up."

Sam recoiled. "I get it." She rose, moving away, then slipped into the Adirondack chair angled at ninety degrees from the bench, creating distance—from him and from the news. She leaned back, staring straight ahead.

"I wish it was different. I wish I wasn't the one to tell you. I wish your father wasn't dead." Kellen peered into the darkness. "I know how much he meant to you."

"You don't know the half of it," she said, emotion choking her voice to a whisper. "I haven't even had time to process Uncle Phil's...disappearance. I'm not sure how to handle both of them gone."

She started to shake.

Kellen shifted down the bench toward her, reaching out.

"No." She shook her head as she held herself in a tight hug, her arms crossed across her chest. "Where is he?"

Kellen let his arms fall. "Galveston County ME's office. Texas City. I took the body there—there's a jurisdictional issue, but we'll work it out." Kellen cringed. More than Sam needed to know. "They're going to ask you to identify the body." Ignoring his self-preservation instinct, Kellen moved to sit on the arm of her chair, looping an arm around her shoulders, pulling her closer. "You don't have to. There are other ways."

Tensing for a moment, Sam acted like she'd pull away, then relaxed into him. She scrubbed at her face with the heel of her hand. She might be able to wipe the tears away, but she couldn't wipe away the look on her face—a look that cut Kellen to the heart. "You think you have all the time in the world," she said, sounding a world away. "He was not an easy man."

"Easy men aren't worth your time." Kellen breathed her in.

"I had so much to say to him." She turned and gazed up at him, the hurt pinching her cheeks and haunting her eyes.

"For what it's worth, just because someone is gone, I don't believe they're unreachable. He knows what's in your heart; he always knew. Ego can cross you up, but the heart isn't fooled."

Sam leaned back to get a good look at him. "You've got a bit o' the Irish in ya', Mister Wilder." Despite her brave smile, a tear escaped and trickled down her cheek. She ducked her head and brushed it away. Patrick Donovan's daughter had spent her life trying to be his firstborn son, the one he'd said he always wanted. But wishing couldn't make it so; emotion overrode control, and tears streamed down Sam's face. "Oh, God, Kellen, what am I going to do?" she asked through tortured gasps.

Wilder brushed her forehead with his lips, then held her close as she cried.

CHAPTER TWENTY-SIX

One Kirby Oaks, a cylindrical tower of steel, glass, and arrogance loomed at the edge of River Oaks—*the* bastion of wealth and power in central Houston. On the outside looking in, but close enough to bask in the mystique. A starter-condo in the building on the ground floor in the back by the garbage bins cost almost a million.

Drayton Lewis lived and worked on the top two floors.

As offices went, Becca Molinari figured it would be hard to improve upon. She had her own large office next to Mr. Lewis's, both cordoned off from the living space by a motorized accordion wall. Today, the walls were open as they usually were when Mr. Lewis wasn't there.

Becca's duties extended through all parts of Drayton Lewis's life. Nothing like two degrees from MIT and a law degree from Columbia to end up making sure the boss man's boxers were properly pressed. But working for Mr. Lewis did keep life interesting.

Perhaps too interesting. After meeting with Jake Walker's sister, Becca felt like a corporate Icarus flying too close to Lewis's sun, the wax on her wings starting to drip. Thankfully the guy in the Dodge hadn't made a move, but he'd creeped her out. If Drayton knew what she'd done...

When she'd started feeding Jake Walker information, Becca had no idea what the stakes were, how far men would go. She had been stupid, really, wanting to poke a hole in Drayton Lewis's reputation, knock him back into the real world. When she'd found evidence that Drayton was investing heavily in oil futures, all the while crowing to the world about the evil of petroleum products and the sanctimony of alternative fuels, it had seemed like it would be fun to see him undressed in public. A little bit of payback.

She never thought anyone would get hurt.

Poor Jake. If he'd just stuck to the script.

They'd been friends in Boston when they both were studying at MIT. A love of coding and craft beer had brought them together, and a serious need to one-up each other had made them fast friends. Jake had won that game. Becca smiled as she let her finger run over the cool glass of the bottle on her desk. Pliny the Younger from Santa Rosa Brewery. One month a year, long lines, sold at the brewery only. Yep, Jake had won.

Becca swiped at a tear. Shelby had assured her that nothing would lead them back to her; her secret was safe. Becca was wise enough to know that smart money wouldn't bet against Drayton Lewis.

What had started out as a game of sorts wasn't a game at all anymore.

"The emperor has landed." The breathy words breathed through the intercom jolted Becca to action. Lewis's helicopter had landed; the boss was back.

And a day early. Not good.

After checking herself in the mirror, patting her hair into place, and applying a quick coat of lip gloss, Becca rushed up the winding glass staircase to the living quarters and strode toward the far end. Pushing through a set of double glass doors, she braced herself for the heat of the day and most likely from her boss—only bad news could get him off the water a day early. She'd only been working for him a short while, but she'd already learned that lesson.

A short flight of stairs, which she took two at a time, and then she pushed into the hazy light of a summer day in

Houston. Lewis had fought a protracted and expensive battle to overcome the delicate sensibilities of the River Oaks' residents to be granted permission to leave and return by helicopter from the top of the exclusive apartment building. But as he always said, everyone has a price; it just takes time to figure out exactly what it is. And this heliport on top of the building had been one of the more expensive.

Hiding from as much of the rotor wash as she could, her iPad clutched with both hands and shielding her chest, Becca watched as the door opened and Drayton Lewis stepped out. With his eyes hidden behind mirrored Ray-Bans, she couldn't read his mood, but the set of his jaw and the tension in his posture indicated it couldn't be good.

Crouching, he moved toward her. Once out of the reach of the rotors, he straightened. Brushing by her, he started right in as she fell into trail. "What the hell is this I hear about Senator Herrera?"

Becca filled him in as she stutter-stepped to keep up with him and not step on his heels. At six feet, she could out stride most men.

"Get Bishop on the horn." He made short work of the stairs and then burst into his apartment, turning right. As he strode into his personal quarters, he started shedding clothes. First his shirt, which he peeled off and dropped on the floor, then his belt. "That ass needs to bring his dog to heel. We need to get a bead on the senator. Without him..." Drayton shot her a quick glance as if he'd said too much. Anger radiated off of him.

Anger and something else, thought Becca, bobbing to retrieve the items, then laying them over an arm as she followed, a mother after a wayward son.

Stepping on the heel, he shucked first one canvas shoe, then the other. "Throw these out. Make sure I have a new pair by tomorrow." Then he dropped his jeans and stepped out of them. He wasn't wearing any underwear. A finger raised, he turned toward her. Then, after a bit of thought, he spun on his heel, leaving her standing there.

As Becca bent to grab his pants, she watched the

muscles in his butt flex as he strode into the bathroom, steam already billowing from the shower his butler had prepared. She wondered if there was a direct correlation between having a nice ass and being one.

Awash in a moment of self-loathing, she pondered just exactly when sleeping with her boss had become part of her job description, but she couldn't put a finger on the exact moment. It simply happened—one night, too much expensive Champagne, and there was no going back. Becca didn't want to think too hard on the things she did to keep her job and her position—that would bring up the ugly question as to how far she would go. Had she stepped out onto the proverbial slippery slope and there would be no stopping her slide into the abyss? She didn't know and that worried her, but obviously less than it should—and that worried her even more.

As she turned to drop the clothes in the laundry chute, something caught her eye—a crusty brown stain on the cuff of his jeans, and another bit swiped down one thigh.

Blood?

Drayton Lewis had just preened before her in his altogether, and she hadn't seen a mark on him. So, if not his blood, then whose? He'd been on the boat. Men sometimes got hurt, although not often. Becca couldn't imagine Drayton Lewis coming to anyone's aid.

With a hasty glance around to ensure she wasn't being observed, Becca folded the jeans and gathered the shoes, tucking them far in the back of one of the lower drawers in Drayton's vast closet. His valet would never look there, and, God knew, Drayton wouldn't bore himself with something so menial as choosing his attire.

"Honey?" Drayton's voice snaked out of the bathroom, bolting Becca upright as if it'd bitten her on the ass. "You still out there?"

She leaned through the doorway. "What do you need?"

"I need you to get in here."

Sex. Drayton *was* stressed. Becca ran through a list of excuses, knowing none of them would work. Jake's death, the blood, self-loathing, all weighed on her, crushing any libido she might be able to summon. "What about Bishop? Don't you want to talk to him?"

"Yeah," came the growl. He stuck his hand out. "Give me the phone."

She recognized Bishop's voice when he answered. Of course, she *had* dialed his cell. "Hold for Mr. Lewis." Bishop said something. His tone didn't sound positive, but Becca didn't wait to hear him out. Instead, she dropped the phone into Lewis's outstretched hand, then lingered within earshot but out of sight. She pulled out her phone and started the voice memo function.

"What the hell is this I hear about Herrera? He was your man. We need him." He fell quiet, apparently listening. "That is total bullshit. Why would they come after him?" Again, silence. "How much did he know?" This time less anger, more something else. Fear?

Becca doubted it—she'd never seen any hint of fear in her boss.

"I see. I have my men in place. We can take Donovan down anytime. And if you don't kill him, I will." He tossed the phone onto his towel puddled at the shower door. "Becca!"

She turned off her phone, stuffed it in her pocket, then started counting to ten. At five he shouted again. Dashing into the bathroom, she pretended to be out of breath as if running all the way there from her desk. "Right here, Mr. Lewis."

"I want you in here...now."

Silently she seethed, as she began unbuttoning her shirt. *One day.*

As she rounded the glass partition and stepped into the steam, Drayton grabbed her arm and yanked her under the water. Hot, almost scalding, it hit her skin with the sting of a slap. Becca knew better than to shrink away or show any weakness. Drayton pushed her against the marble wall, still cool against her back—the two temperatures meeting in the middle, making her feel like she'd explode. His fingers dug into her arm.

"You're hurting me." Becca didn't like the hint of wounded animal in her voice.

Drayton's eyes held the flat intensity of a predator.

Becca braced for what she knew was coming. This wasn't the first time.

One corner of his mouth ticked up as his eyes slid over her face and down her body. She shivered. He grabbed her hands, holding them above her head in one of his.

When his mouth closed over her breast and he bit down hard, she screamed.

The call came through just after two a.m. Drayton Lewis eased out of bed and slipped into a robe. Next to him, Becca breathed the slow steady cadence of sleep. Her blonde hair fanned across the pillow, half hiding her face, but it couldn't hide the bruise blooming on her cheekbone, nor the ones at her throat. Lewis licked his lips, remembering the taste of her blood. The sex had gotten a little rough. His cock swelled at the memory. Becca had been...amazing, taking control. Where had she gotten that riding crop? He traced the red welts on his chest, following the burn of pain. God, that had been...well, he hadn't had an orgasm like that in decades.

Inside that pretty head of hers, she was smart and clever. He'd liked that—it made the victory over her so much sweeter. And when she'd turned the tables in bed...Lewis was surprised to find being dominated and beaten was such a turn-on. A challenge. And an intriguing game, one that had escalated. She'd raised welts; he'd drawn blood. The next level would be interesting.

Careful to draw the pocket doors tightly together to insulate his conversation from the bedroom should Becca awaken, he stepped to his desk.

The red light on his office phone blinked red.

"What the hell are you doing?" the voice hissed.

Lewis recognized him. The workday was just getting underway in London. "Be careful." Lewis's tone was cold with a lethal edge. He could hear the man swallow hard on the other end of the line.

"Our man is dead?"

"Missing." Lewis frowned. He didn't like loose ends. The senator was a loose end.

"Why?"

"He was having a crisis of conscience."

"Any damage done?"

"None that I can't take care of." Lewis thought of Donovan and his huge find. If Phil Herrera told anyone anything, it would be Patrick Donovan. But soon he wouldn't be a problem either.

"And the trader?"

Lewis bristled at the man's lack of accuracy, but didn't feel the need to correct him. "Jake Walker has been silenced." A noise behind him—a small click and a whoosh. He whirled, peering into the darkness; he stilled.

"The trading, our identities, they cannot be known."

"Shut up!" Lewis barked, then he listened. He thought he heard a faint swishing sound, but he wasn't sure. "You are safe. I've got it under control." He slammed the receiver back in the cradle.

Hitching the sash on his robe, he started to knot it, but pulled it loose. He eased to the doors, took a breath, and then with a quick motion threw them back. The room was dark as he had left it. He could see the covers mounding over Becca's body, hear the faint whisper of her breathing. He shrugged out of the robe, letting it fall to the floor.

Easing under the covers, he moved in next to Becca. The heat of her body, the smell of their sex, aroused him. He leaned down to nibble on her ear. Then he bit down hard. "Let's play some more of that game. But this time, I'm in charge."

CHAPTER TWENTY-SEVEN

The Galveston County Medical Examiner's office was on the landward side of the Galveston ship channel in Texas City, an industrial town overshadowed by huge refineries lining the waterfront and famous only for a huge explosion in 1947. Ammonium nitrate on a French ship moored at the dock ignited, spreading to other vessels and oil facilities nearby. The conflagration killed five-hundred eighty-one people, including all but one of the Texas City Fire Department. Although at the mouth of the Houston ship channel and across a narrow strip of navigable water from Galveston Island, known for being wiped off the face of the Earth in 1900 by a hurricane, only to rise like Atlantis, reborn as a tourist mecca, Texas City had done little to rise above its less than auspicious history. The locals tried to spruce it up, but the town couldn't overcome its roots. Industrial, bleak, smelling of raw petroleum, sulfur, and money, Texas City might offer riches, but it exacted a price.

Sam thought it the perfect place to encounter death. As she squinted her eyes against the assault of the morning sun, her fingers played a staccato rhythm on the armrest as she tried not to think about her father, the vibrant, loving, boisterous, bigger-than-life total con artist, reduced to lifeless sinew and muscle. A soulless form in an ignominious place.

"You don't know how sorry I am, Sam. You sure you're up for this?" Kellen darted a glance her way, then flicked his attention back to the road.

Normally one to keep her own business, Sam had, in a moment of weakness, accepted his offer and now found herself bouncing along the highway in the front seat of his F-250. In no shape to fly, she'd canceled her morning lesson in the J-3 and had booked another pilot to fly the St. Charles round-trip. Thank God it wasn't shift change in the Gulf—that was her bread and butter. No, she wasn't up for this. In fact, she felt hollow, emotionless, dull, defeated...and a bit scared. The world without Patrick Donovan in it was somehow diminished. But she didn't want to talk about it, didn't want to admit it to herself. Reality would gut-shoot her soon enough. "What is it about every jet-jockey south of the Red River having to drive a pickup?"

Kellen slipped into the deflecting idle chitchat. "And a motorcycle."

"Now that's just plain stupid."

"Agreed. So instead, I bought a piece of property up toward Brenham. Needed some breathing room, know what I mean?"

Boy, did she ever. Sam thought about the solace she found in the wide-open spaces of the sky. "Yeah."

"Got a grass strip if you ever want to bring that J-3 up. Grass is what that little plane was built for. Ever landed her on something other than concrete?"

"Not that particular plane. That one was abandoned at one of the private strips near Harlingen. Some drug dude thinking he was going to carry a mint in coke or weed. Didn't bother to understand the concept of useful load. Bought it for a song at auction."

"No owner?"

"She didn't want it back. They'd pancaked it in."

"So you fixed it."

"Took it right down to the tubing. I have a Super Cub I

got the same way. I used to take her into the Northern Territories dropping fishermen and hunters at remote sites. That was the plane the drug guys should've bought—it'd carry anything. Heck of a little float plane, too." Sam appreciated him letting her thoughts wander to more pleasant things while avoiding their upcoming appointment with the downside of life. For a moment, she let herself be carried back, losing herself in the memories of flying on the edge with no one around and nothing to save you but your wits and skill earned through experience. Somebody always knew where she was headed, but that was no guarantee.

"Seriously?" A hint of admiration slipped into his normally nonchalant tone. "Flying in the bush, that's some serious shit."

"Serious shit for a girl?" Sam goaded, half looking for a fight. Anything to offload the emotion building like pressure in a capped well.

"You know me better than that."

"True." Sam blew at the curls tickling her forehead. "Like plucking folks off of boats in a storm isn't serious shit."

"Cut from the same cloth, you and me."

Sam didn't know what to do with that. Yes, they were, in so many ways. That's what made their relationship a minefield—always one step from incineration, but spurred by the knowledge it could be navigated. "My dad taught me my bush skills—the ones that can be taught rather than learned, if you know what I mean."

"Best place to learn to really fly."

"If you get out alive."

"If you don't, then you've had one hell of a time, and hopefully, have gone out doing what you love. There are worse ways to leave this adventure." She hoped her father had gone out with a bang, riding some thrill or another. He deserved that. Sam stared out the window, watching the scenery slip past. There was nothing remarkable about this stretch of Texas, sand dunes slipping toward the coast, coastal grasses bent by the prevailing onshore flow, seagulls circling briny tidal pools, the desiccating sun. She rolled down the window and tested the salt breeze, letting it run through her hair and caress her face.

"What happened to the Super Cub?"

"I left her with a friend who runs a small seaplane operation off of Lake Union in Seattle. I just couldn't cut all my ties with that part of the world. I'm going to go back some day. Maybe run a charter service or something."

"Got plans, do you?" Kellen tried for a smile.

"Dreams, more like. And I'm a long way from getting that one. But, if you don't dream." She shrugged. "And the Pacific Northwest is breathtaking. No place like it, even when it rains for months on end. There's just something magical there."

"I get that. Once you fly up there, it gets in your soul. I spent some time up on Whidbey. Did some training with the Navy. Offshore rescue. Those storms can give you a real lummer."

"Lummer?"

"Shot of cold urine right to the heart. A Navy term."

Sam leaned her head back. "You know, Wilder, you're not half bad."

"If you don't watch yourself, you might end up liking me."

Welcoming the distraction, Sam picked up that gauntlet. "Doubtful. You Coasties are the ones wanting to kick my operation off of Ellington. Remember?"

"That decision is way above my pay grade—I've told you that how many times?" His knuckles whitened as he gripped the steering wheel harder. "You know I think that whole national security thing is way overblown."

"Yeah, well, you're their point man."

"It's my job."

"And you're threatening my livelihood."

"You could relocate to Galveston." Like weary opponents, they batted the well-worn argument back and forth.

"After the last hurricane, the insurance companies won't touch that." Sam recited that in a flat monotone as if she'd told him that a dozen times, which, in fact, she had.

Kellen's frown deepened as he looked straight ahead. "Here's our turn."

Sam's thoughts snapped back to the business in front of her. Even though she'd never tell him, she was glad Kellen had come with her. Whether he wanted to be there or felt obligated as the bearer of the bad news, she didn't know and, right now, it didn't matter. His presence lent comfort, and for that she was grateful.

"You okay?" Kellen navigated the turn.

"No." Sam kept her hands balled in her lap.

They rode the rest of the way in silence. Kellen hit his blinker. "This is it."

The Medical Examiner's office was a gray, story-and-a half building hidden behind the Mainland Medical Center on the western outskirts of Texas City, just a stone's throw from the Interstate. As if eroding under the burden of hopelessness and horror housed inside, the unassuming building hunkered at the back of a small parking lot next to a water-control culvert. She wondered if the folks in the hospital knew what they were looking at. She hoped not. That and the large dumpster out front that sent Sam's imagination places she didn't want it to go.

Kellen nosed in his truck at the left end of the building—two receiving bays occupied the right side. A sign in flat metal letters on the front of the building: Medical Examiner. Galveston County. The entrance was on the end of the building around to the left. A short tier of steps led to a single glass door bracketed by a window on one side. A slatted blind hung at an angle, its string tangled, its slats bent. Sam guessed the box to the side bolted to the stair railing was for specimens to be sent out, but she didn't really want to think about it. Clouds had washed in from the coast, muddying the sky and darkening the sun. It looked like rain. Smelled like it too.

"Well, drive-up appeal certainly isn't a priority," Sam

mumbled, as Kellen held the door.

The smell hit her first. Something rank and nasty that wrinkled her nose and roiled her stomach. Linoleum, monochromatic color scheme, furniture that looked like castoffs from an office furniture liquidator, the place was cold, stark, and unwelcoming. Of course, they probably didn't have too many visitors—not any who cared what the place looked like, anyway. Two offices had been partitioned to their left, one to the right. A desk squeezed into the space between them.

Sam took a breath. She felt numb, like she'd been out in subfreezing temps for too long and then the sting of warmth returning, the pain of blood filtering back into her heart. Her feet obeyed, but she didn't really feel attached to them. Her hands stayed in her pockets. Her heart beat as usual, she breathed in and out, her brain replayed the same short loop—Patrick Donovan, larger than life, was dead. After that first reaction, she hadn't cried. Hadn't felt anything really. The last harsh words between her and her father, sandpaper on a thin scab. Were they to be their last? Sam couldn't even remember exactly what they'd fought about, which struck her as profoundly sad. If those words were to be the cross she had to bear, at least she should remember what they were and why she'd said them, but she didn't. Patrick Donovan was as irritating as chiggers in the summer, and as relentless. Sometimes, she just had to push him back so she could steer her own ship for a while.

A quiet assistant clothed all in white, her mask pulled low, hanging under her chin, appeared through a door behind the desk and greeted them. "Ms. Donovan?"

Sam nodded, holding back while Commander Wilder introduced himself. "My crew transported the body. I was the first on site."

The assistant nodded. "This way." She opened the secondary door and led them into a large room, empty tables surrounded by mounds of shrouded equipment hulking in the shadows. One table at the far end of the room wasn't empty. Illuminated by several stalk lights, it supported a body, naked, the skin white and puckered—a curiosity suffering from numerous indignities—the sea, various aquatic life, Medical Examiner's scalpel and saw.

Sam noticed the strong muscles of the thigh, the mound of a belly, the skin loose, some of it mottled, a headful of white hair, matted with... She shivered and averted her eyes as bile rose in her stomach. With a hand on his arm, she stopped Kellen. "Is this what it comes to?"

"Your father is already gone. The body now is just an empty shell."

"Yes, but I remember the twinkle in his eyes, his wicked grin, his touch."

"Yes, but the body is just a trigger for your memories. The flesh withers away, but the memories run much deeper." He took her hands in his and waited until her eyes met his. "You don't have to do this."

Sam could see concern and kindness in those blue eyes, eyes that changed colors as quickly as Kellen Wilder's emotions shifted, which could be dizzying. "There's no one else."

"Your mother."

Sam shut down that thought with a look. Summoning her normal resolve, Sam squared her shoulders and advanced on the table, the body it held, and the man bent intently over it.

He seemed startled to see her. Pushing himself back until half consumed by the shadows, he raised the clear splash-shield covering his face. A narrow face, eyes pinpoints of focus, an intense expression—he didn't smile.

"I'm here to identify the body," Sam said. The steadiness of her voice, the firmness and resolve, surprised her. Especially since she felt like throwing up. Swallowing hard, she kept her eyes raised.

"Oh, Ms. Donovan. Thank you for coming." Worry and sadness flashed across his face as he glanced down at the body. "I'm sorry you have to see him this way. We had no choice." He seemed at a loss. "I'm Dr. Singleton, the assistant ME."

"It's okay." Sam stepped closer and let her eyes focus on the body. Like her father had taught her to scan the sky while flying, she let her eyes rest for a few seconds, then move, then rest again, absorbing details. Crawling inside herself, she tried to remain dispassionate, analytical—a childhood coping mechanism. Her parents, both wonderful people on their own, were volatile when thrust together. Her childhood had been a lesson in survival. "Can you turn his arms so I can see the inside of his forearms?"

The doctor did as she asked. Sam could feel his unspoken question. She sensed Kellen behind her, stepping closer, trying to see what she saw. Sam let her eyes travel the full length of the body. The crabs and birds had done a lot of damage. No wonder they needed her for the identification. No face. No fingerprints. "Dental records?" Sam asked.

"They appear to be missing. That's why we had to ask you to come down."

"Missing?" Kellen asked as he stepped in beside Sam.

"The dentist of record told us his office had been broken into recently. Files everywhere."

"And they couldn't find my father's," Sam said, her voice flat, hiding her thoughts.

"No digital files?" Kellen asked the doctor.

"My father was old school," Sam answered before the doctor had a chance. "Can I see his legs please?"

The doctor moved the sheet.

She fingered the scars on his knees—the skin cold, his life force gone. The oil field was a dangerous place. "What happened to his feet?" The legs ended at the ankle—the feet were gone.

"Happens a lot when a body has been in the water a while."

Sam shivered in revulsion and kept reminding herself that her father, the man she knew and loved, had left. Another sheeted mound on a gurney against the wall caught her eye. "That the guy they found on Senator Herrera's boat?"

The doctor shifted. He looked uncomfortable. "You know I can't tell you anything."

"Did you find the slug?" Commander Wilder asked.

"Yes."

"And?" Sam pressed. "That's my father lying there. Give us something. Please."

He glanced around as if the stiffs had ears. ".308." He raised his hands. "Please, don't ask me any more. And if I hear that tidbit on the evening news, I'll know where it came from. And you'll be wishing for a court-martial when I get through with you." His eyes shifted to Sam. "We have a witness. And that works both ways."

"The senator, now your father," Kellen said to Sam. "I know they were friends, but were they working on anything together?"

Sam fingered the key in her pocket. "I don't know. My father had a sweet lease—stole it out from under the big boys, to hear him tell it. Herrera was the chairman of the committee overseeing leases. That I know. Anything else would be a guess."

"Humor me."

Sam shook her head and shut him down with a look.

"Somebody wasn't taking any chances." Dr. Singleton leapt into the awkward silence.

Sam glanced between the two men. "You're going to rule this an intentional homicide? A murder?"

The doctor didn't look pleased. "It was intentional all right. And somebody went to great lengths to prevent quick identification and allowing the sea and the birds and others to do the rest."

"A gamble," Kellen said.

"Yes, but not much of one. Perhaps the killer was in a hurry. This wasn't premeditated but more unplanned, a surprise. A fisherman hooked the body over twenty miles offshore, right?"

"Yep. He brought it to the nearest rig where I happened

to show up." Kellen shook his head as he looked at the body. "Not much to go on. You said killer? I'm assuming you have a cause of death?"

"Blunt force trauma to the head."

"Really? Someone hit him over the head and then tossed him off the rig?" As much as she didn't like that scenario, it answered some big questions.

"That's the best theory we have so far." The doctor raised his eyebrows in question as he reached for the sheet folded at the end of the gurney. Sam nodded, and he covered the body.

Kellen swiveled to look behind them.

"What?" Sam asked.

"Thought I heard voices."

"My assistant will take care of it." The door opened, then closed behind the woman who'd greeted them and had remained in the background.

"This whole thing stinks." She held up her hand, forestalling the next question she could see on their faces. "No, I don't know exactly what he had gotten himself into, but I intend to find out. And when I do..." She took a deep, steadying breath. "Well, we know the how. Perhaps I can help with the who."

"Over my dead body. The last thing I need in this investigation is a rabid female hot on a witch-hunt. The investigation is my job."

"Really?" Sam eyed him, her voice icy.

"Yeah," Kellen rushed, tripping over his explanation. "We don't know exactly where this happened, but my guess is somewhere close to federal waters and beyond the jurisdiction of Texas and the Galveston police. So, that leaves the Coast Guard. But, the jurisdictional issues are up in the air since we don't know the exact location where the crime was committed. We can let the big boys fight about it if they want to. But this was the nearest forensics lab. That's why the body ended up here."

"You guys do this often?"

"More often than you'd think. But most of the time, the crime scene is more defined."

"What's your best guess as to where this happened?"

"Once we have a time of death," Kellen glanced at the doctor, bringing him into the conversation, "we can track the currents and backtrack to location. It's not exact, but there isn't much out there besides the current operations and an abandoned rig or two. And, if it happened on a boat... " Kellen shook his head. "Boats can disappear."

"For all we know," her voice hitched and she cleared her throat, "someone could've killed him onshore and taken the body out there to dump it."

The doctor nodded. "True."

"So somebody hit him over the head hard enough to kill him and then dumped the body in the water. What else do we know?" Sam asked as she looked at the now shrouded body, but still seeing what lay underneath. "Do you have a time of death?"

"A couple of days. The salt water, the damage to the body, they make accuracy a bit problematic." The doctor stepped back into the light. "Ms. Donovan, I have to ask you this. Is this your father?"

Sam fought a tear as she nodded.

CHAPTER TWENTY-EIGHT

Once out of the Coroner's building and halfway across the parking lot, with a hand on her arm, Kellen stopped Sam, swinging her around. "You okay?" Kellen held up a hand. "I'm sorry, stupid question. I got the impression something back there wasn't sitting too well with you—I mean, besides the obvious."

Sam yanked her arm from his grasp. ".308 That means the shot that killed the assassin—that totally sounds like something out of a B-movie—was taken with a long-range rifle So somebody shot from the shore, maybe."

She'd taken a logic left turn and Kellen struggled to catch up. He thought about it for a moment. "Yeah, that sounds right."

"So then, let's assume they shot from the shore. I saw some tire tracks and bit of matted grass on the north shoreline, which I told the State Police about." She gave him a piercing look. "Don't you sorta wonder where the dead guy came from? I doubt he left with Uncle Phil, and there's no boat."

"He could've been hiding below decks." That had been Kellen's running theory—he didn't have another that held water.

Sam shook her head. "Uncle Phil would have to go down and open up the fuel system. With that much fuel on board,

I'm sure he had all the shuttlecocks closed to prevent seepage and a big bang when he lit the engine." She wasn't sure that would happen, but it sounded good. "And the assassin came on board with no gun?"

"It could've fallen overboard."

"Maybe, but I saw the body. It hadn't been moved; the blood hadn't been smeared. And from where he fell, I'm thinking he would've dropped the gun as he fell back, his head jerked back by the penetration of the bullet."

"So you think someone else was there?"

"Uncle Phil didn't own a .308. His weapon of choice was a SIG-Sauer P227." Sam turned on her heel and stalked to the truck.

She had a point. And the .308 blew his theory pretty much to hell. "What about your father?" He rushed to keep up. He brushed her hand from the handle and opened the door, then invited her in.

"My father is my problem. I don't want you involved. Where I have to go, a commander in good standing has no business going."

"I'm already involved. My jurisdiction, remember?" After he made sure she was all in, he took a deep breath and tried not to slam her door. As he walked around the back of the truck, he surveyed the parking lot. Old habits never die.

Sam stared out the side window—she didn't look at him as he slipped behind the wheel. He couldn't tell whether she was pissed off or crushingly sad—probably a bit of both. And like a wounded animal, she was dangerous and would take special handling.

"Sam, you may see me as the enemy, but, our conflict at the field notwithstanding, I'm a friend. And, if you've a mind to track down your father's killer, I'm the best friend you got."

He gave her a few moments as he found his way back to I-45 and headed north, setting the cruise control at five over. "Okay, spill it. I'm your best shot at solving whatever problem has got your trigger finger all twitchy."

Sam glanced down at the offending digit then clasped her hands together in her lap. "My father has...had...a knack for finding trouble. My guess is this time he couldn't charm his way out. It wouldn't be the first time my father's charm failed him. Usually I was around to pull his ass out of the crack. Luck of the Irish, he said. I remember this time in South Dakota. He'd crashed a Bonanza A-36. I loved that plane. He stole it. Took it without even asking. I should've shot him then."

"You're putting me off with your cute story. It won't work. I need to know everything your father told you. I assume your argument had something to do with where we find ourselves today."

Sam crossed her arms and stared out the side window, avoiding him. "Take me home. Kidnapping is a federal offense."

"So is lying to the Feds." Kellen gave them both time to cool off as he slowed and eased his truck to a stop on the shoulder. Putting it in park, he turned to Sam, who fumed but didn't say anything, preferring to look daggers at him. "You always shoot the guy who happens to be in range?"

"What are friends for?" Sam shrugged but looked a little chagrined, which Kellen accepted as an apology. It was probably the closest he was going to get.

"Is Sam your given name?"

She blinked at him a couple of times. "Seriously?"

Kellen shrugged. "Just thought if we're going to be in bed and all on this one, it'd be nice to know your real name."

"Wishful thinking, sailor." She shot him a look that would've eviscerated a lesser man. "You think Sam is a good Catholic name? Seriously? The Donovans may be liars, thieves, cheaters, and reprobates, but they're good Catholics to a one."

Kellen couldn't find a grin, but he felt his mood lighten a bit. At least he'd gotten her to talk. "I'm not even going to point out all of the inconsistencies in that statement."

"Apparently, you weren't raised Catholic."

"Agnostic."

Sam looked out the window, and when she spoke, there was melancholy in her voice. "We all need to believe in something."

There was truth there, so Kellen let it lie. He didn't know what he believed in. One stormy night years ago had shattered his faith. He shook off the horror that was as real now as it was then. "Tell me what're you thinking?"

"I'm thinking that I don't want to immerse you any deeper into the Donovan family's penchant for finding trouble."

Kellen leaned back and stared at the highway stretching in a straight line to the horizon. "Well, I'm pretty fond of one of the Donovans. And I've already told you that, barring any evidence to the contrary, it's my rodeo. Whether you want to pull me into it or not, I'm in. Might as well give it up—I'll find everything out eventually anyway. Perhaps as a team, we can at least honor your father by catching his killer."

Sam didn't say anything as she turned in on herself, scrunching down in the seat.

Kellen focused on the rush of the traffic going by as he corralled his fears. No way was he going to let her waltz alone into a situation where two people had been killed already and one very important person was missing. "Let me in, Mary Catherine."

Sam swiveled to look at him. "You knew my name all along."

"I'm an investigator. I'm good at my job. When I want to know something, I don't quit until I find it."

"Don't tell me I didn't warn you." Sam shot him a look.

"So tell me exactly what you two talked about last time you saw him." Kellen pushed himself up, looked in the side mirror checking traffic, then hit his blinker and accelerated into the flow of traffic.

"My father was all excited, but nervous. Something had him spooked, like I told you. I'm pretty sure it had to do with his lease out in the Gulf. Deep water stuff. Really big time for a small-time player."

"Did he tell you that?"

"No. Not exactly, but I know him well enough to connect the dots. A find of a lifetime, he'd called it. I can't tell you how many times my mother and I heard *that* before."

Kellen caught the disgust in her voice. "Was he ever right?" Kellen glanced in the rearview. A truck, white, hunting grill, tinted windows, wove in and out of traffic, closing fast.

"Well, perhaps his finds never lived up to the recent hyperbole, but he had a nose for oil. He'd celebrate each new well with a new wife." She paused, closing her eyes.

Kellen could almost see her shake the anger away. A fight for another day, he guessed.

"This time, I got the impression, was different."

"How so?"

"I don't know. Bigger? He'd moved up. Maybe playing with the big boys has a different set of rules?" Sam's voice quivered. "And maybe that's what got him killed."

"Could be. Big money attracts big attention." Kellen kept his voice steady and one eye on the truck behind them. After closing the distance, the truck settled on Kellen's bumper.

"He needed a bunch of money. Leveraged everything he had, including good sense. He was taking on some limited partners that he wouldn't have invited over for dinner."

"Any names?"

"No, but easy enough to access—the limited partnership should be a matter of public record on file with the Secretary of State's office."

"Really?"

"Yeah, the state takes a dim view of a lack of transparency."

"A place to start." Kellen's voice trailed off, his attention captured by the view in his sideview mirror. A low-slung car, dark, weaving in and out of traffic, closed the distance.

"My father has several honorary degrees in innuendo and bullshit. Most of the time I wouldn't have believed him, thinking he was drumming up sympathy—something he was real good at...until he'd burned you a time or two. But this time he seemed like he was looking over his shoulder. Told me he didn't want me to know in case something happened to him."

Sam's eyes, large and round, met Kellen's. She looked like she'd made a decision. Pulling her fist out of her pocket, she extended it toward him and opened her fingers.

A key.

Kellen glanced down, then back to the road, his eyes flicking to the side view. The car was still coming. From the grill, he thought it might be one of the new Dodge muscle cars—all the cadets lusted after them, adorning their small spaces with glossy photos pulled from hot-rod magazines. "What's that?"

The car was almost on them now.

His eyes shifted to the side mirror. "That guy is in one hell of a hurry."

Sam swiveled to look behind. "Aggressive drivers—like cockroaches in Texas."

"Maybe." Kellen kept checking the mirror. He didn't like it.

"My father gave this key to me the other day. He'd said when I found myself looking for answers, I'd know where to go."

"Do you?" Half listening, Kellen switched his focus from the mirror, swiveling to look out the side window, expecting the car to come into view. It didn't. And the white Chevy pickup stayed behind them. He didn't like this, not one bit. All the marks of a setup.

Lost in her memories, Sam kept talking. "What my father actually said was to look where he would keep something he held dear. That was a bit more of a puzzle than I can solve right now. The key seems like a file key."

"Maybe his office?" Kellen's eyes flicked back to his side mirror—the car was in his blind spot. And it had slowed. Matching speed, it settled in at his shoulder where he couldn't see it without turning. Kellen moved up, increasing speed slowly so it wouldn't be noticed.

A growl as the car accelerated, downshifting to lunge forward. The car's side window lowered a fraction. A quick glint of metal.

The commander reached out, grabbed Sam's shoulder, and threw her forward. "Get down."

Keeping his hands on the wheel, one eye above the dash, he folded toward her.

Both flinched away from the loud noise. But it didn't come from the side. No, someone in the truck behind them fired.

A setup. I knew it. Kellen ducked his head.

Glass rained as the back window exploded.

Sam caught a quick look through the side window of the car lowered a few inches. A man, dark hair, military short, Ray-Bans, thick lips, the skin over the planes of his face taut with surprise.

Another boom from behind. The black Dodge swerved. The man wrestled with it before regaining control. The engine growled, the wheels caught, and the car fishtailed, then gained traction and raced into the distance.

"That's his two shots," Kellen muttered as he focused on the truck still following them—an easier target than the car disappearing into the distance. "Would you get your head down?" Kellen shoved Sam lower as he braked hard, closing the distance between his bumper and the trailing truck's grill. He felt the bump—it'd worked. He'd caught the other driver unaware, buying a few precious seconds for Kellen to reach for the gun he kept under the back seat. A sawed-off pistol-gripped Remington 12-gauge pump-action he'd had since he was a kid. Legal then; not so much now. He always had a round chambered.

One glance in the rearview. Then a switch to the side mirror. The white pickup had swerved into the left lane and was matching speed.

Kellen wondered why the guy wasn't closing. "You okay?" he asked Sam, who no longer hunched out of harm's way—not that he expected her to, but it would've been nice. "Just once, do you think you might do as I say?"

"You're dreaming, flyboy."

She had no idea.

Sam shot him a tight look as she pulled her seatbelt snug across her lap, then reached over and did the same for his. "An outlaw gun for one of the white hats. You surprise me, Wilder."

He thought that a good thing. "You know us Coasties, always prepared."

"That's the Boy Scouts." Sam glanced over her shoulder.

"Close enough." Wind whipped around the cab as Kellen lowered his window. "Here we go."

He braked, hard. The driver reacted, swerving to the left. He wasn't quick enough on the brake, and the nose of the pickup jutted just past the rear wheel well of Kellen's truck. Kellen yanked the wheel hard to the left. Metal ground and screeched, as one driver's will met another's. Brakes squealed, and the truck retreated from view. Kellen was ready, slamming on the brakes and turning first into the skid, then against it. The stench of burning rubber and his own sweat filled the air as time seemed to hang. Then it collapsed as his truck came to rest across two lanes, nose to the inner guardrail. He had their pursuer blocked. With quick precision, Kellen fired off two shells, puncturing the two front tires.

At least they'd caught one of them. With one, the other shouldn't be too hard to track.

One more pump and Kellen leveled the gun at the driver's compartment. He felt sure the driver was out of ammo—no way to break open the gun and drive, too. "Let me see your hands," he shouted. "You got your two off. No time to reload." On the off chance he had overplayed his hand and was wrong, Kellen kept himself sheltered behind the door of the truck. "Stay down," he barked at Sam when she raised her head.

"Get out of the truck," he shouted at the driver.

The cloud of dust created by traffic jamming to a stop behind them blew by, carried on a breeze fueled in the Gulf. For a moment time stopped.

The driver's door opened. "Don't shoot." A female voice. Hands, one holding the shotgun, appeared above the driver's side window as one high-heeled foot appeared below, followed by another.

"What the hell?" Kellen didn't sound amused.

"What? You think women can't drive and shoot? Flyboy, you should know better than most that underestimating a woman can get you killed." Sam tossed the accusation as she slid down through her open door.

"And a painful death it would be." Kellen leveled the gun on the woman in front of him. She looked familiar, but he couldn't place her.

Sam leaned into the cab, using the truck as a shield. "You got a gun for me in here?"

Kellen nodded at the glovebox. "A round's already chambered."

Sam popped it open and whistled in admiration as she palmed the Glock. "I'll check the passenger side, make sure nobody's lurking in there ready to blow your big head off."

"You'll probably waste that first bullet on me if I tell you to be careful, right?"

"Not worth the jail time," she said as she slipped out of the truck. "Remember that."

The northbound traffic on the Interstate was piling up. They'd effectively shut down all four lanes.

Kellen waited for Sam to give him a nod; then, with another round chambered but the barrel pointing at the ground, he advanced on the woman. Danger past, Kellen's anger lit. "Nothing like being the center ring in a three-ring circus," Kellen growled. "Hand me your gun, butt first."

Lowering her hands, she flipped the gun around.

"Don't point it at yourself." Kellen sidestepped even

though he was fairly certain she was out of shells. It paid to be careful. "Aim it to the side. Don't you know anything about guns?"

"I'm from New York."

Kellen grabbed the butt. "Where only the criminals have guns."

"And the politicians don't have a clue; I get it." She trotted out the Texas party line as if she really did at least half get it.

Kellen handed the shotgun to Sam, presenting the stock but keeping the barrel pointing toward something unimportant. "Make a note of that serial number." Then he turned back to the shooter. "Who the hell are you?"

The woman, young, chin out, dark hair in a sleek bob, cheekbones carved like granite cliffs over lips lush and red, but hardly kissable, and a body in need of several weeks of all-you-can-eat, stared at him with dark eyes that held a challenge. "Shelby Walker," she said, as if that was enough. She glanced around, then shook her head at all the people who had stopped and were peering at them. "You'd think with gunfire, they'd be a bit more leery."

"You'd think."

"But you'd be wrong," Sam said as she gave the gal the once-over. "Pretty gussied up for a killer."

Shelby Walker gave her a withering look. "You've got this all wrong. But we need to get out of here."

Kellen found his voice. "We?"

"*We* are waiting for the cops," Sam chimed in. She stuck the Glock in the waist of her jeans where she could reach it.

"Look, I work for one of the network affiliates in New York. If we can move somewhere less exposed, I'll give you everything. And you can check me out to your heart's content."

She may have gotten the gun thing, but she failed to understand that trotting out an East Coast pedigree only inflamed the locals.

"Is shooting at folks a new interview technique?" Sam

kept her eyes and Kellen's shotgun leveled on the woman as Kellen moved both trucks to the side. With the truck clear, traffic eased around the three of them standing off to the side as the looky-loos got a full dose.

The girl licked her lips as her eyes darted between Sam and Kellen, who reclaimed his gun when he returned, pocketing the keys to Shelby's Chevy. It wasn't going anywhere with the two front tires blown, but he made sure.

"The guy in the Charger? He had a gun. I've seen him. He's tailed me around town, then showed up on a stakeout the other day. Ran his plates, but they came back a no-hit."

"Stakeout?" Kellen sounded surprised.

"I'm a reporter. Anyway, the guy passed me without a thought, but when he lowered his window a fraction I knew he was gunning for you guys. That much living in New York will teach you." She gave a knowing look at Sam and Kellen as if she'd picked up on all the subtext. "I didn't have time to think."

"Nice try. You were working with him," Sam said.

The woman let her hands sag lower as her face registered her shock. "What? That's preposterous. And, yes, the plates weren't registered, at least not where I could find them. I had a friend of mine check."

Kellen motioned with the barrel of his gun, and Shelby raised her arms up again. "How do you hide your plates?"

"*You* don't. *I* don't. But it can be done. Anybody with a computer and a lot of know-how can make you disappear, so license plates shouldn't be too hard."

"Hard to argue with that," Kellen said.

"Hard to believe, too." Sam wasn't buying it, not for a minute.

"If I was working with him, why would I shoot at him?"

"You didn't," Sam reminded her. "You shot at us."

"That's what you think?" The woman sounded incredulous.

Kellen motioned to the blown-out rear window in his truck.

That took a little of the starch out of her. "I hit you, but I was shooting at him."

"New Yorkers," Kellen growled. "Okay, I'll play. Who was he?"

"I told you, I don't know." She glanced around, taking in all the attention. "If he's the guy I think he is, he assaulted my roommate, probably had something to do with the disappearance of Senator Herrera, and," she swallowed hard, "and he most likely is the guy who killed my brother."

CHAPTER TWENTY-NINE

"You think the guy that shot at us killed your brother." Still standing on the side of the highway as the traffic inched past, Sam ignored all of it—the looks, the sun, the heat—and focused in on the one important tidbit Shelby Walker had dropped.

Shelby blinked furiously as tears welled. She nodded once. "And maybe somebody else. All morning I've been calling a source I had here in Houston. She isn't answering the phone."

"Who?"

"A source."

"If you think she's in trouble, a name would be helpful," Kellen said.

"I'll give it to you, but we need to get out of here. Jake," she cleared her throat, "my brother, knew more than he should have. He sent something to me thinking I would be home. Now my source, who was working with Jake, isn't answering her phone. A senator involved in all of this has gone missing, and there's a dead oilman back there who factors in somehow."

Sam felt her blood start to boil. "And you think one guy did all of this?"

"I don't know, but things are starting to line up. One connection is a coincidence. But two? That starts to get your attention. By three, I'm thinking there is something solid there. I can't prove anything."

Sam thought about the death she'd left at the morgue as she watched Shelby. So twitchy she looked like she'd jump out of her skin, the woman kept darting looks around. "And now you have something your brother had and a killer wants."

"Or someone thinks she does," Kellen added.

"Which is it?" Sam pressed.

"Someone thinks I do," Shelby admitted with a sigh. "Jake liked to play games. He's good at misdirection."

"But not staying alive." Sam put the pieces together. "And that's how the roommate got assaulted?"

"To be honest, I've got pieces and no glue. I'm making this up as I go. The pieces fit, but I can't prove any of it. I sure could use your help."

"You shot at us. Is that any way to ask?" Kellen looked not the least bit amused.

"I'm a bad shot. Sue me. Or, better yet, do me a huge favor and throw me out of this hellhole of a state."

"Why did you shoot at us?"

"The other guy was taking aim; I was sure of it. I've seen him around."

"Where?" Sam pushed hard. She needed some answers.

Shelby once again glanced around. "Look, can we get out of here? That guy in the black Dodge could circle back."

"There is that." Sam looked at Kellen. "You know we are targets standing out here with a crowd gathering. Anyone with a rifle and steady hand could pick us off easy. I've been shot at once today, and, frankly, that's more than enough."

"She has a point," Kellen said, turning to the New Yorker. "Shelby Walker. Why do I know that name?" He seemed intent on keeping Shelby unnerved, letting her stew in the juice of her own fears.

With one lane still not completely clear, the traffic was stacking up behind them. The traffic on the other side slowed as well. Pretty soon the gridlock would have them corralled for hours—like shooting fish in a barrel.

"She's a stringer for that news show, *Straight Talk.*"

"The show that takes everything out of context to present the story they want?" That sounded like it made him angrier than being shot at.

Sam cocked one eyebrow. "So cynical, Commander Wilder."

"After Hurricane Ike, that show was a pain in my ass. Apparently, they didn't appreciate the lives we saved."

"Before my time." Shelby didn't look particularly apologetic, but she didn't try to suck up either. "Are we getting out of here or what?"

Sirens sounded in the distance. It had taken longer than Sam had thought for someone to rally the troops. "Couldn't you have just honked or flashed your lights or something if you'd wanted our attention?"

"Really, you think that would've worked?" Shelby closed her eyes for a moment and took a deep breath. Then she leveled her calmer gaze at the commander. "Shooting was a bad idea. I understand that. But it was the best I could come up with given the immediacy of the situation."

Kellen granted her that one. If she'd flashed her lights, he would've ignored her.

As the sirens grew louder, Shelby grew more agitated. "Look. I've been digging up dirt on, well, I know this sounds crazy, but a group of billionaires who have banded together to protect their collective investment in fossil fuels. My brother...he was in a position to put the pieces together."

"Conspiracy theories?" Sam broke down the shotgun. The spent casings ejected. "You're in Texas—after JFK we've all become a bit skeptical. Got anything better?"

Shelby ran a hand through her hair. "Can we take this conversation elsewhere? Getting arrested isn't on my agenda today."

"Shootings on the Interstate generally attract attention."

"I'm chasing some proof on my conspiracy theory, as you put it. But, if you are interested in the bodies back there in the morgue, I can help you."

Sam watched, weighing the girl's words. She knew something. How much was anybody's guess. And it seemed likely she was promising more than she could deliver. Given the circumstances, if Sam had been in the girl's shoes, she would've done the same. "Your source put you onto them?"

Shelby nodded. "She's someone on the inside."

"On the inside of what?" Kellen still didn't sound like he'd bought in.

"The conspiracy," Sam answered, keeping her skepticism only slightly hidden.

"Keep me out of jail, and I'll tell you what I know." Shelby pressed, her voice worried now. "A commander in the Coast Guard ought to have some sway." She glanced over her shoulder as the sirens grew louder.

"You discharged a firearm on the highway."

She gave him a look. "To save your ass. And, not to point out the obvious, so did you. I've got something to trade. With me in jail, that info will be locked tighter than a virgin's knees. Guess it depends on how important it is to you."

Sam tucked all three guns out of sight in Kellen's truck. They were safe unless the cops got pushy and trumped up some probable cause. Of course, a bunch of flat tires might make them twitchy.

At the last minute, she pulled out the Glock.

CHAPTER THIRTY

Senator Phillip Herrera awakened slowly. Easing his eyes open, he waited while they adjusted to the dim light. Gray metal surrounded him; a lumpy mattress that smelled of mildew underneath him. A small room, no windows—only a closed door on the far wall.

He was alone.

His head felt as if someone had split it with a meat cleaver. He licked his lips, wetting the cracked dry skin. A sharp metallic taste lingered. Had he been drugged? Dizzy, his movements slow, his thoughts and memories muddled, it sure seemed like it. What he would do for a double single-malt. Easing his eyes shut, he listened. Nothing. Maybe the lap of water? He wasn't sure. Snaking a hand over the edge of the mattress, he felt the metal—cool to the touch, condensation slicking the surface. Yes, water. A boat? Not his, that was for sure. He stilled. He couldn't sense any motion. If he was on a boat it was a large one.

The last thing he remembered was the guy coming alongside and leaping aboard. He'd raised a gun, slipped...then his head had exploded. There'd been somebody else. Phillip fingered the back of his scalp, probing the edges of a knot the size of an egg. His fingers came away bloody. Someone had sure gotten a lick in, but who? Squeezing his eyes tight, he searched his memory.

Just the one guy.

Gently, he pushed himself onto an elbow and waited for the world to stop spinning. The room appeared empty, only one way in or out, with a small grate at the top of one wall, flush against the ceiling presumably for air. A nice touch. It took a few minutes, but finally the senator was able to stand—wobbly and on the edge of vomiting, but on his feet. Using one hand to brace against the wall for support, he followed it around to the door.

Surprisingly, the handle turned, and the latch released. With his palm flat against the metal, he eased the door open. After checking to make sure no one was around, the senator stepped into the light, blinking furiously as his eyes teared against the onslaught of the sun fractured into thousands of arrows by the waves below. He stepped out onto a platform, scoured by storms, the welded seams leaking rust that slalomed through the bubbled paint. A small abandoned oil rig, or what was left of it. Nothing more than the one room and a platform about half the size of a football field. After completing a circuit and peering over the side, the senator confirmed he was alone, as abandoned as the old metal structure surrounded by nothing but open ocean stretching to the horizon.

With a hand shading his eyes, he scanned the hazy horizon where it melded into a gauzy sky. Darkness lurked to the south, and fingers of cloud sailed by above, carried on an invisible current.

Except for a few gulls darting and diving, the sea was empty.

Not another soul in sight. No Agent Presley Davis. No FBI.

Off to the left, tucked in next to the room he'd stepped out of, the senator saw what looked to be a soft-sided cooler. Dragging it into the shade, he unzipped the top. Water, beer, several sandwiches encased in cellophane. He polished off one bottle of water and was halfway through the second when he tucked into a sandwich and settled down, his back against the metal building, his legs stretched in front of him.

He thought of his wife, his kids, and of revenge.

CHAPTER THIRTY-ONE

Always good to cultivate the Almighty when the Devil hung so close at his shoulder, thought Farrell Bishop, but today the good preacher was pushing Bishop's tolerance for piety. Making a slashing gesture across his throat, Bishop telegraphed his impatience. In flagrant disregard for the illegality, each day at noon, all of San Rafael Oil's employees were required to attend services on the top level of the parking garage.

Bishop had learned long ago that Houston, hellhole of Texas, was a funny place. Nobody cared who you really were; they just cared about who you appeared to be, never looking deeper than the superficial. So Bishop cultivated his Buckle-of-the-Bible-Belt persona, which wasn't too far from his Catholic upbringing—weekly confessionals kept you on the path to Heaven, no matter what you did in between. Six days of sin worked right into his life plan.

But today he couldn't shake the feeling things were spinning out of control, sin gaining the upper hand. This business in the Gulf had his blood pressure high and his patience low. Besides, it was hotter than hell, the concrete radiating an already blistering heat. The Devil himself would have a stroke, thought Bishop, as sweat beaded under his shirt, wilting the perfect starch job. After the preacher's close, Bishop added his, "Amen, brother," to the throng's responsive chorus and stepped back into the shadows.

One by one, he greeted his staff, the men with a firm handshake, the women with a limp one and then a hug and sly grope, as they hurried back into the comfort of conditioned air. He knew each by name. He also knew their families, their financial situations, their weaknesses, and their vulnerabilities, but they didn't know that.

As the sea of humanity funneled by him, Bishop tried to keep his interest level casual, but every few minutes he scanned the faces in front of him.

On the verge of losing it, he finally caught the bloated, sweaty red face, not of Johnny Halloran, but of one of Johnny's best men, to hear Halloran tell it. Hanging back, he stepped in at the rear of the line. When the other employees in front had disappeared into the comfort of the air conditioned building, he grabbed Bishop's hand and squeezed.

Bishop didn't flinch. "What the hell are you doing here? Where's your boss?"

Halloran's thug, a man north of fifty but not by much, wore the trappings of success poorly—the stench of West Texas oilfield trash still clinging to him despite the bespoke suit, handcrafted shoes, and flash of gaudy at the wrist. In retreat from the onslaught of age, his dark hair had thinned to the point of transparency, no longer covering the freckles that dotted his scalp like age spots on an old man's hands. His body still muscled, his shoulders broad, his waist softening under a spare tire, he looked like he had come up the hard way, which he had. Had it not been for first Halloran and now Bishop, the man would've outlived any usefulness decades ago. "Halloran went out to the rig."

"I thought he was sending you."

"Plans changed."

"Really? Did he say why?"

"Wanted to see for himself, or so he said."

"Have you heard from him?"

"Not him exactly, but another of our guys checked in.

Said he was calling in place of the boss."

Bishop felt of a trickle of worry slip down his side. "And?"

"Patrick Donovan is dead."

Bishop hid a smile. "Confirmed?"

Halloran's man shrugged as if death were weightless. "I'm just relaying, you know."

Bishop did know, and he didn't like it, but, it wasn't the first time. So the deed was done. He allowed himself a small gloat. You hang with the right people, you plant the right seed, and the right weed will grow.

Now he was back in the game.

The entire afternoon had been wasted while the State Troopers puffed out their chests and exerted their power. There wasn't anything Sam, Shelby, or Kellen could do other than play nice, keep their mouths shut, and stick to their simplified version of the truth, which they did.

Cops were cops no matter the uniform. The more you said, the worse they made it until stories could be turned right back onto the victim. If Kellen Wilder were a cynical man, he'd think the cops didn't want to actually *solve* a crime. Why would they when pretending to be all busy trying to solve it was so much easier?

Once seated in one of the Adirondack chairs in front of Sam's hangar, Kellen waited until his beer was half gone and his anger half diffused before he looked at Shelby. Her truck had been loaded on a rollback and carted to the nearest dealer for two new tires. "Why did someone kill your brother?"

"I'm not really sure," she said, acting as if she'd been anticipating a grilling. Then she told Kellen and Sam a little of what she knew and none of what she suspected.

Kellen listened, his eyes half-closed, staring out at the airfield. When she'd finished, he didn't respond right away. "You've got to know how to play the game if you want to get to commander in the Coast Guard. Along the way you hear so much bullshit, you can almost smell it coming. I'm thinking you've pegged us for fools, Shelby Walker, and have overplayed your hand."

"Look at it from my perspective, Commander. I've lost my brother, and my roommate has a bashed-in skull. My source has disappeared. I don't know why, and I don't know who I can trust. I'm seeing killers under every rock."

He cocked his head, not buying it. "But we just established I work for the good guys."

"Didn't we just spend the afternoon being dicked-over by cops?" She turned to Sam. "What's your interest in a stiff at the morgue?"

Sam, leaning against the side of the building next to the chairs, rested her head against the metal and gazed across the field. "He was my father. I'm Sam Donovan. My father is...was Patrick Donovan of Donovan Oil."

"Patrick Donovan is dead?" That took some of the starch out of Shelby. For a moment, her mask slipped and some scared seeped through. "I'm sorry. I hadn't made that connection. So much for being an ace reporter. I was insensitive."

Sam gave her a steely look. "You've been a lot of things. Insensitive is only one of them."

Shelby, to her credit, accepted that with equanimity. "Point taken."

"Why do I get the impression you knew that was my father in the morgue?"

Shelby took a swig of her beer and stared out over the lights of the airfield. "I wasn't sure. I hoped like hell it wasn't."

Sam didn't look like she was buying any of it. "Did your source tell you about him?"

"She just said all this had to do with some strike or

something Donovan Oil had in the Gulf."

"You going to tell us who this source is?"

Shelby glanced at her, then back to staring holes into the darkness.

"Look, we're not on opposing teams here. We both are looking for the truth, right? We're not one of your interviewees that you want to tear the stuffing out of."

"Sorry. I'm used to scratching and clawing for everything I get. Network news is still a good ol' boy network."

Sam scoffed. "Honey, this is Texas, the backwater of the feminist movement. You have no idea."

"Am I going to be shot at dawn for my Y-chromosome?" Kellen asked from the sidelines.

"Oh, lighten up, Wilder," Sam said as she handed him a fresh beer and tossed his empty in the oil drum serving as a trash can. "We'll let you be one of the girls. Won't we, Shelby?"

"Obvious requirements can be waived, at least temporarily."

"So who's your source?" Sam pressed.

"Becca Molinari, Drayton Lewis's personal assistant. I'm really worried. She hasn't answered the phone all day. Not like her. She should be at work."

Kellen drained the rest of his beer as he eyed her over the can. He wiped his mouth with the back of his hand and then crunched the can in one fist before arcing it into the trashcan. "Lewis? He may be a corporate fat-cat who made his money raping and pillaging and who now has found his Messiah in saving the environment, which makes him a hypocrite. But I can't see what he would have to do with oil trades and Donovan Oil. Besides, the guy has enough green to buy half of Houston. So why would he mess with getting his feet dirty?"

"Oil is the counterpoint to his investment in sustainable energy. And he's bet the bank on it, leveraged himself to the max. From what I know, he's very good at hedging his bets.

And he doesn't recognize all the normal boundaries, or so I'm told."

"And how'd you get put onto Donovan?"

"If you look, I think you'll find the list of investors in Donovan Oil to be very interesting. To be honest, I started in a different direction. Hell, Mr. Donovan wasn't even on my radar—he doesn't usually swim with the big fish, the piranha." Shelby looked at the beer Sam had pressed into her hand. "What is this stuff?"

Sam wanted to tell her that piranha were quite small, but she resisted. "Pure Texas and a fer piece from Boston Lager."

Shelby took a long pull, then wiped her mouth with the back of her hand. "I like it. Refreshing."

"That's the point. So Ms. Molinari put you onto my father's company?"

"She told me to look at the money behind Donovan Oil's new project, that's all."

"And?" Sam pressed.

"I pulled up the Limited Partnership Agreement through the Secretary of State's office; it's a matter of public record. Only problem is that most of the partners are hidden behind several layers of foreign corporations. It'll take some digging."

"Foreign?" Kellen asked. "Like not Texas?"

"Yes and no," Shelby answered. "Some states don't require very much information when incorporating. Lots of criminal enterprises hide behind those statutes. And some international corporations skirt the law. It's all a legal shell game designed to protect the guilty. The only one I could ferret out was San Rafael Oil and Farrell Bishop. If I dig a little bit further, *and* if I get lucky, I bet I'll find Lewis's fingerprints all over those corporate investors. But, like I said, time is in short supply."

"So you thought you'd go to my father to get the information?" Sam asked.

"I tracked him to San Rafael Oil, then by helicopter to

his rig. He hasn't come back."

"You've been monitoring the frequencies."

"They're open channels." Shelby nodded toward Kellen. "I picked up your transmissions to the ME's office when you were bringing the body in. I waited to see who might show up. Sometimes you get lucky."

"What exactly is the story you're chasing?"

Shelby shrugged. "It started as just another piece on corporate greed, but something's changed. It's way more than that now. I know it, but I can't prove it."

"Is that why you were here when your brother thought you were back in New York?"

Shelby flinched. "No, Jake sent me here. I got a text from him. Go straight to Houston, don't go home, that kind of thing."

"And you did it?"

"He's my brother. But he knew I was coming here to interview Drayton Lewis. My big break." The disdain in her voice indicated she thought it anything but her big break.

An only child, Sam didn't get it, but she understood it. So many times her father had cried wolf and she'd come running. The things we do for family. "Did you interview Lewis?"

"Poked a stick in his beehive. He ended the interview, stormed off muttering something about having my head on a spike."

"If what you say is true, then I'd be willing to bet you got his attention."

"I can't leave it alone. You understand, don't you?"

"Totally." Sam nodded, her voice like flint, scratching a spark. Sam fingered the key in her pocket. "Maybe we should give my father's office the once-over."

"Oh, no," Kellen said, leaning forward and putting out his hands. "No way you two are going off on some vigilante mission. Sam, you've got work, and, Shelby, one little stinger like that shotgun you got won't stop much."

The reporter looked genuinely surprised. "Really?

Scares the hell out of me."

"Proving you're from New York," Sam added. "My father would use a gun like yours to pepper my butt with rock salt when I crossed the line."

Shelby's eyes grew big. "Seriously?"

Sam shrugged. "Different part of the country. Different way of handling problems. We need to get you something with real stopping power."

"Did either of you hear what I said?" Kellen tried to force his way back into a conversation that had run off without him.

Sam shot him a look. "Either pony up and help or get out of the way." She turned back to Shelby. "I'll help you find your brother's killer, and your roommate's attacker... Could she identify the guy, assuming we had someone to show her?"

"No. She didn't get a look at his face. He had on some sort of mask."

"Why again did he attack her?"

"She's lucky she didn't sign for the package Jake sent me. She sent it on with the FedEx guy to me here. The guy still creased her skull pretty good."

Sam flinched. "Package? Why didn't you mention that before?"

"Things were a bit tense." Shelby's eyes shifted to gaze at her feet.

Sam wanted to believe her, but the gal was making it difficult to tell where prevarication ended and truth began. "And where is the package now?"

"Should be here tomorrow."

"What's in it?"

"Haven't a clue."

"But it's obviously something the bad guys want pretty badly." Sam pushed herself off the hangar siding, then perched on the arm of one of the empty chairs. "We need to intercept that package. Do you have the tracking number?"

Shelby nodded and then scrolled through her phone.

"Reroute it to Kellen." She turned to the commander. "Can you get some guys with guns and intercept the package?"

"That would be across the line for sure."

"Not what I asked."

He gave her a grin. "I know. Just making a point. Yeah, I can."

"Good." She waited while Kellen gave her his address and then started in again questioning Shelby. She wasn't sure whether she liked the girl or not, but she knew she didn't trust her. She was holding out. "Anything else you might have that could shed some light?"

"Jake put me onto Senator Herrera." She held up a hand to stop Sam from riding to his defense. "He could be one of the white hats. I don't know. All I do know is I tailed his Chief of Staff, Grady O'Dell, to a meeting with Ferrell Bishop on the QT out in La Porte." She fished in her bag, pulling out a couple of photocopies. "Then this guy in a black Dodge...curious coincidence, don't you think...shows up and picks O'Dell up after the meet?" She handed the papers to Sam. "Don't worry about checking the plates, even though you'll do it anyway. They aren't on file anywhere. I do have some photos of the tire treads. Maybe they'll give us a connection." She asked for Sam's cell number as she worked through the files on her phone. "There. They should be in your inbox."

Sam read the numbers and letters. She knew them. Same Dodge that had caused them so much trouble today. "How does this factor into your conspiracy theory?"

"Not sure. Like I said, I got pieces but still can't see the whole puzzle." Shelby eyed one of the chairs but, instead of sitting, she stepped in front of Sam and Kellen, pacing like a lawyer delivering a summation. "You know the legislation banning drilling in the northern slope of Alaska? Senator Stevens was a huge proponent to opening those fields up. He died in a plane crash. Your Senator Herrera was instrumental in opening the area where you father hit his strike. He's now dead."

"Lot of time between," Sam said. "Could be a coincidence."

"True. But I'd recently come across some information about a group of men, all incredibly well placed, all of them in the fossil fuel industry. I'm talking heads of major corporations here. Together they control a significant percentage of the world's oil production."

"How significant?"

"Enough to want to protect."

That caught Sam off guard. From the look on his face, Kellen, too. "Protect?" Sam asked. "How so?"

"Look at it this way—up until recently, OPEC carried the big stick. Then Russia got their production back up. The Chinese became a huge player in the world market. Iran is about to come back online. And, with the burgeoning shale play here in the states—"

"The new supply eroded their power base." Patrick Donovan had been crowing about that possibility for years. Sam guessed he hadn't been fully appreciative of the downside.

"They've shut down production of the north slope stuff. The huge reserves off coastal California will never be exploited, if these guys have their way. They've taken out two senators who have dared to cross them."

"And an oilman," Sam added. Kellen reached over and squeezed her hand. "But the price of oil is really low right now, and falling. Doesn't that blow a hole in your theory?"

"No. Keeping reserves from being exploited is only half their game." Shelby took a deep breath and let it out slowly in ragged hiccups. "Right now, they're working at driving out their largest threat."

"What's that?"

"Shale. With the new technology and drilling techniques, a huge amount of previously unreachable oil is now exploitable. But the costs are high."

"And shale is a small oilman's play." Shelby kept pacing, pausing only to make a point. "So you keep the price low, below that threshold, you don't have to do it long to drive the guys to the sidelines. None of them have deep pockets."

"You got it. Right now, the shale industry is in free-fall. Houston is feeling the repercussions—the layoffs have only just started. It'll ripple through the whole economy here."

"And shale will be dead."

"Can you prove any of this?" Kellen injected himself into the conversation.

"Not yet, but I'm obviously making them nervous." Shelby sagged into the chair next to Sam's.

Kellen sipped his beer and stared out over the lights of the airfield.

Sam knew what he was thinking: He loved to fly—there was escape in the wild blue yonder. "Up there it's like none of this exists," she said to him and was rewarded with a slight shocked look then a hint of a smile, or half of one anyway. "They took out my father. That's a departure from two senators and a computer guy. We can assume they all had a hint of the game and the players and had outlived their usefulness, or were being proactive in taking the game down. But why my father?"

"You said yourself, he's sitting on a sea of oil," Kellen said. "If that came on the market...."

"I understand that." Sam snapped. "But there are other large reservoirs—we've named a few—and, to my knowledge, nobody's been killed to keep it off the market. Up to now, these guys have been much more subtle, only resorting to killing when someone forced their hand."

"Maybe he knew more than he should?" Shelby asked.

"Doubtful. He had a nose for oil, but not for much else. I can't imagine my father had that kind of information."

"But clearly Phil Herrera did," Kellen reminded her.

Sam thought back to her father's words. "Yes, and he'd told my father enough to scare him, so maybe they acted fast. But that raises another question: why not just kill Herrera? And why leave your assassin dead on the senator's boat with his head blown out?"

"So what are you saying?" Shelby's voice was sharp, betraying her interest.

"I don't know, just that it doesn't feel right. Something else is going on." She looked around the small group, their eyes wide in the subtle light from the single bulb hanging by the hangar door. "Something that got my father killed." Her gaze lasered Shelby. "What else do you have?"

"Jake sent me a few emails from a secure account."

"Anybody could've hacked that," Sam said. "If what you say is true, these guys are pretty sophisticated."

"He knew that. When we were kids, he devised this rather elaborate code that we used to communicate when we didn't want our parents to know what we were planning."

"A kid's code?" Sam didn't try to hide her doubt.

"The NSA was no match for a ten-year-old Jake Walker—trust me on that one. It was a good thing he was only ten at the time. But an uncrackable code begins with a key, a basis that only the parties communicating know. Think the Enigma machine in World War II. The Brits didn't crack the code until they intercepted enough messages to figure out how they changed the basis of the code each day. Then they had it. Jake and I had a favorite book. We never mentioned the book in any messages, but we both knew it. The code is built on that book."

"What did he tell you?" Sam resented having to keep pumping the woman for information. And she couldn't shake the niggling feeling they were missing something.

"Houston. Senator Herrera. And Drayton Lewis."

"So back to Lewis. How did he get on Jake's radar?"

"Lewis's personal assistant, Becca Molinari."

"Your source who's gone missing?"

"She and Jake went to MIT together. She brought this whole thing to him."

"What whole thing?"

"Not sure of all the details. Jake did say Lewis entered the market, shorting stock right before every major natural disaster in the oil sector. He made a fortune jumping in, letting the market overreact to the bad news, then cashing out."

"Makes these things seem intentional rather than accidental." Kellen voiced the obvious.

"And I can't prove a lick of it." Shelby slumped back in her chair. "Not without Jake." Her voice hitched and she swiped at her eyes.

"What exactly did Jake do?"

"He was the senior security analyst for the New York Mercantile Exchange."

Kellen whistled softly. "He would be in a position to track these guys."

"Yep. And I wouldn't bet against him. There was a weird thing, though, he told me something about a trip to Oklahoma and some operation in Conroe. He was too oblique for me to make sense of it." She looked between Kellen and Sam. "Any ideas?"

"These places have to do with the oil business?" Sam searched through remembered snippets of conversation with her father.

"That would be a good guess."

"Well, there's a place in Oklahoma, a huge storage farm for oil. I remember my father watching those numbers carefully. The inventory numbers are regularly reported to the exchange—traders key off them."

Shelby pulled a notebook out of her purse and started scribbling. "Now we're getting somewhere."

"I don't have to remind you, this is all conjecture," Kellen said. "It all could be coincidence."

Shelby looked up, the expression on her face murderous. "There is no such thing as coincidence. Anything you know about Conroe?"

"A few years back a bunch of the smaller to midsized oil companies, and even some of the large ones based here, pulled their IT departments out of their offices. They set up this huge data clearinghouse." Sam paused. "Any guess where it might be?"

"Conroe," Kellen and Shelby said in unison.

"Man, I really need Jake." Shelby collapsed back in the chair, the murderous look replaced by sadness.

Sam envied the ease and warmth with which Shelby spoke of her brother. There wasn't anything easy about her own family, and the only real warmth came from the heat of battle. Well, that was true when it came to her father, but her mother was a different story. Her mother! The thought bolted Sam off the bench. "I've got to talk to my mother."

CHAPTER THIRTY-TWO

The men moved in the dark, what noise they made hidden in the whistle of the wind as it raced through the rigging on the platform. Lewis had been clear—time was running short. With the tropical storm expected to strengthen into a hurricane and the evacuation order, the crews worked double shifts pumping cement, trying to set the last run of pipe and then cap the well before the storm hit. The crews hurried, cut corners—it would be a disaster either way. The only chance they had of averting it would be to set the pipe, cap it, and hope like hell the blow-out preventer would save them if they'd underestimated.

Which they had.

Lewis's men had seen to that. Numbers fudged. Rechecks not done. Mud, too light.

The pressures were building to the point of no return. This would be even more devastating than the BP disaster. And curiously, but in a stroke of luck the man wasn't going to question, the man himself, Patrick Donovan, hadn't been around. With so much riding on this well, and being a hands-on kind of owner, Donovan would normally be sticking his nose into every aspect of the operation—especially at this critical a juncture. Briefly, the man wondered why he wasn't around, but, then again, he wasn't the sort to question good luck. It wouldn't take much to alter the mud mixing in the tanks. His job was keeping the mud the right consistency, making sure it flowed properly, and then catching it and cleaning it as it came back out of the hole. So no one paid any attention as he opened the lids on the mud tanks. He had it rigged so that he could pour the chemical, the second component to a binary explosive, in a separate bin. The first was already mixed into the mud. When he got the go-ahead, he'd come back to open the bin. Then the chemical would mix with the mud...and that would be that—no stopping it after that. He didn't want to think about the ensuing explosion. An hour or less for the binary components to mix thoroughly and then blow the pipe. And nature would take its course. Another disaster to equal Deepwater Horizon.

He didn't want to think about the consequences, so he didn't. Instead, he thought about the money Drayton Lewis had deposited in an offshore account in his name. Mr. Lewis would give him the access code once the rig blew, and he'd be sitting pretty on some island or something where nobody could find him.

The cement was already running light—he'd made sure of that. Too light and it wouldn't be enough to set the pipe against the pressures of the well, which were off the charts—it wouldn't harden. They'd already lost a lot of mud to the reservoir.

The whole scenario was setting up nicely.

One last thing to do.

Leaning back against the wall, the man took a moment to breathe and then he peeked around the corner. Everyone worked in and out of the checkerboard of shadow and light. Keeping close to the wall, hidden in a shadow, the man inched toward the control room. When anyone glanced in his direction, he'd pause, holding his breath as he pressed back against the metal, cold and dank even through his jacket.

Finally, he reached the control room. Snaking a hand out, he tried the handle.

Locked.

But he'd come prepared.

Pulling a set of picks out of his pocket, he fingered through them by memory, selecting the right one. Then he bent over the lock. Normally, he'd need no more than fifteen seconds, twenty at most, but in the dark and wind he fumbled.

As the lock gave and the handle turned, he eased himself inside. He'd practiced this a million times in his head, so no lights, just by feel and by memory. He could do this.

The blow-out preventer control panel was on the main grid.

CHAPTER THIRTY-THREE

Kellen loaded Shelby into a cab bound for the St. Regis. Sam went to work buttoning-up the hangar. Letting Shelby Walker out of their sight didn't sit well, but, short of kidnapping, there wasn't much they could do...except keep looking over their shoulders.

Sam had locked the office and come back down. Kellen joined her as she surveyed the hangar. She'd never really had to think about intruders before. Of course, with field security on high alert, anything she did was probably overkill, but it made her feel better—like there was actually something she could do that would make a difference. "Did you actually see the guy in the Dodge shoot at us?"

"It all happened pretty fast. The black Dodge racing alongside, the window lowering, the back window exploding. Shelby crowding us from behind." He let out a short huff as he rubbed his eyes. "You know what? I can't say that I did."

"Me, either. I caught a glimpse of him. But, if asked, I couldn't swear he had a gun."

"Shelby swore he did."

Sam chewed on her lip as she looked at him with hard eyes. "How'd she know?"

"Good question." Kellen looked a bit put-out with himself. "I should've—"

"Being shot at sorta changes expectations. Cut yourself some slack. You're not Superman."

"And I thought I had you fooled."

Sam bit back a grin. "Almost. I was damn impressed you knew she had only two shots. How could you have been so sure?"

"I saw the truck in the M.E.'s parking lot. The gun was in the back window. 12 gauge over and under, Benelli fancy. She's at least got good taste in guns. I've seen that sucker in the shop for no less than four grand."

"Good call. Do you trust her?"

Kellen made a disparaging noise.

"Yeah, me neither."

"You're not serious about going alone to your father's office, are you?"

"Hell, yes." Sam disappeared into the dark depths of the hangar. "Word of my father's death hasn't gotten out, at least not in a big way, but I need to act fast. But first my mother's."

"How do you know your father's death isn't all over the airwaves?"

"No one's come sniffing around here. My phone isn't ringing off the hook—it's not like I'm hard to find."

"Okay, but I'm sure the natives are whispering."

Sam darted in and out of the shadows. Finally, he stopped following her, choosing a spot in the idle of the hangar where he could watch her as she eased between planes, her hand trailing across the skin of each machine as if taking its temperature, checking for signs of illness. They hadn't turned on many lights, preferring the cloak of the stars hanging high above.

Sensing Kellen was staying within earshot, Sam kept talking as she flipped on lights. The halogens high above sputtered and spit, then eased to life in a soft glow that would brighten as the bulbs heated. Sam reappeared in front of him. "You've got to run the registration on the gun."

"You told me already."

"I know. Just going over things trying to stop the panic, you know?"

Sam moved toward the hangar door. "I get the feeling her brother was up to something—I'd like to know exactly what. But that fact alone makes her about as trustworthy as a wolf in a hen house."

"Agreed. And, for the record, you were right about needing the handgun to talk the cops back from the ledge. We're a good team, Mary Catherine."

Sam glanced at him over her shoulder. "I'd appreciate you keeping my given name to yourself. It's hard enough to get any respect in an industry where less than two percent of the commercial pilots are women."

"And Sam is a masculine, one-of-the-boys name?"

She angled her head, drinking him in with one long look. Sexy as hell in that flight suit that looked tailored to within a quarter inch of decency and that left not quite enough to the imagination to suit Sam. With him around, it was hard to think clearly. And, yet, being levelheaded was exactly what she needed to be. "It's a darn sight better than Mary Catherine, which I always thought sounded like a nun's name."

"I knew a Sister Mary Catherine once, mean as a rattler and tougher than an old boot."

"I really don't want to get you into trouble." Sam snagged the keys to her ride from her pocket.

"My choice, not yours. And if anything happened to you, that'd be far worse than being forcibly retired from the Coast Guard."

"Jail time?"

"That, too."

Kellen finished his beer and arced it toward the can. It missed, clattering on the concrete floor. Thankfully it didn't break. "You know how you could really impress me?"

"Who says I want to?"

He stepped in front of her, blocking her path as she rounded her desk. "If you got the shooter's plates, the one in the Dodge, I'll be really impressed."

He smelled of jet fuel and heat. Sam closed her eyes as she recited the license plate number. When she opened them, they were dark, unreadable.

Kellen whistled but didn't seem that surprised. "Any reason you didn't share that with the State Troopers?"

"You saw that kid, so young and tripping on power. Sending him after the shooter would be like sending Barney Fife after Al Capone. I couldn't live with myself when he turned up dead."

"That's weak—it's his job."

Sam cocked her head to one side and pursed her lips. "Just a gut feeling. If he shot at us, he didn't hit anything, and he was so close even with adrenaline redlining and shooting from a moving car, he should've hit something."

Kellen didn't argue. Sam couldn't tell whether he thought her foolish or if he agreed with her, not that it really mattered. "You can run the plates, can't you?"

"Sure." Kellen stepped closer. "I wonder if they'll come up a no-hit as Shelby said."

"Not taking that bet." Sam shifted from foot to foot. "And find out if her tire tracks match the ones that I mentioned seeing close to Uncle Phil's boat. Her truck was towed to the dealer, so we should be able to do so pretty easily. The State Police should have photos if not a mold."

"Got it. Anything else you want from me?"

"The gun." Sam's voice trailed off.

"Right, the gun. You said that already."

He stood close, too close. Raw, her emotions in turmoil, Sam did something she knew she'd regret later—she grabbed him by the front of his flight suit and pulled him toward her.

When her lips met his, she fell, drowning in the nearness of him, the touch of his skin. Never had she believed a kiss could be something she felt to her toes. She let the sensations wash over her, losing herself in him.

Kellen deepened the kiss.

For a moment, Sam was lost, then, with two hands to his chest, she shoved him away. "Shit!"

Kellen blinked as if he'd been in the dark and now stared into a bright light. "It wasn't that bad. In fact, I thought we were doing pretty darn good, for a first kiss and all."

Sam gave him a look. "My mother. We gotta go."

"How does she figure into this?" Kellen looked disoriented, like a man struggling for oxygen after being held under water too long.

"I've got to talk to my mother." Sam's voice held a hint of exaggerated patience. "Remember?"

"I thought your parents were divorced."

"They are. Have been for a long time. But when my dad gets his ass in a crack, he runs home to Mom. I need to get to her before anyone else does."

"Okay." Kellen seemed to be catching up, reentering the present. "Truck's around the side."

Sam shared his struggle. One kiss! Holy damn! "I know that. But, Coastie, you're not going." He started to argue. She put a hand to the middle of his chest, swallowing hard at the connection that bolted through her. "After I talk to my mother, I'm going to do a little breaking and entering. I've got to see what my father is hiding. His office is a good place to start."

"I'm not letting you go there by yourself," Kellen said, then softened his tone. "Look, I know you want me to bird-dog our N.Y. friend later, get the FedEx package, but I'm not comfortable with you going alone. Your father's death wasn't an accident. I'll be your wingman."

"And pull her gun registration and run those plates and check the tire prints. And figure out a window in this weather—I have got to get out to my father's rig."

He opened his mouth, ready to argue.

"Help with the door?" She motioned to the hangar door that hung in panels to the sides of the large opening. "It's going to be rusty."

She was right. Kellen mopped at the sweat beading on his forehead after they wrestled the door closed. "I don't want you going alone."

Sam put three fingers to his lips, shutting him down. "I'm not." She reached for the Glock she'd stuck in her pocket. "And I might have to bend a few laws. Not good for a commander's career path."

"Only if we get caught."

"So not happening, flyboy. Deal with it."

"Let me come, and I'll tell you who I think is driving that black Dodge."

CHAPTER THIRTY-FOUR

Shelby waited until the cab had cleared the gate at Ellington Field and left the lights of the Coast Guard Station well behind. Leaning over the front seat, she plucked an earbud out of the driver's ear. "There's been a change of plans."

Brid Donovan struggled with two bags of groceries, shifting one as she dug in her purse for her keys. The garage light hadn't come on when she'd pulled in, and now that the door was shut it was darker than blazes. She made a mental note to change the bulb this weekend. Patrick had bought her some not too long ago; at least she thought he had. He always put them in the cabinet over the washer and dryer. Making sure the door was latched, she locked it as Patrick had convinced her to do. Tonight that was a bit more hassle than comfort.

On the verge of dropping her groceries—one bag had slid halfway down her leg—Brid found her keys in the bottom of her purse, stuffed into the corner. Wasn't that always the case? She shook her head and smiled, her thoughts resting pleasantly on her ex-husband. He'd been coming around more often, which was nice. She'd always found his presence fun and comforting in a way she'd never found with anyone else. The man she wanted was one who couldn't be had. While her head knew that, her heart never gave up hope.

A flicker of worry crinkled her brows into a frown, something unusual for Brid Donovan. The last time she'd seen Patrick...she thought back...when was that? Two days ago? Three? He hadn't been himself. Oh, he'd put on the big load of malarkey he was known for, but she knew him better than she knew her own shadow. He'd gotten himself into something; she could feel it. She'd pressed him, but still he'd put her off. It was best she not know, he'd said. That made her more afraid than watching the news ever could.

Grabbing the bag on her knee as it slipped, she laughed at herself. *You're going daft, old woman.* With one elbow, she pushed the door open and stepped through, kicking it shut behind her. Shadows filled the house. In the half-light she stepped to the kitchen, depositing the sacks on the butcher-block island. Taking a moment, she balanced them, making sure they wouldn't tumble fruit all over the floor. That would be all she needed. Her body ached; she'd been on her feet all day running. The emergency room kept her hopping. She loved the work, but her body paid the price.

And Phil Herrera had gone missing. Above the mayhem in the ER, that had been all the buzz. She couldn't imagine who would do that to Phil. A good man, he was. If Patrick were here, she'd have a strong toddy, a hug, and a good cry. But he wasn't, so she'd have to settle for a long hot bath and some comfortable slippers for her aching feet.

The hug would have to wait, but her nerves still jangled a bit.

Sam. Brid felt the immediate, overwhelming need to call her daughter. If her daughter was okay, then life would settle out.

She'd left her phone on her nightstand this morning.

As she bent down to shuck one shoe, a noise in the front of the house stopped her. Cocking her head, holding her breath, she listened for it again. Silence. She waited. Nothing. Shaking her head, she grabbed one shoe, then switched feet and shucked the other shoe. Years ago, she could breeze through a day then dance half the night away. Not anymore. Her feet hurt; her legs were swollen. Age was tapping at her shoulder, trying to get her attention, but she'd ignore it just a wee bit more. Perhaps it might leave her be.

Enjoying the cool, in sharp contrast to the blistering heat of the Texas summer, she left the lights off, using memory and filtered light to navigate toward her bedroom on the far side of the house. Halfway down the hallway, she sensed movement. Turning, she wasn't fast enough. She gasped. A scream caught in her throat. A hand clapped over her mouth. He grabbed her arm, pulling her to the floor.

CHAPTER THIRTY-FIVE

The offices of Donovan Oil were dark and locked up tight when Grady O'Dell let himself in through a window off the back alley. A little flypaper on the pane to catch the broken glass; an elbow delivered with just enough force, and, voila, he was inside. In casing the joint day before yesterday, Grady had been surprised to find no security system. In this part of Houston just south of the downtown, they'd steal the paint off the walls if they could. Once he was inside, though, he understood there was nothing of any value, at least to the common thief. But Grady was no common thief. He was a lawyer. And he knew what he was looking for.

With a thumb, he flicked on the Maglite but kept it pointed barely in front of his feet. The office fronted a busy street, and lights flashing around inside would attract the attention of the police, who regularly patrolled this neighborhood at the border of inner city and urban gentrification. Grady needed to hurry. He couldn't be the only one who knew that Patrick Donovan was the only person who should be there, and Donovan wasn't coming. His own daughter had identified his body. The M.E. had signed off on the death certificate.

With the word leaking out, Grady didn't have much time.

The light flickered over the office, touching various

surfaces. Donovan wasn't the most organized guy. Papers scattered over the desk, cascading to the floor. Grady fingered through them. Another time they might be interesting, but they weren't what he was looking for.

A photo, laid over on its face, caught his attention. A woman. Red hair. Challenge in her eyes. A shy smile. Wicked cute. Donovan's daughter. She looked like she'd be fun. Another time, perhaps. He tried the desk drawers. Locked. He pulled a small black case out of his shirt pocket and selected the right pick. The lock opened in less than a minute, which didn't make him happy. He was rusty.

Holding the flashlight in his teeth, he fingered through the files. All old stuff. Nothing that could have Bishop in such a lather.

Something was going down. Something Bishop didn't want known. And that was just the kind of information Grady O'Dell liked to have. A born horse-trader, Grady had a knack for finding the stuff folks would kill to keep quiet...and that someone else would pay serious green for. He searched behind the paintings—faded oils of a faded history. No safe. Pulling a knife from his pocket, he flipped it open and headed for the leather sofa.

The muzzle of a gun pressed against his ribs. A voice sounded in his ear. "I wouldn't do that."

Grady lifted his hands high, dropping the knife. The person behind him reached back and flipped on the desk light.

Grady got a look at his reflection in the window glass. "What the hell?"

CHAPTER THIRTY-SIX

"So, how was the 76-D?" Kellen asked Sam after he had settled her in the passenger seat of his truck and he'd slid behind the wheel. In the end, he'd won the argument. To be honest, he thought Sam had relented a bit too easily. She was scared, and sad.

Sam's voice turned wistful. "Better than sex." Riding in the passenger seat, she angled toward him. Wilder had talked her out of her keys. Reeling from emotional overload, she was glad he had. The memory of their kiss still both delighted and horrified her. What had she been thinking? "Look, I was out of line back there. I'm sorry."

Kellen kept his eyes on the road. "I'm not. You can use me to let off some steam anytime."

Sam drew up, indignation straightening her spine. "I was not..." At his grin, she relaxed. It was like the man knew what she was thinking, what she was feeling, better than she did.

"If that copter was better than sex, you've been sleeping with the wrong guys." Kellen gave her a look that warmed her in places she'd thought dead. "But I know what you mean."

He was right. She secretly referred to her last romantic partner as Earnhardt—he thought speed was a trait to be admired. The guy was over and done before she'd even wrapped her brain around where he was going. One trip around the track and she'd sent him on his way. How long ago had that been? A while. It wasn't that she didn't have plenty of opportunities to date. Any night she could have her pick—one of the perks of playing in the boys' sandbox for a living. But most of the guys were just looking for some fun. They didn't understand that for a woman it wasn't fun unless one had some skin in the game, so to speak. And that meant one had to be open to hurt. Not a place Sam wanted to visit again. For now, flying would have to suffice. She was safe there. "That copter would make my life sweet."

"Then what's stopping you?" Kellen had negotiated through the security enclosure and headed for the highway. "I'm assuming we're heading into Houston?"

Sam nodded. "Oh, I can think of eleven million reasons why I can't park the Sikorsky in my hangar."

Kellen gave a low whistle. "Well, if anybody can crack that nut, a Donovan can. Don't you have a big contract or something you're working?"

The lights of Houston cast a dome of light in front of them, which bounced off a low-hanging cloud layer. "Yeah, San Rafael Oil. I'm a small fish compared to their usual haulers. Bishop, the CEO, practically offered to finance a new chopper if I'd take the deal."

"Sweet." Kellen glanced at her. "Why am I sensing you aren't that enthusiastic?"

"I don't know. It'd be a dream. But—and maybe it's listening to my father all these years—I just can't see the business reason behind Bishop pushing this so hard. He's got loads of other operators already in debt to their eyeballs who would love to get even a small portion of the business he's trying to throw my way. I'm new. I'm small. I'm a girl. It just doesn't pass the smell test. And now he turns up meeting with the chief of staff of a recently disappeared senator who has ties to my father? The whole thing is starting to stink like week-old fish."

"I can see that. Sometimes we've got to go with our gut."

The fact that the Coastie seemed to so get her made Sam

uncomfortable. Better to keep him at a safe distance, but that wasn't what her gut was telling her to do. "You don't really know who is driving that black Dodge, do you? That was just to weaken me so I would bend to your wishes, right?"

"Please, I have my standards. And lying to a woman to coerce her into doing my will would undermine every one."

Sam sat up straighter. "You do know?"

"I can't prove it, you understand, but everything points to the Feds."

Sam let that percolate through her overwrought brain. Made sense. "Agent Davis?"

"Or one of his minions. The other night when he so rudely interrupted our Thai dinner—"

"—and you followed him out into the rain," Sam interrupted.

"Yeah. He was driving a low-slung black sports car with tinted windows. Could've been a Dodge, but I didn't look that closely. To be honest, this is the sort of squirrely deal, riding the edge of acceptability, that Davis loves to run."

"Where folks are just collateral damage."

Kellen squeezed Sam's hand that was resting on the seat between them. He didn't let go.

"I wonder what he's running this time," Kellen said.

"And which team he's playing for."

With too many questions and no real answers, silence stretched between them. Twenty minutes put them in the heart of the city. To Sam, those twenty minutes had flashed by in thoughts of her father. He'd liked Wilder. She had to admit, even if only to herself, Kellen Wilder filled the empty silence in the corners of her life in such unexpected ways. Whether that was a good thing or not, she hadn't a clue, but she liked it. And she hoped like hell she wouldn't hurt him.

Sam directed Kellen into Montrose, a bohemian, artsy part of Houston that Sam always thought gave the flat, uninspired city its soul. The streets narrow, the lighting subtle, the trees tall, Montrose was the comfortable overstuffed armchair in a sea of cool contemporary. With small houses, some residences, some restaurants, bookstores, or beauty parlors, the neighborhood would be labeled by many as eclectic. Once predominately traditional families, now it was home to the non-traditional—single-gender households, cohabiting couples, single-parent families, mixed racial couples. Humanity in all of its perfect imperfection. Sam loved it just as her mother did. "This is it."

"Your mother chose an interesting neighborhood."

"Interesting? My mother loves to take in strays—this is the perfect place for that. She's a rescuer. My father is a case in point. It's her one fault and yet her saving grace."

Kellen cut the engine. "You make no sense, and yet you do."

"It's a curse." Sam nodded, her lips a thin line, anger in her eyes. "Are you sure you're up to barging in on the family?"

Kellen opened the door and slid out. "I know this is a difficult time."

"Right." Sam couldn't detect even a hint of light from inside the house. Her mother should be home by now. "You can leave me here."

"I'll see you inside."

The house was a craftsman, restored until it sparkled. A porch with the obligatory swing graced the front—although given the swamp Houston was built in and its mosquito population, the swing was merely an adornment with no functional usage save perhaps two weeks in the spring and another two in the fall. A large door, painted red, beckoned. The bay window invited, though the interior was dim at this time of day, darkness beginning to lay claim to the land. Day was fading into the obscurity of twilight in a humid climate where everything turned gray as the sun sank toward the horizon. If her mother was home, then she'd not turned on any lights other than the two lamps in the front room, which she always left on—not even the kitchen light in the back.

Without knocking, Sam unlocked the front door with a key on her ring, then eased the door open. The front room was a jumble of mismatched, overstuffed chairs, filling space around a bright red sofa and a neon yellow chair-and-a-half with a green ottoman. The artwork was amateurish but bright, the wallpaper a faded purple and gold. From each of two end tables bracketing the sofa, a Tiffany lamp radiated a kaleidoscope of light.

Kellen whistled low. "This explains a lot."

Sam elbowed him in the stomach and he let out a rush of air, grimacing as he clutched his side. "You're stronger than you realize."

"I realize." Sam threaded the narrow path through the furniture. She didn't announce their presence and was glad Kellen followed her lead and hung back just a little.

Sam stopped, extending a hand behind her as a signal to stop. "Something's wrong," she whispered.

CHAPTER THIRTY-SEVEN

Thirty floors above the ground, Drayton Lewis paced in front of the window—a tiger with a pane of glass separating him from his prey. He loved watching night creep over the land, the shadows swallowing the city features, smothering them in darkness. Pausing, hands clasped behind his back, he half-turned so he could see where Becca Molinari used to sit.

Becca. She had been such a disappointment. He'd thought she would be a more worthy opponent, but, like the ones who had come before her, she proved wanting. His dick swelled at the memory, the look on her face as his fingers tightened around her throat. That moment when realization dawned. This wasn't a game.

Taking a chair by the window, Lewis popped open his laptop. Toggling through drop-down menus, he stopped periodically to watch a video clip or read a keystroke log. When he'd finished out the offices, he'd had cameras tucked into every spot that could conceivably hide one. Always best to know what the staff does while he wasn't there—while the cat's away and all of that. His father had taught him that. Of course, it had been him the old man had caught. And the old man hadn't wanted to blow his brains out; he'd taken some convincing.

Becca. He had wondered if she'd beg.

The videos proved his suspicion, but the record of all her phone calls proved the most enlightening. A New York number. A few minutes and the computer gave him a name: Shelby Walker. Jake Walker's sister.

On another screen, he watched the GPS tracker record of her movements. "Oh, Becca. You've been a very bad girl."

CHAPTER THIRTY-EIGHT

Grady O'Dell was afraid to breathe. A bead of sweat trickled into his eye. He blinked against the sting, but didn't move to wipe it away. The air in Donovan's office was dank with the stink of fear. An angry female was worse than a rattler disturbed from sleep. And this one had her gun stuck in his side. She looked pissed off enough to pull the trigger, hence the no breathing thing.

"What the fuck are you doing here?" the woman asked. She patted him down. Not finding anything, she released him and stepped back. "Turn around. Don't do anything stupid. Keep your hands where I can see them."

"A hackneyed phrase if there ever was one. You write for television?" Grady did as she asked, keeping his hands raised, the palms open. The gal's New York accent and her awkward double-fisted hold on the gun told him she was no pro, but she looked nervous enough to pull the trigger whether she meant to or not.

"Cute," she said. She narrowed her eyes. "What's the chief of staff for a missing senator doing in the office of a dead oil man? Now *that* would make good TV, don't you think?"

A smart one. Grady realized he had underestimated. "I could ask you the same thing."

She raised the shotgun until it pointed at his chest.

"They say go for a center-mass shot, right? What are the rules here? The girl with the gun gets to ask the questions?"

Grady moved, a slight step toward her.

In a quick move, she adjusted her aim lower and pulled the trigger. The tight cluster just missed his left foot, although he felt the sting of a few random pellets. It kicked up a frayed tuft of old carpet, exposing the rotting pad underneath.

An over and under, the gun held two shots. She'd taken one. Grady didn't move.

"Shit!" Grady froze, the report echoing in his head. Maybe someone would hear? A flare of hope, then he realized in this part of town, no one would call in gunfire.

"Make like a statue, big guy."

He did as she said.

"This doesn't look so good for you. Your boss disappears. Now a little bit of B and E. Makes you suspicious as hell."

Grady fault her logic. "Agreed."

The barrel again pointed at his chest, and she raised an eyebrow and cocked her head. "Give it up."

"I'm looking for some files." Out of ideas at the moment, it seemed like a good idea to play along. "How do you know who I am?"

"With your boss missing, your mug is on every local channel at four, six, and ten. But I also know you're hiding a few secrets, Grady O'Dell, also known as O'Dell Washburn."

"Note to self: bury you past a bit deeper."

"Don't be disappointed. I'm good, and I'm motivated. Somebody killed my brother and attacked my roommate to get some information. I don't know who's pulling the strings, but you've moved to the top of the suspect list."

"What? Shit, no!"

"But you've shown rules don't mean much to you."

"Long time ago."

"But a hint as to character."

"Yes, but I can use it for the forces of good or evil."

"Now who's writing bad television?" She seemed to relax just a tiny bit, the merest hint. "Why did you meet with Farrell Bishop out in La Porte?"

"That came out of left field. "You tailed me?" She tilted her head, looking rather satisfied with herself.

"Pretty easy."

"I'm rusty." Grady tried to buy some time to think. How much did she know?

"Tell me what you two talked about."

"You tell me what you think we talked about, and I'll fill in the gaps."

She aimed the gun at his left knee. He could see her knuckle whiten as she took up the trigger slack. "Okay. Okay. He was looking for some information."

"There's this group of men. I don't know what they were up to. The senator was one of them. Bishop wanted names."

"So there really is a conspiracy."

He wasn't surprised that she'd sniffed that far down the trail. "I'm not sure. Only whispers of one as far as I can tell. I didn't find anything in the senator's office."

"Of course you didn't. I'm sure he felt the noose tightening. Why else would he go fishing? He was making a run for it."

"Agreed."

"Who was the guy in the black Dodge with fictitious plates?"

Grady made a mental note: she knew people who knew how to push the limits. "A guy I'm working with."

She twitched her finger on the trigger. "A guy in a black Dodge tailed me yesterday."

"A coincidence?"

"Which are as real as the Tooth Fairy. You wouldn't happen to have pinched some dental records, would you?"

Grady grimaced as a bead of sweat trickled down his brow. So much for calm, cool, and collected.

"What game are you playing? And who's running you? The guy in the Dodge?"

"How do you know someone is running me?" He knew her from somewhere. Television, maybe?

"You look too stupid to be playing in this crowd." She drew in a ragged breath. Grady could see all that she had been through was taking a toll.

They both jumped at the buzzing of her phone.

"You going to get that?" Grady asked.

Narrowing her eyes, she let loose of the gun with one hand and rooted in her pocket, keeping the gun leveled, a finger on the trigger, her hand clutching the gun at the balance point.

When her eyes flicked to the screen, Grady closed the distance between them with one stride. He slapped the gun to the side, then landed a left hook to the jaw. He caught her by surprise. She dropped where she stood.

Grabbing her purse, he dumped the contents on the floor next to her.

Shelby Walker, investigative reporter. A New York driver's license. A room key. He whistled. "St. Regis. Pretty pricey for a cub reporter."

Grady touched her jaw where he'd hit her. Red now, it would turn purple tomorrow. He checked her pulse—slow and steady. She'd come around soon. He straightened out her arm, which she'd fallen on, then pocketed her room key and the keys to her car.

With one last glance around, he turned out the light, locking the door as he left.

CHAPTER THIRTY-NINE

Senator Phillip Herrera prowled the edges of the platform. If he could just get his hands on the asshole who dumped him out here. His fingers probed the back of his skull where a tender goose egg bloomed. He couldn't remember much. One minute he was setting his fishing line; the next minute some guy came out of nowhere, jumped aboard...after that things got blurry. A shot. The guy's head exploded. He'd jumped off the flybridge, then lights out. At least they hadn't shot him. But, if he couldn't figure a way off this rusting hulk, he'd probably wish they had.

The place was a better holding cell than Alcatraz. And with the storm brewing...

The wind tugged and pushed at him, urging him to hurry. The storm the weather gurus had been threatening had started to ooze into the Gulf. The dark smudge to the south had turned into an increasing wall of black before the sun had gone down. Now the black blanket above blocked the stars. He needed to get off the rusting pile of abandoned dreams, and now. He calculated the distance to shore at well over ten miles, if not more. Nothing marred the smooth nothingness of all three hundred and sixty degrees of horizon. They could've dropped him on the surface of Mars for all he could tell.

After his third circumnavigation, he'd pulled together

everything he had and put it in a pile in the center of the platform. Sitting, legs crossed, he examined each article.

Not much. His cell phone, minus the SIM card. Some sandwiches and a dozen bottles of water, which told him either they'd be back fairly soon, or they wanted him to die slowly. A life vest. A waste bucket. Two twelve-inch sections of pipe two inches in diameter. He tucked one in the waistband of his pants at the small of his back, securing it with his belt tightened up a notch, then loosened the tail of his shirt to cover it.

Pulling the cooler next to an exterior wall of the small room he'd awakened in, he sat, bracing himself against the wall, stretching his legs in front of him. Earlier, gauging from the false light of the sun through the clouds, he'd guessed he was looking north from this position—north toward home. They would come from that direction...if they came at all.

He downed two bottles of water and then unwrapped a sandwich and ate, ravenous with a hunger food wouldn't satisfy.

And he settled in to wait, knowing that when he got off this bucket of bolts, he'd shoot that son-of-a-bitch Agent Presley Davis when he saw him.

CHAPTER FORTY

Sam Donovan dropped into a squat just inside the front door to her mother's house, motioning for Kellen behind her to do the same. Her voice hushed to a whisper. "Something's not right. Follow me." She pulled the Glock from its resting place. She didn't need to make sure a round nestled in the chamber—if she carried a gun, it was loaded and she was ready to use it, a lesson taught by an angry grizzly when she had to make an emergency landing on a sand bar next to a river in Alaska.

A hint of her mother's perfume fought with lingering scents of boiled cabbage and corned beef, welling memories, and panic. Silence surrounded them, the house hiding its secrets. Sam reached back and tugged on Kellen, then motioned with a nod. He followed her as she eased to the left, still crouched, her gun held in both hands in front of her. The muted glow of the city lights reflecting off a low cloud deck bathed the room just enough for Sam to see. The kitchen. The bag of groceries spilling from the butcher-block island, the oranges rolling on the floor, not like her mother, not like her at all.

Sam fought the urge to run through the house searching, calling. She thought she smelled fear...and blood. The fear could be her own—that thought slowed her down a bit, focusing her thoughts. She'd be no good to her mother if she couldn't think.

Her mother's purse was gone. Her keys, which she hung on a hook by the back door each time she came in, were missing. Sam motioned down the hallway.

Halfway to the bedroom she found the blood.

Her foot slid in the pool, the metallic tang telling her what it was before she tested it with her fingers. Still liquid but coagulating.

Kellen sat on his haunches next to her. "Somebody waited here. I don't think this is your mother's blood."

"Why?"

He pointed to the trail of drops on the other side of the pool. "See those? See how they have a tail pointing toward the back of the house? Whoever was bleeding came from there, then stopped here. And waited."

She didn't ask what for. She knew.

Her mother.

Sweat popped as Sam firmed her grip on the gun and advanced on the bedroom, careful to step around the blood trail. Kellen's breath came in short gasps behind her. Each day her mother drew the blinds before she left as protection from the heat of the day. They remained closed. Only fingers of fading light leaking around the edges pierced the almost Stygian darkness. Sam paused, listening. Silence answered. Circling her hand, Sam motioned for Kellen to ease around to the left. Sam took the right. They checked all the corners and closets, then met in front of the bathroom.

The bedroom was empty.

Sam stood and scanned the room again. "Pissed off and nobody to shoot."

"The bleeder came in here," Kellen said from the doorway leading to the back patio. "Broke out a pane. Looks like he cut himself on the glass."

A dark stain trickled from the jagged edge. He reached for his phone.

"What are you doing?"

"Calling it in."

"Don't—"
Lights arcing behind the house cut her off.
At the tone in her voice, Kellen stopped dialing.
"Someone's coming."

CHAPTER FORTY-ONE

Shelby awakened with a start, pushing herself up on her hands as she twisted her head around, expecting danger. Still Donovan Oil offices, but the room was empty.

He hadn't asked whose dental records. The lying son-of-a-bitch.

The thought was the last thing that had hit her before Grady O'Dell did. A ten-finger guy in the past, she was sure Grady O'Dell had the skill to steal whatever he wanted.

The twilight world around her swam. Her vision blurry, unfocused, she stayed on the floor. Pressing both hands to her head, bracing her elbows on her knees as she sat where she had fallen, Shelby tried to stop the spinning. Breath hissed in through her teeth when she touched the spot on her jaw.

Grady O'Dell was a dead man....when she found him.

And if Shelby Walker was good at anything, it was hunting down her man. With her head cradled in her hand, sitting there in the dark, Shelby thought back. When had she lost the upper hand? What had happened?

The phone. Someone had called.

Gingerly, with the world a bit more stable, Shelby looked around, careful to keep her motions slow. Her brain didn't need any more rattling. On the first scan, she didn't see her phone. Had O'Dell taken it?

Then she caught sight of it—under the desk nestled up against the trashcan. Easing to all fours, she crawled the five feet or so then sat with her back against the front of the desk. Oddly, the wood was cool, which felt good—like a cold compress, it brought her back. Working her jaw—it hurt like hell—she squinted at the numbers.

Becca? She hadn't left a message. Shelby called her back. Someone answered, but they didn't say anything. "Becca?"

Nothing.

Then a click.

The line went dead.

With his hands stuck in his pockets, Grady O'Dell strode through the dark streets and alleyways like a rat on familiar ground. He hadn't planned on hitting Shelby Walker. Of course, it wasn't the first time he'd hit a woman, but still he felt bad about it. He'd made it four blocks when the black Dodge eased to the curb next to him, keeping pace. The passenger side window, the one nearest him, rolled down.

Grady didn't look. He knew who it was. "So the boss man sent his trained dog."

With a hand on the steering wheel and an eye on the empty street in front of him, Agent Presley Davis leaned across the seat so he could see Grady. "No. The boss man came himself. Get in." He flipped the handle and pushed the door from the inside.

Grady weighed his options for a fraction of a second, then slipped inside the car. He didn't ask who Davis had found him. Tracking his phone most likely.

When they'd accelerated to a normal speed, Grady glanced at Agent Davis. He looked like forty miles of bad road. "I thought you said they made this car?"

"We changed the plates. In this state overladen with

testosterone, there are lots of black Dodge Chargers. They can look, but if they find this pearl, we'll be long gone. Things are heating up."

"You don't say." Grady rubbed his knuckles. They were sore where they had connected with Shelby Walker's jaw. He remembered the straightness of her posture, her chin jutting out like a challenge. She had moxie; he had to give her that. Even if she was a damned newshound.

"I'm taking it you didn't find anything?" Agent Davis asked.

Grady contemplated how much to tell him—the bad feeling he'd had the first time he'd met the uber-Fed had only increased with each meeting. "Donovan didn't have the files."

"Fuck." Davis pounded the steering wheel. "We've got to get that proof."

"Look," Grady said as he twisted to face the FBI agent, "I told you when I called I'd seen some info on some bad shit going down. I couldn't put it all together, but I had a feeling the senator was in up to his eyeballs."

"You were trying to do your civic duty, upstanding citizen that you are."

Grady didn't like his mocking tone, but he refused to take the bait. "Think what you will. I paid my debt. I've done what I can; now it's in your lap. Don't you guys specialize in skulking around in the dark?" Grady rued the day he agreed to help them. Cops were cops, the Feds even more so. All bully and bullshit in the name of truth and justice—the line between good and not-so-good very thin. "You got any idea where the senator is?" Grady popped the question, hoping for surprise.

"No." The agent's eyes flicked to him then back to the road.

Fuck. He knew it—the Fed was lying. Big mistake expecting the good guys to play straight. Everybody worked their own angle—Grady knew that better than most, but somehow this time he'd hoped it would be different. Discovering Senator Herrera, one of the white hats, was doubling down with the bad guys had rocked Grady. When idols fall... But now he wondered who was playing whom.

"We need those files," Agent Davis pressed. "The names of the players."

"Then I suggest you keep looking." When the agent slowed for the red light at Memorial, Grady popped the door and stepped out. He dashed around the back of the car then down the grade, disappearing into the park along the Bayou.

CHAPTER FORTY-TWO

Sam and Kellen bracketed the back door as the car pulled into the garage. Sam held the Glock steady, chest-high. Kellen had grabbed an andiron. Time slowed to a crawl, each second a drop of blood oozing from a deep wound.

The driver killed the engine. The occupants waited until the garage door closed before opening the doors.

"Easy there." Her mother's voice.

She was alive. Sam's fear thinned. But she'd kill whoever hurt her.

A groan. Male? Hard to tell.

Footfalls approaching the door.

Sam raised her gun, fingering the trigger to take up the slack.

Kellen raised his arm, the metal rod held high. Sam stopped breathing, but her lips curved into a smile.

The knob turned. The door opened.

A figure stepped through the opening.

Sam didn't lower the gun. "Hello, Da. I thought you might be showin' up here."

Patrick Donovan stepped through the door. Pale and thinner than a few days ago, he nursed an arm cradled in a sling.

"I knew it. You son-of-a-bitch." Sam shook her head.

"What have you done this time? Were you the one who bashed Halloran's head in? That was Halloran on the slab at the ME's office, wasn't it? I recognized the scars on his knees. Not much else to go on. You two always did look like brothers."

Donovan didn't deny it. He didn't look sorry either.

"You did it, didn't you, Paddy? You killed Halloran."

CHAPTER FORTY-THREE

Under the watchful eye of the front-desk clerk at the St. Regis, Shelby Walker rooted through her bag with a shaking hand for the key card to her room. "It's in here somewhere." She glanced up and then kept looking. Grady had taken her keys, which made her laugh. Her truck was at some dealership awaiting a couple of new front tires and release by the cops. She'd been lucky to lure a cab into the bowels south of downtown at this time of night, and she'd been lucky he hadn't run when he caught sight of his fare—a woman with a shotgun. But this was Texas. Open carry was the law, and folks seemed to roll with it.

"Do you need some ice for that bruise?" the clerk asked as if a woman with a black-and-blue jawline was an everyday occurrence. This being Texas, perhaps it was. "Should I notify the police?"

"That would be lovely." Shelby abandoned her search. "The ice, I mean. That would be lovely. No cops. I fell, no biggie."

"Of course." Tall, with an upright posture and an uptight attitude, the clerk's expression didn't change.

Afraid he'd see right through her, Shelby didn't meet his eyes as she kept looking for the key card. On the verge of losing it, she worked to appear normal, to hold it together, but she couldn't stop the shaking. It rocked through her, constant shivers making her jumpy and her movements jerky. *Where the hell is my key card?*

Tears threatened to spill. *Just a little longer, Shel. Hold it together. Oh, Jake...* She shut down that thought. Grady O'Dell hadn't struck her as a killer—more like a lightweight thief who ran when someone turned up the heat. But he knew something...

The damned key card must've fallen out in the scuffle at Donovan Oil. She thought she'd been very careful to get everything, to erase any hint of her having been there except for the hole in the carpet and subflooring. No way to fix that. Apparently, she hadn't been as thorough as she'd thought. And that could be a problem. "I can't seem to find my key." She tried to hide a swipe at a bold tear leaking down her cheek. "Could you make me another one, please?" Shelby dipped her head so she wouldn't have to look at him. If she did, she might reach across the desk grab the guy by his lapels and scream. His complete control highlighted her own lack that left her teetering on the brink. Maybe that's what pissed her off. Well, that and the look of sympathy in his eyes, and yet he said nothing. She showed him her driver's license, and he did as she asked. As she took it, she said, "Sometimes you gotta get involved. You gotta ask. Otherwise the bad guys win." Hurrying to the elevators before the flood of emotion broke through the dam of control, weakening by the moment, Shelby didn't hear his response. Carrying her shotgun, she brushed by a startled couple as they exited the elevator.

The suites at the St. Regis were everything they should be—Shelby's in particular. Once through the doorway, she dropped her purse on a nearby couch, laid the gun across the arms of a chair, and started shucking clothes on the way to the bathroom, propelled by an overwhelming desire to wash the dirt of the day away. The tears flowed freely; she didn't bother with wiping them away. They were tears of sadness for sure, but tears of anger, too. Her brother. So young, so full of potential. The emotions ambushed her; she couldn't hold it in any longer.

She turned the taps on the jetted tub to scald and rid

herself of the remaining items of clothing. That Coast Guard commander could show up to stick his mug into her business anytime—he wanted her with him when they tackled FedEx. She'd have to do an end-around somehow. No way would she share before she knew what she had.

Becca hadn't left a message. And she still wasn't answering her phone—other than that weird hang-up. Something had happened. Shelby could feel it in her bones. When they'd met, Becca had been scared. Oh, she'd tried to hide it, but Shelby could see the fear in the way she had constantly checked the surroundings, noted everyone who came near.

There was a lot of that going around. She herself was guilty. Her hands shook as she ran fingers through her hair, working the tangles loose. When she was busy, she was fine. But when the quiet closed around her, she heard Jake's muffled screams. Who else had they killed? Patrick Donovan? Senator Herrera? Who would be next?

Waiting for the bath to fill, she poured herself a stiff dose of whiskey from the bar and threw it back, reveling in the fiery path it traced. The second dose she sipped. Turning to head back to the bathroom, she spied a white rectangle on the buffet in the foyer.

Her key card. Not her new one—that she had made sure to secure in her purse.

This must be her old one. She hadn't remembered leaving it there. She must've put it down on her way out.

Odd. Of course, with...everything...she hadn't been herself lately.

Shelby grabbed her gun, opened the breach, then stuffed in two rounds. Snapping it closed, she took it with her, placing it next to the tub.

Drayton Lewis fingered the laptop. Jake Walker's laptop.

Becca had rerouted the package. He'd gotten that much out of her. He had intercepted it.

The FedEx clerk had feigned disinterest when he'd torn into the package right there on the counter. The laptop fired right up. Encrypted. Not that he was surprised. Jake was a security nerd, after all. The fact that he'd gotten the thing out of the NYMEX building despite being bird-dogged by the best in the business had surprised him, though. Jake had never impressed him as the resourceful type, but, then again, people often were not what they seemed. Lewis flexed his fingers, remembering Becca's pulse pounding under his fingers as he squeezed tighter and tighter. He lingered a moment in the memory as he adjusted his rising erection.

Shelby would know the cipher. Becca hadn't told him that. She hadn't had to.

"The St. Regis," he ordered when he'd settled himself in the back of the limo. The driver, his usual—a man who did what he was told and who saw nothing—nodded, his eyes resting on Lewis longer than normal as he stared at him in the rearview.

The St. Regis nestled on a discrete street just off of San Felipe in the Galleria area but inside the 610. A small property, it reeked of money and class, business deals worth billions, and euro-trash on a toot to see cowboys and shoot guns. Decorum was a Texas tradition, even if class was often overlooked, but this particular hotel had both. Drayton stepped through the door that the valet held for him. He graced the valet with a cool smile then strode through the double doors, taking a left past the registration desk to the elevators on the right as he ignored the attention his presence generated.

The staff nodded in recognition.

"Third floor, Mr. Lewis?" A bellman exiting the elevator with an empty luggage cart asked.

"Second."

The bellman hid any surprise behind an air of fastidious competence. He pressed the button for the second floor and then retreated.

Double doors at the end of the hallway opened into a foyer protecting the entrance to the suite.

Lewis let himself in with the key he'd found in Becca's purse.

Shelby, still flushed from a bath, appeared through the doorway from the bathroom, trailed by a billow of steam. Her hair turbaned in a towel, and wrapped in a terrycloth bathrobe several sizes too large and cinched tightly at the waist, she looked like a child. Red ringed her eyes, and spent emotion puffed her face. Her eyes held a haunted, hateful look. Lewis, standing in the middle of her suite, brought her up short. "What the hell are you doing here?"

"Ms. Walker. We meet again."

CHAPTER FORTY-FOUR

"You lied." Kellen threw the words at Sam.

Satisfied that her parents were alone, Sam eased her finger off the trigger and placed it at the ready along the side of the Glock. But she kept the pistol aimed at her father, holding him in the doorway, her mother behind.

"I'm sorry," Sam said to Kellen. "Standing there looking at that body, I was sure of two things. My father wasn't murdered, but he most likely was a murderer. I had to keep the cops off his tail until I found out the truth."

"You could have trusted me." Kellen didn't say more, but it was clear, although he might have understood, he hadn't forgiven.

Sam didn't blame him. "So, Paddy, let me hear it. Did you kill him?"

At the sight of his daughter training a gun at his heart, Patrick Donovan opened his arms wide—well, one arm anyway. A sling cradled the other, a heavy bandage around his forearm. He tried his patented grin on her. "Now, is that any way to treat your father, back from the dead?"

Sam kept the gun trained on him. "One squeeze, that's all it would take."

He dropped his arms and looked crestfallen. "As you always told me, not worth the jail time."

"But you're already dead." Sam caught the smile playing on her mother's lips as she waited behind her former husband. "No law against killing a dead man."

"Mutilating a corpse, maybe?" Kellen asked, leaning his andiron against the wall in the corner.

Donovan cringed. "You're supposed to be on my side," he said to Kellen.

"Because of a shared chromosome? Hardly. You've gotten yourself in quite a crack, Paddy. You better start talking and talking fast before your daughter perforates your hide because, for once, she can get away with it."

Sam lowered the gun, but she didn't put it away.

Patrick Donovan seized the opening, wrapping his daughter in a hug. "Mary Catherine. I can't tell you how glad I am to see you."

Sam didn't relax into him; instead, she kept her posture rigid, resisting. If Patrick Donovan sensed a weakness, a chink in the armor he could exploit, she'd never get the truth out of him. Caught in her father's arms, Sam let the hurt, the fear, fall away. But the anger remained. Working both hands to his chest, she pushed him away. He let her step back but kept her close with a hand on her shoulder.

Her father gave her a peck on the cheek, then eased past her. With a groan, he sank slowly into one of the chairs around a circular kitchen table.

Sam tucked the gun away and relieved her mother of several of the bags she was holding. "Where have you been?"

"Your father was bleeding from various perforations," Brid said as she fussed over him. "Not that that bothered me, mind you. But he was making a bit of a mess, what with the gunshot in his shoulder and then the shredding he did to his arm breaking the back window." She waggled a finger at her former husband. "You'll be puttin' that right, Patrick Donovan."

Sam's parents always staggered her—people were dying, and they were arguing about a window. Then the words caught up. "Wait. Gunshot?"

Patrick motioned for everyone to join him around the table.

"You're harboring a fugitive," Sam said as an aside to her mother as they all chose a chair. A tall woman, with porcelain skin dotted with freckles and bright red hair she wore swept up in a loose knot, Brid Donovan gave her only child a knowing smile. "Aye, but I knew that before I married the man."

Sam's brow creased. "Do I know that story?"

"There's a lot you don't know," Patrick said as he settled in for a story. "Take a seat, girl. You too, Commander. Good to see you again, by the by. You two look like you've seen a few ghosts today. I'm thinking my wallet washed up somewhere and they called you, Mary Catherine."

"Your wallet, in the front pocket of a jacket worn by Johnny Halloran. Clever switch by the way."

"I'm sorry you had to see that. Clever girl, you are. What made you think it wasn't me?"

"The knees."

Paddy shrugged. "I figured you'd know it wasn't me." His hand shook as he motioned to the open bottle of Tullamore Dew in the middle of the table. "Pour me a snort of the good stuff, would ya'?"

Sam took a seat and motioned to her mother for two glasses, then did as he asked, meting out a healthy dose for each of them. Her mother and father accepted theirs. Kellen shook his head. She pushed a glass toward him. "It's bad luck to turn down whiskey from an Irishman."

Normally the offer of whiskey on an empty stomach would've gotten her a lecture from the buttoned-up Coastie, but not today, which made Sam smile. She, on the other hand, had no such high moral ground. Whiskey, an Irish breakfast tradition. "You think you're so smart, don't you?"

Paddy's grin faded at her tone.

"With you out of the way, they came after me." Sam leaned forward, her hand capturing his bandaged arm.

He winced, even though she applied only light pressure.

"What's with your find out there, Da? Why are all the sharks circling? What do you have?"

Paddy threw back a quick hit of Dew, then refilled his glass. The flush in his cheeks told Sam this drink wasn't her father's first and, knowing him, doubtful his last. "Spill it, Da. There's a man dead on a slab in the Galveston County Coroner's office, and everybody thinks he's you."

Patrick's blue eyes shifted to his daughter's. "Did ya' tell 'em different?"

"No."

"I knew there was something weird at the morgue," Kellen said.

Sam ignored him.

Relief flooded across her father's face. "For that, I'd be grateful."

"You'll be grateful for a lot more before I've finished with ya'." A hint of her heritage crept in when Sam was angry. "How did Johnny Halloran wind up dead? You've been swearing on every Bible this side of the border that you'd kill him the next time you saw him. Did you?"

Donovan gave his daughter a look, leaving out the other two at the table.

Sam's eyes widened. "You did."

"Self-defense, and it wasn't me rightly. He came poking in the operations room, shot me in the shoulder." He gently touched the part above his heart. "Benji creased his skull with a length of pipe."

"You've told some grand tales, Da."

"Aye, that I have. Your mother has a wicked right cross." Affection glowed in his smile as he looked at his first wife...his true wife.

Brid gave him a stony look. "And I'll be using it again if you don't pipe down and tell it to them straight. This one's too big for you to charm your way out of, Paddy. You need their help."

Patrick polished off the contents of his glass in one quick motion. "I'll not cross your mother again, Sam. I've made my promise." He pushed his empty glass toward her, giving a nod.

"More, Paddy?" Brid asked, sounding none too pleased. "Not a good idea with the pain meds and all." At an impasse, the two glared at each other for a moment, then Brid broke and did as he asked.

Sam wasn't surprised. For all her bluster, Brid Donovan had never been able to resist her husband, no matter what he did. God knew, if St. Peter had been toting up his sins, the list was quite long by now.

"This Halloran guy took a shot at you?" Kellen asked. "Why? What did he want?"

He'd been so quiet and her emotions so jumbled, Sam had almost forgotten he was sitting next to her. Almost.

"He got off a shot all right. If Benji hadn't walloped him, I'd be but a memory."

For the first time since she'd arrived, Sam focused on her father's appearance. Underneath the ruddy lurked a bit of pale. His eyes, normally sparkling with mirth, were now dimmed with pain, the hint of a bandage just hidden at the edge of the left armhole. Her anger faded into fear. "You've seen a doctor, right? You're okay, right? You're not bleeding inside or anything?"

"Fine, lass. Didn't see a doctor—a gunshot raises all kinds of questions I wasn't ready to answer. Your ma bandaged me up. Never a better nurse, I've always said. She's put me back together a dozen times or more through the years. Why do you think she went to nursing school?"

"She went to nursing school because you left us." Sam's voice flattened.

But her mother shut her down. "My fight, Mary Catherine."

Truth of it was, both Sam and her father were a bit afraid of Brid. And even though Sam thought the fight wasn't entirely her mother's, Sam recognized it was a fight for another day.

A brave man or a foolhardy one, Kellen stepped in. "Mr.

Donovan, I appreciate you not wanting to bring your family into whatever it is you've gotten mixed up in, but it's a bit late for that. Your best option to keep them safe is to tell us what's going on and let us help. The body...Halloran?" He glanced at Sam for a confirming nod. When he got it, he continued, "Is my problem."

"How's that?" Donovan eyed Wilder, an appraising look.

"As I see it, the death took place on a vessel on territorial waters. Coast Guard jurisdiction. Am I wrong?"

Donovan's gaze shifting from his was all the answer Kellen needed. "Okay, then. Start at the beginning. Don't leave anything out."

Sam thought the possibility of the unvarnished truth from an Irishman was a long shot, but she settled back to listen to the story. Prevarication was one of her father's strong suits. She'd heard enough of his lies through the years she ought to be able to separate out the truth. Of course, her mother might be a better judge, but, when it came to her father, her assessment wasn't to be trusted. Sam took a slug of the whiskey and almost choked. Irish whiskey needed preparation, reverence as her father always said. In her haste, she hadn't been properly reverential.

Her father smiled at her as if he knew what she was thinking, which she was sure he did. *Damn him.*

Paddy moved his shoulder slightly, then grimaced. "Oh, girl, I never meant for them to come after you. But, then again, I never meant for my find to change the world."

CHAPTER FORTY-FIVE

Drayton Lewis moved quickly, closing the distance between them before Shelby could react. He backhanded her, and she crumpled to the floor.

She put a hand to her cheek. Blood dampened her fingers. His ring had left a gash across her cheekbone.

"You fucking bitch!" He straddled her, glaring down at her. Then he grabbed her by the arms, dragging her up and setting her on her feet. "Who else is here?"

"No one." She felt the trickle of blood ooze down her cheek. "How dare you barge in here?" Shelby let her anger override her fear as she drew herself up, pulling her shoulders back. "If you're still steamed over the interview, take it up with my bosses."

A tic worked in his cheek as he looked at her with dead eyes. His voice held the knife-edge of a threat. "I think you know why I'm here."

This time she was ready for the backhand. She turned, absorbing the sting of a glancing blow.

He grabbed her by the arm and dragged her to the couch, where he threw her down. Thrusting the laptop at her, he said, "Open it. Tell me what your brother knew."

"How..." Shelby started to ask but then realized men like Drayton Lewis had the power to do whatever they wanted. Fear and rage coiled inside her. She booted up the computer to give herself time to think. Even though it didn't feel like it, she really did have the upper hand. Without the base of Jake's cipher, Lewis would never break the code. And she was the only one who could tell him what he wanted to know. "The Internet here isn't secure."

Lewis stood still, his eyes stone-cold. If he was breathing, he hid it well.

Shelby barely snatched her fingers out of the way before he slammed the computer shut. "The truth is, I don't need you to tell me what's in the computer. I already know, or at least have a good idea. Your brother hacked into some information that puts me at risk. But what I do need to know is how much he told you." Grabbing her, he hefted her to her feet. "We'll do this on the boat. Everything is secure there. No one will know."

Those last words, pregnant with subtext, weakened Shelby's knees. Wasn't the first rule never leave with your attacker?

As if he could read her mind, Lewis backhanded her again, then once more for good measure. "Get your clothes on. You're coming with me. The only way you can stay alive is to do what I say."

Shelby put her clothes on, but she knew Lewis's comment went only so far.

Once he got what he wanted, she was dead.

Grady O'Dell counted to twenty after the door slammed before easing the closet door open a crack. He'd let himself in with Shelby's key card, the one he'd taken after he'd knocked her out at Donovan's office. He still felt a little bad about it, but taking the card, coming here, it was working in Shelby's favor. As far as Grady knew, she didn't have anyone else stupid enough to ride to her rescue.

Grady had been casing the room when she showed up.

The closet had seemed like a good idea while he figured out his next move, but he hadn't banked on Lewis showing up.

Grady listened, then opened the door a bit wider. As he suspected, he was alone.

Lewis! Fuck! Who would've thought? But now Grady knew who.

And he knew where.

CHAPTER FORTY-SIX

Sam and Kellen leaned back in their chairs and eyed Paddy.

"You mean to tell me you think you are sitting on a vein of unlimited oil?" Sam didn't even try to hide her skepticism. She glanced at the commander, but she couldn't read his thoughts—he wasn't wearing them in his expression anyway. But the tilt of his head indicated a question.

"I don't know. The logs are saying that's what we've got. More tests and time will give us the full scope of the field. But," he gave her a wink, "you do know there's that theory that oil is made in the furnace at the center of this big rock we live on, then filters its way up, riding all that heat and pressure."

"You've been filling my head with that bit of fringe science for as long as I can remember."

"Preposterous, I know," her father said, unable to hide his grin.

"But feasible," the commander said, as if he bought in.

"Great, two crackpots to deal with." Sam put her hands up, willing everyone to silence as she composed herself. "Da, whether you've hit the Fountain of Renewable Petroleum Products or you've just tapped into a mother lode, the result is the same, differing by degrees, nothing more."

"I knew you'd see the problem."

"Problem?" Kellen asked, clearly not following. "You're sitting on a boatload of oil, and you call this a problem?"

Paddy lifted his chin toward his daughter. "You tell them." His voice had weakened, his face paled.

Brid clucked over him as she checked his bandages. "He's lost a bit of blood. A pretty rough go of it."

He brushed her concern away. "You can tend to me later. Right now, I can't be flaggin'. I have a feeling the snakes will be coming out of their holes."

"He's right," Kellen agreed. He turned to Sam. "Can you give me the short version?"

"Balance of power. Russia, Iran, Iraq, Saudi Arabia, hell, the whole Middle East, along with several other players south of us—they all depend on a stable price of oil. If oil goes too low, Russia is bankrupt, the Middle East can't pay the stipend every citizen lives on, Venezuela is bankrupt, and Iran will be."

Realization dawned across Kellen's face. "And the world goes kaboom."

"Something like that," Sam said. "This is serious."

"So, what do we do?"

Sam shook her head. "I'm flying in the fog here, but I do know we need to get Da someplace he can't be hurt, or found, for that matter. Hell, he's already dead—let's keep him that way. Maybe with him gone, the snakes will show themselves."

"I don't like it," Kellen growled. "That means, as your father's heir, you are the target."

"Snake bait." Sam laughed at a private joke. She didn't elaborate.

"I'm guessing word of your find has leaked out?" Sam asked her father, finding it hard to swallow that now that her father finally had the find of a lifetime—the pot of gold he'd been chasing since he was a teenager—and it just might kill him.

Paddy touched his shoulder. "Halloran has been a

strong-arm man for San Rafael Oil ever since he and Farrell Bishop stole my first find. Those two love to get folks in a financial bind, then twist until they sign away their interest for pennies on the dollar. Unethical capitalism as taught at most of our finer institutions of higher learning. But I never thought him a killer."

"San Rafael Oil?" Sam thought about the contract carrot Farrell Bishop had been dangling. She shot Kellen a look—they'd just been talking about the contract she was negotiating with them and Sam's unease over the whole thing. Talk about validation. "What's their play?"

"They're a limited partner."

"Haven't you learned about inviting snakes into your nest?"

"Do you have any idea how much it costs to drill a deep-water well?"

Sam conceded the point. There was no use rehashing it anyway. "What about Uncle Phil? Have you heard from him?"

"No, he was trying to get out to the rig when he disappeared."

"Any ideas?"

"Only worries. He'd said we'd stepped into a viper's nest, but wouldn't elaborate until he was sure he was not followed and they weren't listening."

"They?"

"That's the question. I haven't a clue."

Sam poured her father another drink. Pain pinched his face. At her mother's look, Sam said, "Medicinal." Then to her father, "Da, we've got you being shot at, a dead software engineer who'd discovered something amiss in the trading programs at the Merc, and a mole at Drayton Lewis's office feeding information about the trading anomalies to the sister of the dead programmer, who happens to work for one of those network news shows. Oh, and the senior senator from Texas, the Chairman of the Natural Resources Committee and the one responsible for your lease in the

Gulf is missing after a failed assassination attempt. Oil's at the heart of it, but what's the play?" The table fell silent.

It didn't take long for Sam to come up with a theory. "Someone's pulling a Hunt Brothers but with oil."

"What?" Kellen said out of the side of his mouth.

"They tried to corner the silver market back in the seventies. Feds changed the margin requirements midstream. Damn near bankrupted a big Texas oil family. Still a lot of bad blood."

"Someone's trying to corner oil?"

Paddy shook his head. "No, that would be virtually impossible. Too many sources and too much product."

"A price play, then," Sam said, warming to the idea. "Think about it. Lewis with his investment in alternative fuels will see his stock rise if oil stays high—everyone will be looking for a viable alternative."

"And Phil?" Paddy asked.

"He holds the keys to your lease."

"My lease." He snorted. "Everybody thought I was crazy. They were right, just in the wrong way."

"News of your find will destabilize the price pretty dramatically. It'd be hard for anyone, Drayton Lewis or whoever else is working with him, to place enough money in futures to drive the price up."

"So they needed to get rid of me and shut the find down." Paddy stared over Sam's shoulder.

She could only imagine the thoughts of homicide tumbling through his head. "Uncle Phil must've played along. Then when he'd outlived his usefulness, they tried to kill him."

Paddy slammed a hand on the table, making him grimace in pain and everyone else jump. "Never."

Sam regrouped quickly—she didn't believe Phillip Herrera would sacrifice his legacy and shame his family any more than her father did. "Okay, another theory. He played along planning to expose the game and the players when he had enough on them."

"That's more like your Uncle Phil," Brid said in a quiet voice filled with conviction.

"Either way, we need to find somebody who knows a way into all this." Sam glanced at her watch. "Not much we can do now. I'm sure we all need some sleep." She leveled a stern look at her mother. "Do you have a gun?"

Paddy answered for her. He hiked up his pants leg, showing a compact semiautomatic tucked in an ankle holster.

"Where'd you get that?"

"Off of Halloran. It's what he shot me with."

Kellen leaned in. "That's evidence."

"That is the least of our worries at the moment," Sam said, trying to steer Kellen in a different direction. "The list of felonies is already enough to send him away for several lifetimes. I'm not sure a tampering charge would amount to much one way or the other."

Paddy looked insulted. "What felonies?"

Sam shot him a narrow-eyed look. "That innocent game doesn't work with me, Da. Accessory to murder for starters. Then accessory after the fact in disposing of the body."

"It was self-defense." If Paddy did anything well, indignation had to be at the top of the list.

"So you want us to believe that Halloran stowed away and managed to lose himself in the shift change on your rig?" Sam found her words first. Like the others, she had been mesmerized by her father's story.

"Girl, outta the whole story that's what you find hardest to believe?" Paddy gave her a look that told her he didn't believe that for a minute.

She stared at the bottom of her glass, thought for a moment, then poured herself another shot. Medicinal, she told herself. Keeping her wits was crucial. "Seriously, Halloran gets a shot off at you, then Benji wallops him over the head, killing him. And you two fools thought it would be a good idea to toss him over the side." She held up a hand, quieting her father as he opened his mouth to speak. "And then you decided to let the world think it was you who got his head bashed in. Remind me again, why is it you thought you'd be better off dead?"

Her father shifted in his seat. "I thought if no one was looking for me, then I'd have freer rein to figure out who the hell is trying to blow the lid off the world."

Sam let that sink in for a bit. "I hate to admit it, but it sounds logical." Sam shrugged when Kellen shot her a look. "By Donovan standards."

"I know, Mary Catherine, but as God is my witness it's what happened." Paddy sounded sincere.

Sam knew that didn't count for much when it came to her father. "And your dental records? Did you have Grady O'Dell steal them?"

"What? You mean like I was planning for Halloran to gun for me? You hurt me, girl. I might cross the line from time to time, but I have my standards."

"And we haven't yet found out just how low you will stoop."

"Not that low."

Kellen shook his head. "Man, a limitless supply of oil." Clearly, he'd gotten left in the dust as the conversation had galloped off without him.

"Fringe science," Sam reminded.

"Fortunes have been made by the crackpots, or by those who prove them right." Donovan's voice was level, his expression serious as he kept a steady gaze on his daughter.

"Let's assume your oil well is as you advertise," Kellen said. "Perhaps we should be focusing on a solution rather than the enormity of the problem. Do you have a plan, sir?"

"We can't let the news get out."

"Who else knows?" Kellen's voice was hard.

"As far as I know, just Benji."

"Your engineer?" Kellen waited until he got a confirming nod. "How far are you willing to trust him?"

"He saved my life."

"Well, I'll give you that." Kellen shrugged in

capitulation.

"Pretty big news to keep under your hat, Paddy," Brid remarked.

"What are you saying?" Paddy turned to his wife.

"If only the two of you knew, and you didn't let it slip..." Donovan pressed back in his chair, his arms braced on the table, then winced and collapsed into his hurt shoulder. "If he told someone, I'll kill him myself."

"And that would make things *so* much better." Sam had heard all she wanted to hear. Processing all of it would take the rest of the night. "You better hope Benji stays alive. A corroborating witness would be a good thing to have, all things considered." Sam rose. "Not the time for grandstanding, Da." She motioned to Kellen. "Let's go. Ma, don't let him leave here. Everyone thinks he's dead. No one will come looking, I shouldn't think."

"I need to get to the rig." Despite the whiskey, Donovan looked pale, his cheeks drawn.

"Not tonight." Sam softened. "Being dead isn't all it's cracked up to be, is it? Mom has some pills for the pain. I think you should take some."

"Just one, I think," he said, surprising her.

She retrieved a Diet Coke from the fridge to wash down a pill her mother had produced from a pocket.

Paddy grimaced. "You know, these things can kill you." He looked at her over the top of the can as he drained it.

"Shouldn't matter to you; you're already dead." She took the can. "Sleep now. Tomorrow will be soon enough to slay dragons."

"I need to talk to Benji. We should be at well-depth by now. It's a critical time." Donovan's eyes fluttered as he talked.

Brid helped him struggle to his feet. "Come, Paddy. For once, do as she says."

He let her lead him toward the back of the house. "The storm. The men."

"You're not fit to help them now, Da. The commander

will handle the evacuations. Benji and the men know what to do." Stopping in the front hall, Sam watched her parents, her father leaning on her mother, as they headed toward the bedroom. It had always been that way. When Patrick Donovan lost his wife, he'd lost his way.

Kellen waited until they were outside, the door closed, before turning on Sam. "Are you sure they'll be okay?"

"My father loves my mother desperately. Leaving him with her is best. He won't do anything stupid to put her at risk." Kellen didn't seem convinced. Sam stepped around him. "I can't exactly call the cops. I don't know for sure what he's guilty of, but, knowing him, it's something that's going to be hard to get him out of."

Kellen had no choice but to follow her. "Now you're harboring a fugitive."

Pausing before she opened the door, Sam took a deep breath. "He's dead, remember?"

"Cute." Kellen opened the door for her, then walked around to slip behind the wheel. "We both know he's not dead, he's guilty of something, and, given the right motivation, he will do something stupid." Kellen eased away from the curb.

The neighborhood was quiet, the streetlamps casting pools of warm light. A nice neighborhood, with normal people, doing normal things. A place where nothing bad happened. A place where secrets hid behind closed doors.

And, she prayed, just for a bit longer, please let our secret be safe.

"Are we going to your father's office?"

"Hell, no, he'd never keep anything important there." Sam could feel the heat of his rising anger.

"Why have you kept saying we should look there?" A tic worked in his cheek.

"For Shelby Walker's benefit. Not sure I trust her."

"That makes two of us." The hard set of his jaw eased a bit. "You've been playing fast and loose with me."

"I told you not to get involved."

An awkward, angry silence stretched between them. If her father really had done something he couldn't worm his way out of, what would she do? Family. She'd always wanted a normal family, whatever that was. She'd done everything she could to keep the three of them together.

And maybe that was the problem. Saving her father from himself was out of her reach and not her obligation. He was what he was, and she couldn't fix it. What she could do is figure out a way to live with it.

Family. She shot a sideways glance at Kellen. Both hands on the wheel, eyes straight ahead, a tic working in his cheek. "It's not good to clench your jaw."

He didn't respond, but the tic stopped.

Sam moved over, resting a hand on his thigh. "I'm sorry."

The tension released him; his posture sagged.

"You've done nothing but treat me with kindness and consideration," Sam continued. "And I've not been a good friend in return. I just panicked, to be honest."

"It's been a hell of a few days." He snaked an arm around her shoulders and pulled her close.

Sam interpreted that as an acceptance of her apology. "What if my father really killed Johnny Halloran?"

"To quote a very smart friend of mine, don't worry about the what-ifs."

Sam relaxed into him with a smile—a small one, but a smile nonetheless.

"You do realize that, with your father out of the way, they will keep coming after you."

CHAPTER FORTY-SEVEN

Benji Easton balanced a plate laden with barbecue, beans, and potato salad in one hand as he fought the wind, making his way to the control room. His shift long over, he knew he was running on fumes; but with the storm approaching, he had to get the last section of pipe laid or the whole operation would be jeopardized. Food would help. A day of sleep would help even more, but the weather gurus gave them five hours to tighten everything down and get off the rig.

Head down, rounding the last corner, and thinking of food and everything that had to be done, Benji almost mowed over a guy coming the other way.

Wes Craven. The mud man. Farrell Bishop's asshole. The guy who'd played him. The reason why Benji now found himself in a bad mess. Leaking drill logs to a limited partner was one thing. Attempted murder—hell, real murder—was a whole other thing. And now the guy was lurking around the control room, a place he had no reason to be.

"What are you doing here?" Benji didn't even try to hide his anger.

Wes cowered back. "Wanted to know what you wanted to do with the tender." The tender had been tied up alongside to catch the mud and the cuttings.

"Well, hell, secure the damned thing as best you can.

Losing mud and cuttings in the storm doesn't matter much. It's letting loose a bunch of oil that has me all hot and bothered."

"Yes, sir." Wes ducked his head.

As he moved to step around Benji, the big man grabbed him by the arm. "Now that I think about it, let's you and me have a talk."

Wes tried to pull his arm free, but Benji held on with an iron grip.

"You seem worried." He pressed the handle, surprised, but not really, to find the door unlocked. Benji knew he'd locked it when he'd left—he'd checked it twice. He'd been a fool—more than once. That stopped now.

With all his anger uncoiling, Benji threw the man through the control room door. He landed with a thud, sliding into the bolted leg of the large table in the middle of the room with a grunt. Benji glanced around, then slammed the door shut, locking it behind him. He set his food on the table and narrowed his eyes at the man unwinding himself from around the table leg. As he advanced on him, Wes crabbed away from him across the floor, holding his side where flesh and bone had met metal.

With one meat-hook hand, he grabbed the guy by the front of his shirt, then yanked him to his feet. "I need to know what exactly it is that you've done."

The man flinched away from him. "I don't know what you're talking about."

Benji fisted his other hand, raising it. The man cowered, covering his face with raised forearms. A heavy jab to the stomach doubled him over.

"Tell me."

"Just my job, man," he gasped as he sucked in air.

Benji thought there was some truth to that. "No doubt."

"I was told...you was...one of us."

Benji waited until he felt the man relax just a bit as he lowered his guard to peer upwards at Benji.

Another fist to the gut drove the breath from him. When

Benji let go, he dropped to all fours, struggling to pull air into his lungs.

"You were told wrong." The thought that there was some truth to that burned away at him. He'd thought he was leaking information to a partner. So he got it a little early. Where was the harm in that? Benji couldn't connect the dots, but he knew that his leak had set off some sort of chain reaction. First, they came after Donovan. Now he had a feeling they were coming after the rig.

"Which job, exactly, have you been doing?"

"Don't know what—" A boot to the ribs cut off his words, the steel-toe threatening to crack ribs as it connected.

"Try again."

He'd worked the guy to within an inch of his life when Benji Easton found his limit. He couldn't go any further. Blood oozed through a large split in Wes's upper lip. Both eyes puffed up and would turn all shades of blue and purple. A couple of times when he'd hit him, Benji had felt a few ribs crack. Wes's breath came in shallow gasps as he cringed against the pain.

But still the guy wasn't talking. He looked up at Benji through the open slit in one eye. "We gotta get off the rig."

"Why?" Benji grabbed him by the hair, pulling him up.

"You can't stop it."

"What?"

"They always get what they want."

"Who?"

Wes went limp, surrendering himself. An uppercut snapped his head back. He collapsed at Benji's feet.

Benji took him below decks and locked him in the infirmary. He probably should call the doctor, but he thought the doc had already been evacuated. As he tested the door one more time, he thought he heard Wes mumbling about having to get off the rig.

Back in the control room, Benji checked every control, then double-checked everything. Patrick's files were still locked. Everything showed in the green. All was as it should be. But it didn't feel like it was. What had Wes done?

He made one more circuit of the control room. Everything still checked out. Maybe the storm had him ready to jump out of his skin. Maybe what he'd done didn't sit too well either, scratching him like a thorn through the sole of his boot. How he'd gotten talked into it...

He choked down a few bites of his now-cold food.

First, he had to secure the rig. If he didn't do that, nothing else would matter.

***

Grady O'Dell was making this up as he went. He didn't know what he'd been expecting, but he sure hadn't figured Drayton Lewis to show up at the St. Regis, slap around a woman, then drag her off at gunpoint. In retrospect, however, he should've seen it coming.

Business was business and the law either an impediment or an artifice. Grady thought he actually preferred working with guys who didn't pretend to be anything other than the thieves and reprobates they were.

Lewis had stuffed Shelby in the back of a limo, which Grady now followed. Half a mile back, but keeping them in sight, he tucked up behind a cement truck, only dipping to the side to get a bead on the limo every minute or so. Grady was betting Lewis wanted privacy, and the best place for him to get it would be his boat. Too large for the Houston Yacht Club, the *Vengeance* would be berthed in Galveston.

Tuning the radio to a country station, O'Dell settled in for the ride.

CHAPTER FORTY-EIGHT

Nothing moved on the airfield when Kellen parked under the lone bulb by the small personnel door to Sam's hangar. Another squall had blown in. Rain pelted the truck like shrapnel. The security guy had been surprised to see them, but even more surprised at the barrage of questions they had for him about what and who he'd seen. Despite the grilling, he hadn't been able to offer them anything, not that Sam expected him to.

"You going to invite me in?" Kellen asked as he met her at the door, both of them huddled against the rain under the overhang.

Sam fumbled through the keys on the ring, trying several before finding the right one. As the door swung inward, she faced him. "Do you really think that's a good idea?"

"We're not going out to the rig in this weather. I'm betting that's where your father would keep anything important he might have." He waited for Sam to nod. "Your father is stashed, safe for now. We both need some shut-eye."

She raised an eyebrow at him.

"They're going to come after you. If we're right, they've already tried twice." He took a deep breath. "I need to know you're safe. No way could I sleep over there." He motioned toward the Coast Guard hangar. "Not when I know you're over here, alone, baiting the bad guys."

She still looked unconvinced.

"I just want to hold you. Can I do that?"

"I fell for that once, in high school."

"I mean it."

Sam motioned him through the door and she followed him in out of the rain. "I love the sound of rain on the tin of the hangar. So soothing. And this is home, my safe place." She paused. "Or it was."

Kellen knew how she felt. "It will be again. Once all this is over."

"I'm glad you're here," she said, surprising him.

He tripped on one of the steps up to her apartment, making Sam smile.

The space was small but comfortable—a twin bed, an overstuffed couch along the far wall, a kitchenette in the corner, and a whole hangar full of airplanes right out the door. Heaven by way of Kellen's thinking, and he knew Sam felt the same way.

Sam seemed unsure with him there. He tried to make it easy, peeling back the covers on the bed. "You in first? I'd really prefer you against the wall and me on the outside."

Sam kicked off her shoes, pulled off her socks, put the Glock within reach, and climbed in. Kellen settled himself partially on his side, folding her in his arms, her head resting comfortably on his shoulder. "You okay?" he whispered.

"Hmmm."

Kellen could feel her start to relax as she let him pull her closer. She molded into him, then started to shake as the adrenaline dissipated. Running low on food, sleep, hell, everything, she was drained dry.

Kellen tightened his arms around her, brushing his lips against her hair. He didn't offer a platitude about everything being okay. He knew Sam didn't want one. It would be what it would be, and they'd figure it out.

Chilled, Sam sought the warmth of him, craving his touch, the connection. Her fingers found the zipper on his flight suit, pulling it down to his waist. He took in a sharp breath when she pressed her hand to his warm flesh. She looked him in the eyes. The tic once again worked in his cheek, this time not from anger. Intensity sharpened his features. His skin grew even warmer under her touch.

"Do you think this is a good idea?" he asked, his voice tight.

"Probably not."

Then his mouth closed over hers, feasting, plundering. Sam wound fingers in his hair, holding him tight as she kissed him back, taking what she wanted, what she needed. Abandoning herself to the sensation of his touch, his need, his want, her own desires inflamed, Sam lost herself. Working his zipper down, she fumbled, and his hand closed over hers. His forehead pressed to hers, his breathing labored, he whispered, "Slowly. The first should be savored."

Her eyes widened as she raked her hair out of her eyes. "Seriously?"

Holding her hand in his, he kissed it. "Trust me."

And she did. Implicitly. Thinking back on it, she wouldn't be sure when her mind had let go and her heart had taken over, but it had.

Gently, he pushed her back. Shucking his flight suit, he tossed it on the floor. Then he turned his whole attention to Sam, covering her body with his. "Close your eyes." She did as he asked. She gasped when he pressed his lips first to one eye, then the other.

Arcing back, Sam reveled in the sensations as he feasted on her neck, nibbled on her ear. Frissons of excitement. Heat, lingering like the brush of hot metal where his skin touched hers, then released it, moving on. A path of touch-points. Desire curled in her belly. She moaned, a sound, that, had she been aware of it, would have embarrassed her.

Raising her arms Sam let him ease her shirt up and over her head. He stopped just short of taking it off, capturing her hands in coils of cotton, and held them there. When his mouth closed over her exposed breast, Sam gasped as bolts of desire shot to her core.

Kellen eased his legs off the bed so he was kneeling and he could have the whole of her. Teasing one nipple hard with his tongue, he moved to the other as he worked her pants loose.

She kicked them off, opening herself to him.

He pulled her around, lifting one leg over.

Sam held her breath, her eyes still closed, waiting for his touch. As his mouth consumed her, her back arched in pleasure. His tongue teasing, darting in and out, then stroking. Her fingers found his hair, pulling him tight to her. Stomach clenching. Back arching. Muscles tightening. Pleasure spiraling, rising. Exploding in sweet release. Her body trembled, exquisite aftershocks bolting through her.

Moving over, making space for Kellen, she still didn't open her eyes. Seeing would only compete with feeling. He settled in next to her. She could smell herself on him as her hand reached for him. Closing around his hardness, she felt him shudder. "Your turn, flyboy."

She pushed him down. Rising up, she straddled him, one foot braced on the floor, holding herself above him. Slowly, she opened her eyes, capturing his as she lowered herself onto him, absorbing his heat, his hardness within her.

As she started to rock and lift herself up, then lower back down slowly, Kellen was the one who closed his eyes. His fingers dug into her flesh, urging her into a rhythm. She resisted.

"No. This is all about you."

CHAPTER FORTY-NINE

The price of sweet west Texas crude took a dip in after-hours trading. No one paid much attention. So much of the futures trading was triggered electronically by programs with specific price points at which to buy or sell, short or long, the market fluctuations occurred without much human input.

Nor did anyone pay much attention when a string of trades, all futures puts, slid the price even lower. Oil had been falling for the better part of the spring and now into the summer, so traders were used to it.

Except Farrell Bishop. He damn sure noticed. And he didn't waste any time calling the emergency number to connect him with the Consortium. This was not part of the plan.

The man with the odd European accent answered swiftly, his tone a little less smug than normal. "We are working to control the problem," he said without preamble.

"You said safeguards were in place."

"We will take care of it."

"So you don't know the origin of the trading anomalies?"

The sound of the line being severed was final.

Farrell Bishop paced in front of his desk, a huge

mahogany monstrosity that had been rumored to have belonged to Sam Houston himself. No one quite believed it, but the rumor persisted. Hands clasped behind his back, a rosary trailing through his fingers, Bishop ran through the litany prayers by rote.

He'd mortgaged not only his financial future but his life as well, putting them both in the hands of shady figures with way more at stake than he had. He'd thought that was enough.

A new player had entered the game.

Bishop didn't know where the trail might lead, but he knew where to start.

The newest player he could think of was sitting on an oil reservoir of unheard-of proportions—enough oil to shake the balance of power to the core. Donovan Oil was the leverage Bishop needed. He held the largest minority stake—and a Limited Partnership Agreement that gave him control if something happened to Patrick Donovan.

Time to pay a visit to the new head of Donovan Oil. Without Patrick, that title fell to his daughter.

After shrugging into his favorite western-style jacket with the gold stitching, he reached for his Colt 1911 with Ivory grips, securing it at his side.

The silent vibration of his phone caught Agent Presley Davis in a rare moment of uncertainty. His team was chasing their tails through the millions of lines of code in the trading programs at the NYMEX. The storm in the Gulf had intensified quicker than anticipated, making Senator Herrera a bit more of a priority. They'd lost one agent in the storm already, and he wasn't about to lose a senator. Grady O'Dell wasn't picking up his phone, and he'd ditched their tracking bug. He doubted things could get worse.

"Yeah," Davis barked. "Tell me you've cracked this

thing."

"I got a piece of it." Andy Jeffers sounded as tired as Davis felt. "I'm chasing the money all over the world. I'll crack it eventually. But there's this other input coming out of Conroe, just north of where you are. Apparently, there's an IT operation there."

"What kind of input? A financial funnel?"

"No. Information."

"What kind?"

"Inventory numbers from the looks of it. Someone is intercepting the numbers, then changing them before they are passed along to the trading desks. And here's the deal; a bunch of trades get placed right before the numbers go public—all placed on the right side of that information equation. And none of them are high enough to trigger any of the security protections."

"Good work. Keep chasing the sources." Davis rang off. They were closing in; he could feel it. Before he had time to stash it in his pocket, his phone vibrated again.

"Davis."

"Sir, we picked up something interesting on the tap you got the other day." The agent on the other end of the line played the recording of Farrell Bishop's call. Wiring up O'Dell when he talked with the oil man had been a random cast. And now they'd hooked a big one. Bishop was part of whatever was going on. Davis would love to get his hands around the guy's neck. "Time to reel him in."

"You want us to grab him?"

"No. I want you to get out to that rig and grab the senator. Be careful—don't underestimate him. If he has the chance, he'll beat you like a redheaded stepchild."

"Want me to take the chopper?"

Davis glanced at the sky, felt the wind as it whipped around the corners. "No, I may need that. Take the boat. You've got time, but don't waste it."

"And Mr. Bishop?"

"I'll take care of Mr. Bishop. Where is he?"

"He just left his office. Got on I-45 driving himself. A Ferrari Mondial, early nineties. Red. Sweet ride."

"Heading south, I bet."

"Yeah."

"How many guys on him?"

"Two. Do you want me to call back up?"

"No, have them keep a safe distance. I don't want them spotted. If they spook him, I'll bust them all back to desk duty. Keep me updated on his location. I'm pretty sure I know where he's going. Tell them not to engage until I get there. You got that?"

"Yes, sir."

"And go get our senator before he gets washed out to sea." Agent Davis tossed his cold coffee and slid behind the wheel, accelerating out of the parking lot, then screeching through a U-turn.

Once again Donovan Oil was the eye of the hurricane.

The howl of the wind had stepped up a few decibels and the night had deepened when the first alarm went off, jolting Benji to his feet. He'd grabbed a couple of hours of shut-eye sitting in the chair at the control panel. Pulling out the string was a job he didn't have to lord over—the men knew what to do and when to call him.

Nothing he could do until they'd logged the well. After that, they'd test the hole one more time circulating the mud, then set that last section of casing and cement it. After that, they could shut it in until the storm had passed. After that, they would move the drilling rig and set the production platform in place. Then the whole thing was Donovan's hot potato.

He checked the dial. "A kick. Goddammit. That's the last thing we need right now." The pressure in the well was high and rising. Not too fast, but fast enough. And not yet too high to trip the blowout preventer, thank God. But they needed to get heavier mud in the hold fast.

He grabbed a slicker from one of the pegs and bolted through the door. The rain and wind made the going treacherous, turning the oil on the deck into a slick slurry.

He reached the hole, his foreman hunched over his panel. He had to touch the man on the shoulder before he knew he was there. Leaning in, he still had to shout. "Whatcha got?"

"Pressure rising. Where the hell is Wes?"

"He won't be helping."

The foreman jumped like he'd been hit with a cattle prod. "Why? Where is he?"

"Unavailable." Benji glared the questions down.

The foreman swallowed hard. "We're pumping heavier mud as fast as we can."

"Is it holding the pressure?"

"Not yet, but it's slowing it down."

"And the last section of production casing?"

"Ready to go in the hole."

"How many men do we have left here?"

"The last load. I don't think the helicopter will be able to get back to get us."

"Agreed. Grab them. Get in the pods. Strap yourselves in tight." The rig was fitted with large seaworthy escape pods for just this kind of emergency. They'd have quite a ride in the hurricane, but it'd be better than immolation in a blowout.

Benji didn't have to say it again—the man turned and ran.

As he charged off to find the mud engineer, he reached for his phone and dialed Patrick Donovan's number. "Boss, we have a problem."

CHAPTER FIFTY

Hyped on sex and worry, Sam couldn't sleep.

Kellen breathed softly next to her, but the moment he sensed her stir, he was awake. "What is it? You okay?"

"Gotta go to the bathroom." That was the truth, as far as it went. Sam eased herself over the commander. Grabbing the clothes she had shucked the night before, then the Glock as an afterthought, she padded to the small bathroom. Gazing at herself in the mirror, she thought she looked exactly like what she was—a woman who had had the most incredible, mind-blowing sex. And that wouldn't do. So, she set about trying to normalize her appearance, scrubbing her face, brushing her teeth, and smoothing her hair back into a ponytail, making as little noise as possible in the process. Then she eyed herself critically. Better. But her lips were still slightly swollen. She fingered a red mark on her jaw and tried to think when that had happened. Details disappeared into a haze of orgasmic hangover, not that that was a bad thing.

Opening the door slowly, she eased across the room, grabbing shoes and socks as she went. Kellen breathed the even cadence of sleep when she let herself out, locking the door behind her.

Needing air, she unlocked the hangar door and tugged a panel open, stopping when it squealed in protest. The opening was just large enough for her to shimmy through. Her hand on the butt of the gun tucked at the small of her back, she checked the perimeter, peering into the shadows. A man stood just out of the light to her left. On a normal night, she wouldn't have noticed him. But nights had been anything but normal lately. She drew her gun. "Show yourself."

He didn't seem bothered by her or the gun as he shouldered himself off the wall and stepped into the light.

Farrell Bishop.

"What the hell are you doing here? It's the middle of the night."

A quick glance at her, then he took a last drag on a cigarette, dropped it, and ground it out under the toe of his boot.

The cigarette butts littering the ground around his feet indicated he'd been there a while.

The 1911 holstered on his belt caught the light.

"That's far enough. How'd you get in here?"

"I keep one of my corporate jets at the FBO."

That explained getting onto the field, but not getting into the secure enclosure where Sam's hanger sat protected between the Coast Guard and NASA, but Sam played stupid, knowing that's what any Texas man would expect. "And why are you here? It's late, well past business hours, and even too late for a social call."

He stopped, holding his hands out from his sides. "I just want to talk."

"Then talk."

He glanced at the sky. Low clouds scudded across the haze of a moon. "Storm is going to be one for the record books."

"You're opening with the weather?" The guy oozed slime, and Sam couldn't figure why her father had let the guy in the door, much less taken his money. Deep-water wells were huge investments, but her father was scraping the bottom with this guy.

"That contract is still on the table."

"The contract?" For a moment, Sam had no idea what he was talking about.

"Your helicopter service contract with San Rafael."

God, that discussion seemed like a lifetime ago. And life had certainly put a new spin on it. The irony that Sam had been contemplating taking the guy's money just as her father had wasn't lost on her. "It's not a contract yet. But it's the middle of the night. Why would you think this was a good time to talk about it?"

"Are you going to put that gun away?"

Sam was surprised to see she was still pointing the Glock at his heart...if he had one. "No."

"Suit yourself." Bishop shifted, but kept his distance. "I'm very sorry to hear about your father."

Sam heard the squeak of the door opening upstairs. She ignored it and prayed Kellen was smart enough to stay out of sight. But she was thankful he was there just the same. "It's a shock."

"He will be missed."

If he trotted out another insincere platitude, Sam thought she might grab a wrench and test just how thick his skull really was. If she shot him, that would bring the cavalry and take more time than she could allow for explanations.

Bishop cleared his throat. "I'm really here about the drilling operation. I have a great deal invested in the project. Without your father at the helm, and at this particular point in the operation, the limited partners have asked me to step in."

"I see." Sam crossed her arms but didn't trust herself to look at him. "And what are you proposing?"

"First, you need to secure the rig. That hurricane is really winding up to throw one hell of a punch. My firm owns the rig. To lose it would pretty much sink us."

That wasn't what Sam was expecting. "I'll talk to the men. I'm sure you understand that there are certain points in the drilling of a well at this depth where you can't just button it up and leave. The consequences of a shoddy job could be disastrous."

"Of course, of course."

"I'm assuming that's not really why you're here. You could've taken care of that with a meeting of the limited partners and a call to the rig."

"I'm assuming you are your father's heir and executor?" Bishop didn't wait for confirmation. "I'd like to buy out his interest. The well, of course, is unproven. The partnership agreement lays out the parameters for the valuation and the sale in just this instance."

"I see."

He reached into his inside jacket pocket but slowed when she raised the gun. With two fingers, and in plain sight, he pulled out a sheaf of papers, folded vertically in half, then extended them to her. "In case you don't have a copy."

Sam took them, then tossed them in the trash can. She ignored the noises from the landing outside the apartment as Kellen moved.

Bishop grabbed Sam's arm, digging his fingers into soft tissue. The gun didn't even slow him down—he ignored it. Perhaps he knew she wouldn't use it. Sam was smart enough to know he wouldn't hurt her—not until he'd gotten what he wanted. She staggered as he pulled her close, but she didn't wince. She wouldn't give him the satisfaction.

"You'd be advised to do as I ask." His breath, hot on her cheek, smelled of whiskey, but the rest of him reeked of desperation.

"Or what? If I don't hand over control to you, it'll take you a long time to get it through legal channels."

"You think you're a match for me? You are playing a game you can't even begin to comprehend."

For a moment she thought she saw a flash of fear. "What game is that?"

His expression closed, the dead look returned to his

eyes. "You need to sell me your father's interest, and you need to do it quickly, before..."

"Before what?"

"Just do it. I can save us all."

"Save your ass, more like."

"Look, you'd be wise to play along with me. I'm the best chance you have. You have no idea the forces at play here, the lives that hang in the balance."

"And if I don't?"

"I'll get what I need, and I'll take you out of the game. Airplanes are dangerous things. A tailwheel spring. A safety wire."

"Are you confessing to sabotaging an aircraft? That's a felony...or two."

"Just saying, things can happen."

Agent Presley Davis, his gun at the ready, stepped out of the shadows. "Yes, they can."

Bishop whirled at the sound of his voice. Sam stepped away from him.

Kellen came flying down the stairs. Caught off guard by the attack from two sides, Bishop was slow to turn. Kellen hit him chest high. Both men fell in a tangle, Bishop underneath. As he hit the floor, the commander pile-drove a shoulder into his chest, forcing his breath out in a rush.

The fight was over before it began.

Pistoning his feet underneath him, the commander dragged the oilman up by his lapels. The Fed's gun kept him from doing anything stupid.

Still trying to process...everything...Sam took Agent Davis's presence as somehow expected. "How much did you hear?" she asked the Fed.

"Enough to haul his ass in on various felonies. Sabotaging an aircraft is quite frowned upon, Mr. Bishop."

A young cadet came racing through the door, skidding to a stop at the scene in front of him. He swallowed hard. "Commander?"

"Yes?"

"You're needed, sir. That storm has turned into a motherfucker." He colored, then nodded at Sam. "Sorry, ma'am."

She rolled her eyes.

"And, sir," the cadet continued as he held out what looked to be photocopies, "you asked for these? The State Police sent them over."

"Thanks. I'll be right behind you." Kellen scanned the papers, which were indeed photocopies.

Sam got a good look at them over his shoulder. She pulled up the photos of the tire tracks Shelby had emailed to her. She and Kellen, heads bent together, compared the two.

They were the same. The tire tracks from where they'd taken the senator and the tire tracks from the black Dodge. Their eyes met as realization dawned, but each kept their thoughts to themselves. Not the place or the audience for airing as yet unfounded accusations. Bishop for sure played for the wrong team, but Davis? Anybody's bet.

Kellen grabbed her shoulder. "I've got to go." He ignored the two men and the cadet. "Are you going to be okay?" At the look on her face, he said, "Forget I asked that. Try not to kill anybody. It just creates a paperwork nightmare." He planted a very warm kiss, holding her lips hostage for a bit longer than comfort dictated. With that he was gone, the cadet trailing behind.

Bishop crossed his arms and leveled a gaze at the agent. "Who the hell are you?"

Davis flashed his badge.

Bishop lost a bit of his starch but not his bluster. "You'd best be watching who you're dealing with. We don't cotton much to Feds around here."

"Are you threatening me, Mr. Bishop?"

"Of course not." His lie hung there. "Ms. Donovan can attest to that."

"You want me as a character witness?" Sam would've laughed if she had had any laugh left.

"I am here to negotiate a couple of contracts."

Sam had no trouble interpreting his look. A light sheen of sweat glinted on his brow. A bullshitter, a liar, was it too far a reach to murderer? "Did you have my father killed?"

Bishop reeled backward, slapped by her words. "Me? Why would I do that?"

Sam answered to the agent. "You heard him trying to strong-arm me into transferring my father's general partnership interest in the well to him?"

"Yeah. What is so goddam incredible about that fucking oil well?"

Sam and Bishop both clammed up, staring at the Fed. Sam wasn't about to tell anyone about her father's find or the extent of it. She assumed Bishop wasn't going to incriminate himself further.

"I'll be telling ya' if you really want to know." Patrick Donovan strode through the door.

Sam whirled. "Da. What the hell?"

Bishop looked like he'd seen a ghost.

"Surprised to see me, Farrell?" Donovan took the stairs one at a time, holding tight to the railing.

Knowing it was impossible to stuff a cat back in a bag, Sam said nothing. The agent shot a questioning look her way. "My father. He's always had a flair for the dramatic." Then she turned and hissed at her father, "How the hell did you get here? And why did mother let you out of her sight?"

He started to explain.

Sam raised a hand. "Rhetorical. That way you don't have to bother to lie."

"Aren't you supposed to be dead?" Davis asked.

"A minor misunderstanding."

Sensing Paddy weakening, Sam rushed to his side. He held on, but he didn't lean on her.

"You all better start talking, or I'm going to bust the lot of you."

Sam held her father's arm as he sank down on the lowest step with a groan, then sat next to him. "Careful of the shoulder."

"Shoulder?" Agent Davis asked.

Donovan hitched his head toward Bishop. "He sent his goon after me. Darn near sent me to the Great Beyond."

"Me?" Bishop's voice cracked like a twelve-year-old soprano's.

By Sam's way of thinking, Bishop overplayed the mock indignation, but scared was written all over him, and, in her experience, where there was fear, there was guilt.

"Halloran has been on your payroll ever since you had him set up our first stake twenty years ago, so don't waste this good public servant's time with bullshit."

Bishop wasn't the only one overplaying, thought Sam, but this wasn't her show. Besides, she felt powerless to affect the outcome—but her mother would kill her if she let her father end up in a federal slammer.

Donovan sobered, his voice turning lethal. "Make sure you keep this bit of trash," he hooked his thumb at Bishop, "in your sight and away from any communication device, or the blood will be on your hands."

"What's he got?"

"Names." Donovan stared him down. "Information. I don't know. But what I do know is the boys you're playing with," he focused the words on Bishop, "they're going to come after you. You've really screwed this one up, and I have a feeling you've been working your own angle in this game, something you always were good at. You like stealing other people's oil. And you came here tonight to steal mine. You're going to inherit a whole bunch of interesting attention if you succeed. But if you fail, you're a dead man. So, either way, it isn't going to be good for you."

Bishop didn't argue. As he mopped his brow, he looked like a marked man weighing his options.

"So what's it going to be?" Davis asked. "You flip on these guys and whatever their plan is, and I can probably keep you alive. You don't help us, well, God help you."

"Okay. Okay. I'll tell you what I know. But that's how

the Consortium works—those not in the inner sanctum, so to speak, only know bits and pieces."

"Bits and pieces will get us started."

Sam could feel the anger as her father tensed. "Agent Davis, you need to tell me where you've got Senator Herrera stashed. And I need to know right now."

"On a derelict platform ten miles off shore. I've sent an agent to get him." Agent Davis reached for his radio. "How'd you know?"

"I didn't, not exactly. But this whole game has the stink of a con on it—trust an old con to know it."

The agent almost smiled as he shook his head.

Donovan turned to Sam. "I need your chopper. I've got to get to the platform. Benji called. Pressures are rising. With that hurricane, if we don't get it fixed..." He left the threat between them.

"You're in no condition to fly. Pale as a ghost, you are." Sam glanced at the clouds. Now growing thicker, they'd obscured the moon. The ceiling was still just high enough. "You can't get there. The hurricane."

"I can make it."

"And leave my helicopter to be washed away. I think not."

"Sam, the rig, the oil, the Gulf. I can save all of it, but I have to go now."

"Benji and his crew, whoever is left, why can't they save it?"

He visibly worked to control his temper. "Because experience has to teach you something."

Something else, she could feel it. "What aren't you telling me?"

"Let it go, girl."

"You're asking me to risk my ass, yours, *and* my chopper. Don't you think I deserve to know the whole story?"

"At the last crew change, new faces started appearing—not our normal guys. Their paperwork checked out, but still,

Benji's sure something's going down. But he was sure that whatever it was, it was going to be spectacular."

"They've rigged it to blow?" He didn't have to spell out the disaster that would be. BP had already shown the world the devastation of a blowout on a deep-water well.

"And I've got almost no time left to figure out how."

With the very real possibility the thing could blow up around them. "Great. Glad I put on my fireproof underwear this morning."

"Spoken like a Donovan. But it'll be just me, girl. You drop me and skedaddle back here. Your mother would kill me if anything happened to you."

And she'd kill me if anything happened to you, so, really there's only one outcome—we both come back. Sam didn't want that bet; she didn't want that one at all. "Life wouldn't be worth living if we didn't try. Mom will have to live with the consequences. But, Da, we're going to need a whole lot of that Irish luck you're always crowing about."

He didn't smile. "Well, then?"

"Have you checked the storm?"

"Benji said forty-mile-an-hour gusts at the rig." He paused a moment. "We'd better hurry. It's only going to get worse."

She shook her head. *A fool you are, Sam Donovan.* "Flying into the teeth of that storm, we're going to need a bigger chopper with a bit different rigging." She thought of the Sikorsky and smiled. "Agent Davis, how do you feel about commandeering a helicopter?"

CHAPTER FIFTY-ONE

The wind gusted now, whistling around the small steel structure. Waves crashed against the pilings. Spray whistled on the wind, liquid shrapnel. Low, scudding clouds erased the feeble light that had smudged the western horizon. A shiver chased through Senator Herrera, but he wasn't cold. He saw the searchlight before he heard the thrum of the twin diesels.

A boat.

The senator didn't know whether they were coming to rescue him or to stage a murder scene. He didn't feel like waiting to find out which. Pulling the steel pipe from its hiding place against the small of his back, he hefted it in his hand. Heavy enough to crush a man's skull. He tucked it back where he'd had it secured, making sure his shirt wouldn't get in the way. Then, with both hands grasping a rusted cable slick with water and gritted with salt, he eased over the side of the platform, bracing his feet on a strut three feet below. He crouched, unsure how long he could hold himself there against the wind and gravity. He prayed it would be long enough.

The young agent, standing in the bow, his feet spread, rode the waves as the boat climbed the face of the next roller, then squatted and braced as it slipped over the crest to slide down the back. At the top, the kid tried to flash the light at the platform, an eerie skeleton, its limbs bent and deformed, whistling in the wind.

Soaked through by the spray washing over him and trickling down his neck, the young agent wiped his eyes, then squinted again into the spray as the captain and his one lone crewman maneuvered the vessel alongside the abandoned platform. The engines growled above the increasing fury of the storm, thrumming through the metal under the agent's feet.

Most people don't think of senators as particularly dangerous—neither did the agent. That was his first mistake. Leaving his gun tucked safely in its underarm holster was his second.

"Senator Herrera! FBI. I'm boarding your platform. My instructions are to take you back to Houston."

Only the howl of the wind answered him.

The screech of metal on metal as the roiling sea threw the boat into the platform leg. A wave breached the side. A moment of fear. Then the power of the sea unleashed across the deck. The agent grabbed a cable. The fact that he stood in the bow and that the platform kept the boat from rocking too much saved him.

"Kid, we've got to hurry," the captain said over the speaker. "I can't keep tied up here too long. The waves are shifting, the wind coming up."

The kid cinched down the hood on his slicker and reached for the ladder that hung from the platform just within reach. He timed the ride up and over the swells, looking for a moment of stillness to transfer his weight. For a second, the boat hung on the crest, and he swung himself over to the rusty metal.

Slick with salt water and neglect, the metal flaked, his hands slipped.

DEEP WATER

Shifting weight from one foot, he reached for a new purchase on the next rung. He found it just as his lower foot lost its grip. Grunting as one shoulder took the bulk of his weight, the agent clung to the ladder as his feet searched for a rung that would hold him.

The rain came in sheets now, blinding him as he struggled up the ladder. More careful now, his breaths coming in gasps, he worked his way up as the wind tried to pluck him from his tenuous hold and then fling him into the sea boiling below.

He looked down once. That was all he could take. Acrophobia hadn't been on his intake eval, and he'd chosen not to mention it.

After several lifetimes had passed before him, he felt the solid base of the platform. Slithering onto it, he offered up a whispered Hail Mary. Rolling onto his back, he abandoned himself to waves of fear and nausea, taking deep, gulping breaths. His radio crackled to life, Agent Davis's voice over the speaker—somehow he'd lost his earpiece.

"Status? What the hell is all that noise?"

The kid laughed, a choked sound, but a laugh just the same. Agent Davis was a total nut-job, and the minute he got back on *terra firma,* the kid promised himself he'd take any reassignment he could get as long as it was not within spitting distance of any body of water larger than the pond on his parents' farm.

"On the platform. No sign of the senator, but I haven't gotten very far. There's a hurricane out here, in case you haven't heard."

"He's there. Get him and bring his ass back here."

"What'd he do, fuck the wrong intern or something?" the kid asked, but he got no reply.

His world a bit more settled, he rolled over then pushed himself to his knees and hands.

That was his third mistake.

CHAPTER FIFTY-TWO

In a low squat, Grady O'Dell moved between the crates on the dock, staying hidden but keeping Drayton Lewis in sight. He and his thug manhandled Shelby Walker, pushing and prodding her toward the sleek black vessel moored alongside. The *Vengeance,* Grady assumed. The name fit. Backed in, low to the water, built for speed, the boat reeked of menace—the perfect ride for a modern-day pirate. Especially with the small helicopter lashed to the bow deck and the closed doors in the stern that probably held all kinds of fun sea toys.

The threat of the storm rode the wind, whipped into a frenzy, lathered and foaming like a rabid animal. The threat whistled through the bare masts of denuded sailboats, tethered to ride out the storm. Other boats, snug in their slips, banged and shook, animals rattling their cages, as if they knew. The storm breathed down on them, a predator playing with its prey. Every instinct shouted at Grady to run, to find solid shelter to fight the wind, high enough to be safe from the storm surge. But he couldn't leave Shelby.

The three of them angled up the gangplank, Lewis and the thug behind corralling Shelby. The guys above trained their weapons as added incentive. Still, Shelby fought, which Grady liked. Didn't she know it was better to fight your attacker than go with him? The thug cold-cocked her and she sagged against him. He loaded her over his shoulder like a sack of flour.

Twice in twenty-four hours—that girl was going to have one hell of a headache.

Lewis paused on the gangway, hurling an object into the water. Flat and black, it looked like a computer, but at this distance, in the weak light and sheeting rain, it was hard for Grady to tell.

One thing he could see with clarity—he needed help. The police had been unable to respond. An evacuation order for Houston had just been issued, and the place was gridlocked. Sacrificing the few to save the many. Grady had always thought that idea had merit...until now. Until he'd become one of the few. And Shelby, too. And that wasn't right. He didn't know anything about her really. But she had guts, and he liked that.

Maybe he could call the Coast Guard.

He abandoned that idea as quickly as he'd thought of it. With the hurricane, they'd have a hell of a mess on their hands. Right now, he figured they'd be moving all their assets to be best prepared to come in right behind the storm. The boats would trail the storm. The helicopters would hunker down and wait. With a longer range, a faster giddy-up, and only really good for the search part of search and rescue, the planes would be secreted inland to ride it out.

This one was on him.

Lewis could take Shelby out to sea, dump her in front of the storm, and her body would probably never be found.

Single sodium bulbs, at barely adequate intervals down the dock, cast weak pools of light. No cameras. Once Lewis and his guest disappeared inside, the two guys toting automatic weapons patrolled the upper deck of the *Vengeance*.

Nobody guarded the back deck. Lights were on inside.

As if answering a prayer, the rain started. Sheets of it, almost horizontal as it rode the wind. Grady smiled.

Storage lockers along the dock sheltered him as he moved toward the boat. The rain and the darkness did the rest. Ten seconds and he'd made short work of the ancient lock on the gate to the dock. A ten-year-old lock to protect a fifty-million-dollar asset. Of course, there were the goons with the M4s.Indiana Jones and the three tests. All things being equal, Grady would rather be James Bond with a healthy arsenal from Q. But, alas, he was neither.

The engines firing vibrated through the dock. He thought he heard them above the storm as the captain added power, but he wasn't sure. And he didn't figure the guy at the helm was the law-abiding type—so he'd blow right through the five mile-per-hour harbor speed limit.

Men on board unwound the mooring ropes from the bollards and tossed them up to the deckhands. Power to the props churned the water behind.

He had ten seconds, maybe fifteen. And he'd have to time his leap perfectly.

Crouching down, he gathered himself. Then he stood and ran. Nobody shot at him; at least he didn't think they did. With the storm roaring and his blood pounding in his ears, he'd only know if they hit him.

The vibrations increased. The boat responded to the power input, pulling further away.

In a flat-out run, his toes just at the edge of the dock, he launched himself, clawing into the darkness.

The young agent was still out. Senator Herrera had hit him harder than he thought. The senator felt around in the dark for a few precious seconds for the kid's gun. Finally, his fingers touched the metal—still in the holster. He secured the weapon, then stuffed it in his pocket. The agent didn't move as the senator grabbed him under the arms. He fell twice struggling to pull the kid over to the ladder; he was all muscle. The rain made the old metal as slick as snot. At the edge, he motioned to the captain peering through the glass. He'd have the answer to his question as to what they intended to do with him in a minute. Either the guy would shoot at him or help. One way, he'd be dead.

The senator eased the gun out of his pocket and held it by his leg, hidden, his finger on the trigger.

The captain ducked into the rain. He bent down. Senator Herrera tensed. The captain raised up, a coil of rope in his hands. It took him two tries in the wind to catch the captain's toss. The senator looped the rope through the ladder and then tossed it back to the captain, who pulled it tight, keeping the boat close as best he could, man against storm. Thankfully, they had the waves and wind working in their favor—until the storm turned, or moved past and the wind shifted. They'd have to be quick.

He'd have to get the kid down three rungs before the captain could help. Easing first his legs over, Herrera sat bracing against the weight, his feet against the upper looped rungs of the ladder. Slowly he absorbed the weight as the storm lashed at him, the rain pelting him. His muscles screamed. He focused on the pain, using it.

Finally, at the breaking point, his muscles shaking, his grip loosening, he felt the load lighten. He eased his hold, letting the rest of the agent's body slip into the waiting arms of the captain. Actually, the young agent fell on the man below, who absorbed some of the kid's fall, probably saving him one hell of a concussion.

While the captain struggled under the weight, the senator scrambled down the ladder. Breathing hard, water cascading down his face, he swiped it out of his eyes as he leveled the pistol on the captain. The young agent was starting to stir, which presented another problem, but Herrera was glad for the signs of life—killing the kid had never been his intention.

"You know where Donovan Oil is drilling out here?" the senator asked the captain.

The captain's eyes widened as the full reality of what

Senator Herrera wanted hit him full face. He nodded.

"Set a course and get there as fast as you can. The men on that rig are going to need our help."

"Yes, sir."

"Then, when you can, get that asshole Davis on the horn."

CHAPTER FIFTY-THREE

They caught the salesman Sam had ridden with before as he was sliding into the right seat of the Sikorsky.

"A little late getting this bird to safety," Sam said, as she stepped in so he couldn't pull the door closed.

"Yes, and I need to go." The wind tugged and pushed at the helicopter as it swirled, heralding the advance of the storm.

Davis opened the other door. Leaning in, he flashed his credentials. "I'm commandeering this chopper. Government business. National security." He backed up his request with his pistol, pointing it at the pilot.

Sam stepped back a bit, removing herself from the danger zone in case Davis actually pulled the trigger. She made just enough room for the salesman to get out.

He waffled for a few precious seconds, then slid down and past Sam. "You're not FBI," he said as he watched her climb aboard.

"How do you know?" Her eyes scanned the instruments, familiarizing herself with them once again. "If you've got a problem with all this, call 202-382-5633. They'll be able to help you."

The salesman drifted back and Sam shut the door.

"What number was that?" Davis asked.

"202-FUCK OFF."

"I like your style." He started to climb aboard.

Sam swiveled and planted both feet in his chest, then pushed.

Surprise caught him, but he was able to hang on with one hand. He struggled, then fell into the darkness. Paddy's pale face appeared and his body followed as he climbed aboard and slammed the door before Davis could stop him.

Sam had the RPMs up. "What did you do with Bishop?" She reached over, helping him shrug his bleeding shoulder into the harness.

"He's sleeping a bit tied to the railing in your hangar. He's Davis's problem. Sweet machine, this."

"It's not ours."

Paddy added the coordinates to the GPS.

Even firmly planted on the ground, the machine rocked as wind and the rain buffeted it, the wipers barely able to keep the windscreen clear enough for Sam to see. Not that it would matter—once in the air, the instruments would be her eyes.

The tower controller seemed unsure when he cleared her for takeoff, a warning hanging in the space between his words. She could identify—she wasn't feeling all that committed either. But life had narrowed the choice to one.

Thankfully, her father didn't say a word as she eased up on the collective, lifting the machine into the first buffet of an angry storm. He did, however, reach for a handhold, his knuckles whitening as the chopper rocked and swayed, the engines fighting to steady what amounted to little more than a kite in the wind.

With all the lights strobing and the landing light a weak beacon to at least lighten the gloomy darkness, Sam swung around to the south, following an invisible path into the mouth of the beast. The rain peppered the windscreen and then streamed to the side as Sam added power, gaining speed.

"This isn't the time to hold back," her father said.

She glanced at him. His face ashen, his lips moved in silent prayer.

His eyes shut, his arm outstretched, Grady O'Dell hung in the air, his fingers reaching for a hold, something solid. Time stopped. The sound of the engines thrummed through him. He braced himself. The wind tore at him, pressing him down.

Then he hit. Hard. His breath left in a whoosh.

He scratched, scrabbling in the darkness. His hand slid as gravity yanked him down. Then he felt it. The aft gunnel.

With one hand, he grasped it, the metal slick with rain.

But he held on. He kicked around until he could get his other hand on it, too. Then he hung there, the propulsion of the ship pulling his body away from the cold metal of the stern like a breeze catching a flag.

His arms shook. His fingers numb with pain, he held on. When the boat reached speed, he'd have his chance.

His right hand cramped first, the fingers failing. The left one started to go. If he fell now, he'd be sucked into the props—if this thing even had props. Fancy yachts weren't part of his purview. Either way, he'd be in the water, and the girl would be dead.

A hint of renewed strength rode in on that thought.

Finally, the boat settled in. They must be out of the harbor now. With his body flat against the metal, he could feel the roll of the swells, which would only get worse. A few seconds, he had them timed. Pulling with every bit of strength he had left, he swung until he got one foot hooked over the railing, then the other. With his legs to help, he levered his body up and over, falling on his back on the aft deck.

The light streaming out of the stateroom didn't reach to the aft railing, Grady's first bit of real luck this evening. He lay in the shadows, gathering himself, working his fingers to get blood back in them. The pain told him he was alive. Keeping still, he mentally tested all his parts. They seemed to be returning to function—although his brain had sure led them astray. Stupid thing to do. Now here he was, one waterlogged pistol—thankfully it was designed to take this kind of punishment—against fresh muscle with automatic weapons. How many, he hadn't a clue. Two for sure. Probably more. But, once at sea, it wouldn't take an army to protect this boat. An open ocean and hurricane would do the job better than anything man could devise. Grady actually was happy about that.

Keeping still, he rolled his head so he could see into the stateroom. Lewis was alone with Shelby—the thug had apparently been sent away. That was a good thing. Shelby lay on the couch.

Lewis poured himself a drink at the bar, then threw it back in one gulp.

Lewis.

Grady had spent a lifetime working with and around guys like him. Smart to the point of arrogance. Used to getting his way, to fooling everyone. In the past, the best way to deal with them had been to wait for them to step one step too far, make a move that would give him an opening, but Grady didn't have time. He focused on Shelby. On her back, one arm dangling off the couch, the other laying across her face, she didn't move.

Come on, Shel. You gotta be able to help. I can't carry you and get us out of here.

A phone sounded in the darkness, so close, Grady panicked for a moment, thinking it was his. Patting his pockets, he remembered he'd left his in the car. Good thing; he didn't think Steve Jobs had designed his phone for this sort of punishment.

"Yeah. Hang on." The deep voice was right above him on the top deck.

Footsteps receded. Grady angled a look as the man attached to the voice stepped into the stateroom, thrusting the phone at Drayton Lewis. Banking on the other guard being forward, Grady rolled to his stomach, then pulled his feet under him. Keeping low, he eased down the narrow walkway between the side railing and the interior of the boat. Ducking below the side windows, he could barely make out the raised voice above the howl of the wind. The boat rose on a swell, hung there, then slid down the other side. Spray broke over the bow.

Grady hated small boats on big, roiling seas. His stomach clenched as he fought waves of nausea.

The raised voice belonged to Drayton Lewis, who was yelling into the phone now. Something about getting out to Donovan Oil's rig and "doing it himself."

If Lewis left, Grady figured his problems might just become manageable.

A lone figure stood on the foredeck, the dim light from the bridge barely illuminating him. Grady inched closer, thankful for the power of the storm, the crash of the sea. When the boat rode up the next swell, Grady crouched, waiting for the moment of balance before it angled bow-down. As it crested, Grady lunged, ripping the gun from his hands. Caught by surprise, the man turned. Grady slammed the butt of the gun into his head. Instinctively, the man raised his hands as he staggered back but didn't go down. Flipping the gun, Grady jabbed it in the guy's stomach, doubling him over, then the butt in an uppercut to the chin. That finally dropped him.

Grady contemplated how to keep the guy from being trouble when he came to. Life vests filled the box next to him. Grabbing them, he slung a handful overboard. Reaching back in, his hand hit something soft, cold.

He peered into the box. Cold, sightless eyes stared at him. Limbs twisted, bruises around the throat stark against blue tinted skin. A woman. Young. Blond. She'd been beautiful once. Grady tossed the last life vests overboard—there was room for one more body.

He'd just managed to work the dead weight of the thug into the box and secured the toggle latch when voices behind him had him darting for the shadows. A thin beam of light probed the darkness.

Grady pressed himself back into the darkness as he lowered his head, blinking against the rain. Hard to tell who or even how many. But if they came this way, there'd be no place to hide. The automatic weapon at least evened the playing field, but he didn't want to use it. For all he knew, a whole army could be waiting below-decks.

Holding his breath, he held the gun at high-ready, his finger on the trigger.

Halfway to him, the men took the stairs to the upper foredeck.

The helicopter.

Lewis must have steel balls. Better him than me.

With the two guys working to launch the helicopter, there was a good chance he'd find Shelby alone. Grady slipped from his hiding spot and hurried toward the back of the boat.

He leaned around to look in the sliding glass door to the rear. Yes, Shelby was alone...at least as far as he could see. Still out on the couch. Easing back into the darkness, he retraced his steps back to the side door Lewis and his goon had used. He tested the handle. Unlocked.

Gun at low ready, he raised it as he slid the door open. Stepping inside, he turned.

One thug, two hands wrapped around the butt of a pistol aimed at his crotch, stopped him cold. "That's far enough."

CHAPTER FIFTY-FOUR

The sound of rotors spooling up caught Kellen Wilder's attention. "Who approved a flight?" he shouted.

Bates ducked his head in the doorway. "Wasn't company, sir."

A thought sucker punched him. "Oh, she didn't. Tell me she didn't." He bolted to his feet and strode out of the door. Bates was smart enough to keep his mouth shut. By the time he reached the hangar doorway, the helicopter was just a light spot in the clouds as the storm swallowed it. "Get the tower on the horn!" he shouted to anyone within hearing distance. One of the mechanics extended a handset toward him. A short conversation confirmed what he already knew. Sam had done something truly stupid. And this had Paddy Donovan's fingerprints all over it.

"Sir, there's nothing you can do." Bates had followed him and now appeared at his elbow.

"I don't need you to remind me of my duty." Kellen closed his eyes and breathed deeply. "Sorry."

"No need, sir."

"Keep monitoring the emergency channel while I figure out how we are going to deal with the mess this monster leaves behind."

"We've received confirmation that all but one of the rigs has buttoned up and all of the crews have been transported to safety."

Kellen worked at containing his temper. "You don't have to tell me which one is still occupied."

"Only a skeleton staff, sir. And I just received a message from one of the foremen that the rest of the crew is abandoning in the pods."

"See if we have a cutter close enough to get them, then outrun the storm."

"Already *en route*, sir."

"Good job, Bates. Tell them there are two fools *en route*. If they get there, see if the cutter will be able to get them. If they can get close enough, tell our guys to use whatever force necessary to get everyone off that damned death trap." Kellen had been watching the isobars tighten as the pressures plummeted, the storm winding up. The last satellite photo showed a well formed eye lurking between Yucatán and Cuba as the storm slipped into the Gulf. The Hurricane Center's best guess had the storm gaining strength over the warm waters, heading north/northwest, putting Corpus Christi in the bull's-eye. But a cold front dipping down could sheer it off to a more northeasterly direction, hence the evacuation of Houston. "What a fucking mess."

"Yes, sir."

As Kellen watched Bates go, he knew that the cutter wouldn't be able to dock.

And Sam would be on her own.

"How long do ya' think?" Paddy broke the silence between him and Sam.

She glanced at the computer display. "Twenty minutes." He didn't ask if she could hurry—he could see as well as she that temps were holding just below the redline.

Mud was pumping as the foreman had said. Benji checked the gauges. Nothing he could do at this point. He hoped to hell Paddy got here soon. If he didn't, he'd have to blow the BOP and grab a pod himself—not something he looked forward to. He'd ridden out a storm before in one of those, emerging safe but covered in vomit and sweat. Maybe a better outcome than dying but not by much.

He thought he heard the beat of blades above the roar of the wind. "Thank God!" In this wind, the landing would be a challenge, so he headed toward the helipad.

Lewis peered through the glass bubble of the Robinson R-66 as he closed in on Donovan Oil's platform. He chambered a round and tucked his Sig P229 back in its holster under his arm. In that spot and under his slicker, not that it would matter—the pistol would fire wet or dry. The small helicopter with its turbo-shaft engine barely held its position against the wind. The tiny machine rose and fell, bucked and shimmied, a leaf riding a gale. He'd have one shot at this.

Fighting the wind, the darkness, and the slick deck, Benji had taken far longer to get to the helipad than he thought it would. The wind was playing tricks on him—he thought he'd heard a chopper close in, and he had. But the little Robinson that rested there, the wind buffeting it like a cat swatting a toy, was unexpected.

Donovan wouldn't come in that. Nobody but a desperate man would come in that—not in this wind.

Nobody was on the platform—he could see right through the chopper—so Benji climbed the last couple of steps and circumnavigated the small machine. Empty. No hint as to who had ridden it in.

But whoever it was, he was loose on the rig.

Sheltering his eyes from the rain with a hand over them, he scanned the skies. A small light to the north, growing brighter. The chopper closed quickly, then hovered just off the edge of the helipad. A Sikorsky. Not sure how they scored that ride, Benji was sure they had.

Sam and Paddy! Thank God!

Paddy's face appeared in the window—Benji could barely make it out through the rain. He motioned to Benji—he didn't have to ask twice. The big man put his shoulder to the small machine. Using the wind to help push, legs driving, he gained momentum. The helicopter slid on the wet deck. When the machine hit the edge, it went over, hanging for a moment as a skid caught the edge. Metal tore with a shriek, then the chopper disappeared into the darkness below.

Benji crouched, watching as Sam maneuvered into the wind, starting out over the water and letting the wind push her back slowly. Over the landing area, she set it down abruptly. And killed the engines.

Benji rushed to add his weight to the machine—extra help to hold it against the wind as the rotor spooled down. Sam made quick work of tying the machine down as best she could, then ran around to open the door for her father, helping him to the deck.

"You've got to go back," Paddy shouted above the wind.

Sam reached inside the helicopter, opened the fuse cover, and pulled three fuses, which she pocketed. "Not without you two." Tucking herself under her father's arm, she steadied him as they met Benji at the ladder.

"Whose ride was that?" Paddy speared Benji with a sharp look.

"I don't know. Whoever he is, he's five minutes ahead of you, no more."

"That's enough."

Benji filled him in with what he'd learned since they spoke last as he helped him down the ladder then followed him. He started with the mud engineer and finished with the pressure issue. "We had a kick. Pumping mud, but we need to secure the well and get out of here."

"Let me take a look."

Sam followed her father and Benji down the ladder and across the deck. They ringed the mud control panel. While the two men looked, Sam took in her surroundings. It had been a while since she'd been this close to the drilling operation, preferring to stay out of the way whenever she brought supplies or employees. She kicked at a sack that wrapped itself around her leg in the wind. Bending, she retrieved it. Unmarked but empty. "What's this?"

Her father opened it and took a sniff. Nothing he recognized. White powder caught in the oil on the deck. He followed the trail, finding the powder on the lip of the mud tank. Someone had added something to the mud. "You know anything about this?" he asked Benji.

"No. And it wasn't here a little bit ago. I was checking the mud right here when I heard your chopper...or thought I did."

"We have a saboteur." Paddy looked around, his head on a swivel. "Anybody else left here?"

"I didn't count heads as they left, but, no, I don't think so." He'd told them about Craven locked below. He hoped someone had gone to get him. The mud man. "Do you think they put this stuff in the mud?"

Paddy mashed the kill switch, stopping the pump. "How long ago?"

"I was standing right here twenty minutes ago, so not long."

Paddy motioned for Sam to get under a shoulder and help him. "We gotta run, girl. I think I know what they've done. And if we're going to save the well and ourselves, we have to hurry."

CHAPTER FIFTY-FIVE

"You don't understand," Grady tried to use his most sincere voice as he stared down the ugly eye of the thug's pistol. "I'm the new guy. Came aboard with Mr. Lewis."

"Right. Put the gun down and kick it over."

Grady gave a short, derisive laugh as he laid the gun on the ground and then kicked it to him, sliding it on the hardwood floor. With the rolling of the boat a bit more pronounced now, the gun actually came to rest halfway between them.

"Mr. Lewis is going to have your ass." Out of the corner of his eyes, Grady thought he saw movement on the couch. Shelby was coming to. He eased to his right.

"Stay put." The thug left the gun between them as he turned, following him, keeping the gun leveled at his chest now.

A darn sight better than his crotch, Grady reasoned. "It's been a hell of a day. I think I broke a rib trying to get on this bucket of bolts. I just want to sit. A condemned man's last wish?" He propped one butt cheek on the closest bar stool. Shelby's eyes opened, but she didn't move. Grady focused on the thug, trying to capture and keep his attention. "So, what are you going to do with us? You kill us both, that'll be pretty bad for you." His words sounded weak even to him—the guy looked like he was born to snap necks with his bare hands.

"The thug shrugged. "It's not like you're going anywhere. Pretty stupid thing you did, sneaking aboard."

Grady couldn't disagree. "Stupid becomes me; at least that's what my mother always says."

Still prone on the couch, Shelby reached up, pulling a harpoon off the wall above her. Some decorator's idea of nautical art.

But it would do, thought Grady, as he worked to keep his eyes off Shelby. He eased around on the stool and reached over the bar. "Mind if I have a drink?"

The thug took a step toward him, unwittingly presenting his back to Shelby.

"Oh, come on, be a sport." Grady hefted the crystal decanter of amber liquid he'd seen Lewis pour a drink from.

Gripping the harpoon, Shelby eased to a seated position, gathering herself.

The thug shot once. The crystal shattered in Grady's hand.

In one move, Shelby rose, and thrust, driving the harpoon through the thug's back.

Caught with his mouth open and his eyes wide, he flexed toward the pain, grabbing the shaft behind the point of the harpoon that stuck out of his stomach. Grady dove for the floor as the thug raised his gun. Slugs traced a line across the bulkhead above him. Then, the gun clicking on empty, the thug dropped to his knees, his arms falling to his side.

Shelby rose up behind him, something hard and heavy in her hand. She swung. A meaty thunk. The thug's eyes rolled back and he toppled over.

"That's for Jake." Breathing heavy, still a bit wobbly on her feet, Shelby stared at the man for a moment. When she looked up, her eyes were dry. Then they widened with fear. "Watch out!" she shouted.

Grady ducked behind the bar as the shot rang out. The guy who'd gone topside with Lewis. Grady whirled and got off a shot of his own. The guy was fast, but not fast enough. Grady winged him, which slowed him down.

Grady's next shot hit the guy center mass.

As the light in his eyes faded, he staggered to the bar. The next shot hit him again, this time under his left arm. A dead man still hell-bent on a mission, the guy reached out as he fell. Grady lunged to stop him.

Too late. A hidden panic button.

An alarm screamed. Red lights flashed.

A heartbeat, then footsteps thudded from below.

Grady grabbed Shelby's hand. "Can you run?"

CHAPTER FIFTY-SIX

Donovan, adrenaline overriding pain, hit the control door at a dead run. Sam was at his shoulder, Benji trailing behind. Donovan skidded around the corner, stopping in front of the control panel. After punching in a series of numbers, he opened the cover over the dead man's switch that would fire the blowout preventer and pressed it.

Nothing.

"Fucking fool," Benji berated himself. "*That's* what Wes did."

Donovan moved to the electrical panel. The lock had been jimmied—someone had taken care to hide their handiwork, but scratches in the metal gave them away. Not that it mattered at this point. They knew who. They needed to know what. Donovan looked at the tangle of wires. Even he didn't have the knowledge or time to try to connect the right circuits. "Come on. We've got to get to the remote vehicles. We can use them to put the blow-out preventers in place."

As he moved toward the door, he stopped Sam with a hand on her arm. "You got that key?"

"The key?"

"The one I gave you."

"Sure." She fished in her pocket. "Right here."

"There are some papers in the top drawer of the file over there against the wall." He motioned with his chin. "Grab them. Protect them with your life, girl. Give them to Davis."

"Davis?" Sam asked. "What's he got to do with this?"

But her father was gone. Benji right on his heels.

Sam's hands shook as she aimed the tiny key at the lock. After two tries in the half-light of the emergency lights, she was no closer to getting the damned thing open. A deep breath. She held it—and finally got the key into its equally tiny hole and turned. A sheaf of papers—drill logs it looked like. And some other letter-sized papers with an official-looking logo at the top. The Office of Senator Phillip Herrera.

Sam folded them and stuck them in the waistband of her pants under her shirt up against her stomach. With her hand on the knob, she paused.

Something wasn't right.

The angry wail of the wind, the lashing of the frenzied ocean...something else underneath the storm. Then she felt it—a shudder, a tremble like an earthquake.

No!

She launched herself through the door.

A wall of flames exploded in front of her. She dove under a platform—the landing on a set of stairs—as superheated metal, mud, and oil rained down. *Da!* Several times she tried to dart toward the fire, trying to find a way through. Each time she was driven back. Debris, hissing in the rain, pelted down. The fire, a billowing, snapping, angry beast, fueled by gas and oil expelled by the massive pressures inside the reservoir, rose in great hissing towers of flame, feeding, consuming the petty man-made structure.

No way she was getting through.

But she had to get to her father. He had to be okay. He'd made it this far. They both had come a long way. Life couldn't stop them now. Of course, Sam wasn't thinking about the fire, the well, the oil. That would come later.

Now all she could think about was family. *Her* family.

The spur to her side. She would not let her father die before she had her say. And no way would she go back to face her mother without her father.

He was alive. He had to be.

CHAPTER FIFTY-SEVEN

At the door to the salon, Grady paused, holding tight to Shelby's hand and listening. With seconds to spare, they bolted out the door as guys, guns at the ready, piled through the door on the opposite side. The first one sprayed the spot where Grady and Shelby had been.

He ran toward the stern. Shelby panted behind. Even though he could move more quickly if he let go of her hand, he wouldn't. At the forward stairwell, Shelby jerked him up short.

"We need the computer."

"What?"

"The computer my brother sent me. Lewis has it."

Grady pulled her forward. "No, he doesn't. He threw it overboard."

"What?"

"It's gone. In the drink. We gotta go, Shel."

"He knew what was on it," Shelby said, almost to herself.

Grady had no idea what she was talking about, nor did he care. "Come on."

Again, Shelby jerked him up short, nodding toward the stairwell in front of them. "That's where the men came from."

"Yes, and they aren't there anymore. They're right behind us."

Another spray of bullets, and Shelby dove after Grady. The staff would be berthed in the lower decks. So, one set of stairs down, and Grady took a hard turn down the middle hallway toward the stern.

He smiled when he saw the set of double doors. The playroom. Probably not the technical term. The doors weren't locked.

Grady tugged Shelby in after him and slammed the doors behind him as the men filed down the stairs behind them. The doors had a bolt on the inside, but it wouldn't hold against the muscle and firepower on their tail.

He motioned to the outer doors. "Open those."

Shelby stood, transfixed by the two gleaming Waverunners housed in the small compartment. "We're going into a hurricane on those?"

"Hurricane's not here yet. You got a better idea?"

Gunfire erupted, splintering holes in the door. Grady ducked. Shelby jumped to open the hatch. Wooden shrapnel cut them as the doors succumbed to the barrage of lead.

A button near the outer door angled the floor into a slide. Putting all he had left into it, Grady pushed the machine as the doors opened. The big machine slid toward the darkness, the water lashed into a fury, the wind and the spray pushing and pelting them. Grady straddled the machine. Shelby, her eyes wide, jumped on behind him, her arms clamping around his waist as she tucked into him.

"Here goes nothing." Grady pressed the starter and the machine roared to life.

The door behind them gave way. The men pressed inside, still firing.

Shelby slumped against him as he opened the throttle.

The SOS came in on the Coast Guard Emergency Channel, VHF 16. Bates transcribed it, then bolted out of the room. He caught Commander Wilder pacing from one side of the hangar doorway, then back again. The rain came in waves now, riding an almost horizontal wind. Lieutenant Bates caught him mid circuit. "Sir, we have some...folks...on a Waverunner unable to make shore."

"Where?" The commander eyed the skies.

Bates consulted his notes and read off the lat/long for his boss. "That's about ten miles out, a bit less."

"What the hell were they thinking?"

"I don't know, sir, but the gal who called it in asked for you specifically. Said her name was," again he consulted his notes, "a Shelby Walker."

"Get me a swimmer. I'm flying this one." The commander turned toward the load-out room on the opposite side of the hangar. "And, Bates, get the chopper ready. We need to roll. That storm isn't going to go quietly."

The boat's captain extended the ship-to-shore phone to Senator Herrera. "Storm is fucking with the connection. But I got Davis for you. And now I gotta move this boat away from that rig, or we're going to end up with a hole or worse in the hull."

The senator nodded, keeping the gun trained on the captain as he pressed the receiver to his ear. "What the hell kind of game are you playing here, Agent Davis?" He spat the name like an epithet.

"One that clearly has gotten out of control. Where are the papers you promised me?"

Herrera felt his anger gel into a white-hot resolve. The guy had cojones, or was a sociopath; either way, the guy redlined his pissed-off meter. "What, no apologies? No, gosh, bet it was really unpleasant to be stuck out in the Gulf on a platform in the path of a hurricane?"

"I saved your fucking life, Senator."

"You put my fucking life on the line."

Davis paused. "You're right. I'm sorry. The papers?"

The senator wasn't sure whether he liked the asshole or the patronizing iteration of Agent Davis better. "I'm taking your boat and your agent there now."

"Where is *there*?" Davis asked.

The senator killed the connection and tossed the receiver back to the captain. "Set a course." Then he rattled off the coordinates of Donovan's platform. "How far is that?"

"Not far, sir. But we better hurry."

CHAPTER FIFTY-EIGHT

Benji dove for the deck when he felt the explosion rumbling up the string. The concussion ripped through him, throwing him forward, sliding him across the deck. He'd covered his head with both arms and rolled up against the housing to one of the big diesels. Now, flames licked at him. A spot on his shoulder burned. He couldn't feel his lower legs. The smell of burned flesh filled his nostrils. But he was alive. He had no idea whether Donovan could say the same. Opening his eyes, he blinked against the smoke. Donovan had been in front of him. Ten feet? No more.

Now all that remained was twisted metal, smoke, and the fire.

Donovan was gone.

Her father had to be alive. He *had* to.

Sam pushed that fear aside as she tugged the Glock from her waistband. Someone else was on this rig. Someone who was trying...and damn near succeeding...at blowing them all out of this world and into the next.

Before he succeeded, Sam aimed for a bit of revenge.

Perhaps St. Peter would go easy on her, but at this point, she didn't really care about another black mark on her soul. Checking her pistol in the shelter of the operations room, she stopped to think.

The saboteur had done what he came for.

He'd be trying to get off the rig. Short of swimming for it, there was only one way left.

Ducking her face into her shoulder against the rain, she stepped out into the storm. The cloak of the rain obscured all but the bright finger of flame curling, hissing, and licking, like a serpent rising from Hell. But the light from the fire pushed at the storm, allowing Sam to navigate through the debris. With the wind blowing the fire toward her, Sam eased around the far side of the control center. In the shadow of the fire now, she felt for the first stair as her hand closed around the railing. Keeping the gun in front of her, bending low, she worked her way up the stairs. She flinched at an explosion behind her. A huge ball of fire lit the sky as the tall metal tower used to hoist sections of pipe collapsed. Holding tight, she braced for the concussion but kept moving.

He was here. Close. She could feel it. The hairs on the back of her neck rose, her hand slick with sweat and rain as she re-gripped the pistol. She'd made the top step when she caught a movement out of the corner to her right. A man, running, silhouetted against the flames. Through the rain, it was hard to tell if she knew him or not. But he wasn't thick enough to be her father nor tall enough to be Benji.

She aimed, her finger squeezing tighter. Blinking against the rain, swiping a hand across her eyes, she struggled to focus, to identify the figure hurrying toward the helipad.

Knowing where he was going, Sam threaded her way around to the other side of the helipad. Time worked in her favor—he wasn't going anywhere. She allowed herself a small smile as she thought of him trying to start the engines without the fuses.

Easing up the side staircase, the gun held in front of her,

Sam reached the top rung. Crouching, she stopped, her eyes scanning for movement. He had to be here somewhere. The storm raged around her. Her chopper groaned under the assault but remained rooted. She made a second pass; if the guy was here, she couldn't see him. He had to be in the helicopter.

Bent at the waist, using the walkway to at least partially shield her, Sam kept to the perimeter. The storm, the darkness, were the perfect shroud—the guy could be anywhere. Making her way to the other side of the helipad where the guy would've come up the stairs, she eyed the gamble of making a run across the open space to the helicopter. As she eased back to come at it from the rear, an arm caught her around the neck, jerking her back.

Surprise. A jolt of fear. She fought the urge to fight him.

"You're going to get us out of here." A voice rasped.

Lewis.

Sam stepped back, pushing into him. She threw an elbow behind her, the hard point connecting with soft flesh. Lewis grunted. His grip loosened. Sam buried a heel into the top arch of his foot, then pulled away. Whirling, she raised the gun.

He'd disappeared.

Shit! With both hands wrapped around the gun, her finger tight on the trigger, Sam squinted against the assault of the rain. *Where would he go? What would he do next?* She eased to the railing, then peered over. A few feet of the walkway below was visible, but then darkness swallowed it. Her breath coming in short gasps, her hands shaking, Sam inched her way around the perimeter. He had to go this way, there were no other options if he wanted the helicopter.

Something clattered behind her. She whirled. Nothing moved in the dancing light of the flames riding the wind. Pain exploded. Her knee buckled as she staggered. From below, Lewis must've swung a piece of pipe, connecting with her kneecap. Blind, she fired into the darkness. She thought she heard a grunt. Had she hit him?

With one hand on the railing, she bolted over, letting her good leg absorb most of her weight. The walkway vibrated beneath her. Lewis was running. But which direction? Cocking an ear, she tried to catch the sound, but she couldn't figure a direction. Fifty-fifty chance. She'd shot in front of her and below, so she ran that direction. Her knee hurt like a mother, but she managed to coerce it into action, a stagger, then a stride. Not the best, but it worked.

Scanning the darkness in front of her, she kept the gun at the ready. The vibrations stopped. Lewis had stopped running. She whirled, raising the gun above to point toward the platform, but she was a fraction too late. Lewis hurtled out of the darkness.

They fell in a tangle. Sam's gun caught between them. Half underneath Lewis, she wiggled and shoved. His weight held her. He reared back. She flinched. His fist glanced off her jaw. Not sure where her gun pointed, she closed her eyes and pulled the trigger.

Lewis yowled and rolled to the side.

He reached for her gun. Sam pulled the trigger again. This time Lewis fell back, clutching his knee. A dark stain seeped through his fingers. His eyes were wild, the look of a feral beast. Sam crabbed backward away from him, her gun sighted on his chest.

Pain contracted his muscles and contorted his face. Keeping the gun pointed at him, Sam scrambled to her feet. The bullets had hit his knee and shattered his shin from what she could see. As she took careful aim, calm settled over her. She pulled the trigger.

His other knee exploded.

Instinctively, Lewis reached for his freshly injured leg. Sam stepped in and kicked him in the head.

He went limp. Pulling the laces loose from her tennis shoes, she tied him to the railing.

"I figure you want to see your plans through to the end," she said, though she doubted he could hear. She tried not to think about what she was doing. Leaving him to a sure death. He deserved it; that much was certain. But was the punishment hers to impose? Life had put her here now, so she took that as a sign.

Hurrying, she reinstalled the fuses and fired up the engines. No time for warm-up, she would have one shot at this, and she'd better get it right. Trying to gauge the speed of the wind was impossible—it whirled and gusted. Whether the chopper could even hold position in these conditions was anybody's guess. The storms Sam had conquered before were nothing like this one. *Paddy, send me some of that Irish luck.*

The left door flew open and a body hurtled across the seat, pulling himself inside.

Sam whipped the gun around.

Benji!

Thank God, she'd paused that fraction of a second. She tossed the gun aside then grabbed his shirt with both hands and pulled. He couldn't help much; he didn't say anything. Half upright, his weight on one haunch, he used both hands to lift his legs and swing them inside. A foot hit the side of the door and he yowled.

Blood stained his jeans—a fainter darkness against the dark of the water soaking them. Both legs had taken a hit. One looked like a compound fracture jutted through a tear in the denim, but Sam couldn't be sure.

Benji leaned back, his eyes shut, his jaws clenched as he let Sam strap him in. His hair slicked to his head, his skin tight with pain, his eyes were wild when he looked at her. "Your father," he said through gritted teeth.

"Is he alive?"

Benji shook his head as he panted against the pain. "I don't know, but I know where he is."

A glimmer of hope—something Sam could work with. She brought the RPMs to redline, counted to three, then yanked up on the collective.

CHAPTER FIFTY-NINE

Grady O'Dell kept the throttle on the Waverunner wide open. It was a sweet machine—more power than he could imagine and a bright light. Rich men and their toys. For once he was thankful for Lewis's excesses. Leaning forward, willing the machine up the face of the next wave, he had a moment where he thought they wouldn't make it. They'd slide back and founder.

But, hanging on the edge, finally the machine crested the wave, the strong beam of its light bouncing off the dark angry clouds swirling above, then off the white of the roiling sea as they aimed down the other side. Shelby, her hands fisted in his shirt, leaned heavily on his back, her chin bouncing on his shoulder.

As they rode up one wave, he felt her fall away from him. He grabbed her hands, holding tight. "Hang on!"

But there was no reply.

With the nose down and engines maxed, Kellen Wilder screamed into the storm. The GPS, locked onto the coordinates of Shelby Walker's cell phone, guided him in the dark. His swimmer sat silently behind, ready. His co-pilot monitored the radio and scanned the water. This is what they paid them both for.

Come hell or high water. Kellen found humor in that. He figured this mission qualified as both. "Five minutes." Although his heart pounded, his voice stayed calm.

The swimmer opened the hatch and peered down into the darkness.

Kellen's eyes scanned the sea. As he came on position, he held the chopper just above the angry waves, and Kellen descended toward the water. He couldn't go too low—a rogue wave could take him out without warning. "See anything?"

After receiving an update from Bates, he moved a hundred yards to the north. A small watercraft, huge waves—they'd get a brief window. Damn near impossible. He fought to hold their position against the wind. The storm was strengthening. He watched his fuel. A few more minutes, then they'd have to turn for safety. Corpus Christi to the west was out of the worst of the storm.

"I have a light. Two o'clock. Wait for it," the co-pilot said. The swimmer shrugged into the rest of his gear and readied the basket.

"Got it." Wilder moved the chopper overhead. A Waverunner. Two passengers.

The co-pilot unbuckled and moved to the rear to work the winch.

The Waverunner struggled up the face of a wave. Paused near the top. Then went over backward. The riders fell.

The swimmer jumped.

CHAPTER SIXTY

The wind caught the chopper, lifting the nose dangerously high. If the blades struck the deck...Sam instinctively let the wind carry her, using it as she threw the chopper over to the side. The helipad sitting high gave her a hundred feet or so to play with. Not much, but it would have to do. The chopper rolled. Sam flinched, but the blades missed the deck. Once away, she yanked again on the collective and stomped on the rudder as she eased the stick back.

Holding her breath, she still descended. Blackness engulfed her. Then the blades caught, and the machine responded, lifting her as if on the backs of the angels. That was close, so close spray had salted her windscreen.

Away from the rig and now in control, Sam steadied the machine and eased around to the other side of the fire. The heat, the wind, everything was playing havoc with her ability to control altitude.

Once under control, using the term loosely, she turned to Benji. "Where?"

She followed where he pointed. "You wouldn't know how to fly one of these machines, would you?"

Benji, his head supported by the headrest, rolled his eyes her way and gave her what she thought might be a grin.

"Didn't think so." She fought to stay close to the rig, the heat of the fire and the drafts it created combined with the storm in a whirlwind of ever-changing speeds and directions. "You gotta get to the back. I can't fly and work the winch." She peered across him a t the tangle of metal and cables and debris on the rig. "We both no there's nowhere to land."

Sam could see him working up his courage against the pain. She gave him a short course in operating the winch and basket—it was pretty obvious, even for an engineer.

He pressed his lips together and nodded. "Got it. Keep working your way around. If he got through, he has to be on the other side of the rig." He pointed. "See over there where the hut blocks the fire? He'd find shelter there."

Not for long. The flames licked around the small building like a tongue—an animal looking for food.

As she pressed tightly to her door as she could to give him room to maneuver, she resisted the need to hurry. They'd not get too many chances. *If her father was alive.*

While not religious, Sam was Irish and she asked the angels to add the beat of their wings to help her.

Benji wedged himself around her, working the leg he could put weight on in front of him. Facing the back, with a hand on each of the seats, he pulled air into his lungs, then screamed as he launched him into the rear.

Sam pivoted to look. He'd rolled and landed on his back. The thumbs up sign made her smile.

While Benji readied himself, Sam focused on flying.

Finally, his voice sounded in her ear—he'd found the headset. "Keep coming around. Can you get in tighter?" He slid the side door in the back open, then swung the beam of the winch out and locked it in place. He hooked the basket as she'd instructed him.

If her father was alive, Sam had no idea how badly he might be injured. Plucking someone off the platform in this weather and with the maze of twisted metal below left by the explosion would've been a feat with a whole team in the chopper working together. At least she had Benji—she never could've managed this on her own.

"Keep coming," Benji's voice, thin with pain, sounded calm.

They could do this.

The chopper climbed and fell, like a rollercoaster dropping out from under her in the heat as she got as close as she dared to the flames. Once or twice she was sure the wind would throw the blades into the bent metal of the superstructure—once Sam actually cringed. But still they flew.

The landing light and her searchlight painted the deck below, already illuminated by the fire. She scanned for movement.

Nothing.

No one.

Come on, Da. You're too close to pack it in now.

Sam's stomach clenched as she scanned the empty deck.

Please, Da. She fought the helicopter, trying to hold it against the wind. The storm was bearing down. Time was slipping away.

A few minutes longer.

Sam felt the tight heat of tears, of fear. The pain of loss singeing her heart.

As the wind pushed and shoved, she held the chopper for one more pass.

Then she saw it. Movement below. Blinking hard, she leaned forward and focused. A man. She focused the spotlight. "Do you see him?" Her father, crouched against the heat shield of the building.

On his feet. He could move!

"Yeah, got him. Come right, ten feet."

"Do I have clearance?"

"We'll find out."

Sam eased over as much as she dared. The whine of the winch was barely audible above he roar of the storm.

Breath escaped her in a rush. Her heart started beating again. And then a new flush of fear.

Paddy squinted up into the light as he held onto a piece of metal, the storm raging around him. He motioned to her, pointing to his left to a clear space. Sam eased away from the rig.

Concentrating on the instruments, she focused all her senses on the helicopter. The chopper would tell her everything she would need to know.

She could feel it list slightly as the wind caught the line and the basket, dragging it. A touch on the stick to correct as she danced the chopper back toward her father's position. A few feet at a time, then steadying, the process painstaking.

Finally, the weight eased, the helicopter rode lighter. The basket was on the deck.

Working all control surfaces, fighting, praying, Sam didn't dare take the time to look behind her.

The craft listed slightly as it took weight.

"Basket fell off the side. Lifting it. Gotta come back in again."

"Fuck."

She eased back in for another try.

CHAPTER SIXTY-ONE

The eye of the hurricane passed over Houston, then moved inland, flooding the eastern half of Texas to the Oklahoma border. Corpus Christi had escaped the worst of it—some rain and wind, a few downed trees and power lines, but no major damage. Sam's hands shook as she paced. Too many cups of coffee to count, no sleep, no real food, and a boatload of worry had her running on fumes. The hospital looked like any other, smelled like any other, and reeked of fear with tinges of hope, like any other.

Grady O'Dell stretched out in the cup of a plastic chair. His hands, the fingers laced across his belly as he twitched in fitful sleep. His hair caked with salt, his face, too, he'd waved off the opportunity for a hot shower and food to remain where the doctors could report when Shelby got out of surgery. Two bullets, one had nicked a kidney. The other, no one was sure. She'd lost a lot of blood.

They'd airlifted Benji to another hospital—they weren't sure whether he'd lose one of his legs. He'd most likely sacrificed it to save her father. Sam couldn't process that, not now, maybe never.

Paddy was in another surgical suite, but his injuries weren't life threatening, at least not until his wife got here.

Nothing like a near-death experience or two to bring a family together.

The fact that she left Lewis with two shot-out knees tethered to a rig that probably wasn't there anymore caused Sam nothing more than a passing thought or two, surprised her. Sometimes life put you in the position to deliver a karmic payback. Today had been her turn. And she was okay with that.

Kellen appeared in front of her with another steaming mug. He looked as bad as she felt. "Here."

"I can't do any more coffee."

"I know. This is chicken noodle soup."

Why did he have to do the right thing at the right time almost always? Sam grinned. She and Wilder were probably destined to irritate each other for a good while yet. What did her father always say? Payback was a bitch and karma was her stripper name?

At the first whiff of the chicken soup, Sam's hunger kicked in. The first sip scalded her tongue. Blowing on it didn't help much, but she managed a few sips. Her body practically sighed. "Thank you."

"There's a whole pot in the cafeteria. Cornbread, too, if you want some. Probably the only thing I could get used to in the South. Any word yet?"

"No. Mom's stuck in Houston, which is probably a good thing."

Kellen smiled in understanding. He tipped his head toward Grady. "How's he holding up?"

"Pretending to be strong."

"I know the feeling." Kellen eased the now half-empty mug from Sam's hands and set it on a table nearby, then he wrapped her in a hug. "You scared the hell out of me."

Sam tucked into his embrace. His arms, his presence, his caring felt good. "Me, too."

"Hell of a brave thing you did."

This man so got it—she was his equal. "Not brave. Necessary. I'd rather die knowing I tried."

"This time you succeeded."

"Luck O' the Irish."

"I've seen you fly. No luck involved there."

"There's always luck involved with flying. When you forget that, you are on a quick trip to being a statistic."

"Yeah, I'm just not comfortable to abandoning you to Lady Luck each time you fly." Sam started to say something but he quieted her with a finger to her lips. "But I'll deal with it."

"Any word on Benji?" Sam asked.

"No, they said his left leg was like a jigsaw puzzle."

"He made it worse to save Da."

"You don't know that and, besides, that's between them. I think the two of them have some scores to settle. The storm is moving north. I've got to go. Hell of a mess it left behind."

"I know." Sam wrapped her arms around his waist and pulled him tight.

"You going to tell me what happened out there?" His breath was warm in her hair. His heart beat a steady pace as she pressed her cheek to this chest.

"I already did." She leaned back and looked up at him. "Why?"

"After picking up Grady and Shelby, hearing their story, we moved to intercept the *Vengeance*. They ran into the heart of the storm. Got a mayday from them a bit ago. A cutter went out there. The ship had breached. We got all the crew that was left before the thing sank. They said Lewis went to your father's rig and never came back. Did you see him?"

"Seriously? The storm. The explosion."

"Did you find the bodies?" Grady asked as he pushed himself up in the chair.

"One body, Becca Molinari, and one really pissed bit of Lewis's trash. We turned him and his pals over to the State Police. I'm sure they're trying to put their story together."

"Damn." Grady slumped a little. "Shelby's gonna take Becca's death hard. That's all she kept whispering about. 'Find Becca,' she kept saying."

"I'm so sorry," Sam said, not knowing what else to say.

Kellen pulled her tighter. "I'm still amazed you were able to pull in your father even with Benji manning the bucket."

She could feel the warmth of his breath in her hair. "You and me both. It wasn't his time, I guess." She let go and stepped away, shivering in the touch of coolness where there had been heat. "Be safe." He leaned in, capturing her mouth with his.

His kiss left her breathless.

And, with that, he was gone.

Sam had reclaimed her soup, downing the rest of it as she tried to deal with the vacuum left by Kellen's departure, when Senator Phillip Herrera strode around the corner, his eyes scanning. Sunburned, a bit ragged, he actually looked pretty good for disappeared-presumed-dead.

Sam gagged on the soup mid-swallow.

At the sight of her, the senator broke into a grin. "Sam! Your father?"

"Patching him up now," she managed to gasp as she struggled for air. "Will be fine. Where did you come from? I couldn't get any information out of the FBI other than you had taken one of their ships."

"You wouldn't believe me if I told you."

"Try me."

His eyes took in the people milling around waiting for news. "I will, but not here."

"Okay."

"I'm really glad your father is okay. Things got..."

"Out of control?"

He gave her a grin as he put a hand on Grady's shoulder. "I hear you're a hero, son."

Grady moved to stand, but Senator Herrera pressed him back down. "Our plan worked. No thanks to Davis. Where is the asshole anyway?"

"Not sure, sir." Grady leaned back, looking up at his boss. "We've got enough to fry Bishop, but not the others.

Davis has Bishop. And last I heard, he was singing like a bird."

"Good." The senator wiped a hand across his eyes. "I hope it's over."

"I'm sorry I doubted you, sir. We have them on the run."

Sam could tell neither of them thought this would be enough. "Who is on the run?"

"The less you know about them, the better," the senator said. "Trust me."

"I always have. Can I ask you a question?"

"Fire away; not sure you'll get a straight answer, though." He summoned a bit of his patented charisma, but it cost him. Weariness rushed in behind the diminishing adrenaline.

Sam knew the feeling—they all were rowing that boat. "Why were you trying to get out to the rig?"

"Proof. I'd given some papers to your father. We figured that was as safe a place as any. We underestimated."

"We all did." Sam pulled out the papers, which she had transferred to her flight bag once the danger was over. "I think I might have what you're looking for."

The senator scanned them, then, his eyes alight, he focused on Sam. "You got them off the rig?"

Sam smiled. She loved it when everything came together. "What happened out on your fishing boat? How did you end up being stashed out in the Gulf?"

Senator Herrera rubbed the back of his head. "I really don't know."

"I believe I can answer that question," Agent Davis said as he walked into the room.

Sam thought if it were possible for time to diminish a man, then it had done just that to Agent Davis. Gone were his ass-hat swagger and condescension. Something akin to relief shaped his features into a smile, which looked garish on the normally somber agent. Spurred by emotion, Sam dropped her cup, rushed over to him, and threw an elbow catching him in the jaw. He dropped like a stone.

No one moved. No one rushed to help the agent. They all stared down at him.

Groaning, he worked his jaw as he pushed himself to his knees. Pausing, he shook his head a bit as if dispelling cobwebs. "You throw a good punch."

"You're lucky she pulled it." The senator reached a hand down and yanked the agent to his feet. "You deserved it."

"Can't argue."

"We matched the tire treads to your car, Davis." Sam stepped into him. "You were out there watching, or someone who worked for you. You knew they were going to make a play for the senator."

"I knew he was running. And if I knew it, chances were good they knew it, too." He focused on Senator Herrera. "We had an agent on you and one waiting out by Donovan's rig. Unfortunately, my agent on you was on the shore—he was in the Dodge, not me—but, fortunately, he had a rifle. When the other boat closed on you so quickly, all our guy could do was lay down and set up a shot, in case he needed to. When the killer jumped on board and pulled a gun, he took the shot. You ducked as you came down the ladder and fell. Hit your head. My guy worked his way around until he could get to you, tossed you in the killer's boat, and took off."

"Then you drugged me and stashed me on that platform."

"Something for the pain." Agent Davis looked like he enjoyed that part of the story. "I sent someone to get you."

"Is that how you got here?" Sam asked the senator.

"In a roundabout way."

"He damn near caved in my agent's skull, then commandeered my boat."

Sam gave Davis a flat look. "Seems only fair."

No one argued.

"Did you come straight here?" Sam asked the senator, sensing there was more to the story.

"I went back to your father's rig looking for these

papers."

Davis reached for them. "I'll take those."

Senator Herrera folded them, then handed them to Grady. "Not just yet. You and I have some further negotiations to do." He turned to Grady. "Keep these in a safe place." They both laughed, but no one else saw the humor.

"You got on the rig?" Sam's voice sharpened. The senator nodded.

In his look she saw that he knew.

She stepped away from the group to stare out the windows. Daylight lightened the sky. Clouds still hung low, scudding on the wind, but the rain had stopped.

Senator Herrera joined her. He lowered his voice so only she could hear. "Found another bit of trash I took care of." He reached out and took her hand, putting something in it.

Shoe laces. Cut.

Sam's eyes widened in question.

The senator nodded. "Lewis won't be a problem...to any of us."

CHAPTER SIXTY-TWO

Two days and Patrick Donovan had charmed all the nurses and convinced the doctors to let him go. Brid cooed and clucked over him. He pretended to be disgruntled, but preened under her attention as she plumped the pillow behind him.

"Woman, quit fussing," he said with a wink to his daughter. "Where's that sorry Coastie with my whiskey?"

Kellen appeared in the doorway as if on cue. "You talk about me that way, and I'll drink your share myself." He had poured a drink for everyone, including Grady and Shelby, who appeared in the doorway as if silently summoned.

Grady, cleaned up and looking no worse for wear, pushed Shelby in a hospital wheelchair. Thin, a bit wan underneath a healthy grin, Shelby gazed around the room, then up at Grady. She'd lost a kidney and a couple of feet of intestine, but, amazingly, her vital organs had been relatively unscathed except for a crease across the back side of her liver. Millimeters, Sam remembered the doc saying.

Sam had no trouble interpreting what she was thinking—she'd been feeling the amazement and the gratitude for two days now. "Good to see you, Shelby. Hell of a ride, huh?"

"We got them, though, right? The guys who killed Jake."

"That's what Agent Davis says," Kellen said as he handed her a drink. "But we may never know for sure."

Sam stepped back into the corner and leaned against the wall. From there, she watched everyone, joking, reassuring, taking strength from each other and giving it back. Family and chosen family. That's what she'd wanted all along. But, whether her father went off on another harebrained scheme, or he and her mother could find a large enough patch for the holes in their relationship, it didn't really matter anymore. They were still family. And friends were family by choice. So, sort of like Dorothy, she really never had to leave home to find what she was looking for.

Her father's voice brought her back. "Kellen, Sam here has told me my well is shut in. We got the BOPs to fire and no oil escaped. Is that true?"

"Flew over your sight today, sir. No surface sign of oil. Benji has ordered a crew to send a submersible to check it out, but with the mess out there, it might take a while."

"And the rig?"

"Overturned in the storm. A total loss, I'd say."

"Bishop's problem," Donovan said with a satisfied smirk.

"There's still the issue as to who came after you, Da," Sam said from her corner.

"I'd say Bishop. Halloran was his boy. And the two of them loved stealing finds out from under the rightful owners. Not sure I can prove it, though."

"Davis can sweat it out of him."

"Maybe. Attempted murder would go a long way to keeping him from doing any more harm to us innocent folks."

Kellen caught Sam's eye. "There is the matter of a dead guy found floating in the Gulf."

"Surely you can't be thinking of laying it off on me?" Donovan overplayed the role of the innocent to the amusement of everyone. He eased his legs over the side of the bed. Brid helped him to stand. He leaned heavily on her arm. "Come, woman. Grab a drink for Benji, then take me to see him. We need to get our stories straight."

Once her father and mother were out of earshot, Sam turned a worried look in Kellen's direction.

"Don't worry—clear case of self-defense. Benji will corroborate."

"Yeah," Sam sighed. Benji'd made it through. The leg was still touch-and-go. They wouldn't know for a while yet. Regardless, they'd all made it through. "The guy should've known that it would take more than one shot to bring down a Donovan. So," she turned to Grady, "tell me if I've figured this right. You and Uncle Phil were working with Davis to bait the guys who were messing with the markets and trying to buy senators."

"I didn't hear a question."

Sam lasered him with a look.

"Yeah, the senator was playing along. I was his backup. He didn't trust Davis."

"A wise man," Kellen growled. "The guy is working every angle, I'm just not sure for whom."

Weeks had gone by. Sam was back to flying a semi-regular schedule. Life was returning to normal, whatever that was. The Gulf would need months to recover, maybe even years. And curiously, the storm had done what the oilmen had been trying to do all along—brought the price of oil up to a respectable level. The whole supply-and-demand thing proved to be almost as immutable as physics.

Sam pulled her truck into her mother's driveway, then gathered the flowers she'd brought for her mother and the whiskey she'd brought for her father. Even though fully healed, he had yet to move out of his former wife's bedroom. Sam took it as a good sign.

A black Dodge with government plates sat at the curb.

She let herself in. "Anybody home?" she shouted, more as a warning than a request for an answer.

"In the kitchen," her mom called back. She sounded happy.

Agent Davis had joined her father at the table. Her mother rushed over to give her a hug. "Tulips. My favorite. Thank you, dear." She changed her tack and bussed Sam on the cheek rather than crush the flowers.

Sam put the bottle in front of her father. "The good stuff."

"You've forgiven me, then?"

"Forgive, yes; forget, no," she said with a smile as she kissed him on the cheek. She greeted the agent as she joined the men at the table while her mother found a vase for her tulips. "Agent Davis, to what do we owe the honor?" Her cold tone stripped the nice from her words.

"The man came with his hat in his hand, girl." Paddy didn't seem angry. "He wants to make us a deal."

"How so?"

"Our silence for the lease, and—" Paddy pushed a paper napkin to her "this amount of money, per year, to be deposited in our accounts. A royalty of sorts."

"But no one is to know the extent of the oil reservoir you found." Davis hammered home the point.

Sam eyed the number scribbled on the napkin—the last of a series of numbers, all the rest had been crossed out. She swallowed hard but kept a neutral expression. "Never dicker with an Irishman, Agent Davis."

"I carry the scars."

"Da, it's your oil. You're sitting on a huge amount. Could be worth a whole lot more than this." Sam didn't say it, but the amount Agent Davis was offering was staggering.

"Aye, but it's mine at the largesse of the government. And I think we've seen protecting it will take more firepower than I've got. Besides, that amount of oil spilling into the market...well, you know what it will do to the economy."

"With our hand on the spigot, Ms. Donovan, the United States will have leverage in the marketplace against OPEC and the other big players that we've never had before. We can work it to keep the world stable and life at the optimal levels for everyone."

"Half of that goes to you, Mary Catherine. Then, when I'm dead and gone, and your mother, too, it'll all be yours."

"And then your grandchildren's."

Her father's eyes lit.

She held up her hand. "Not saying there will be any."

That didn't diminish his glee.

"It's a perpetual claim against the government," Davis said. "My authority to offer it comes from the highest level."

"An Irishman trusting the government." Sam didn't have much confidence in Davis or his deal, but she figured, as her father probably had, they didn't have a lot of choice in the matter. "Anything you've learned these last few weeks that you can tell us?"

To her surprise, he nodded. "The State Police have Lewis cold for the murder of Becca Molinari and an agent I had on a Waverunner out watching Donovan's rig, waiting to pick up the senator...before we nabbed him from his boat. My man disappeared a few days before the storm. Now I know what happened to him. We found some of his blood on a pair of Lewis's jeans stashed in his apartment. Now we just have to find Lewis." He tilted his head as he looked at Sam. "You wouldn't have any ideas as to where we should look, do you?"

"Not a one," Sam said, her calm voice surprising her.

Sam left her father and Davis to their negotiations and Brid to referee. Lost in thought, trying to absorb all that had happened, and how life had changed, she drove for a while. Her truck eventually carried her back home to the airfield. She found Kellen nursing a beer in front of her hangar. Without a word, he pulled a beer from the cooler at his feet and handed it to her as she settled into the Adirondack chair next to his, stretching her legs in front of her.

Home was once again home.

When he reached for her hand, Sam allowed herself a satisfied sigh. "It's over."

Kellen turned her hand over, lacing his fingers through hers and squeezed. "It's just beginning."

EPILOGUE

Shelby Walker, Jake's terrycloth bathrobe wound around her, her feet bare, padded through her parents' midtown apartment. Her parents had been hovering, worn thin with worry and sadness. Shelby finally convinced them to go to the pub at the corner, eat with their friends, re-engage with life. Although it would never be quite the same, it was the one they had. They hadn't wanted to leave her, her father especially, but she'd managed to push them out the door.

So, for the moment, the apartment was hers...and Jake's. The echoes of their childhood taunted her. And the silence, when she stepped into Jake's room, crushed her chest, taking her breath. They'd buried Jake, but he still lingered. Shelby could feel him, pushing her, whispering, trying to tell her to hurry.

The same place. He'd used those exact words in his text.

Shelby pulled in a deep breath, then opened his closet. The smells of him wrapping around her, a shield that hit her heart. In the back corner, she knelt down. Pushing aside the detritus of Jake's youth, she pried a panel out of the floorboard.

It was there, as she knew it would be.

A small laptop.

Turning, she leaned against the closet wall. Opening the laptop, she pressed the button to bring it to life. Pulling a pad and pen from the pocket in her robe, she began reading and decoding.

Jake had won.

She had her story.

Her progress was slow. She hadn't gotten very far when she heard a car pull up out front, a door slam. Using the curtains to shield her, Shelby peeked through a gap.

A black Dodge.

THE END

Thank you for checking out *Deep Water*. For more fun reads, please visit www.deborahcoonts.com or drop me a line at debcoonts@aol.com and let me know what you think. And, please leave a review at the outlet of your choice.

Also by Deborah Coonts

The Lucky Series

"Evanovich....with a dose of CSI"
—*Publisher's Weekly* on *Wanna Get Lucky?* A Double RITA(tm) finalist and NYT Notable crime Novel

WANNA GET LUCKY?
(Book 1)

LUCKY STIFF
(Book 2)

SO DAMN LUCKY
(Book 3)

LUCKY BASTARD
(Book 4)

LUCKY CATCH
(Book 5)

LUCKY BREAK
(Book 6)

LUCKY THE HARD WAY
(Book 7)

Lucky Novellas

LUCKY IN LOVE

LUCKY BANG

LUCKY NOW AND THEN
(PARTS 1 AND 2)

LUCKY FLASH

Other books by Deborah

AFTER ME

DEEP WATER

CRUSHED